BURIED SECRETS

ELISE NOBLE

Published by Undercover Publishing Limited

v3

ISBN: 978-1-912888-48-1

Edited by Nikki Mentges, NAM Editorial

Cover design by Abigail Sins

www.undercover-publishing.com

www.elise-noble.com

Sometimes when you're in a dark place you think you've been buried, but you've actually been planted.

— *CHRISTINE CAINE*

Deadly emotions, buried alive, never die.

— *JOYCE MEYER*

1

ROMI

Rain streaked the windows against a grey September sky as the airplane descended toward Portland. Figured. The weather matched my mood, and that mood reflected my life in general.

Miserable.

Not that I could admit it. Wasn't I living the American dream?

The world sure seemed to think so. I had millions in the bank, a wealthy silver fox on my arm, a body made for the runway, and—as of last month—my own accessories line.

I also had an ex-boyfriend who refused to get the message, more addictions than I cared to think about, and what my therapist termed "father complex" but society called "daddy issues."

Most of the time, I felt as if I was living in a house of cards, just one gust away from the walls collapsing on top of me.

And a storm was brewing in Oregon.

Home.

Funny I should still think of it that way when I'd spent the first eighteen years of my life counting down the hours until I could get the hell away from there. In the past eight years, I'd set foot in Baldwin's Shore precisely twice, both times for funerals, and this visit was no different.

There were three things I wanted from this trip—firstly, to get justice for my mom, secondly, to catch up with my brother and a few old friends, and thirdly, to keep far, far away from Aaron Bartlett. Which was easier said than done when he was my brother's best friend and his fiancée's only sibling.

Davis reached across the armrest and squeezed my hand. "We can leave whenever you want. Just say the word."

"Probably it would look bad if we skipped town after an hour."

"Let's try to stick things out overnight?"

If I could have sent flowers and a card, I would have, but this time, the deceased was my mother. I owed it to her to be there, and to my brother as well. How long did it take to arrange a funeral? A couple of days? A week? As for her death, we all knew who'd killed her.

Our father.

Davis's personal assistant was on standby to assist with anything we needed, and she was an organisational genius. She'd already scheduled our flights, hired a car, and booked a room at the new resort that had opened on the outskirts of Baldwin's Shore since I last visited. The Peninsula got five glowing stars in every review, thank goodness. The only other options were the Starfish Motel or my brother's guest room, and the thought of setting foot in the Starfish filled me with horror considering the number of health citations the place had received over the years.

My brother's guest room? Well, I'd rather stay at the motel.

The woman across the aisle glanced at me again—a look I'd seen a thousand times before. She was wondering if she recognised me, curious but too polite to ask. Hardly surprising since my face graced the cover of the magazine in her lap. On another day, a better day, I might have struck up a conversation, but today, the attention made my skin itch. The cabin crew hadn't left me alone either. Next time, I'd listen to Davis when he suggested taking a private jet.

I'd also learn to pack lighter. Despite dressing impeccably at all times, Davis had managed to fit everything he needed into only one suitcase while I needed three, and after fifteen minutes of waiting, there was still no sign of the third on the baggage carousel. Tell me they hadn't lost it? The whole damn world was being sent to try me this week.

"Excuse me? Are you Romina Mendez?"

I turned to find a pair of teenage girls staring up at me, nervous but hopeful. The smaller of the two looked as though she might run away if she didn't get the answer she wanted.

"Romina would rather—" Davis started, but I put a hand on his arm.

"It's okay." I remembered being a teenager, star-struck when I thought I'd spotted Hugh Jackman in an airport. Except it wasn't Hugh Jackman, it was an accountant called Steve, but I'd felt bad for stopping him, so I'd asked for a selfie anyway. He'd laughingly agreed. Probably told the story at parties now. "Sure, I'm Romina. Do you want pictures?"

Davis took their phones and obliged while they giggled and I smiled a humourless smile, one I'd practised enough times to know that it would look good on camera.

"Are you in Oregon for a photo shoot?" the taller girl asked.

"Just visiting the beach."

A bland reply that gave no meaningful information. I used to blurt out everything, but Davis had been coaching me over the past three years, and I'd learned an important lesson: if you didn't give people anything personal, they couldn't use it against you. These days, I second-guessed the questions I'd be asked and prepared canned answers or sometimes lies.

"Which beach? Cannon Beach?"

"Oh, there's my suitcase." Thank the stars. "Great meeting you."

I flashed one more smile as Davis hauled my case off the conveyor and stacked it onto the cart. Dread settled in my stomach. Too late to run, too late to make some pathetic excuse and fly back to New York.

I had to bury my mother, make sure my father ended up in jail where he belonged, and answer awkward questions about why I hadn't been home for so long.

Oh, and avoid Aaron.

The arrivals hall was a sea of heaving bodies, businessmen hurrying between hugging families, backpackers carrying their worlds in oversized bags, tourists scanning the rows of guides and drivers holding up placards. I sidestepped a particularly amorous couple, and my heart jumped when I spotted my brother beside a coffee stand. When I'd called Luca with my flight details, I'd told him not to worry about picking us up, that Davis had rented a car so we wouldn't be dependent on others, but of course Luca had insisted on meeting us anyway.

That made me happier than I'd ever admit.

Yes, I prided myself on my independence, but there were times in a girl's life when she really needed a hug from her big brother, and this was one of those times. He was the only person in the world who truly understood how I felt right now. Which was...mixed up. Sad, angry, guilty... Our whole lives, we'd been told our mom had abandoned us when in truth, she'd been dead. *Murdered.*

"I've missed you," I mumbled against Luca's neck.

"It's been too long."

Over a year. Back then, Luca had been on a break between security contracts, and I'd flown to meet him in the Seychelles for a long weekend. Just the two of us. Davis had stayed in New York, Luca had refrained from picking up random women, and the hotel was far enough off the beaten track that the paparazzi couldn't find me. We'd eaten too much, drunk too much, and talked about past, present, and future.

Then everything changed.

Luca had done the unthinkable and moved back to Baldwin's Shore.

Crazy.

He hated the place.

And he hated our father, as did I.

But he loved Brooke, and Brooke lived in Baldwin's Shore, so... Here we both were.

Brooke grinned at me, and I extricated myself from Luca's embrace and hugged her too. A part of me hated that he'd moved back home to marry Aaron's sister, but the bigger part of me was thrilled because secretly, I'd always hoped they'd end up together. They were perfect for each other. Aaron had done his best to derail things by making some stupid pact with Luca that they wouldn't touch each other's sisters—a pact that Aaron had broken first, by the way—but thankfully, Luca had seen sense and made a move. Which led to yet another problem— Brooke wanted me to be a bridesmaid at their wedding, and of course I'd had to say yes, but then Luca had asked Aaron to be best man, and now I had to come up with a plausible reason to miss the entire thing. Because no way was I going anywhere near an aisle with Aaron "Backstabber" Bartlett.

But that was an issue for another day.

"Brooke, you look great." Radiant. "You've got this glow about you."

"I've got your brother to thank for that."

My mind went from zero to "holy fuck" in nought-point-five seconds. "You're not...?"

"Not what?"

I leaned back and glanced at her stomach. "You know..."

Her jaw dropped. "Oh my gosh, no. Luca makes me happy, that's all."

"So, uh, that's good. Terrific."

And just like that, I was back to my old gawky self. There was a reason I rarely gave interviews, and that was because I was scared of putting my foot in it. An ex-boyfriend once told me I had the face of an angel, the body of a goddess, and the brain of a cabbage. We'd been in the middle of a break-up fight at the time, but his words still stung. Probably because my GPA had been nothing to write home about, but not everyone could be academically gifted, okay? And who needed to learn about algebra and Shakespeare and glaciers anyway? If the teachers had explained how to balance a chequebook or change a tyre or ace a job interview, I'd probably have paid more attention. Schools should replace chemistry with lessons on how not to date an asshole—it was a far more valuable life skill, one I'd sadly struggled to master.

And now people were staring at our little reunion.

"Maybe we should leave?" Luca suggested. "Go somewhere quieter."

"Good idea. The hotel?"

"You don't want to see our new place?"

"Of course I do!" Was that too much fake enthusiasm? "How about tomorrow?"

"Brooke's cooking dinner tonight."

"We're both very tired," Davis tried, protective as always.

"But you've gotta eat," Brooke said. "Right? The food's ready to go in the oven."

And she sounded so disappointed that guilt punched me right in the chest.

"Just us?" I asked.

"Sure. Well, we invited Colt and Brie too. We figured you'd like to meet her, seeing as they'll be your neighbours at the hotel."

I'd actually already met her, several years ago at a fashion show in Denmark, but she probably didn't remember me. She clearly hadn't wanted to be there, and her small talk had been perfunctory, albeit delivered with a smile. Colt Haines was another old school friend of Luca's, and now a colleague in the sheriff's department too.

"So it'll be the six of us?"

"Colt and Brie will bring Kiki. You remember Colt's daughter? She'd have been two years old the last time you came back here."

How could I forget? Not only was Kiki the cutest kid ever, but we'd been introduced at her mom's funeral.

"What about Addy?" Adeline Crowe had been Brooke's best friend since we were kids. "Is she coming?"

"She has a hot date tonight."

"Where does she live now?"

"Coos Bay. One of the big apartment buildings in Shoreside. She said she'll drive over tomorrow, and then we'll have the whole gang back together." Brooke's smile faded. "Apart from Hannah, but everyone else."

Hannah, Colt's late wife, was with Mom now, both physically and spiritually. We'd buried her in the same cemetery six years ago.

"What about Aaron?"

Was it too much to hope he'd gone on vacation?

Of course it was. Aaron was a workaholic. If he wasn't lawyering, he was busy fixing up his apartment, so Luca told me, and I had to concede he was good with his hands. Good in every possible way. Dammit, why had I been so stupid?

"Oh, sure, he'll be there tonight. I'm planning to borrow his kitchen since it's bigger than ours, plus his dining table seats twelve."

They all lived in the same building. Not even a big apartment building with dozens of units, but a converted car dealership, just the three of them. Aaron had the entire first floor, and Luca shared the second with Brooke.

Luca's expression morphed into worry. "Romi? You okay?"

And so it began... *Smile.*

"Not really. I mean, Mom..."

"Hey, are you Romina Mendez?"

I turned to see a teenager with a smartphone at the ready. Couldn't I get two damn minutes to myself?

"Please, not now."

The girl backed away, and as she hurried off, I heard her friend say, "Told you she was a bitch."

Great.

Details of that little interaction would undoubtedly be on social media within five minutes, further cementing my reputation for being difficult. Why was it always the bad stuff that made the news?

2

ROMI

The last time I'd seen the building formerly known as Deals on Wheels, I'd been eighteen, and I'd run out of there screaming with Hannah Haines—or Hannah Willmer as she'd been called back then—at roughly three a.m. after we got dared to spend the night there. We'd taken sleeping bags and flashlights and huddled behind the dusty remains of an old desk until we heard footsteps in the early hours. *Tap, tap, tap, tap.* Hannah tried to convince me it was just one of the boys playing a prank, but as my heart threatened to hammer its way through my ribcage, I'd made an executive decision—we were getting the hell out of Dodge. Fast.

Of course it *had* been the boys, but thankfully, their photos of our not-so-elegant escape had turned out too blurry to identify our faces. Otherwise, those would have come back to haunt me as well.

As things stood, Deals on Wheels was still the stuff of nightmares, but for a very different reason.

"Not too late to back out," Davis murmured as we approached the door.

But it was. I couldn't hurt my brother like that. And besides, I needed answers.

Two days had passed since I'd gotten the call from Luca telling me a body had been found in a deserted old cabin in the forest. A skeleton. He'd been the one to find it—find *her*—and when he called with the news, I'd heard the hitch in his voice. My brother, my tower of strength, former Army Ranger and current Sheriff's Deputy, had been on the verge of tears. I'd been on a break in the middle of a shoot, and when he told me how he'd recognised the dress she was wearing, the one with the hibiscus flowers that she'd made herself, I'd ruined my make-up. I'd loved that dress. Mom had sewn most of her own clothes—partly because she'd been talented, but mostly because we were dirt poor—and she'd made me a matching outfit.

The first time I put it on, she'd done my hair and painted my nails, and I twirled in front of the age-spotted mirror in her bedroom.

"I love it! But I don't understand—why are the flowers called 'his biscuits'?"

She'd laughed that tinkly laugh of hers. "Not 'his biscuits,' chiquita. *Hibiscus*. My mom used to grow them in our yard when I was little."

"Can I see them?"

"Nana's in heaven now, but maybe we can grow the flowers ourselves?" Mom had twirled alongside me. "Now we're twins."

It was one of the few memories I had of her. And after she left, I'd never worn the hibiscus dress again.

The day Luca called, I'd messed up the shoot. Intergalactic space maidens weren't meant to cry. I'd tried to pout my way through it, but after half an hour, Ishmael, the designer, had taken me aside and said we'd reschedule.

Okay, what he'd actually done was wave his arms around and inform everyone that the vibe was wrong, *all wrong*, and then skateboarded out of the studio, but that was just his way. He acted like a lunatic, but I'd known him for years, and underneath the endless drama, he had a good heart. The best.

My agent had grudgingly cancelled a couple of appearances and pulled me out of a runway show, Davis had rescheduled his meetings, and now here we were. Ready to sit down and discuss my mom's murder over dinner with my oldest friends, a bona fide princess, and the man who'd stomped all over my heart.

Luca opened the door and pulled me into a hug.

"Hey, you only saw me an hour ago."

"Can't I give my little sister two hugs in one day?"

"Less of the 'little.' I'm as tall as you are."

"Yeah, well, I'm wider."

Perhaps not for much longer if the smells wafting in my direction were anything to go by. Garlic, tomato sauce, bread... I'd barely eaten since I got the news about Mom, but now my stomach grumbled. Brooke appeared behind Luca, casual in jeans and a pale pink sweater with two cherries printed on the front. My brother hadn't gussied up either, but after Davis and I had unpacked at the hotel, I'd changed into a plum pencil dress with an asymmetric neckline and studded belt, teamed with high-heeled pumps and full make-up. Perhaps I should have worn pants? I'd considered it, but I'd figured a power dress would send a better "fuck you" message to Aaron. And Davis had worn a suit, so I wasn't totally overdressed.

"Okay, fine, you can hug me."

"I wasn't asking for permission."

Davis got another cool handshake. I could tell Luca

wasn't his biggest fan, although he'd never said as much in words. I suspected it had something to do with our age difference—seventeen years—or the fact that every news article ever written about us referred to me as a trophy girlfriend. But the journalists didn't understand our relationship. Davis was the best thing that had happened to me since my modelling career took off. He supported me, grounded me, kept me sane. It was Davis who'd helped me to pick up the pieces after Aaron tore me apart, and I'd forever be grateful.

Luca finally let me go, and I followed him into Deals on Wheels. An open door to the left led to Aaron's apartment, and the giant ramp cars had once driven up to reach the second floor stretched ahead.

"I'll give you the tour while Brooke finishes dinner. Start upstairs?"

"Sure."

Anything to put off the inevitable.

We trailed Luca up the ramp to the apartment he and Brooke called home. It was smaller than Aaron's—although still expansive—thanks to the roof terrace that took up a third of the top floor. Luca turned on the outside lighting as I peered through French doors securely bolted from the inside.

"We haven't finished the terrace yet. Brooke wanted palm trees, so I got her palm trees, but it's still a work in progress."

"It's a good space," Davis commented. "Got a view of the ocean from here?"

"Not the best view, but we can see the water from the far side."

"You could put a grill over there. Or a hot tub."

"Aaron's got a hot tub on his wish list, but that'll have to wait for a few years. We don't have the budget for luxuries at the moment."

If Luca and Brooke had wanted a hot tub, I'd have bought them a hot tub, but Aaron could go fuck himself. Or drown himself—either worked for me. I managed a non-committal shrug.

"It'll look great when it's finished."

"You given any more thought to buying an apartment?"

Translation: how serious were things with Davis?

"I travel so much that I'd barely use it. When I'm in New York, I can just stay in Davis's penthouse."

Judging by his, "Hmm," Luca didn't much like that answer, but I ignored his disapproval and made the right noises while he showed me around his new home. And it *was* a great place. Light, airy, generously sized rooms. Brooke's artwork decorated the walls, and she'd made the place homey with cushions and candles. She always did have an eye for colour.

When Luca showed me the guest bedroom, I felt a pang of regret that I wasn't staying there. The suite at the Peninsula was comfortable and opulent, the same as in every other five-star hotel I'd stayed in, but no matter how many personal touches they added—the slippers, the selection of herbal teas, the fashion magazines—it wasn't home.

Sometimes, I missed having a home.

"Dinner's ready," Brooke yelled from downstairs, and I stiffened on instinct. Bracing for what was to come.

"You okay?" Luca asked.

Dammit. He always had been observant, but he also only saw what he wanted to see. He'd remained mercifully oblivious to my crush on Aaron all through high school, and that was the way it needed to stay.

"Absolutely fine."

"Don't worry about meeting Brie. She's surprisingly down to earth."

Oh, thank goodness, he'd misinterpreted. "I'm sure we'll get along."

"Fashion royalty versus blue blood," Davis murmured.

"What does that make you? The King of Wall Street?"

He flashed me a grin. "More of a duke."

Aaron wasn't seated at the dining table, but there was a place set for him. Waiting for him to appear was like slow torture when all I wanted to do was rip off the Band-Aid.

Colt rose to greet me with a kiss on the cheek, and he had a genuine smile for Davis too. He'd been my brother's other partner in crime growing up, a regular guy until he'd taken his duties as a sheriff's deputy to the nth degree and saved a princess—twice—as well as falling in love with her. My brother, a freshly minted deputy himself, had given me a blow-by-blow account of the gorier elements of the drama, and I'd followed the rest in the papers.

At least the press was being a little kinder to Gabrielle now that she'd starred in her own fairy tale. The paparazzi could make a girl's life a misery. They'd done several hatchet jobs on me over the years, but in the early days, I hadn't known how to handle the attention. Back then, I'd been a slave to the old adage of "no publicity is bad publicity," but in recent years, I'd followed Davis's advice and kept a much lower profile. No drunken parties, no wild vacations, no running my mouth at people who provoked me. New Romi went to bed early, ate healthily, and embraced teetotalism.

Fuck, it was hard.

"Good to see you. Both of you," Colt added, but his focus was on me. "How've you been keeping?"

"Busy, always busy."

Not entirely true—Davis made sure I scheduled downtime—but easier to fib than to explain why I'd barely been home for eight whole years.

"I'd like you to meet Brie, and do you remember Kiki?"

"I do, but she was just a baby when...before." When I'd flown in to attend her mom's funeral and then flown straight out again. "Hi, Brie."

What was the proper etiquette for greeting a princess? Should I have used her title? I'd asked Davis during the flight to Portland, but he'd been clueless, and Google had been no help either, not for a private setting. At the fashion show, we'd been briefed not to say "pleased to meet you" because that was meant to be a given, and she'd offered a bland smile and a few pleasantries as I curtsied. No touching. Dammit, I should have asked Luca, but my mind had been on other things. So I bobbed in a sort of curtsy, and Brooke burst out laughing.

"Don't curtsy," Kiki whispered, and my cheeks burned. "You're really tall. Are you a princess too?"

"No, I'm just Luca's sister, but thanks for the tip."

Brie's smile seemed genuine. "Honestly, I wish the curtsying would go the way of codpieces and court jesters, but my mother's big on tradition. The whole greeting thing is a minefield. Do I hug people? Give them a high five? Deon from the grocery store does this weird thing with fist bumps, and I get it wrong every time."

This wasn't how I'd expected Gabrielle to be at all. She seemed so...down to earth.

"I've never loved the hugging thing. When you get poked and prodded by strangers daily, the last thing you want is more strangers squeezing the breath out of you."

"No curtsies, no hugs from strangers. We're set.

Although we have met once before, I believe. You probably don't remember."

She remembered? "No, I do."

Luca looked surprised too. "You've met Brie already?"

"Very briefly."

"At a fashion show in Denmark," Brie explained. "Sorry if I didn't seem thrilled to be there. As I recall, my sister was meant to go, but she felt unwell, so I had to step in. And fashion really isn't my thing. Although it's an admirable pursuit," she added hastily. "It's just that I like to sail, and there isn't much call for haute couture on a boat. Anyhow, it's lovely to see you again, and I'm so sorry to hear about your mother."

When I first heard that Colt had hooked up with Princess Gabrielle, I'd checked the calendar to see if it was April first, but now that I saw her away from the spotlight, I understood why they'd ended up together. Colt was a good man, the best, and Brie was easy to like.

"The identification isn't official yet," Colt reminded us.

"We all know what happened." Luca's voice sounded hollow. That he should be affected more than me wasn't a surprise—I'd barely been six when Mom disappeared, and the fleeting memories I'd stored away had faded with time. Luca had been eight, and although he'd confided that it hurt to think of what we'd lost, he'd kept those pictures of her in his mind.

"Yes, we do know what happened. Have you arrested Dad yet?"

"That's not the way things work."

"But you're a deputy. It's your job to arrest people."

"I am, and it is, but I'm not working this case."

What? Why the hell wasn't Luca investigating Mom's murder? Didn't he want her killer to pay?

"But there are only two deputies in Baldwin's Shore. Colt's working the case on his own?"

"Neither of us is working it. It's a conflict of interest. We just had a meeting with the state police this afternoon, and a detective from the Roseburg office is gonna take over."

"Roseburg? But that's crazy. You know the town. You know the people."

"The sheriff didn't give me a choice in the matter. I'm not allowed to be involved."

We'd see about that. Who had more passion to investigate, to see the case through to the end than Luca?

"Who's the sheriff nowadays?"

"Mort Newman."

"What, still? He had one foot in the grave when I was in high school."

"Yeah, well, people keep electing him."

"Maybe he's gone senile? I'll speak to him tomorrow."

"No, you won't."

"I'll be diplomatic, I promise."

Luca just groaned. Okay, so I'd lacked tact as a teenager, but that was ages ago. And during the intervening years, I'd mastered the art of pretending to be nice to people I didn't like. Only two weeks ago at a movie premiere, I'd told Emiliana Sardo that her outfit looked fantastic when in reality, she'd reminded me of an anorexic cassowary.

"This is the way it has to be," Colt told me. "We don't like it either, but if this investigation leads to an arrest—which everyone hopes it does—the investigator will end up on the stand testifying. A defence attorney's gonna search for any signs of bias or favouritism and use that to sink the case, and the fact that Luca and his father aren't on good terms counts as a major bias."

"So he just gets sidelined?"

"He'll be a witness. You'll both be witnesses. I'm sure the detective from Roseburg will want to sit down and ask you a few questions before you leave."

"Are you sure there's no way…?"

"We ran it past Aaron, and he agrees with the sheriff."

"Oh, and Aaron's so fantastic at everything. Try asking someone else."

Luca gave me an odd look. Shit.

"Well, he *is* a lawyer. Romi, did Aaron do something to upset you?"

Yes. Aaron had done *everything* to upset me. But I couldn't tell my brother that, so I forced what I hoped was an innocent expression.

"No, no, everything's fine. I'm just a little upset in general at the moment."

"Hell, we all are. Where *is* Aaron, anyway?"

Nobody answered because Brooke walked in with a platter of hors d'oeuvres. Brie managed to grab a breadstick before Luca and Colt fell on the snacks like a pair of starving seagulls.

"I made appetisers," Brooke said, stating the obvious. "Marinated mozzarella balls, prosciutto bruschetta, and *spiedinis*, which are breaded beef and onion kebabs."

I knew what *spiedinis* were. After all, I'd spent a *lot* of time in Milan. Which led us to a bigger problem. Not quite Aaron-sized, but it sure had the potential to be awkward.

"Luca didn't tell you I'm a vegan?"

The colour slowly drained out of Brooke's face. "What? But you used to love cheeseburgers?"

"I thought it was just a phase," my brother mumbled.

To be fair, so had I, initially. Going vegan had been all the rage in the fashion world several years ago, and as so often happened in those days, the peer pressure had gotten to me and I'd jumped onto the bandwagon. But after a photo shoot with a bunch of baby goats, I'd picked up one of the pamphlets lying around, and now I'd never eat animal products again. Plus I steered clear of leather. Sure, that closed off some opportunities, but it also opened the doors to others, with the added bonus that eating a bunch of veggies helped me to keep my weight down. Appearances were everything in my world.

"I haven't eaten animal products in six years. When we met up in Casablanca for my birthday last March, we ate at a vegan restaurant, remember? The waitress asked how your food was, and you made a crack about it needing a good steak to go with it, but she didn't see the funny side?"

"Oh, yeah. Shit."

Brooke rolled her eyes. "I can't believe you forgot to tell me. Uh, we've got olives. And salad."

"You put parmesan in the salad," Brie reminded her.

"Dammit, and there's beef in the lasagne. And cheese, and milk, and eggs."

Yes, definitely awkward. "I can eat the breadsticks."

"Why didn't *you* tell Brooke you'd turned vegan?" Luca asked.

"Because I'm hopeless at keeping in touch with people, okay?"

Luca used to say my memory was like a sieve, but it was more of a colander. Sometimes, even important stuff slipped away. I'd gotten slightly better in the last couple of years since Davis's assistant got involved—she organised birthday and Christmas gifts, sent flowers whenever a friend was feeling down, and commented on my social media posts—but I still tended to block Baldwin's Shore from my mind. Especially after the Aaron debacle.

Although he'd always remembered my dietary

preferences, at least. The last time we'd been out for dinner, he'd picked out a vegan burger joint in the East Village, then insisted on splitting the check even though I earned twenty times more than he did. Aaron was one person I *had* kept in touch with, and although I never wanted to speak to him again, a twisted part of me still missed our weekly chats.

Chats I was almost certain Luca knew nothing about.

"Let's not argue," Brooke said, ever the diplomat. "I'll call Aaron and then whip up something vegan for Romi. You can eat pasta, right?"

Now wasn't the time to complain about carbs. "As long as it's not the kind with egg in it."

Brooke patted her pockets until she found her phone. She'd lost weight since I'd last seen her. Not a huge amount, but enough to nip her waist in an inch or two.

"Oh, wait, Aaron sent a message." Her face fell. "He says he's been delayed at work and not to wait for him."

"Guess he's got an important case to deal with," Colt said.

Either that or he was avoiding me. And if it was the latter, I could only be grateful.

3

AARON

*E*ven though I'd broken the glass deliberately, the tinkle of the shards falling into my trash can still made me wince. The gift had been a joke—from Romi, ironically—a miniature bottle of Scotch in a red box, with a tiny hammer stuck to the side and "IN CASE OF EMERGENCY BREAK GLASS" written across the front in block letters. The box had sat on a shelf behind my desk for the past five years, first in New York and then in Baldwin's Shore, and only once before had I been tempted to drink the contents. I'd resisted, but now memories of that night had come back to taunt me.

Because Romi was in town.

A town she'd sworn never to set foot in again.

I understood why she'd come, applauded it, but that comprehension did nothing to ease the tension between us. Even though I'd kept my word, kept my mouth shut about what had happened between us three years ago, Romi still hated my guts, my dick, every fibre of my being. I couldn't entirely blame her. Now that I'd had time to reflect, I saw there were a dozen other ways I could have handled the situation that night. Smarter ways. Ways that wouldn't have involved lying to my best friend and losing the girl I'd had feelings for since puberty.

Even back then, I'd known she'd break my heart. Romi had a way about her, a layer of feistiness over a core of vulnerability, sass that hid sweetness. Plus she was a free spirit.

A dangerous mix.

That was why I'd made a pact with Luca—I'd stay away from Romi if he kept his hands off Brooke. At the time, it had seemed like a win-win situation. Luca chased anything with breasts, charmed girls from Coos Bay to Coquille out of their panties, and then "forgot" to call them afterward. I'd hated the thought of my sister getting hurt, and I'd also wanted to protect myself from whatever havoc Romi might wreak.

Years later, I'd cracked and taken a taste of her, spent one forbidden night doing all the things I swore I never would. A mistaken night. A night that had ended with me dropping her off at the Maple Mountain Recovery Center in upstate New York. Not a mountain or a maple in sight, but the place had an excellent reputation, although at eighty thousand bucks a month, I'd have expected nothing less.

The media reported that Romi had been suffering from exhaustion.

Luca believed she'd checked in to get help with her alcohol problem.

I knew her issues ran far, far deeper.

She'd always had problems with drinking, but alone and away from home, under pressure from the wrong crowd, her one-too-many-at-parties habit had morphed into full-blown alcoholism, and that was before she got started on the coke.

Maybe I should have told Luca about the drugs. In the

years since my showdown with Romi, I'd had plenty of time to regret the decision not to, but at the time, Romi's argument that landing a bombshell on him in the middle of an op would be distracting had made enough sense for me to stay quiet. In those days, Luca had been an Army Ranger, and in that line of work, distractions could prove fatal. Plus she'd agreed to go to rehab as long as I kept my mouth shut, and more than anything, I'd wanted her to get help. To get off the drugs and stay healthy. Stay alive. I'd known all too well what drugs could do to a person, had even attended the funeral to prove it.

Well, I'd gotten my wish. Romi had changed her lifestyle. I read more news articles about her than was healthy, scanned the gossip websites most mornings, tried to filter out the bullshit. At first, she'd dropped out of sight save for the occasional modelling appearance. But then she'd popped up on Davis French's arm at some art show with a new haircut, a dress that could only be described as demure, and a tight little smile. Hell, I'd barely recognised her at first. She'd always been a butterfly—colourful, eye-catching, not to mention fragile—but no longer. It was as if French had arranged her as he wanted her, then pinned her to his arm to fade in the sun. A rich lepidopterist.

How rich? The jury was still out on that one. Rumour said he'd been a billionaire once, but he'd lost a chunk of change to his ex-wife in the divorce. Although he'd probably make the money back soon, and more. That was how the world worked—the rich got richer while the poor were left scraping around behind the couch cushions for their loose change.

Not that I was bitter or anything. I had a comfortable enough life—I just disliked flashy, Machiavellian hedge fund managers in general and Davis French in particular. I'd crossed paths with too many of those pricks when I lived in New York. In my time as a student assistant at the New York State Office of the Attorney General, I'd come to understand the dirty tricks they played, and over a summer internship at the NYPD, I'd heard stories about what they got up to after hours. They fucked around, found out, and then...poof. The charges disappeared. It wasn't *what* you knew, but *who* you knew. And who you could pay off.

At first, I'd worried the asshole would push Romi onto drugs again, but I'd watched her from afar over the years, and as best I could tell, she'd stayed clean. If she went to a party, it was with French, and they tended to be the kind of stuffy red-carpet affairs that one walked out of at the end of the night rather than crawling. Hell, I never even saw her with a glass of wine in her hand. So I had to give French credit for keeping Romi on the straight and narrow, but I still didn't have to like the guy.

He had what I'd lost.

Davis French's presence in Baldwin's Shore was the second reason I'd cried off dinner tonight. The first reason? I had no idea what to say to Romi. And considering I made my living by knowing the right words to use at any given time, that was a pretty big problem.

My phone buzzed across the desk, and a message popped up.

Brooke: Aw, work sucks! I'll make up a plate for you to reheat when you get home, hope the case prep goes okay x

Shit. I hated lying to my sister.

I twisted the cap off the bottle of Scotch, took a long swallow. Coughed as the fire burned down my throat. I'd never been much of a drinker—beer, sure, but not hard liquor. How long would Romi be in town? A week? Two weeks? She'd want to bury her mom, but the ME didn't seem to be in any hurry to release the body. *Body*. There hadn't been much left of Serena Mendez, just a pile of bones arranged where she'd fallen. Or, more likely, where she'd been dumped. Nobody believed she'd ventured into that crawl space of her own accord.

Fuck, Romi must be hurting, and I couldn't even give her a hug. Couldn't offer to assist with the funeral or tell her how sorry I was. At least Brooke would help out. And Luca, although I saw the pain in his eyes every time he spoke about his mom. Plus Colt was around, and Brie, and Addy. And Davis. I might not have been able to stand the guy, but I had to concede that he was probably good at organising. Or he had staff to do that shit. Either way, Romi wouldn't be on her own.

But being cut out of her life still hurt. I'd tried to call her after she got out of rehab, of course I had, but she'd changed her number. My emails bounced back. I couldn't even resort to a pen and paper because Romi didn't have an address. For years, she'd travelled the world as a nomad, staying in hotels when she had a job to do or occasionally renting an apartment if she needed to stick in one place for longer. That night in New York, she'd borrowed a penthouse from a friend who was out of town, a photographer, and every wall had been covered in moodily lit pictures, including half a dozen of Romi herself.

She'd found me checking them out in the early hours, padding up behind me on silent feet, her hair still damp from the shower. Caught red-handed, or rather, red-faced since she'd been posing practically nude. I'd tried to pretend I was admiring the view of the city, but Romi wasn't stupid. Naive, sometimes, and too easily led, but not stupid.

"It's okay; you can look."

"I didn't mean to... These are personal."

"I was just doing my job." She paused, studied the pictures herself. "Does it make you uncomfortable, looking at me like this?"

"No, not— A little," I admitted.

"Why?"

Because now I had a semi and she was standing in front of me in a silk kimono.

But that wasn't an answer I could give, so like every good law student, I'd dodged the question.

"Doesn't posing like that make you uncomfortable?"

"For Quentin? No, not in the slightest. He's a master behind the lens. Plenty of photographers are creeps, but I avoid working with them." A shrug. "I'm lucky that I don't need the money. Anyhow..." She took a step back. "Look all you want. I know you won't touch me because you made some stupid agreement with my brother."

She knew about the pact? "How did you...?"

"Find out? Luca told me one night when I questioned why he didn't man up and ask Brooke to go on a date with him. So even if I was standing right in front of you naked, you'd keep your hands off." Romi flashed the dirty smile that had gained her a whole damn fan club and slipped the robe off one shoulder. "Hey, I'll prove it."

"Romi, don't."

I made a grab for the top of the robe, but it slipped farther down her arms, and then she beat me to the sash and the whole thing pooled on the floor. Romi strutted away from me on tiptoes, one hand on her hip, ass swaying as if she were on the runway. I groaned out loud. Was she trying to kill me?

"Romi, put the damn robe back on."

"Make me."

She'd been drunk earlier when I rescued her from her

friend's place, but dammit, I thought she'd sobered up. I'd made her vegan grilled cheese. Poured a carafe of coffee into her. And now...now she'd turned into a monster. A temptress. I told myself I needed to tuck Romi into bed and then get back to my sister—I'd abandoned her at a Broadway show when I got the panicked call from Luca that Romi was in trouble—but my traitorous dick had other ideas. As Romi twirled and sashayed back toward me, it turned to rock, and of course she noticed.

"That really was a stupid agreement you made. We could have had so much fun together, you and me."

I found myself nodding in agreement. "Yeah, totally fucking dumb."

Damn, she had perfect tits. Small, but high and firm, just begging to be sucked. And she waxed *everywhere.*

Stop staring, asshole. I stooped to pick up the robe, then averted my gaze as I held it out.

"Put this back on."

"But it's so hot in here. Don't you think it's hot?"

"Romi..." I practically growled her name. "This isn't funny."

"I'm having a great time. You should loosen up. Take that stick out of your butt every now and again. Do you need a hand?"

Since I was still looking away, she caught me by surprise when she squeezed my ass. When I jerked my head around, her lips were three inches from mine and I was staring straight into mesmerising brown eyes. In bare feet, she stood half an inch taller than me. The perfect height for... *No, don't even think about that.*

This. This was what I'd been afraid of all those years ago. That Romi would break down my defences and leave me raw. Exposed. Bleeding. But at that moment, I didn't think. Couldn't think. When she kissed me, I kissed her back, and soft soon turned into frantic. My shirt disappeared. Romi rubbed herself against me like a cat, lithe and practically purring, then her hands went to my belt buckle.

Holy fuck.

4

AARON

"Wait, wait." I fisted a hand in Romi's hair, then tilted her head back so she had to look at me. "Wait."

"Why?" Slowly, deliberately, she bit her lip in what had to be a practised move. "We've waited a decade already."

I had no answer for that. In fact, I had no coherent thoughts at all. Romi got my pants undone, and then she was on her knees, and I lost the ability to speak entirely when she took me into her mouth. Hell, if the wall hadn't been there, my knees would have given way. The woman was a goddess. A siren. A beauty who lured men to their doom. Even now, the image of her sucking me off was burned into my brain like a brand. Close my eyes and I was transported right back there, forever doomed to teeter on the edge of hell.

But she didn't finish. No, she waited until I was nearly there, then rose gracefully to her feet and sauntered over to the nearest floor-to-ceiling window. Bent at the waist. Placed her palms against the glass.

"You can't be serious," I choked out.

"Relax. Quentin told me there's a coating on the outside so we can see out but nobody can see in. I've always wanted to do this."

She had? In all the fantasies I'd had about Romi, all the daydreams, I could honestly say the idea of screwing her against the New York skyline had never entered my head.

"With you," she added.

Fuuuuuck.

"I don't have a condom," I told her, my brain finally coming up with a coherent thought.

"Oh." She bit her lip again, but this time she came across as worried rather than alluring. "Uh, I'm on the pill. And I'm clean, I swear. I've never had sex without a condom. Never." A giggle. Yeah, she was definitely nervous. "If I got pregnant, it would ruin my career, so I get a little paranoid."

"So why would you do anything different with me?"

Her voice softened, and just for a moment, I saw the real Romi. The insecure woman lurking beneath the brash exterior.

"Because you're the one man who would be worth it." Then her confidence returned. "Are we gonna do this, or aren't we?"

I'd forever regret not backing off. Not wrapping her up in the silk robe, carrying her to bed, kissing her on the cheek, and running the hell back to my apartment. Instead, I did what only a fool would do. I took three long strides, then sank my dick into her hot centre even as curses slid from my throat.

This was Romi—enchantress, femme fatale, destroyer of men.

And I didn't stop there, oh no. After I'd fucked her against the window, after I'd emptied myself into her and watched my cum run down her legs, I staggered into the bedroom with her and did it all again.

The guest suite had a skylight above the bed, a window to other worlds. That night, the sky was clear, and as a sleepy Romi lay beside me with her head on my chest, I wondered if maybe I'd died and ended up in heaven. She was fire, pure fire, but for five whole minutes, I'd actually dared to think I might not get burned.

"The portraits aren't a patch on the real thing," I murmured, skimming my hand over her bare back in the moonlight, nape to ass. She must have some kind of treatments. Surely no woman's skin could naturally be that silky? "You have no idea how long I've been wanting to do that."

"Sure I do. Since Tania Fry's party when you were sixteen. Remember? Easton Baldwin truth-or-dared you to feel me up, and instead of touching me, you told everyone you'd pooped your pants one Halloween. I don't know why you didn't just squeeze my boob. You nearly did, didn't you? I saw the look in your eyes."

"You were fourteen, Romi. And you didn't deserve to be a pawn in some stupid game."

"I wouldn't have minded."

"*I* would have minded." She sighed as I kissed her dark hair. "Anyhow, you were worth the wait."

"I don't want this night to end."

"Me neither."

"Give me a minute."

She swung her legs off the bed and headed toward the en suite, and this time, I didn't bother to look away. Now that the dam had broken, I wanted every piece of her that I could get. What the hell was I meant to tell Luca? If this was gonna be more than a fling—which I hoped it was—we couldn't hide it. He'd probably punch me in the face, and I'd deserve the bloody nose. But I'd take the hit. Romi was the one woman who would be worth it.

I found my phone, tapped out a quick text to Brooke while I waited for Romi to finish doing whatever it was women did to freshen themselves up at three a.m.

Aaron: Romi split up with her boyfriend, and she's not feeling herself. I'm gonna stay in the spare room so I can check she's okay in the morning. Meet you for lunch?

That high-priced NYU law education was paying off already. Technically, everything I'd written was true. *Technically*. Romi wasn't feeling herself, she was feeling me. And we were both staying in somebody's spare room. But, yeah... I was still going to hell.

Brooke: Lunch sounds great! Can we go to that noodle bar you told me about?

Aaron: Sure, anywhere you want.

The bathroom door opened, and Romi strode toward me, silhouetted against the light as if she'd stepped from the opening credits of a Bond movie. When I heard she'd been scouted as a model, it hadn't surprised me in the slightest. She always had known how to move. I sat up to take a better look, but she quickly pushed me down onto the bed and straddled me.

"My turn on top. Although if you're good, I might let you roll me to finish."

"You want to... Again?"

Five minutes ago, she'd been yawning, practically asleep. I'd wanted her to drift off first so I could watch her at peace, which, now that I thought about it, made me sound like a creeper, but it was what it was.

"Where's your stamina?" She grabbed my dick in her

hand and began jerking it roughly. Too roughly. "It's only, like, three o'clock? The night is still young."

"Aren't you tired?"

"Nuh-uh, I'm good to go again. Ready to par-tay. But just the two of us, Romi and Aaron, Aaron and Romi. A private celebration." She giggled, but not nervously like she had earlier. No, now she sounded...well, crazy. "Want some champagne? Rocki always keeps a bottle on ice."

Rocki was her ex. The one she'd just split up with. "I thought you said this place belonged to Quentin?"

The laughter grew hysterical. "Oh, yeah, right. *Quentin.* He's not allowed to watch us. No cameras, not tonight. Aaron..." She gave a sulky little pout. "Why won't your cock work?"

"Romi, what the hell is wrong with you?"

"Nothing! Everything's right. You, me, together. It's *perfect.*"

I reached out and fumbled around for the bedside light switch. When the lamp blinked on, it took me two seconds to spot the white powder around her nose. The dilated pupils. The madness dancing in her eyes.

Fuck.

"What have you taken?"

"Taken? I'm a giver, baby."

"Don't bullshit me."

"Okay, okay. It was just a little coke. You want some? I have plenty."

"What the hell? I don't do drugs, and you know it. Where are they?"

"Why do you care if you don't want any?"

"Because I need to get rid of them."

I was halfway to the bathroom when she caught my arm, but I shook her off. Last year, I'd been powerless to stop my former roommate's coke habit from spiralling out of control, but I'd be damned if I was going to let Romi suffer the same fate. Where had she hidden her stash?

I pulled open the top drawer of the vanity as she shrieked at me, but it was empty. Same for the next drawer. Then I noticed her glance toward her purse, and I dumped the contents out onto the counter. Phone, lipstick, make-up compact, ponytail holders, tampons, and...holy shit...a ziplock bag full of white powder. I wasn't an expert on drugs, but I knew the law, and there had to be at least an ounce in there.

"You've been carrying this around New York? Have you lost your mind? If you're caught, that's a Class B felony. You could get nine years in prison."

"Well, I didn't get caught, and it's cheaper if you buy in bulk." She tried a smile, but it didn't work. "Nonna always said saving the pennies was a good thing."

"Don't you bring my grandmother into this. She was talking about a Costco membership, not illegal substances."

I flipped the toilet lid open, and Romi pounded on my back as I poured the contents of the baggie into the water and flushed. In the morning, I'd have bruises to go with the earlier scratches from her fingernails, but I didn't care.

"Hey, that cost me two grand!"

That would've paid my rent for a month. "Next time, buy a diamond or something."

"I'll buy whatever I damn well want. You're not the boss of me."

"No, I'm not. I only came to pick you up tonight as a favour to Luca, so you're his problem now."

"You can't tell my brother!"

"Watch me."

Her tone turned pleading. "But it's the middle of the night. He'll freak out and make me go to rehab."

That was a good point. The first part, not the second part. I didn't know what time zone Luca was in, whether he was on some kind of mission or not. Certainly, he hadn't been able to stay on the line for long earlier, and I'd heard what sounded like gunfire in the background.

"Fine. Then how about we cut out the middleman?"

"Huh?"

"You go straight to rehab, do not pass go, do not collect two hundred dollars."

"And then you won't tell Luca?"

"You can't hide this from him forever."

"I can. *We* can."

Romi argued, bitched, wheedled, and even offered to fuck me ten times over in a position of my choosing if I'd brush the problem under the carpet, but I refused to back down. We negotiated. In the end, she consented to check herself into rehab if I promised never to tell Luca the real reason why she was going, and so help me, I'd agreed. At the time, I'd believed it was the best option for everyone. Romi was right—Luca would freak out if he knew, and it was safer for him to remain blissfully unaware of his little sister's mistakes.

"I'll sign up as soon as I have a gap in my schedule," she promised. "Happy now?"

Not in the slightest. The best evening of my life had turned into a nightmare. "You'll go tomorrow."

"No way. I have shoots booked. Shows to walk in."

"Cancel them."

"I can't."

"You can, and you will."

"I hate you."

"Well, I love you too much to stand by and watch while you kill yourself slowly, so this is the way it's gonna be."

I spent the rest of the night mainlining coffee and researching rehab facilities while Romi crashed from her high and passed out on the bed. The next morning, I rented a car and drove her to Maple Mountain. She didn't speak to me the whole way. Lunch with Brooke turned into dinner, and as I listened to her scene-by-scene account of everything I'd missed from last night's musical, I steeled myself for a life without Romi.

More than anything, I missed her friendship.

Whenever I'd felt tired after a hard week of work and study, she'd always been at the other end of the phone, ready to beam a few minutes of sunshine into my life. Sure, she could be mercurial and difficult, but her nervy exterior hid a sweetness few dug deep enough to find. Plus she was fun. Romi always made me smile. And I knew damn well she'd paid off Nonna's medical bills, even if she'd played innocent and shrugged whenever I tried to thank her.

Romina Mendez was one in a million.

The day after she reappeared on Davis's arm, she'd modelled Ishmael's latest collection in a show billed as his edgiest yet, and considering the designer had once propped up corpses along the runway—actual corpses—that was saying something. Romi strode out wearing a ball gown covered in opium poppies, turned, pouted, then practically snarled as she gracefully extended her middle finger to a waiting camera. I'd just known that gesture was meant for me.

And I'd probably deserved it.

Just like Romi deserved an apology. That night, I'd been the one to panic, and I'd acted too harshly. I took another swig of whisky and picked up a pen. Wrote half a sentence.

Wadded up the page from my yellow legal pad and tossed it at the trash can. Missed.

Story of my life.

I tried again.

Romi,

I realise I'm the last person you want to hear from right now, and I wish I didn't have to write to you this way, but I need to say...

ROMI

"Ma'am, if you could just take me through events on the day your mother went missing."

"Romina, please."

"I'm sorry?"

"My name is Romina or Ms. Mendez, not ma'am."

I never used to correct people, quite the opposite. One time, I'd introduced myself to a photographer's assistant as Romina from Stellar Wild—the agency that represented me —and she'd gotten confused and called me Stella for the entire day. But Davis had taught me to be more assertive.

"My apologies, Romina. Would you mind taking me through the day?"

"Hasn't Luca already done that?"

"He has, but I'd like to hear it in your words."

"I was only six years old. I don't remember a whole lot."

"Anything you can recall could prove useful."

Detective Payne settled back in his seat and took a sip of coffee. He seemed congenial enough, but he kept clicking his pen rather than using it to take notes, and in the time it had taken to get the introductions out of the way, he'd checked his watch twice. I couldn't blame him for wanting to leave, though. Who'd want to work surrounded by this mess? His office was such a jumble of papers and files and empty coffee mugs and stacked-up boxes that I didn't know whether to start tidying or run screaming. I liked order. Everything tucked away in its place.

"It was just a regular Thursday. Luca and I went to school, and I guess Mom went to work. But she wasn't there when we got home. The day before, everything was normal. She had dinner waiting, grilled cheese. The last..." My breath hitched. "The last meal she ever made for me."

The last meal Aaron had ever made for me, too. My comfort food. When I turned vegan, he'd found a bunch of recipes for "cheese" sauce and tried one after another until I found one I liked. I'd tried making it myself since, but I never could get it to taste the same.

"Did you see her in the morning?" Payne asked.

"She helped me to get ready for school."

"And did she give any indication of her plans for the evening?"

"Not that I can remember."

Payne made a note on his pad. "You travelled to school alone?"

"Yes, on the bus."

"Where was your father that day?"

"He worked too. I think... I think something to do with trees?"

Payne consulted his notes. "According to the file, he was employed by a lumber company at that time."

At that time. Dad never managed to hold a job down for long. Sooner or later, he showed up drunk or cussed someone out or started a fight, and Luca and I would have starved if Brooke and Aaron's Nonna hadn't made us dinner every day after Mom disappeared. Aaron used to sneak me food out of his lunch, too. An apple here, a package of chips there. Those days had been hard, but in a weird way, also easy. Adulting was tougher. Twenty-six years old, and I still had no clue what I was doing.

"That sounds right," I told Payne. "He worked in the daytime, and in the evening, he drank."

"At home?"

"Sometimes. Mostly he went out, though."

"The file says your mother worked in the evenings as well as during the days?"

"Yes."

"So who looked after you?"

"Luca."

We'd shared a room in those days, a room smaller than my current closet at Davis's place. Our whole house had been small. One storey, five rooms. Two bedrooms, a tiny bathroom that didn't actually have a bathtub, a kitchen, and a living room with a dining table in one corner. When Luca turned fourteen, he and Aaron had boarded out the attic and installed a light, then moved a mattress up there so we could each have our own space.

But at the time in question, our room had been next to Mom and Dad's, the walls thin enough for us to hear their arguments, her tears, and other things I couldn't bear to think about.

"Luca looked after you? But he was only eight years old?"

"We had rules. Stay in our room after seven o'clock, don't turn on the lights, don't make a sound."

Detective Payne made a sucking noise against his teeth. "And what happened that night?"

"Nothing different from any other night. Mom went out to work—or so we thought—Dad went out to drink, and Luca and I went to bed."

"Or so you thought?"

"We didn't actually see her that evening. I guess... I guess we just assumed..."

"Did you hear them come home?"

"I don't think so? Usually, I was asleep. But I woke up the next morning expecting to see my mom, and she wasn't there."

"Your father was there?"

"Yes, and I do remember that he was angry. He kept slamming doors and shouting, and Luca had to help me get ready for school. I tried to make my own breakfast, but I dropped the Krispi Puffs on the floor, and they spilled everywhere, and I knew Dad would be mad, so, so mad..." Suddenly, I was back in the kitchen, scrabbling around on my hands and knees, trying to stuff all the cereal back into the box. He'd yell at me. He'd slap me, always so vicious with his hands. "And that was when I found the note. On the floor, sticking out from underneath the refrigerator. I couldn't read it, so I called Luca."

And he'd sounded out the words I didn't want to hear. That Mom had gone. That she was sorry, but she just couldn't stay any longer. My whole life, I thought she'd left us behind to suffer at our father's hands in order to save her own skin, and I'd been so damn angry all the time. But now I knew better. And that...that left me hollow inside. She'd been lying dead in the woods, and I'd hated her for it.

"What happened to the note?"

"I don't know. I guess Luca gave it to Dad. He stayed furious for weeks after that. And I think Mom took the car, because we didn't have it anymore." Wait. "Only she couldn't have taken the car if she was dead, could she? What happened to the car?"

"We don't have an answer to that question at the moment."

"Dad probably crashed it somewhere on the way back from hiding Mom's body. Did you check for reports? I bet he was drunk that night. He got a truck afterward, an old white pickup that smelled nasty inside."

Of oil and body odour and stale tobacco. Bile rose in my throat just from thinking about it. I'd dreaded riding in that truck, squashed in the middle between Luca and Dad, constantly on edge as he cussed at other drivers for some perceived slight. One time, he'd leapt out at a stop light and hammered on another guy's windshield while I wished I could sink into the filthy seat and disappear. I always got nervous in cars now. Hell, I'd never even learned how to drive.

"I'll be looking into that."

"I don't know why you're wasting the morning asking me questions. Why aren't you asking *him*? It's obvious what happened—they had a fight, and he went too far and killed her. She had bruises all the time. *All the damn time.* Ask anyone who knew her back then, and they'll tell you."

"Rest assured, I'll be looking into every available lead."

"Have you talked to Dad yet? What did he say?"

"I'm not at liberty to discuss that right now."

"So that's a no? How can you call yourself a detective when you haven't even questioned the most obvious suspect?"

"We're still waiting on a formal identification of the body. Ms. Mendez, we need to let the experts do their jobs."

"Aren't you an expert? Why aren't you doing *your* job?"

Payne had the gall to look put out. "I've already begun

researching the history of the cabin, but nobody here can recall its existence. There's no registered owner, no utilities connected, no red flags with the authorities. It's possible the place was only occupied seasonally. Maybe it's an old hunting shelter."

"What about forensic testing? DNA, that sort of thing?"

"It's underway. The results should be back in around six weeks, and I'll call you as soon as I know anything."

"Six weeks? You're gonna let my father get away with this for six more weeks?"

"The lab has a backlog."

"Can't I pay to have the testing done faster? I have money. Surely there must be a private lab that does that kind of thing?"

"I'm afraid that's not possible. State crime labs undergo a stringent certification process which gives their findings credibility, plus if we let families cut in line, it would also give the appearance that justice can be bought. Here at the Oregon State Police, we believe that equal justice under law is important. And I feel it's best to manage your expectations —any forensic evidence is likely to have degraded over time, and even if we find your father's DNA on, say, your mother's clothing, there's a perfectly reasonable explanation for it being there. They *did* live together, as you're aware."

So what he meant by equal justice under law was no justice for anyone?

"Why didn't the police investigate this twenty years ago?" I asked. "My brother said her disappearance got reported."

By Mom's boss, not my father. Because Dad had known exactly where she was.

"At the time, there was simply no evidence that your mother had come to any harm. And she did leave a note to say she'd departed of her own accord."

"She left her kids behind. She left us with a monster."

"That would have been an issue for the Department of Human Services, and I understand that nobody filed a report." Payne's expression softened. "I sympathise with your frustrations, Ms. Mendez. Too many abused children slip through the cracks. We try our best, but we just don't have the manpower to fix every problem. I do promise to update you as soon as there's any progress on your mother's case." Another glance at his watch. "I'll show you out."

***

"Why is everything so slow?" I asked Luca as we headed back toward Baldwin's Shore. "Twenty years to look at the case, six weeks to get lab results... Did you know Detective Payne hasn't even questioned Dad yet?"

Luca had bought himself an SUV since he moved back home, not a brand-new one, but it still had that newish-car smell lurking under a faint floral scent. A sunflower-shaped air freshener dangled from the rear-view mirror, and dollars to donuts, Brooke had put it there.

"Sheriff Newman told Dad we'd found Mom's body."

"And what did he say?"

"Not much, by all accounts. Basically shrugged and said she wasn't his problem anymore."

"Just when I thought it wasn't possible to hate Dad more than I already do..."

"Colt and Aaron had to stop me from going over there. When we found her, I mean. I wanted to knock his head off his damn shoulders."

"Have you spoken to him since you moved back to Baldwin's Shore?"

"Spoken to him? No. Seen him in the grocery store a

handful of times, though. He looks like shit. And one night, I went with Colt to break up a fight at the Cave, and he was there in the corner, drinking with Herb Pettigrew and Frank Swallow."

"Some things never change."

"You're right about that. Herb and Frank didn't look much better than Dad. Frank uses one of those oxygen tubes now."

"Does he still smoke?"

"Probably. Not easy to quit when you're addicted." Luca reached across the centre console and squeezed my hand. "I've never said this before, but I'm so proud of you for getting sober. It can't have been easy to take that first step to rehab."

"It wasn't."

"How's it going? The whole not-drinking thing?"

"You mean have I relapsed? No, but I came close after you called me about Mom. Davis talked me out of it."

Last night at dinner, the wine had been conspicuous by its absence. Everyone had been drinking mineral water, choice of sparkling or still. I always picked the sparkling. Now that I couldn't drink champagne, I had to get my bubbles somehow.

"I wasn't sure about him at first, what with the age difference and everything," Luca admitted. "But he's been good for you."

"I couldn't have got through these last few years without him."

Another squeeze. "Some people come into our lives for a reason. Thank fuck you never got started on anything stronger than alcohol, eh?"

I stiffened. Did he know? He couldn't know, could he? I risked a glance across, but Luca was focused on the road.

No, he genuinely didn't know. Aaron had at least held up his end of the bargain and kept quiet about just how dark a path I'd gone down.

"Yes, thank goodness."

"When I was away, I'd see all those stories online about this celebrity or that getting hooked on drugs, and I won't kid you—there were times when I was worried. I should've realised that underneath the glitz, you'd stay sensible."

"That's me. The sensible one."

"No more wild parties, huh?"

"Nuh-uh. I don't even hang out with the other models anymore."

"It's not just models. Anyone can get hooked on drugs. Hell, Aaron's roommate died from an overdose, and he was some farm kid from Iowa, six months off taking the bar exam. Guess upholding the law doesn't mean much when you get hooked."

What?

"Aaron's roommate died? He never mentioned that."

"Yeah, maybe a couple of weeks before you went to rehab. He was real cut up over it." Luca shook his head. "What a damn waste."

Why hadn't Aaron told me? If I'd known I might touch a nerve, I'd never have snorted coke that night. I'd just... I'd just wanted to stay awake for a little longer. To get as much of Aaron as I could. We hadn't spoken about the future, and I'd been scared that when the sun came up, he'd button down his emotions again, the same way he always did. Backpedal and insist that everything we'd done had been a mistake.

And in a way, he would have been right. I'd been such a freaking mess that evening. First, I'd caught Rocki sucking on Sylviana Maniotti's tonsils in the bathroom at Klaus's birthday party, and then I'd thrown the nearest thing to hand at his head. Which happened to be my glass of red wine. In school, I'd always been picked last for softball, so it had come as no surprise that my aim was off, and the glass hit Sylviana instead. There'd been a fight. I'd pulled out Sylviana's hair extensions, she'd punched me in the boob, and somewhere in the scuffle, my wallet had fallen out of my purse.

Ordinarily, that wouldn't have been a problem—I didn't keep much in it, just a few hundred bucks and a credit card. But when I found myself sobbing on the sidewalk as people gave me dirty looks and crossed to the other side of the street, it meant I had no money to pay for a cab back to Quentin's place, and no way was I going back inside the building. So, because I'd been a screw-up from the moment I was born, I did what I always did and drunk-dialled my brother.

He'd called Aaron for help, the same way *he* always did, and the rest was history.

My friendship with Aaron, that was history too.

"Yes, what a damn waste."

"What time are you coming over this evening? Brooke was up half the night looking at vegan recipes."

"Honestly, I don't want to cause any trouble. Davis and I can just go out somewhere."

"No trouble. Brooke likes to cook, and we've both missed you."

Well, it was worth a try.

"Uh, seven?"

"Seven's good."

"Are the others coming too?"

"I hope so. Although Addy'll want to tell us all about her date, and I sure could live without those details."

"It'll be good to see her again." I meant that. "I should get better at keeping in touch."

"Yeah, you should. Phone, email... Hell, write me a letter once in a while."

Write a letter... Aaron had written me a letter yesterday. The hotel receptionist had handed it to me when we arrived back after dinner, and I'd recognised his writing. Aaron's printing was painfully neat, each letter upright and uniform. I always used to kid that he'd make a terrible doctor.

When I realised where the letter had come from, I'd told Davis I wouldn't read it. Said I'd flush it down the damn toilet. But instead, I'd stared at it for a long minute and stuffed it into my make-up bag, then wiped my tears and flushed the damp tissue. Davis was the only other person who knew what had happened between Aaron and me. I'd confessed my sins, one painful secret at a time, even though I didn't have to. Maple Mountain had a rule that secrets were allowed but lying wasn't. If you couldn't tell the truth, then you shouldn't say anything at all.

But last night, I'd lied to Davis.

Because I knew I'd read Aaron's letter.

ROMI

"You're sure you want to go tonight?" Davis asked. "We can fake an emergency if you'd like. Blame everything on me."

In private, Davis was a sweetheart. His public persona was a whole other ball game, but he used the fierceness as a defence. If people were scared of him, they didn't dig too deep below the surface. But when we'd found ourselves sitting next to each other in group therapy, day after day, I'd learned to see the real him.

Strangers would look at us together and make a snap judgment about our relationship. It was so obvious, wasn't it? Davis was the wealthy financier, freshly divorced and ready for his midlife crisis, and I was the airhead girlfriend, so easily bought with shiny baubles and trinkets.

In reality, we were both fighting addiction, doing our best while living a lie. Unlikely as it seemed, we'd become friends during our time at Maple Mountain, and when we'd gotten out—or finished doing our time, as Davis put it—we'd agreed to support each other. To keep each other on the straight and narrow.

What was Davis addicted to? Work. With nobody to come home to, he'd stay in the office twenty-four seven, relentless in his quest to make ever more money. Money he didn't even need. Davis fully admitted he had more cash than he could ever spend, and his tastes weren't particularly expensive. No island, no mansion, no private jet, although he'd rent them all on occasion. My tastes weren't expensive either. Yes, I liked nice clothes, but I got those free via work, and now that I'd ditched the drug habit, my biggest indulgences were fresh flowers and beads. There was a lot of standing around on shoots, and the beads kept my mind and my hands occupied. I'd started making necklaces, and thanks to Davis's help, that had spawned Ryse, an ethical accessories line with fifty percent of the profits shared among the women I hired to produce the pieces.

Maybe now I was a tiny bit addicted to work as well.

Helping people felt good.

Maybe even better than coke.

But we weren't working today. I'd locked Davis's laptop in the suite's safe as soon as we arrived, and only I had the code. He'd been reading a paperback when I left for Roseburg with Luca, and I noted that the bookmark was nearly at the end now.

"Luca's expecting us, and Brooke's cooking up a special menu. It wouldn't be fair to cancel."

"Well, if you feel uncomfortable and want me to get us out of there, you only need to say the word."

"I will, I promise."

Davis studied me, assessing. "You're still stressed. How did the trip to Roseburg go?"

"Frustrating. Luca says there's a process, but it's just so slow, and the detective... He's... He's..."

"Incompetent? Lazy?"

"I'm not sure. He seemed to know what he was talking about, but it's as if he's got a bunch of boxes to tick, and he's gonna tick them."

"Anal? By-the-book?"

"Yes, those."

"Want me to speak to his boss?"

"Would it do any good?" I slumped onto the couch. Or should I say *into* the couch? They sure hadn't skimped on cushions at the Peninsula. "What if they're all like that? If we start making waves early on, it might get their backs up and make things even worse."

"I know how to be tactful." Davis took a seat in the armchair opposite and steepled his hands. "If you want, I could get in touch with him right now."

Something about the way he said it... And the fact that he'd found the time to read most of a novel while I was out...

"Have you done your exercise today?"

"I thought I'd wait until you got back."

And now he was trying to come up with an excuse not to do it at all. Nice try, pal.

If he didn't keep his blood pressure under control, the heart problems he'd experienced before he finally admitted he had a problem with work might just kill him. That meant taking regular exercise, cutting down on salt and alcohol, and avoiding stress. The problem was, Davis hated the gym, and he was no fan of the great outdoors either.

"We're going for a walk. Where are your boots?"

"Boots? You're planning to go somewhere we need boots?"

"There's a whole network of hiking trails just waiting to be explored."

Davis shuddered. "Sidewalks are so much more user-friendly."

"Fine. We'll compromise and go to the beach."

"The sand will get in my shoes."

"So walk barefoot."

"You're a cruel, cruel mistress."

I smiled at that. It was for his own good, and we both knew it.

"But you love me anyway."

Now Davis smiled too. "Always."

Romi,

I realise I'm the last person you want to hear from right now, and I wish I didn't have to write to you this way, but I need to say...

Okay, I'd cracked and opened Aaron's letter. Davis was soaking in the tub in his en suite after our three-mile amble along the beach, and I'd just gotten out of the shower in mine. The letter was short, the writing a touch messier than usual, as if Aaron had written it in a hurry.

...that I'm sorry. Sorry for what happened that night in New York. I took advantage of you when you were vulnerable, and I'll always regret it. And afterward, I was too harsh on you. I was going through some personal shit back then—not an excuse, there is no excuse, but I let it cloud my judgment.

I'll always miss what we had, but I understand why you don't want to know me anymore. And while you're in town, I'll keep out of your way. Enjoy your dinners with Luca and Brooke.

And Addy, because you know damn well she'll always show up for a plate. I'll stay at the office.

I've got a lot of regrets, Romi, but you look good. Healthy. So I can't regret everything. Take care of yourself, Buttercup.

A x

Buttercup. Aaron had called me that since we were teenagers. It started at the diner on the outskirts of town, the Steak and Shake, our favourite after-school hang-out. Luca, Aaron, and Colt, me, Brooke and Addy. The Steak and Shake was trapped in a time warp, straight out of the fifties. A metal counter along the back with stools, booths with vinyl bench seats in front by the windows, little round tables in the middle, a jukebox to one side. Probably all original, and Viola May, the owner, kept the place spotless. Was she still around? She'd be in her late sixties now, but she struck me as the kind of lady who'd go on forever. A bit like the diner, really. Her great-great-grandfather—I might have missed out a "great" or two—had started the original restaurant in the 1920s, and the place had survived a world war, a fire, a flood, and too many presidents to count.

One day while the rain was lashing down outside, I'd played "Build Me Up Buttercup" on the jukebox, only for a lightning strike to take out the power. I screamed. Brooke screamed. Addy swallowed her milkshake the wrong way and had a coughing fit. And as Luca and Colt thumped Addy on the back and wiped up the spluttered mess, Aaron had danced around singing the rest of the song to lighten the mood. He hadn't been so serious back in those days. And he sure could sing.

Secretly, I missed what we'd had too.

The connection.

But that was the past, and this was the present. Aaron's heavy-handed actions had caused my career to falter, pissed off my agent, and gotten me blacklisted with several designers who I'd let down. It had taken a full year plus help from Davis to get things back on track.

The apology, now that it had finally come, helped a little, and maybe someday I'd be able to forgive Aaron. But I couldn't simply forget.

Davis knocked softly on the bathroom door, making me jump.

"We need to leave in twenty minutes." He hated being late. "Anything I can do to help?"

Invent a time machine to take me back three years? But then I'd never have met him, and painful as that night in New York had been, it had resulted in Davis coming into my life. Like Aaron, I couldn't regret everything.

"It's under control." A lie. My emotions were all over the place. "You think I should dress more casually tonight?"

"I'm wearing slacks and a dress shirt."

Which was about as casual as Davis got. I'd once kidded that he'd worn a suit and tie to kindergarten, and when we went to visit his parents, his mom had fished out the old photo albums and it turned out I'd been absolutely right. She'd bought him the outfit to attend a wedding, and he'd insisted on wearing it every day until he tripped over and tore a hole in the pants. "Oh, the crocodile tears," she'd told me, eyes crinkling. Davis hadn't seen the funny side.

I teamed a pair of high-waisted tapered pants in pale grey with a turquoise silk blouse and royal-blue pumps. A beaded necklace from my new collection completed the ensemble, seven strands in varying shades of grey and silver. I'd made that one myself, the prototype, but most of the production was done overseas in developing countries.

Davis was already waiting by the door when I walked out of the bedroom with one minute to spare.

"Do I look okay?"

"Beautiful." He offered me his arm. "Shall we?"

Dinner went better when I wasn't waiting for Aaron to walk in at any moment. And I almost enjoyed the next few days in Baldwin's Shore. Almost, because I still had Mom's death hanging over me like smog, waiting to choke me up at awkward moments.

Detective Payne called to say Mom had finally been identified through dental records, so that was some sort of closure, at least. But the forensic anthropologist wasn't finished with her remains, so she had to suffer the indignity of lying on a steel table in a lab somewhere for a while longer. And still Payne hadn't talked to my father. Wanted to get all his ducks in a row first, so he claimed.

"I'm meant to shoot a perfume ad in Bermuda the day after tomorrow," I told Luca as we sat down for lunch at the Peninsula on day five. Davis was in the suite working—until six and no later, he promised—and I knew he was starting to get twitchy. Big deals were done in the city, not the ass-end of nowhere.

"How hot is Bermuda at this time of year?"

"Eighties to nineties. It's the whole 'girl on a boat with a hot guy' vibe."

"Davis isn't stirred up by that?"

I cracked a smile. "Maybe just a little." Though not for the reasons that Luca thought. Maxwell, my co-star, was gay, and he looked perfectly edible in a sailor suit. "But it's work, and I'm a professional. Do you think I should cancel?

Or try to postpone? There's the funeral to arrange, and Mom—"

"Mom would want you to focus on your career." Luca swallowed hard and reached across the table to squeeze my shoulder. "Brie and her assistant are gonna help with the funeral, plus Nico's offered a room here with catering for the wake."

"Nico?"

"The owner of the Peninsula."

"You've made some good friends."

"Yeah, I have. Fuck, this was the last place I saw myself settling down, but everything just jelled. Brooke, the job, the apartment..."

"I'm glad you're happy here."

"Reckon you're gonna settle down with Davis?"

"Uh... Uh..." I gawped like a guppy. Personal questions threw me off balance, even when they came from my brother. *Especially* when they came from my brother. "Uh, I don't know."

"He seems to really care about you."

"Yes, he does." How could I explain to Luca that we didn't have *that* kind of relationship? The answer: I couldn't. I'd rather walk over red-hot coals than discuss my non-sex life with my brother. "I was lucky to meet him. You honestly think I should go to Bermuda?"

"I promise I'll call if there's any news."

"I'll come back for the funeral."

"When we've got a date, I'll let you know."

"And when they finally lock Dad up, I'm gonna open the damn champagne."

Luca narrowed his eyes.

"Uh, non-alcoholic champagne."

"Better. And I'll be buying."

7

———

AARON

"*S*on of a bitch."

Luca threw his cell phone onto the couch and stalked to the other end of the great room, spitting curses in his wake. I watched from behind the waist-high counter-slash-breakfast bar that formed the boundary of my kitchen. There'd been plenty of similar outbursts in the month since we found his mom's body, but today's "son of a bitch" seemed particularly emphatic.

"Was that Detective Payne on the phone?"

"How'd you guess?"

If anyone deserved the insult, it was Aldrich Payne. I'd crossed paths with him at work, and he'd always struck me as a man who carried the badge for the wrong reasons. He liked the power it gave him, but not the work that came with it. His paperwork game was top notch, according to various acquaintances, but his investigative techniques needed improvement, and given that Payne was on the slow coast toward retirement, upskilling wasn't on his to-do list. I'd hoped that since the victim in this case was the mother of a fellow law enforcement officer, he might put in a little more effort than usual, but judging by Luca's sour expression, those hopes hadn't come to fruition. I put down the knife I was using to chop carrots for dinner and prepared to sympathise.

"What did Payne have to say?"

"He finally got around to interviewing my father. Only took him a fuckin' month. And—get this—Dad has an alibi."

Luca's roll of the eyes told me all I needed to know about his thoughts on that.

"What alibi?"

"Herb Pettigrew says that on the day Mom disappeared, the two of them were drinking in the Cave from mid-afternoon until closing time."

"How the hell would Herb know? His brain's fried, and the night in question was twenty years ago."

"That's what I said. Herb claimed he remembered because the next day, Dad was complaining that Mom had upped and left, and how was he meant to deal with two kids on his own? Swears on the Bible that it's the truth."

"Herb hasn't been to church this side of puberty. Asa told me he got kicked out of Sunday school for spiking the orange juice at snack time."

Asa was my boss, and he'd been an attorney in Baldwin's Shore for as long as I'd been alive.

"Dad asked Herb to cover for him, I know it, but Payne won't follow up. Says it'd be a waste of police resources because the DA would never prosecute, and he's waiting for the DNA results to come back."

"It's true that the DA wouldn't prosecute the way things stand. Anyone who knows Herb would consider it more likely than not that he's just doing a friend a favour, but a jury of strangers? The claim's enough to create reasonable doubt."

"Are you taking Payne's side?"

"No. It's still a cop-out, if you'll excuse the pun. He needs to dig deeper, but I'm not sure he has the aptitude, and he certainly doesn't have the inclination."

"So, what the hell do we do now?"

"Way I see it, you've got two choices—you wait and hope, or you look into things yourself."

"Which means I'm stuck between a rock and Sheriff Newman. Son, I understand you're upset about this," Luca mimicked in a passable impression of the sheriff's drawl. "But we can't have deputies runnin' around town on some sorta vendetta. There's been quite enough drama in Baldwin's Shore this year already. Sit back and let the state police do their job."

"What if they're not doing their job?"

"Maybe I could try speaking to the sheriff? But I've been working at the department for less than six months, and I'm still in my probationary period. I can't afford to rock the boat too much. There aren't many employment opportunities around here, and I have to think of Brooke too. If I fuck this up, we're screwed. Did I tell you Elmira Fairbanks complained about me and Colt?"

Elmira Fairbanks? Figured. If Satan ever needed an assistant, she'd make a great candidate.

"Why'd she complain?"

"Number one, we trespassed on her property. Number two, we accused her of being a criminal. Number three, we were rude."

"You mean you knocked on her door and asked a few questions about a wrong she absolutely committed?"

"Exactly."

"Did you show Newman the video of said wrong?"

"Yeah, but he said because it was a civil matter rather than a crime, his hands were tied. And then he went off on a tangent and started complaining about vigilantes. He wants to know who the Bad Samaritan is."

Ah, yes. The Bad Samaritan. In Baldwin's Shore, we had the *ultimate* vigilante. As well as playing videographer in order to out Elmira Fairbanks as a catnapper, he'd lent a hand when my sister got targeted by a psychopathic stalker, and when Brie got abducted, he'd stepped in again to assist with her rescue. But his actions had left one man in the hospital and another dead, so understandably, Sheriff Newman was twitchy about the whole thing.

"You got any ideas?"

"One or two."

"Which are?"

"Okay, one. Nico."

Couldn't deny I'd had that thought myself. The vigilante shit had only started after Nico arrived in Baldwin's Shore, and Brie's security team had discovered that he had a dark past. Plus he liked cats.

"Fits. What are you gonna do about it?"

"Right now? Nothing. If he hadn't gotten involved when he did, Brooke would've gone through hell and there's a good chance Colt and I would be dead. That doesn't give us much of an incentive to unmask him. Plus Brooke would be pissed. She likes Nico. So does Brie, and don't even get me started on Addy."

"Addy likes his money."

"Yeah. He seems pretty tolerant, though."

Polite, even a little flirtatious, but he wasn't the type to fool around with a friend. If Nico was the Bad Samaritan, I couldn't see him hurting her. Or any of us, in fact.

"So Sheriff Newman's gonna have to keep on wondering, then?"

"Yup. Me and Colt are agreed on that."

"And what about your mom?"

"I wanna go right over and break that motherfucker's face, but as I said, I've got Brooke to think of now. If I raise hell, where would that leave our future?"

"You know I'd represent you gratis, but I think that's the right decision. For now."

"Sure as shit I'll re-evaluate if Detective Payne doesn't pull his finger out."

Which meant Luca would be re-evaluating a month down the line, no question. But hopefully with a cooler head. Emotions were still running high, and it was my duty as a friend to try to keep him from doing anything rash.

"Again, I think that's the right decision."

Luca sighed, heavy and deep. "Yeah, I know. But I don't have to like it."

"Want a beer?"

"Just one. I have an early start tomorrow. Gotta take a drunk and disorderly over to the courthouse. Deputy Dawkins tripped over his kid's skateboard last week and broke his wrist, so they're short-handed over in Coos Bay."

I opened the refrigerator, took out a bottle.

"Here you go. I've got the morning off." Which meant that this evening, I could drink a whole damn bottle of wine if I wanted to, but I started with a glass. "My schedule's packed for the rest of the week after that, though." Romi was coming back tomorrow afternoon, so I might as well get my excuses in early. "Evening appointments, court prep, documents to draft."

"But you'll come over for dinner, right?"

"I'll see what I can shuffle."

"You didn't even keep one day clear?"

"I blocked out Friday."

No way could I miss the funeral, not if I wanted Luca to speak to me again. Romi would just have to deal with it.

"What about the weekend?"

"The firm's busy at the moment, and I can't afford to turn down work."

Although thanks to the money Luca had chipped in toward the renovation project after he decided to move in with Brooke, I was in far better shape financially than I'd anticipated. Funny how life worked out, wasn't it?

When I finished law school, I'd planned to work at one of the big firms in New York for a while, long enough to get some experience before I moved back to the West Coast. But the competition for those positions was intense, and despite graduating in the top ten percent of my class, I'd lost out every time. Coming home to Baldwin's Shore, I'd felt like a failure. But I'd been offered the derelict building that had once been an indoor car dealership for a song, Asa had hired me with the intention that I'd take over his law firm when he retired, and I had a great group of friends. My love life was a mess, but I was only twenty-eight. I still had time to fix that.

I just had to get through the next week first.

I'd had to let Asa in on the secret, at least partially. Having a fold-up bed delivered to the office was bound to arouse his curiosity, but my back wouldn't take another night on the couch. In the end, I'd kept it vague—simply told him that I'd fallen out with Romi a few years ago in New York—and he'd been smart enough not to ask questions. He also understood the importance of confidentiality, so I wasn't worried about Luca finding out. Not from Asa, anyway.

Luca folded his arms and fixed his steely gaze on me. "If I didn't know better, I'd say you were trying to avoid Romi and Davis."

I choked on a mouthful of wine, turned it into what might have passed for a laugh. "Not at all. We're just at that difficult stage where there's too much work for two people but not enough for three."

"Things are going well, then? You're picking up new clients?"

"Yeah. I negotiated a couple of good divorce settlements, and word got around. Now my appointment book's full of bitter women ready to bitch about their exes."

"Romi always said you were a good listener."

Once, perhaps, but Romi sure wouldn't say that anymore. Luca's words were a punch to the gut.

I picked up the knife and went back to chopping carrots. One week, and life could get back to normal. One week... This time, I'd planned ahead. Stocked the office kitchen with food, stashed a suitcase full of clothes in the coat closet, remembered to pack a toothbrush. No problem. I could get through this.

Or so I thought.

***

"Buddy, I need a favour."

"Sure," I said automatically because this was Luca. I'd always help him out. Plus he'd woken me up at...five thirty a.m.—what the hell?—and I wasn't thinking straight. "What's up? You want me to walk the dog today?" Brooke's mutt, Vega, was lying at my feet, snoring quietly. Occasionally he farted. He'd taken to sleepovers when the mood struck him, but he made a better companion than my ex-girlfriend, so I couldn't complain. "Run an errand?"

"Can you pick Romi up from the airport? Her flight got rescheduled."

Ah, fuck.

"I thought she was flying in with Davis and he was gonna rent a car?"

"That was the original plan, but the baggage handlers in Paris announced a strike, so she jumped on an earlier flight and came straight here. She texted me in the middle of the night and asked if I could arrange a ride."

"When does she land?"

"Four hours."

"I might not make it in time. How about I book her a cab?"

"You know she hates getting in cars with strangers."

In case they drove the way her father always did—which was to say too fast, too close to the vehicle in front, and occasionally under the influence. I'd seen her get out of a cab shaking, although she'd never openly admit to the problem.

"I could pay extra to have them drive slowly."

"Is there a reason you can't go? I thought you had the morning off?"

"No reason." Shit. "I'll leave right now."

8

ROMI

ou've got to be kidding me.

When my brother replied to my desperate "Help, I'm about to jump onto the nearest plane" message with "Ride arranged" and a smiley emoji, I'd assumed it meant he'd shuffled things around to pick me up himself. Either that or Brooke had offered to come. But when I walked into the arrivals hall and saw a once-familiar face, I almost turned around and flew right back to Paris.

What the hell was Aaron doing here?

He was holding up a handwritten sign, cab-driver-style, and I squinted to read it.

I SWEAR THIS WASN'T MY IDEA

There were more words underneath, and when I got close enough to read them, I almost smiled. *Typical Aaron.*

Give me one finger if you want to ride with me, two if you want me to find you a cab.

I hated cabs, really hated them. First, there was the stop-start-stop-start, let's-beat-the-damn-lights attitude, and then there was the road rage. Maybe I'd just been unlucky? Or maybe I gave off "drive like a lunatic" vibes? Whatever, one dose of whiplash from a perfectly avoidable accident was quite enough, thank you.

But four hours stuck in a car with Aaron... Was that better or worse? At least he wouldn't try to make small talk. Or get lost.

Aaron smiled when I flipped him the bird, and my heart skipped. I hadn't seen that smile in three long years, and the tightening of my chest was an involuntary reaction I needed to train myself out of.

"Sorry, Luca asked me to pick you up, and I couldn't think up an excuse fast enough," Aaron said. "And he already questioned whether I'm avoiding you."

"You could've warned me."

"How? I don't have your new number, and I figured a tweet would be inappropriate."

Valid points, much as I hated to admit it. "I'll sit in the back."

"Need a hand with your bags?"

"No, I'm perfectly capable."

One day, I'd learn to travel light, I swear. But today wasn't that day, and the extra suitcase full of clothes I'd been gifted from yesterday's shoot quickly put an end to my idea of riding in the back seat. By the time we'd stuffed two suitcases into the trunk and jigsawed a third plus my carry-on, laptop bag, and oversized purse into the vehicle, the only place left for me was next to Aaron with the seat jammed forward so my knees were wedged against the dash.

"Don't say anything," I warned him.

"I didn't."

"You're judging."

"I'm just wondering how long I'll have to sleep at the office, that's all. That sure is a lot of luggage."

"Why would you sleep at the office?"

"To keep out of your hair."

Oh. "A week. I'm planning to stay for a week."

Aaron glanced in the rear-view mirror. "Okaaaay."

"You *are* judging. I wasn't sure what the weather would be like, so I had to bring clothes for every eventuality, and some of the stuff is gifts for Brooke and Addy. Why do I have to justify myself to you, anyway?"

"You don't."

Aaron pulled away—slowly—and we lapsed into silence as I studied the passing scenery. The only noise came from the classic rock-and-roll songs on the radio. Even though I'd only known Mom for a short time, I'd inherited her love of the oldies, and the more I'd thought of her these past weeks, the more little snippets of life with her had come sneaking back. The way she used to duet with Elvis as she prepared dinner. Dancing around the kitchen while we waited for the food to cook. The contrast between her sunny personality and my dad's surliness.

How had they ended up together? How had she been fooled by his dubious charms? Objectively, I had to concede that my father was handsome, but his veneer of charisma quickly wore away to reveal the asshole underneath. Over the years since Mom's death, he'd had a steady stream of girlfriends, but none had lasted longer than a few months. Mom had *married* him. And it wasn't because she'd been pregnant with Luca—he hadn't been born until eleven months after the wedding.

She'd come from Idaho originally, a small town I either hadn't known or couldn't remember the name of. My grandmother on her side had died young, and Mom's father had never been in the picture. As for the grandparents on Dad's side... Let's just say it was clear where his winning personality had come from.

City gave way to country, neat fields of crops with wooded hills in the distance. Although I'd grown up in Oregon, I'd spent so long away that I felt like a stranger now. Was this how Luca and Aaron had felt when they came back to Baldwin's Shore? As if they'd moved on in one direction and the town had moved on in another? Aaron had been tense when we started driving, knuckles white where he gripped the steering wheel, but as the hours passed, he seemed to relax a tiny bit. At least he kept his speed steady along I-5. I used to wonder if he only drove sensibly when I was in the car, if he was a speed demon the rest of the time, but Brooke said he always preferred the brakes to the gas.

The journey gave me time to think, too much time. This month's shoots and shows and fitting sessions and interviews and business meetings had allowed me to block out the storm brewing in Baldwin's Shore for a while, but now I had a mostly clear schedule and a mind filled with questions. Why had Dad killed Mom? True, they hadn't gotten along for, like, my entire life, but he'd spent the next several years complaining about household chores and childcare, what little of it he bothered to do. Why had they gone to the cabin in the woods? Did he plan her death in advance? Or had it been a spur-of-the-moment attack, the tragic result of frayed tempers and ready fists?

And more importantly, when was he going to pay for what he'd done?

I'd called Detective Payne almost every day since I met him, and on the occasions he deigned to speak with me, he'd had little to report. Forensic evidence was still being reviewed, Dad had some bullshit alibi and denied everything, no sign of the murder weapon, blah, blah, blah. Mom had died of a head injury, that much we knew. Someone had hit her hard enough to crack her skull.

We trundled through Coos Bay, heading for Baldwin's Shore. When I'd driven the route with Luca, we'd been too busy talking for me to pay much attention to the scenery, but now I noticed the little things. A miniature pagoda advertising a Japanese garden with authentic tea ceremonies, a solar farm in the field where old Mr. Hardesty used to keep cattle, a cluster of barns behind neat green paddocks that looked like a new horse farm. The Steak and Shake came up on our right, and at least that looked familiar.

"Does Viola May still own the diner?" I asked without thinking, then cursed myself inwardly for starting a conversation I didn't want to have.

"The only way she'll leave that place is feet first. Nothing's changed. Same menu, same counter, same tables." Aaron cut his eyes in my direction. "Same jukebox."

"I bet you don't sing along with it anymore."

"You got me there."

We lapsed back into silence, but it wasn't quite as uncomfortable as before. If Aaron was trying to be civil, then I should try too, for appearances' sake. If Luca really had asked Aaron whether he was avoiding me, then we needed to be careful not to raise his suspicions further. No way did I want the details of my sordid past finding their way back to my brother.

I also suspected that Luca was trying to hide things from me, not about his past but about Mom. Well, not hide them exactly, but gloss over the unpalatable reality. Would Aaron do the same?

"If I ask you a question, will you tell me the truth?" I asked.

Another glance. "Probably."

"Probably?"

"If I believe telling the truth will result in bodily harm, I reserve the right to plead the Fifth."

"You sound like such a lawyer."

"There's a good reason for that." A pause. "What's the question?"

"Do you think Detective Payne is good at his job? Luca says that there's a process to be followed, and we should allow it to run its course, but..."

"But what?"

"But Payne doesn't strike me as being particularly competent."

"Why do you say that?"

"He doesn't seem to do much apart from dodging my calls and hiding behind stupid rules."

"Have you spoken to him at all in the past several weeks?"

"Once or twice, but... Wait a second... Why am *I* the one answering all the questions?"

"Sorry, bad habit." Aaron drew in a long breath. "No, I don't think Detective Payne is good at his job."

"And why do you say that?" I mimicked, which got a chuckle out of Aaron at least.

"I've run across him a couple of times, and he feels to me like a guy riding out the clock until he can collect his pension, doing the bare minimum to get by. And after I formed that opinion, I asked Asa what he thought, and he was slightly more..." Aaron grimaced faintly. "Scathing. Mutual acquaintances say Payne's strength lies in paperwork, but he's not even great at that. Asa got a client off on a technicality a while back after Payne filled out a form incorrectly."

Well, wasn't that just wonderful? "Why the heck did they give him Mom's case? Don't they want to see it solved?"

"Another question I discussed with Asa. As best we can ascertain, they saw a twenty-year-old homicide with no significant evidence and figured it was gonna be a bitch to clear. So rather than take up a good cop's time at a point when crime is on the increase and they're hunting a serial rapist over in Douglas County, they gave it to Payne to tick his damn boxes."

"So what now? What happens when he can't connect the dots and arrest Dad?"

"Are we still going for honesty here?"

My stomach dropped. "Yes."

"Then the file will most probably sit on the corner of Payne's desk, gathering dust until he collects his pension."

I thought back to my visit to Roseburg, to the mess in Payne's office. There had to be two hundred other files in there already.

"No. No, no, no. That's unacceptable. This needs to be fixed."

"Only way you'll fix it is by getting a competent investigator to do the legwork."

"Can't Luca get the case back?"

"Luca's in a difficult position. He's a trainee deputy, and he's been expressly forbidden by his boss to get involved. And much as I hate to say it, he doesn't have investigative experience. Enthusiasm can only take you so far. A seasoned investigator learns how to read suspects, picks up on clues that others might miss."

"Can't we get Payne's boss to reassign the case?"

"You can try. But there's a reason Payne gets away with doing very little, and that reason is his boss is an asshole."

"Thanks for the warning, but I'll have to try speaking with him. I can't let this go." Aaron opened his mouth to speak. "Please, I don't need a lecture."

"I was only gonna say that in your position, I couldn't let it go either."

Oh. Right. Aaron's support surprised me. I'd expected him to take my brother's side.

"Thanks for understanding, I guess."

"Just telling it the way I see it. And I'd suggest waiting until after the wake before you start making waves—Luca's hurting too, and he doesn't need the extra stress."

The funeral was tomorrow, and then we were into the weekend. Did Payne's boss work Saturdays? Grudgingly, I had to concede that Aaron was right about Luca, and I wasn't going to disagree out of sheer bloody-mindedness. I could wait until Monday if necessary.

"Fine. I won't meet with the man until after Mom's buried."

I'd had plenty of practice at dealing with assholes, and although it wasn't something I enjoyed, I wasn't scared of them. A decade in the fashion industry, working daily with designers and photographers and journalists who needed their egos massaged at every possible opportunity, had taught me when to push, when to back off, and when to do an end run around them.

"Do you want me to drop you off at the Peninsula or at Luca's place?" Aaron asked.

Since Luca's place was also Aaron's place, the hotel would do just fine.

"The Peninsula."

"Got it."

"And Aaron?"

"Yeah?"

"Thanks. Thanks for picking me up, and thanks for not making this more painful than it needed to be."

His lips flickered up in what might have been a smile or a wince. Since I didn't want to stare openly, I couldn't be sure.

"No problem."

9

ROMI

Baldwin's Shore had three churches. St. Luke's was the prettiest, on the edge of town with a view of the sea. We'd chosen the cemetery there as Mom's final resting place. She always had loved walking on the beach, and this was the closest she'd ever get to it now.

St. Luke's was also the smallest church, but we figured Mom's funeral wouldn't draw a big crowd. The people who'd known her would come, and maybe a few other folks would show up out of morbid curiosity, but it wouldn't be standing room only. Baldwin's Shore had a transient population—people came and went all the time—and most of Mom's friends had moved away years ago. Not that she'd had many friends. Two small children plus two jobs and Dad's constant demands hadn't made it easy for her to have a social life. I could still hear his voice in my head. *Why isn't dinner on the damn table? What do you mean, we're out of beer? Get these kids out from under my feet!*

I'd agonised over what to wear. The last funeral I'd attended had been for a flamboyant fashion designer, so everyone just picked one of his outfits and the whole event took on the air of a runway show, albeit a slightly subdued one. According to the official story, the one fed to the press, Massimo had died in the hospital after a short illness. Those of us who were connected knew he'd been beaned with an Anish Gormley sculpture entitled "Three Lovers" after his wife caught him in bed with his girlfriend. The resulting head injury had caused the blood clot that killed him, and the world had lost a priceless piece of modern art. But of course, we hadn't been able to talk about that at the wake, an affair made all the more awkward by the scuffle between his wife and girlfriend after the burial. Davis had been with me on that day too, and when I'd questioned the wife's choice of attire—palazzo pants—he'd pointed out that she needed something to hide her ankle tag. Still, with the money she'd inherited, she could afford a good lawyer.

In the end, I'd picked out a simple black wrap dress for Mom's funeral. Calf-length, plain apart from a thick purple ribbon at the waist, and the neckline was demure enough that I couldn't get accused of being inappropriate. And I'd swapped my usual stilettos for kitten heels. Waterproof mascara? Check. Nude lipstick? Check. Sensible chignon? Check. If any morbid freak decided to snap a photo of me for Twitter, I was ready.

Picking out Mom's casket had been harder than choosing my outfit. The mortician had suggested a child's coffin because there was nothing left of her but bones, but that was just...wrong. We'd picked out a full-size casket in dove grey, and I'd bought flowers in every colour of the rainbow. Mom had loved flowers.

Davis got out of the car first and opened an umbrella. The rain fell in a steady drizzle against a grey sky as we hurried toward the church, not so much as a glimmer of blue in the distance. Luca was waiting outside the door, and he gave me a quick hug.

"Holding up okay?"

Not even a little bit, but I shrugged. Colt was standing next to Luca, and he gave me a hug too. And then there was Aaron. Of course Luca had asked him to be a pall-bearer—they were best friends—but that left me in a difficult position. I could hardly shake his hand, but I didn't want his arms around me either. And if I blanked him, Luca would want to know why. In the end, I closed my eyes and offered a cheek, suppressing a shiver when Aaron's lips brushed against my skin for the merest second.

"I'm sorry," he whispered, and I wasn't sure whether he was apologising for the unwanted contact or for the loss of my mother. Either way, I didn't answer.

The fourth pall-bearer was a guy I didn't know, Decker, so I offered him a cheek as well. He'd never met Mom, but he was a friend of Luca's and also the right height, so I had to be grateful that he'd stepped in.

"Sorry for your loss, Ms. Mendez," he said.

"Please, call me Romi. Thank you for being here today."

"Be lying if I said it was a pleasure, but it's not a chore."

Inside, I did a quick headcount. Over fifty people were waiting in the pews.

"Do you know everyone here?" Davis murmured.

"Maybe half of them?"

Brooke, Brie, and Addy were at the front, perfectly coordinated in black, black, and black, and Addy waved us forward.

"We saved you seats."

I looked beyond her to the couple sitting at the end of the row. The woman was wearing a voluminous dark-grey dress that hadn't been fashionable for at least six years, and the guy clearly hadn't gotten the message about it being a funeral because he was rocking a flamingo-pink suit with the hair to match.

Brooke followed my gaze. "These are my colleagues, Darla and Paulo. They came for moral support."

Darla gave me a sad smile, and Paulo rushed over with his arms flung wide.

"It's so amazing to meet you! I love your dress. And your shoes, and your hair. The whole look, really. Are those earrings from your accessory collection? Brooke's told me all about it." He squashed the air out of my lungs, and Brooke must have given him a glare because he hurried to apologise. "Sorry, sorry, shouldn't mention that right now. And I'm sorry about the pinkness. It's the only suit I have."

Davis's lips twitched, but his amusement quickly turned to shock when Paulo hugged him too. In the whole time I'd known Davis, nobody had ever greeted him that way.

"And you must be Davis? I've heard about you too." Paulo turned his head my way and mouthed, "Very nice." Then he released Davis and clapped his hands over his mouth. "Oh! I'm so sorry for your loss. Should've said that part first."

I wasn't quite sure how to respond. "Uh, thanks?"

Brooke elbowed him in the side. "Paulo, stop."

He did, thankfully, and I turned to Davis, widening my eyes a fraction in a silent expression of "Holy crap, he's something else," but Davis only gave the merest hint of a smile and said, "Hmm."

The pastor arrived, another newcomer whom I'd met last month when we tentatively began planning for the funeral. Dad had shown no interest whatsoever. Technically, he was next of kin, but he hadn't said a word when Luca claimed Mom's body. According to my brother, who'd plugged himself into the local gossip network, the pastor's predecessor, Father Jacob—who'd piously told twelve-year-old me that bad girls went to hell when he saw me holding hands with Aaron—had quit religion and run off to live in sin with Phoebe Gilmore's mom. Phoebe was here today, sitting near the back with her hands neatly folded in her lap.

Right behind the Baldwins. Yes, *those* Baldwins, or three of them at least. Easton Baldwin Junior—EJ—the current patriarch of the clan, his second wife, Marianna, and EJ's older son, Parker.

"Why are the Baldwins here?" I whispered to Brooke.

"Probably because your mom used to work for EJ."

"She used to work for Skip too, and he isn't here."

"Because he's in jail."

Oh, yeah. Right. My mind was mush today. At least the other three Baldwin siblings hadn't shown up. Lillian and Kayleigh, the twins, had called me "beanpole" all the way through high school, and when I started modelling, they'd gotten ahold of my email address and actually expected me to send them tickets to shows. And Easton the Third, he was just a jackass.

People kept filing in, more than I ever thought would come. I recognised Tad, who owned the grocery store, Annie from the hair and beauty salon, and Rufus Biggins, who ran the ranch where Dad used to work until he'd gotten fired. Dick Horton shuffled in, leaning on a pair of walking sticks, and Dylan Rodwell followed, the first time I'd seen him wear anything other than a plaid shirt and jeans. A woman waved to me from several rows behind, and I waved back, although I couldn't remember her name. Her face looked vaguely familiar, as did twenty or so others, but there were so many people I could swear I'd never seen before.

Turned out it *was* standing room only.

And at least one of the attendees was a reporter. I didn't recognise her, but I did recognise her type. Unashamedly nosy, more interested in getting a story than tiptoeing around grieving relatives. She locked eyes with me, held my gaze until I looked away.

Coward. You know better than to flinch first.

The opening bars of the funeral march played, and although I'd promised myself I wouldn't cry, an extraordinary sadness welled up inside me. Davis put an arm around me, lending me his strength as Mom began her final journey. Luca and Aaron, Colt and Deck, they carried her in grim-faced, their backs rigid. Only when Luca took a seat between Brooke and me could I breathe again. Aaron had the sense to sit with Addy on the other side of the aisle.

Mom's funeral was made all the sadder by its brevity. There were no heartfelt readings, no amusing anecdotes, no tales of the past. Luca got up to say a few words, but they were about the future we'd missed out on with her rather than the time we'd actually spent together.

The future that had been stolen by a monster.

I felt him before I saw him.

First, my gut clenched, then a knot of fear tangled in my belly, and when I looked around, I knew what I'd see.

Who I'd see.

My so-called father.

He'd slipped in at the back, and now he was standing by the door, leaning against the wall with his hands in his pockets. Why? Why had he come? Did he want to rub our faces in it? I'd read enough of Davis's detective novels to know that killers often returned to the scene of the crime. Was that why he was here? To gloat? To feel the thrill again? To relive past triumphs?

Anger flashed through me, red-hot and molten. Not just today's anger, but a lifetime of fury and resentment. I tried to push it away, to tamp it down, but it was like trying to hold back the ocean with my bare hands. By the time we got outside, it had become a tsunami. While everyone else followed Mom's casket to the waiting grave, I veered off to the left. To where *he* was standing under the spreading branches of an old cedar tree.

"How dare you? How dare you come here today?"

"Thought I'd pay my last respects to my wife."

"You had no respect for her. You had no respect for any of us."

"What's to respect? Surprised you came back, child, after the way you hotfooted it out of town."

I'd always been "child." Sometimes I wondered if he even remembered my name.

"She was my mother! Serena June Mendez was my mother."

"She turned into nothing but a two-bit whore and you followed in her footsteps, prancing around in your underwear all day. Fucking a man old enough to be your father."

For a second, I forgot where I was. Forgot everything—the crowd, the pastor, the casket—and my world narrowed to a sharp point. I was a little girl again. A little girl standing in front of a father who'd never loved her and never would love her, scared but stoic, waiting for the inevitable. Long ago, I'd learned to twist to the right as his fist connected, a way to lessen the damage.

Except I wasn't so little anymore.

My palm cracked off Dad's cheek as I slapped him, but he didn't flinch. No, he just barked out a laugh and grabbed my wrist in a vice-like grip so I couldn't do it again.

"How dare you raise a hand to me, child? I'm your father."

"You're no father."

"Hey!" Davis appeared beside me. "Don't you speak to her that way."

"Or what?"

"Or you'll come to regret it."

Dad just laughed again and used his free hand to shove Davis in the chest, hard enough that he stumbled backward with his arms windmilling and landed on his ass. I didn't miss the look of shock on Davis's face. *Nobody* treated him that way. Was he okay? Please say he was okay.

"Let go of me!"

But Dad didn't loosen his grip, and I found myself trapped, stuck at the mercy of a father who used fists and intimidation in place of kindness and encouragement. I tried to pull away and failed, but before I could make another attempt, a fist shot past me and connected with Dad's biceps. His arm fell away, limp.

Aaron cradled his fist in his other hand. "Keep your hands off her, motherfucker."

Dad recovered quickly. He always had been good in a fight. "You little..."

But then Luca was at Aaron's side, and Colt, and Deck, a wall of muscle that even a brute like Rey Mendez couldn't bulldoze his way through.

"You've got some nerve showing your face today," Luca growled.

"Got as much right to be here as anyone."

Dad still couldn't move his arm properly, and I hoped there was permanent damage. It would be nothing more than he deserved. In my peripheral vision, I saw Aaron offer his good hand to Davis and help him to his feet, but I couldn't take my eyes off Luca standing up to Dad.

"Why? Because you caused this? Someday, you're gonna get what you deserve."

"I already went through this with the cop, son. It's bullshit."

"I may have your genes, but I'll never be your son."

"And I'll never be your daughter," I put in.

"Take a look in the mirror, child. You're my daughter, all right."

"Get the hell away from here," Luca told him. "Stay out of our lives, and stay out of Mom's death."

Dad gave a careless, one-shouldered shrug. "Hot-blooded and heartless. Guess the apple didn't fall far from the tree with either of you."

And then he sauntered off.

10

ROMI

What a mess. What a damn mess.

The water scalded my skin as I sank lower in Davis's tub, but I ignored the sting. Deserved it. What if I just slipped right under? Took a deep breath? Anything was better than facing the shitstorm awaiting me on social media. Nothing was private anymore, *nothing*, not even a funeral.

Gardenia-scented bubbles tickled my nose, and I fought back a sneeze. The bath hadn't been my idea. I didn't even like baths, which was why I'd picked the room with the family-sized shower stall, but Davis was fond of unwinding with a hot bubble bath after a hard day—something he'd never admit to anyone else—so when I'd arrived back in our hotel suite and headed straight for the minibar, he'd blocked my way, talked me off a ledge I couldn't climb down from alone, and provided me with an alternative way to de-stress. *His* way. Me? I still craved vodka to numb the horror. Needed it.

He'd bruised me. My father had bruised me. Not for the first time, but today he'd done it in front of everyone because he didn't care about the consequences. Why? Because he'd thought there would *be* no consequences. His whole life, he'd gotten away with knocking us around because nobody had done a damn thing. Once, I'd tried reporting him. Just once. When I was nine or maybe ten, I'd climbed out of the window while Dad was whaling on Luca, run to the police office attached to the tiny library on Main Street, and sobbed in front of Colt's predecessor, a portly old guy named Edwin Kidd, if I remembered right. Kidd had given me a pat on the head and a "there, there" and marched me straight back home again. Luca had been gone, and Kidd left me there with that monster. Just the two of us. Dad had loosened one of my teeth that day, as well as knocking another nail into the coffin that held my spirit. Despite the bathwater being hot enough to boil shrimp, I shivered from thinking about it.

And his words from this morning echoed in my head—the apple didn't fall far from the tree. Dad was right. Much as I hated to admit it, he was absolutely right. My temper came from him, and most likely my taste for alcohol too. That slap today had been a misstep, a huge one. If he'd made the first move in grabbing me, I could have pressed charges. My arm had purple finger marks. Assault was the poor relation to homicide, but at the moment, I'd take anything I could get as long as he ended up in a cage.

At least he hadn't escaped completely unscathed today. That punch from Aaron... I hadn't seen it coming, and neither had Dad, clearly. Probably because Aaron rarely showed that side of himself. Usually, his lawyer persona won out—calm, controlled, some might even say cold. But heat lurked under the surface. I'd seen flashes of it over the years, both when we were kids and in a different way on *that* night. My thighs clenched involuntarily as my thoughts spiralled off into a direction I absolutely didn't want them to go in.

Maybe I could just have one drink to take the edge off? A single shot, no more. Yes, it would represent failure, but I'd been a fuck-up my whole life, so why change now? Luca was over in the conference suite, noshing on canapés, reminiscing about Mom, and apologising to the guests for his sister's outburst. Davis had headed over there as well, to do what he termed "damage control." If I rearranged the bottles in the minibar after I'd taken one and hid the empty, nobody would ever know. Although it *would* appear on the tab, so I'd have to head over to the lobby and pay it off in cash. And swear the receptionist to secrecy.

Just one drink...

I was halfway out of the bathtub when the door opened. I jumped out of my skin, water and bubbles slopped everywhere, and Davis's current paperback met a soggy end.

"Shit!" I fished around blindly, and it came out dripping. "Shit, I'm sorry."

What was the title? I'd have to order a new copy, yet another thing to add to my to-do list. *Hard Tide*—a surfer, a private investigator, an age-old mystery. Huh. A private investigator...

"It'll dry out." Davis pulled a towel off the heated rail and wrapped it around me. Pressed his lips to my forehead in that calming way of his. "How are you feeling?"

"Honestly?"

"Didn't we promise to always be honest with each other?"

Yes, and the guilt hit again.

"Okay, I'm annoyed. Annoyed that Dad had the gall to show up and ruin what was already a horrible day, but even more annoyed with myself for losing my cool." I closed my eyes for a second, then asked the question I really didn't want to know the answer to. "How bad is it?"

"It's fixed."

"Thank you, thank you, I—"

"Not by me, by Bartlett."

"Huh?"

Davis's smile was meant to be encouraging, but the hardness in his eyes said he was irritated that he hadn't gotten there first.

"A reporter was close enough to photograph the altercation, but Bartlett called in a favour, apparently. The picture's gone, and there won't be any further mention of the incident."

Why? Why had Aaron done that? Out of guilt? Or to avoid becoming the subject of gossip himself? Lawyers weren't meant to punch people, I was certain of that. But he had. He'd caught Dad by surprise and given me a precious moment to regroup.

"What if somebody else got a photo?"

"The consensus is that she was the only one. I offered your apologies for skipping the wake, but we're both expected for dinner this evening. Want me to come up with an excuse for that too?"

Tempting. And it would be oh-so easy to feign a headache and hide away in my bedroom for the weekend. But Luca would come looking for me, probably Brooke too, and I didn't want them to think I was a coward who always ran away from things. Even though I was.

"We should make an appearance. Stay through the main course at least. Everyone's going to be discussing Mom's case, and I want to find out what's happening." My stomach roiled at the mention of food, and I knew I wouldn't be eating much, if anything. Cue imminent speculation over whether Romina Mendez had an eating disorder. "But there's something I want to talk to you about first. Do you have a minute?"

"For you? I have all the time in the world. Let me get us drinks while you put your clothes on."

"Make mine a mango juice? There's a bottle in the minibar. Uh, I only glanced in there. I didn't touch the alcohol, I swear."

"Yes, I know." This time, Davis's smile was sly. "I counted the bottles, and you didn't have time to hotfoot it over to the lobby and charm the desk staff into covering up the evidence." He watched me closely, and I didn't hide my guilt fast enough. "Ah, you did think about it."

Davis hadn't gotten to his position in life by being a pushover, although Dad might beg to differ. No, Davis had clawed his way from Bayonne, New Jersey, to Wall Street through grit, determination, and no small amount of cunning. Beneath the sharp suits, beneath the kindness he showed me and his generosity, he was a wolf.

But seeing as he was *my* wolf, I had to take that as a positive.

My phone was the latest model, a dinky little thing gifted to me by the manufacturer in the hope that I'd get photographed using it. But right now, it felt like a brick in my hand as I turned it over and over. To text or not to text? Davis was still in his bedroom—sometimes he seemed to spend longer on his hair than I did—but I didn't have long to make up my mind.

Mom's voice played in my head. *Say thank you, Romi. You should always say thank you if somebody helps you.*

And today, Aaron had helped me.

I might have cut him out of my life and spent the past three years cursing his name and mentally running his magic cock through a mincer, but I'd never quite been able to bring myself to delete the last digital traces of him. He didn't have my number, but I still had his. Assuming he hadn't changed it, of course. What if he'd changed it? What if he'd gotten a new phone to go with his new life and his new job? Maybe I was going through all this "Should I? Shouldn't I?" for nothing.

I tapped out a message. Read it. Read it again. Deleted it. How the hell did a girl thank a guy for thumping a blood relative? A guy she'd once hungered for and now mostly hated? What if I just sent him a fruit basket?

Me: If you spend some time at home this week, I won't throw a hissy fit. Or a punch. Nice left hook, by the way.

It was kind of a thank-you, right? Whatever, it would have to do. I added an "R" at the end, just in case Aaron thought some other random person was congratulating him on his boxing skills.

Send.

Well, it was done now. A part of me wished I could take the words back, but it was done. And I didn't have to speak with him. I hadn't made any promises about talking.

My phone beeped.

Aaron: Who are you and what have you done with Romi?

Asshole. I carefully selected the middle-finger emoji and fired it back at him.

Aaron: Aaah, there she is.

This was going to be a long, long evening.

11

ROMI

"Another glass of...whatever that is?" Nico asked. "Orange juice?"

"Mango juice. Yes, please."

At some point between the funeral and dinner, we'd lost Darla and Paulo but gained Nico, much to my relief and Davis's disappointment. I quite liked Nico's quiet confidence, but Davis had researched his background during our previous visit and found that not only had Nico inherited most of his wealth, he'd inherited it from a Russian father who was shady as fuck. Davis didn't have much time for men who rode the family gravy train. He'd preferred Paulo for the entertainment value.

And Davis had grown even more irritated by Nico when he'd taken a seat on the other side of me and engaged me in small talk while we waited for Brooke to serve dinner. I'd offered to help in the kitchen because that would have been easier than playing Switzerland-in-the-middle while Russia and the USA sniped at each other, but Brooke had waved me away, saying she had everything under control. Well, kind of. What she'd actually said was, "Romi, you burn water. Leave this to the professionals," but the sentiment was there. And she spoke the truth. Dad used to yell at Luca and me if we used the stove while he was out—which was most of the time—so I'd never mastered the basics. Nonna Bartlett had cooked dinner most nights, for Aaron and Brooke, for me and Luca, and often for Colt and Addy too. The rest of the time, I'd lived on cereal. Left to my own devices, I'd probably still live on cereal.

In fact, I wished I was eating a bowl of Lucky Charms at this very moment, squirrelled away in the hotel suite. But no, I had pasta, and if you counted the dog snoring at Brooke's feet, the men around the table outnumbered the women by two to one. Luca had already pulled me aside for the "What the hell were you playing at?" talk-slash-lecture, and now he was ignoring me while he, Colt, and Aaron discussed the "next steps" at the other end of the table. I'd been earwigging carefully, and the "next steps" seemed to consist of waiting and bitching.

Nico set a glass of juice down in front of me, and I took a sip to moisten my dry mouth. Then I cleared my throat.

"What you're talking about, it concerns me too, you know."

"We've already discussed the plan going forward," Luca said.

"No, we haven't. You told me what you were going to do, which is basically nothing, and just expected me to go along with it."

Frustration warred with sympathy on my brother's face. Both were expressions I knew well, but they didn't usually come together.

"We're limited on options right now."

"*You're* limited on options. I'm being proactive and hiring a private investigator."

The frustration won out. "You're damn well not."

"Somebody has to get justice for Mom, and as you've pointed out many, many times, your hands are tied. But mine aren't."

"Do you realise how this will look? Sheriff Newman will assume that I'm circumventing his orders by having you sign the paperwork."

"Well, just tell him I've gone rogue." I shrugged. "It's the truth."

If Luca clenched his jaw any harder, he'd crack a tooth. "Aaron, talk some sense into her."

"Uh..."

"Don't you try to talk me out of this. Besides, it was Aaron's idea."

Aaron shrank back three inches as Luca glared at him.

"What? How was this my idea?" Aaron asked. "I never mentioned a private investigator."

"You said, and I quote, that the only way we'd fix this was by getting a competent investigator to do the legwork."

"I meant that you could speak to Payne's boss and request the case be reassigned."

"You said Payne's boss was an asshole."

"You've had plenty of experience at dealing with those."

"Yes, I have." I spread my arms wide. "Behold, exhibits A, B, and C."

"Hey," Colt said. "Why am I included?"

"Because the only thing necessary for the triumph of evil is for good men to do nothing." Some Irish guy had said that, and when I heard the quote, it had resonated. How many people had stood by while Dad abused us as kids? "And you're just sitting there."

"Can't get a word in edgewise," he muttered.

Luca closed his eyes for a second and took a deep breath. "You're not hiring a private investigator."

"Yes, I am. Davis and I already discussed it, and we're gonna go halves." Davis said it was the least he could do, throw some pocket change at removing the problem that was Rey Mendez. He'd even offered to contract with one of the big global investigation firms, but I wanted someone local. Someone familiar with Baldwin's Shore and its quirks. "Aaron, do you use an investigator for your legal stuff?"

"Don't you dare help her," Luca warned.

That was Aaron's thinking face. Brow slightly pinched, eyes unfocused as he turned all his attention inward. Puzzled over the problem. *How the hell do I tiptoe out of this minefield without losing body parts?*

"It's not a terrible idea," he tried.

No, Luca didn't like that answer. "Are you kidding me? We spoke about this before, and you said that family involvement in the case could jeopardise a prosecution."

"That was nearly a month ago. And so far as we can ascertain, Payne has made zero progress in that time. Yes, family involvement might cause issues for a prosecutor, but let's be realistic here—with Payne in charge, there won't be a prosecution."

"But—"

"I'm not finished. Your father has spent his life pissing every cent he earned up walls. His only assets are a shitty house and a half-decent truck. And even if he sold the truck, that wouldn't raise enough cash to pay for private representation in a murder trial. He'd be stuck with a public defender. And I can tell you from experience..." Aaron's lips curved into a smile. "That ninety percent of the attorneys working out of the public defender's office in Coos Bay come out of the same mould as Detective Payne. Show up, tick the boxes, do the bare minimum, get paid. The DA's office, on the other hand, is staffed mainly by sharks. And if you"—he pointed a fork at Davis—"have any political influence, which I suspect you do, you'll pressure the DA to have a Great White assigned."

"Objection," Luca said. "Take that stick out of your ass."

"Overruled," I snapped.

Aaron stayed perfectly calm. "It's not a stick, it's a tightly rolled bar certificate."

"This is fucked up, Romi." Luca shoved his chair back and stood. "Don't you care about my job?"

"I do, but I also care about Mom. She never saw us graduate high school. Never had to listen to our hopes and fears for the future. Never found out which careers we'd choose or how we'd spend our spare time. She'll never see you get married, Luca. Never get to hold her grandchildren. I owe this to her. I have to stand for her because nobody else can."

More support came from an unexpected source: Nico. "Sometimes, it's necessary to take matters into your own hands in order for justice to be done."

"And you'd know all about that, would you?" Luca asked.

Nico ignored the...question? Insinuation? "When I was planning the resort, I used a private investigator in Coquille to do some research. Don Stevens. He's very discreet. Would you like his number?"

"Yes, please."

"Do you have an iPhone? I can Airdrop the contact details."

Luca huffed, exasperated. "Don't I get any say in this?"

"If you have a recommendation for a PI or an idea to push the case forward, then I'm all ears. But if the only thing you want to do is stop me from going through with a decision just because you don't like it, then no. You can tell Sheriff Newman I'm being 'difficult.' The media accuses me of that on a daily basis, so it would hardly be a stretch." Now I stood too. "You're my brother, and I'll always love you, but I don't always have to agree with you. I'm going back to the hotel now. I've lost my appetite."

With Davis by my side, I strode to the door. Luca didn't come after me. Good. And as we were on our way back to the Peninsula, my phone buzzed with a message.

Aaron: If Nico's guy doesn't work out, try Mike McDonald. Lives over in North Bend, but he knows the area well.

I hadn't imagined that Aaron would take my side in this, but secretly, I was glad he had.

12

ROMI

"Murder's not my area of expertise, ma'am. And a twenty-year-old cold case..." Mike McDonald's sucking breath left me under no illusion as to what he thought the chances were of solving it. "Wouldn't feel right taking your money."

"I appreciate your candour."

"Reputation's everything in this game, and I pride myself on being upfront with my clients. But if you ever need surveillance work done or assets located, you have my number. Infidelity's my specialty."

The sense of déjà vu was strong. I'd just had more or less the same conversation with Don Stevens, except he'd told me he specialised in corporate research—which, reading between the lines, meant he worked out who to bribe. Yeah, that definitely fit with Davis's assessment of Nico's shadiness. He sure had proven himself to be a better judge of character than me. Character, markets, investments... At this moment, he was pacing his bedroom with a headset jammed into his ear, trying to buy a small country by the sound of it.

"My partner hasn't been unfaithful."

"If I had a buck for every time I've heard that…"

Wasn't this a cheery conversation to be having on a Saturday morning? Outside, rain from an inky sky skittered against the floor-to-ceiling windows, and the gardens were deserted. A lone figure walked on the beach in the distance, shoulders hunched in determination. *I've paid for this vacation so I'll damn well enjoy it.* I should have been in the South of France right now, modelling shoes. Never had I missed my job more.

"Do you know any other investigators who might be willing to take on an old case?"

"There's Don Stevens over in Coquille."

"I've already tried him."

"Brent Dallerup's on vacation, won't be back for three weeks. What about one of the big firms? Blackwood or Sentinel? They got plenty of people."

"Do either of them have a branch in Coos Bay?"

"Blackwood's got an office up in Portland, I believe."

"I'd really prefer a local. Somebody who knows the people and the places involved. Folks in Baldwin's Shore don't like strangers nosing around."

Locals usually took a while to warm to newcomers. To open up. Trust was earned, not bought. I hadn't missed the suspicious looks Nico received at the funeral, and the Peninsula had been open for over a year now. The town's inhabitants generally fell into two categories—people who were born there and wanted to leave, and people born elsewhere who wanted to stay. There was little overlap. Luca, Aaron, and Brooke were notable by the fact that they'd all escaped, only to bounce right back again. Brooke or no Brooke, I still found it difficult to fathom that Luca had returned to Baldwin's Shore voluntarily.

The things one did for love.

Me? I was counting down the days until I could fly back to the East Coast. Hell, the hours.

Anyhow, Baldwin's Shore seemed to attract more than its share of questionable characters. People running from their old lives, looking for a quiet place to hole up for a year or two. Skip was a case in point. Mom's boss when she'd worked the evening shift at Beer Me Up, and a card-carrying member of the tinfoil-hat brigade. Eccentric but harmless, or so everyone had thought. I'd nearly choked when Aaron told me he'd gone to prison for robbing an armoured car. He'd whacked a colleague over the head, taken four million bucks in gold coins, and run. Run to Baldwin's Shore and opened a damn bar.

I'd always wondered why the drinks were so cheap there, but now I knew the answer. Skip hadn't exactly been worried about his 401(k). Or the legal drinking age, a policy I understood had contributed to his downfall.

Mike chuckled through the phone, and I pictured his jowls wobbling. The picture on his website showed a droopy-faced man in his forties, arms folded, his expression serious. He was being friendlier than I'd anticipated.

"The old Baldwin's Shore probationary period, eh? Gotta do your six months before you qualify to join the local network."

"Something like that. Do you know of any other local investigators?"

"Good ones? With availability?"

"Yes."

"No."

Great. "Well, thanks anyway."

"Unless... Hell, she's not even working as a PI anymore."

"She?"

"Blue Carver. A few years ago, her instincts were as good as they get. Methods were a little unorthodox, but the instincts... Trained with John Roper, God rest his soul, but then she married a jackass, moved to New York, and nearly ended up in jail. She's back in Coos Bay now, but..."

I had no idea who John Roper was, nor did I want to get involved with a criminal. "Jail? For what?"

"Heard she caught her husband with some bimbo and set his car on fire. Threatened to do the same to him if he didn't draw up divorce papers right that minute."

Which sounded like a perfectly reasonable course of action to me. "That's all?"

A pause, and Mike guffawed. "Her ex didn't see it that way."

"They never do. But Blue Carver isn't an investigator anymore?"

"As I said, reputation's everything in this game, and hers is trashed. Her ex, he bad-mouthed her from coast to coast to anyone who'd listen, and some of that shit st—pardon me, ma'am—some of that mud stuck. Even before that, she wasn't the easiest woman to work with. Last I heard, she'd moved back in with her momma and taken a job at Hot Diggity Dog. Uh, that's a restaurant near the Pony Village Mall. They serve—"

"Let me guess. Hot dogs?"

"I was gonna say the best footlongs this side of Portland. But yeah, hot dogs. Always hella busy in there. But if you make Blue a good enough offer, maybe she'd get tempted to go back to her old job."

"You really think she has a good chance of resolving this case?"

"I'll be honest with you, ma'am. I don't think anyone has

what you'd call a *good* chance. But Blue, she's got as good a chance as any."

And that was all I could hope for.

Hot Diggity Dog was an easy place to find. Firstly, the odour of overcooked sausages permeated the air for a full block, and secondly, there was a six-foot-tall hot dog complete with fake mustard and ketchup handing out "buy one, get one free" coupons on the sidewalk outside. It thrust a coupon in my direction, and I took a hurried step back.

"No, thank you. I'm actually a vegan."

"Then you're in luck. Not much meat in those sausages," it said, voice muffled by layers of red-and-yellow foam.

"That's a pleasant thought."

"They don't pay me enough to bullshit. Have a nice day."

Doubtful. I tried not to breathe too deeply as I walked inside, blocking out thoughts of "mechanically separated meat." If I hadn't already been vegan, the hot-dog production process would have turned me. The place was clean, at least, and also three-quarters full. Guess a lot of people shared Mike's dubious taste in food.

The guy behind the counter beamed when I reached the front of the line. "What can I get ya? We have a special on— a footlong and all the fries you can eat for five bucks."

"Just a bottle of sparkling water."

"We got still. Or soda?"

"Still will be fine."

"What're you eating?"

"I'm actually looking for Blue Carver."

"What about our pizza dog? Comes with shredded

mozzarella and pepperoni slices. I'll throw in the drink for free."

"Really, I just want to speak with Blue. Can you tell me if she's working today?"

"Sure, she's right outside." He gestured toward the window, and I did a double take. *Blue* was the hot dog? "If you have a sweet tooth, could I tempt you with one of our churro dogs?"

A churro dog? No, I didn't even want to think about that. I dropped a ten-dollar bill onto the counter and smiled. "Only the water, and keep the change."

"Gee, uh, thanks. If you take a seat, I'll bring it right—"

"Please, just give me the bottle."

"No ice?"

"No ice. In fact, you know what? Keep the water too."

"Wow, I mean—"

I had no idea what he meant, and I didn't care either. I was already halfway to the sidewalk, trying to work out the best way to approach Blue. Usually, eye contact and a smile worked, but I couldn't see a thing beyond the googly, oversized eyes and grinning cartoon mouth.

"What are you looking at?"

My turn to stumble over my words. "Uh, Blue?"

She put her hands on her hips, or roughly where I assumed her hips would be. It might have been comical if the situation wasn't so serious.

"Who's asking? Do I know you? I don't know you."

"I'm looking for a private investigator."

"Then you're looking in the wrong damn place."

"Mike McDonald gave me your name."

"Mike always did have a big mouth. Look, I'm leaving town in a couple of weeks. I got out of that game, and I'm not getting back into it."

"There's been a murder."

"Yeah, well, there's gonna be another one if I have to live with my mom for much longer. Got a job waiting for me overseas. As soon as I can pay for my flight, I'm out of here."

"Which country?"

A pause. "France."

Flights to Europe didn't come cheap. I knew that from experience. For three years, I'd scrimped and saved and walked dogs and mown lawns and babysat until I had the cash to buy a one-way economy ticket. Even if Blue was staying with her mother, she had to have living expenses. And I bet being a hot dog didn't pay more than minimum wage.

"A couple of weeks? Or a couple of months? If you'll help with this case, I'll buy you the ticket as a bonus." When Blue didn't reply right away, I sweetened the offer. "Business class."

"If we're talking homicide, you should let the police handle it."

"Already tried that. Detective Payne doesn't seem particularly inclined to put the effort in."

"Aldrich Payne?" For the first time, I thought I detected a hint of sympathy, although that could just have been the deadening effect of the wiener suit. "Figures. Who died?"

"My mom."

"I'm sorry."

"Could we just talk for a minute? I mean somewhere other than the sidewalk? It's awkward with the whole..." I waved at the costume. As well as being ridiculous, it meant I couldn't read her face. See where her thoughts were going. "Can I buy you lunch?"

"Not in this place." She paused to hand coupons to a

group of teenagers heading past. "Okay. Okay, you get ten minutes. Wait here."

Inside, I heard her tell the guy behind the counter that she was taking a break. After some gesturing, followed by some head shaking, and she headed toward an "Employees Only" door at the back.

"Bobby, for crying out loud, just don't tell him then," she shot back over her shoulder.

Blue was blunt as a rusty butter knife, and she definitely had a rebellious streak. Not the easiest person to work with, Mike McDonald had said. Was it weird that I kind of liked her?

13

ROMI

"One month. You get one month. If I can't dig out anything useful in a month, then I won't be able to find anything useful at all."

I'd told Blue the basics of the case and the situation. The price we agreed on wasn't cheap, plus I had to cover expenses, but she didn't particularly want to do the job, so she said that lack of enthusiasm had to be taken into account in her fee. And she'd get the business-class ticket whatever happened. While she might have acted indifferent, I knew who'd gotten the better end of the deal—Davis and I would be shelling out thousands of dollars with no guarantee of results. Good thing modelling paid more than wearing a hot dog, although I had to admit that on occasion, the outfits were just as laughable.

Out of the hot dog, Blue had been something of a surprise. I guess I'd been expecting a hard-nosed PI, maybe a little butch, sturdy, mid-forties, a female version of Mike. Blue wasn't that, not by a long shot. She was closer to Brooke's height than mine, which was to say a smidgen taller than average, all tits, ass, and attitude. When I was a kid stuffing my bra with toilet paper, I'd dreamed of having boobs like that. Now I was glad I didn't because they would have sunk my runway career, but still... I could appreciate her assets. She wore her dark hair piled on top of her head in a careless bun, and even with no make-up, she was pretty. Not perfect—her eyes were set a smidgen too far apart and her mouth was a touch too small—but she could certainly turn heads if she wanted to. Those eyes, though... Those eyes were tired. And she couldn't have been more than thirty.

"When can you start?"

"No time like the present."

"Don't you have to give notice at the restaurant?"

"I'll just tell Bobby I'm not coming back." That struck me as a tiny bit unprofessional, and my expression must have given my thoughts away because Blue explained, "My uncle owns the place. Trust me, I'll be doing him a favour by quitting. He only gave me the job so I wouldn't tell Aunt Edith I saw him coming out of the strip club on Edward Avenue while she was at her quilting circle."

"You blackmailed him?"

"Think of it as negotiation. We'll have to take your car because I don't have one."

"I don't have a car either."

"Not even a rental?"

"No, because I don't have a driver's licence. But I can call Selwyn. He's a cab driver in Baldwin's Shore."

And he'd driven me to Coos Bay because Davis had to dial in to a board meeting for a company he part-owned. Something to do with shipping, he'd said. Selwyn was as chill as cab drivers came, and I'd arrived at Hot Diggity Dog with only minor anxiety.

Blue muttered a curse under her breath. "Guess we've

identified your first expense. Gotta have wheels. Can't tail someone in a fuckin' cab."

"You think you'll need to tail someone?"

"Who the hell knows? But if your father gets antsy and decides to take a trip, wouldn't you want to find out where he's going?"

"I guess I would."

"Come this way. I know a guy who'll rent us a car that doesn't look like we picked it up at the damn airport."

We ended up with a Honda Civic that had seen better days. Say, around a century ago. Rust spots dotted the wheel wells, and the rear bumper had a dent in the middle. Stuffing spilled out of the back seat, and when I reluctantly folded myself into the passenger side, I caught the telltale whiff of marijuana.

"I have to hand it to you—my father certainly wouldn't expect to see me in a car like this."

"More of a Ferrari girl, are you?"

"I prefer SUVs. They're better in terms of both comfort and anonymity."

"Depends who you're trying to hide from. Sure, the paparazzi might not be able to see you inside, but drive past in a fancy-ass SUV with tinted windows and people in a town like Baldwin's Shore would remember the vehicle."

My head snapped around at the "paparazzi" comment. "You recognised me?"

"Nope. But I googled you when you went to use the bathroom. Got curious."

"Why? I mean, why would you think I was worth googling?"

"You've got this air of entitlement about you, which says you're used to getting your own way. You're obviously well off, and the way you focus on your appearance suggests new money rather than old money. As we were leaving, you put on a big fake smile when two teenage girls approached—probably didn't even realise you did it—and you tensed up. Relaxed when they carried on past. That told me you expected to be recognised. Your age suggested actress, pop star, or social media influencer were possibilities, but your height and build say 'model.' So Google really only confirmed what I already knew."

"I am *not* entitled." But Blue was right on the rest. Did I really do all that stuff? "Am I?"

Having her analyse me that way, having her break down what came naturally and highlight my component flaws, made me squirm in my seat.

"Like I said earlier, I don't get paid enough to bullshit. And right now, you're asking yourself whether you really do all that stuff, aren't you?" Blue started the engine, which miraculously caught on the first try. "Hey, maybe I'm lying. Maybe Bobby recognised you and told me who you were? Maybe he's a fan? Maybe he has a life-size poster of you on his bedroom wall, and every night, he lies in bed and—"

"Enough! Don't you even want to know where we're going?"

"I know exactly where we're going. To the Peninsula Resort. Where else would a gal like you stay?"

"I wish you'd stop making so many assumptions about me. I could be staying at my brother's place."

"But you're not."

"How do you know that?"

"Because if you were staying at your brother's place, you'd have said, 'I'm staying at my brother's place,' not that you could be. Plus I saw your room card in your billfold when you went to pay for lunch."

Blue was sharp. Exasperating too, but anything was better than Detective Payne's polite indifference.

"Fine, so I'm staying at the Peninsula." I gripped my seat belt as Blue swung out into traffic fast, too fast. "Could you slow down some?"

"I'm doing the speed limit."

"Actually, you're slightly over."

"Did you know that most speedometers have a tolerance of plus or minus ten percent?"

"Why on earth would I need to know that?"

"So that you understand when complaining is pointless." Blue sped up instead of slowing as a light turned red, and I closed my eyes. "You've given me an outline of the case, but we need to sit down and go over the details. With your brother too. Is he available today?"

"He's working right now, but I could see if he'll come this evening. And I should probably mention that he wasn't keen on me hiring a private investigator."

"Why?"

"He's worried it might jeopardise any future prosecution."

"With Aldrich Payne working the case, there won't be any prosecution."

"That's what Aaron said."

"And who's Aaron?"

"My brother's best friend. He's a lawyer."

Blue glanced sharply across at me. "Prosecution or defence?"

"Defence, I guess, but he does a bit of everything. Family law, corporate stuff. He works at a small firm in Baldwin's Shore."

"Then I guess *I* should probably mention that I'm not keen on lawyers."

"Any particular reason why?"

"Because they screw you, and then they screw you over."

Wasn't that the truth.

"Was your ex-husband a lawyer?"

"Who told you about him?" Before I could come up with a smart remark, Blue answered her own question. "Mike McDonald. Am I right?" Another glance across. "Yeah, I'm right."

"Are you *always* right?"

"It's one of my better qualities."

"I both love and hate that about you."

Was that an actual smile?

"Yeah, I lost my damn mind and married a lawyer. He fucked me over in every way possible, and the only good thing about being back in Oregon is that I'm now two and a half thousand miles away from him." She lowered her voice and muttered under her breath, "Can't cut the fucker's balls off if I'm not in the same state."

Hmm. Perhaps I should warn Aaron to wear a jockstrap?

14

AARON

"So, you're the lawyer."

The investigator Romi had dredged up—who looked more like a WWE ring girl than a PI—practically spat the final word as she sent daggers in my direction through narrowed eyes. Had Romi told her about the animosity between us? Or did Blue Carver just hold a grudge against the legal profession in general?

"I'm *a* lawyer."

"Figures. Always nitpicking." She turned to Luca. "And you must be the brother."

"I'm here under duress."

"Honey, we're all here under duress."

Romi stepped forward, a fake smile plastered across her face. "Luca. His name's Luca. And this is Brooke, Luca's fiancée and also Aaron's sister, and Colt. He's a sheriff's deputy."

"I thought you said it was Aldrich Payne's case?"

Colt held out a hand. "I'm here as a family friend."

Blue shook hands, briefly, almost disdainfully, then pulled out a seat at the eight-person dining table in the corner of the hotel suite. She'd been marginally politer to Davis. Probably shrewd enough to realise who was funding this wild goose chase.

Two minutes ago, the concierge had wheeled in a giant whiteboard, and he'd been followed by two waiters carrying platters of gourmet snacks. At least this shitshow came with food, although that was scant consolation for being glared at by not one but two women. There was less tension during a capital murder case.

If I could have sat the meeting out, I would have, but I owed it to Luca to help in whatever way I could. And I still remembered the way Serena Mendez had comforted me after my own momma died in a car crash. Brooke too, one of us on each side as Nonna sobbed in the chair opposite. Serena's life might have been difficult, but she'd never been short of love for us kids, always there to fix up a scraped knee or hand out the homemade cookies she somehow found the time to bake around holding down two jobs and cleaning up after Rey. When she'd vanished without so much as a goodbye, I'd felt some of the same bitterness as Luca at her leaving, and now I had to shoulder some of the guilt. I owed it to Serena to help as well.

"Let's start with a timeline." Blue picked up a pen. "Serena disappeared twenty years ago in September, correct?"

Colt spoke up. "According to the file, she was reported missing on Friday, September eighteenth."

"You have the file?"

"Only the original missing persons file from the sheriff's department. I might have made a copy before I was told not to."

Carver's lip quirked, and she nodded in what could have

been admiration. "Okay, you can stay. Who reported her missing? Rey Mendez?"

"Not Rey. Her boss."

"Interesting. Where did she work?"

"During the day, she cleaned vacation rentals for the Baldwin family, and in the evenings, she waitressed at Beer Me Up. Are you familiar with the place?"

"Every kid who grew up in these parts is familiar with the place. Where else could you get a drink at seventeen, no questions asked? Plus you could hardly miss the flying saucer in the parking lot. Skip was the one who reported her missing?"

"No, Easton Baldwin Junior, when she didn't show up for work in the morning. Which means she most likely got killed on the Thursday. Nobody saw her after three p.m."

"Who saw her at three?"

"Marianna Mayer, office manager at Baldwin Estates. Serena cleaned the four properties she'd been assigned, then dropped by after her shift to check which properties needed to be attended to the next morning. Did that each day by all accounts."

"Marianna Mayer is now the second Mrs. Baldwin," Luca added. "From what I recall, EJ was still married to his first wife at the time Mom disappeared. We were in the same class as Easton the Third, and she used to pick him up from school in a top-of-the-line Mercedes while the rest of us took the bus."

All the Baldwin kids had been spoiled, which was probably why most of them had turned out unbearable. Sara was okay, but she was EJ's niece rather than his daughter, taken in after her parents died, and Parker was tolerable on a good day. Quite frankly, I'd rather have had a root canal without anaesthetic than spend an hour in the company of Easton the Third or his twin sisters. Paulo had nicknamed the former "Easton the Turd," which fit him perfectly. EJ himself was a wet lettuce leaf of a man, firmly under the thumb of first Justine and then Marianna, but at least he'd bothered to contact the sheriff's department and report Serena missing. Nobody else had.

"So we can narrow Serena's death—or possibly her abduction—down to a small window," Blue said, writing the date and times on the whiteboard. "That's useful."

Colt helped himself to a mini cheese soufflé. "We can narrow it further—she didn't show up for her six o'clock waitressing shift that evening."

"Skip didn't think that was weird? Was Serena usually unreliable?"

Everyone looked at each other.

"I don't think so," Romi volunteered. "I mean, she went to work every day."

"Yet on Thursday, she didn't. What happened when you got home from school? Nobody was there to meet you?"

"We headed to Aaron and Brooke's place, same as always. Mom often ran errands after work, so we'd all walk from the bus to Nonna's together, and when it was dinner time, Luca and I would walk home."

"On your own? You were, what, eight and six?"

"We only lived three houses away, and Nonna would watch us from the yard until we went through the front door."

"Who let you in?"

"Luca knew where the key was hidden."

"And what time was dinner?"

"Five o'clock. Mom always had dinner ready for five o'clock, and then she'd go to work."

"Talk me through the evening."

"There's not much to tell. We let ourselves in, and nobody was home. Which was unusual, but it had happened once or twice in the past, so we didn't freak out. Mom told us that when we were home alone, we should stay quiet, pretend we were little mice and creep around and she'd be home real soon."

"And Dad told us that if we made any noise, Child Protective Services would take us away and throw us in kiddie jail," Luca added.

Seeing Romi now, I sometimes forgot just how hard she'd had it as a child. It hadn't only been the fact that her father was loose with his fists. She'd been a latchkey kid since Luca was tall enough to reach the kitchen counter, expected to fend for herself after Serena disappeared because Rey hadn't been interested in parenting. Nonna had stepped up, but she'd been getting on in years, not in the best of health, and dealing with four teenagers had been hard on her. In hindsight, I wished I'd done more to help, but I couldn't turn back the clock. Time only went one way. Too late, I'd learned to be grateful for every single minute of it.

"Seems like one hell of a guy." Blue nodded to herself. "Yeah, I can see why you want him behind bars. But being an asshole isn't a crime, although it should be—" Why did she look at me when she said that? "—which means we need to find evidence. At this stage in the proceedings, that evidence is likely to be circumstantial rather than physical, but a good prosecutor can sell a decent circumstantial case to a jury. What else happened that night? What time did your dad come home?"

Romi shrugged, so Luca took over. "We don't know. Barely even remember how we spent the rest of the evening. If it was like every other time we were home alone, we scavenged whatever food was left in the kitchen, watched TV, and went to bed. Dad was back when we got up the next morning."

"And he was in a foul mood," Romi added. "Worse than usual. When we found the note, I thought he was gonna explode."

"The note saying your mom had left?"

"Yes."

"And it was under the refrigerator?"

Luca nodded. "Yeah, but it probably blew off the counter in the draught when he came in the back door."

"You're sure he would've come in the back? Wouldn't the front have been more convenient?"

"He always smoked in the backyard last thing at night."

Sat on an old, broken-down office chair set among the weeds, puffing away. When I looked out of my bedroom window late in the evenings, I used to see the smoke rising behind the Mendezes' kitchen. And every night before I fell asleep, I'd said a prayer that he'd succumb to lung cancer before Romi turned eighteen, but no one up there had listened. At least last month, I'd achieved my childhood dream of punching that fucker, even if it was only in the arm.

Nobody could take that away from me.

"So, timeline." Blue stopped chewing the end of a whiteboard marker and uncapped it. "Serena disappeared sometime between three p.m. and six p.m., and this fact was reported the next day at...what time?"

Colt consulted the notes on his tablet. "Check-out was at ten, check-in was at three. Serena serviced the properties in between. Vacuumed, dusted, changed the linen, cleaned the bathrooms and any other mess left by the previous occupants. So I'd estimate by around eleven when it became clear she was a no-show."

"Who were the occupants of the properties she cleaned on the day she vanished?"

"File doesn't say. Does it matter? She was seen in the office afterward."

"Maybe she forgot something and went back? And even if she didn't, one of them might've spoken with her, been able to gauge her mood. These things always matter."

"I doubt the folks at Baldwin Estates will have the records after all these years."

"I'll ask anyway. Occasionally you get lucky and there's some old gal in records who's obsessed with keeping every piece of paper they ever printed, wrote on, or folded into an origami sunflower." Blue began chewing away on the pen again. Someone buy that woman a pack of gum. "I get that the main thing is to break your dad's alibi, that's your goal, but I have questions. How did Serena Mendez get to the cabin where she was found? How do we know the former occupant isn't our culprit?"

"Detective Payne says it was probably a hunting shelter," Romi said. "No utilities, no registered owner. I bet nobody lived there at all."

"I looked it up, and it's in the middle of nowhere. Who *did* know about it? And if Serena went there voluntarily, why? Come to think of it, why did the sheriff's department go there?"

"There were cats," I started, but Blue gave me such a cutting stare that the remainder of the tale died in my throat. "Colt can tell it."

Romi found my discomfort amusing. At least I'd made her smile, even if it wasn't in the manner I'd have preferred.

If Colt noticed the tension, he ignored it. "We got a tip

that there were stolen cats located at the cabin. When we attempted to retrieve them, Luca fell through a rotten section of floor and landed right next to...you know. The remains."

"Ouch. Who gave you the tip?"

"The Bad Samaritan."

"The what?"

"Baldwin's Shore's answer to the Punisher."

Colt outlined the Bad Samaritan's work so far—one man dead, another in the hospital, and eighteen cats returned to their rightful owners. Oh, and he'd let himself into my apartment twice, a fact that left me twitchier than I cared to admit. Even though I'd installed locks on every door and window and put in an alarm system, I still found it difficult to sleep at night.

Blue gave a low whistle. "That's some résumé. You got any idea who this person is?"

"Well—"

"No," Luca said before Colt could start speculating. "We don't. And we're not gonna go looking either because none of us wants to be his next victim."

"Then how will we find out what led the Bad Samaritan to the cabin? It's not the sort of place you'd stumble across."

"The answer's easy—he followed the catnapper."

"And do you know who the catnapper is?"

"Yes."

"Please, let's carry on playing twenty questions—*who* is the catnapper?"

"Elmira Fairbanks."

"So has anyone asked *her* how she found the cabin?"

Colt, Luca, and I all looked at each other.

"On second thought," Colt said, "maybe finding the Bad Samaritan wouldn't be such a bad idea."

Romi rolled her eyes. "Don't be such a coward. Elmira's a cranky old witch, but she's not gonna put a curse on you."

"Then you can go talk to her."

"Fine, I will." Well, better Romi than me. Perhaps the time away from Baldwin's Shore had dulled her memories? "Wait... Why do we need to talk to her at all? We're meant to be breaking Dad's alibi, not worrying about a bunch of cats that got found anyway."

I opened my mouth to explain, then figured it'd be safer to leave that to Blue. Our new PI might have the personality of a flaming cactus, but I had to concede she knew her stuff.

"Because just breaking the alibi isn't enough," she said. "Circumstantial evidence generally isn't as compelling as physical evidence, so we'll have to build up layers and layers of it in order to convince a jury that your father killed your mother and not, say, some other random stranger. Means, motive, and opportunity. The lack of an alibi would give him an opportunity, a window of time in which he *could* have killed Serena. If we can show that was available, we then also need to show motive and means."

"He knocked her around all the time," Romi said. "I can't remember a time when she didn't have bruises."

"So he was an asshole. A violent asshole. But what gave him the motive to escalate to murder? Without a good reason, he could easily argue it was a disagreement that went too far. Say she fell and hit her head, and he panicked and hid the body. Second-degree murder versus second-degree manslaughter. Which brings us to our next issue: means. Did he have the tools to commit the crime? The head wound's a no-brainer—" Everyone except Blue winced at that, and Davis reached out to squeeze Romi's hand. I hated that he was the one to comfort her. Hated that it wasn't me. "—because he could've whacked her with a rock, but the cabin... Why did he hide her *there*? How did he even know the place existed? What was the connection? Without finding that, it's easy for him to deny everything. And the car's bugging me too. You say it never showed up?"

Colt shook his head.

"Why? Why would he ditch it? Nobody would've blinked a damn eye if he'd parked it back in the driveway. Did he kill her in the car? Were there bloodstains? Where is it? Did he have a buddy who owned a scrapyard, someone who'd dispose of it no questions asked? How'd he get home that night?"

Romi was biting her lip now, and I knew she'd been so fixated on her father's guilt that she hadn't considered any of these questions. And why would she have? Her background wasn't in law. She'd never had to worry about the ins and outs of the criminal justice system, and I was thankful for that.

"Want me to speak with Elmira?" I offered, and Luca looked at me like I'd grown another head. One that had undergone a lobotomy, clearly.

But it appeared Blue hadn't crossed paths with Elmira. "If I want your help, I'll ask for it, frat boy."

Take a deep breath, Aaron. Don't throat punch Romi's investigator.

"I'm not and never have been in a fraternity."

"Then why d'you dress like you are?"

What was wrong with chinos and a button-down shirt? "Some of my clients get intimidated by a suit, and nobody would take me seriously if I showed up for a meeting in jeans."

"Luca's wearing jeans."

"I wasn't talking about this meeting."

"Then you should be more specific."

"Guys, guys..." Colt stepped in as the voice of reason. "Let's not argue. We're all on the same side here."

Blue folded her arms. "Are we?"

"We have to be. Luca and I can't be seen to do any legwork, but we'll assist where we can, as will Brooke and Aaron."

"Add my name to that list," Davis said.

"Noted. And safety has to be a priority. When a killer's been walking free for twenty years, no consequences, he won't take too kindly to the idea of jail."

"I can take care of myself," Blue huffed.

"I'm sure you can, but we also need to take care of each other. Act as a team. This isn't an easy case, and infighting only makes it tougher."

"Nice pep talk. We've got good cop, bad cop, cheerleader, lawyer."

"And you're the bad cop?"

Finally, Blue Carver cracked a smile. "Well, obviously."

Obviously.

15

ROMI

"I don't know nothin' about any cats."

"Mrs. Fairbanks, nobody's asking about cats."

Blue hadn't wanted me to come along, but somebody had to be good cop, right? And I was paying the bills. Well, half of them, plus I was curious to find out how Blue worked. I'd only ever seen investigations on the TV, and everything on TV was bullshit. Cameras lied all the time.

Blue might have been bright, but she'd proven yesterday that she was also abrasive, so I'd figured it would be best if I made the introductions. That way, we stood a chance of getting over the threshold. Blue versus Elmira would be like...like a death match between two grinding wheels. But the moment I'd mentioned the cabin, Elmira had tried to slam the door in my face. I'd managed to get my foot in the gap, and now I very possibly had a fractured toe.

Please don't let it swell up.

"First, your brother and Colton came around accusing me of things I never did, and now you're here."

"I'm not accusing you of anything, just—"

"Say, is that a lesser goldfinch?" Blue asked from behind me.

What the hell? I wasn't paying her an hourly rate to birdwatch.

"Is that really important?"

"You don't see many of those around here. Does he visit often?"

Elmira opened the door a crack. "Why, yes. They nest in the fork of that there maple tree every year."

"Fascinating. And did I spot a hummingbird feeder? They come too?"

"Yes, black-chinned hummingbirds."

"Such amazing creatures. My dream is to travel to Ecuador and see a black-breasted puffleg in its natural habitat."

What was wrong with Blue? Was she even speaking English? What the heck was a black-breasted puffleg? Her demeanour had softened too, I noticed. Gone was the sandpaper quality, replaced by something meeker and almost...friendly?

And Elmira opened the door a foot. "My Gerald refuses to travel farther than New Mexico for a vacation. Says it's too dangerous."

Too dangerous? But the man was married to Elmira—surely just going downstairs for breakfast in the mornings was riskier than crossing a live minefield?

"You could travel on your own," Blue suggested.

"Oh, no, I'm too old for all that."

"Not a bit. And there are tour groups you could join if you don't want to go completely alone. But your age... It's possible you might be able to help me out with a few questions."

Elmira bristled again. "I already told you, I don't know anything about the cats."

"Me neither. Between you and me, I can't stand the pesky things. Always shedding hair and chasing the birds. Why do they always latch onto people who aren't keen on them? My neighbour's cat jumps the fence every freaking morning and sits on the windowsill, staring at me." Blue gave a quiet giggle. "But I guess I'm getting sidetracked. My name's Blue, and as Romi mentioned, I'm a private investigator. I expect you heard that Romi's mom was found recently?"

"That has nothing to do with me."

"Neither of us thought for a second that it did. But Serena Mendez was found in an old cabin to the east of town, deep in the forest, and we're really struggling to find any information on the owner. So we figured we'd ask everyone who's lived in town since those days whether they might have been familiar with them. You know, bumped into them at the grocery store, that sort of thing."

"They didn't have anything to do with her death."

"So you *do* know who lived there?"

"Nobody."

"Nobody lived there?"

"Not when Serena Mendez upped and disappeared."

"You're certain?"

"Are you questioning my memory, young lady?"

"No, no, just— Oh my gosh!" Blue pointed at the sky. "Was that a pileated woodpecker?"

"It may well have been. We do have them in the area."

"Spending time outdoors in Baldwin's Shore is a real treat. Usually I'm stuck behind a desk. Anyhow, where were we? You were telling me the cabin was empty when Serena died?"

"The paper said it happened twenty years ago. Ralph passed two years previous, and Julie-Anne a year before that, God rest their souls."

"Ralph and Julie-Anne?"

"My great-aunt and great-uncle."

"I'm sorry for your loss."

I wanted to tiptoe backward and leave Blue to her weird brand of magic. She'd managed to bewitch Elmira into something resembling human, and I was terrified of breaking the spell. Mike McDonald had been right—her methods *were* a little unorthodox, but they worked.

"They were good people, although why they cared to live all the way out in those woods was beyond me. Ralph used to say humans were destroying the planet, ruining everything. If he were still alive, he'd be one of those eco-warriors." Her tone said she wasn't impressed. "But as it was, he built that cabin out in the sticks and lived there with no phone and no electricity. Used candles. *Candles.* Grew his own vegetables and hauled water in from a stream. He'd have been a vegan too, sure as eggs is eggs."

When her nose wrinkled in disgust at the thought, I kept my mouth firmly shut. Great-Uncle Ralph sounded like a guy I wouldn't have minded meeting, although granted, his lifestyle left a lot to be desired. What was wrong with solar power?

Blue mock-shuddered. "I do like my creature comforts. Do you know who moved into the cabin after they passed?"

"No one. It sat empty for years and mouldered away."

"What about the land? Nobody wanted to use it?"

"Walt Baldwin owned the land, so I guess it went to East when Walt passed too. And now EJ. Walt and Ralph were good pals, you see, and when Ralph wanted to try his 'free-living experiment,' as he called it, Walt said he had just the place. But those younger Baldwins are all about the rental income, and who wants to live like that nowadays? Nobody with a brain, that's who."

"Can you remember Ralph and Julie-Anne having any regular visitors? Whoever hid Serena's body in the crawl space knew the cabin was there, and I don't suppose it's the sort of place a person stumbles over by accident."

"No, it is not. Although kids found it soon enough and trashed the inside, so my pop told me. He used to check on the place every so often, said it was his civic duty what with Ralph's and Julie-Anne's ashes being scattered on the hillside."

"Do you recall any visitors?" Blue prompted again.

"They had friends, of course they did. But they're all long dead. And they were good people too, so if you're going to come here making accusations…"

"I'm not accusing anyone." Blue paused for a second, then took on a conspiratorial tone. "Can I be straight with you, Mrs. Fairbanks?"

"People should always be straight. Liars is why this country's going to hell in a handbasket."

What a freaking hypocrite!

"Okay. Okay, so we have an idea who was responsible for Serena's death—Rey Mendez. But we're struggling to connect the dots to prove it. Can you think of any reason he might have gone to the cabin? I understand from Romi that he did odd jobs as a handyman back in those days."

"Great-Uncle Ralph wouldn't have let a scheming low life like Rey Mendez anywhere near his home." Elmira seemed to recall my presence, and she turned her sights on me. "I can see why you got out of town when you did, missy, but you should keep your clothes on. Getting photographed half-naked the way you do is demeaning. And I don't want my Lydia getting ideas."

Oh, for goodness' sake. Lydia wasn't gonna strip to her panties and take to the runway. The Lydia I'd gone to high school with had two loves in life, candy and binge-watching TV, and neither would lead to a successful modelling career. But Elmira just had to get her digs in where she could. Plus she was a prude. Lydia might have been my age, but Elmira had come to motherhood late in life, and her beliefs were still stuck in the Stone Age.

"I'll take the advice under consideration."

"But your daddy did it, no question about that. A real piece of work, he is, slippery as they come. Figured he'd get away with it. The only surprise is that he didn't move his other woman into the house once your momma was out of the picture."

What? *What*? Was Elmira saying what I thought she was saying? I always knew my father was a prize-winning asshole, but an affair? I racked my brain, but I couldn't remember another woman around that time. Sure, he'd dated casually in later years, but...an *affair*? Luca didn't suspect either. He would have told me.

"A mistress? No. No, you're lying."

Wrong thing to say. Elmira drew herself up to her full height, which put her head level with my chin, and skewered me with her gaze.

"What did you just accuse me of?"

Blue kicked me in the shin.

"Romi had no idea her father might've been having an affair. I'm sure you can understand it's a real shock to find out this way."

"Well, she should have paid more attention to what was going on under her nose."

"I was six years old!"

"Yes, well, a man like that..."

This time, Blue's fingers dug into my arm.

"Do you have any idea who the other woman was?"

"Around that time? Either Jaycee Billings or Gerilee Kroger, but I think Jaycee came to her senses a few months previous."

Dad had *two* affairs?

"Is that the same Gerilee Kroger who worked at the gas station on the road to Coos Bay?"

"She'd spread her legs for any cowboy passing through. Girls like that have no dignity."

"And Jaycee... Is she still in Baldwin's Shore?"

"Buried in the cemetery not three plots from Romi's momma. Had enough illegal substances in her blood to kill a horse, so I heard. You'd think she'd gotten too old for that nonsense, but some people never learn. Back when I was a teenager—"

"Do you find the finches prefer sunflower hearts or nyjer seed?" Blue asked, and I could've kissed her, in a purely platonic way, you understand. I definitely didn't need to hear about Elmira Fairbanks's teenage years.

"Sunflower hearts, but the advantage of the nyjer seed is that the bigger birds don't eat it. Although the sunflower hearts don't sprout everywhere when the finches drop them. My Gerald has to weed constantly."

"Both excellent observations, but on balance, I think I'll stick with the sunflower hearts. I'm not real big on weeding. You and Gerald sure have created a beautiful yard. Well, thank you so much for your time, Mrs. Fairbanks. It's been great talking with you. Here's my number—if you think of anything else, would you call me? And if you happen to get any interesting feathered visitors in your yard, I'd appreciate a heads-up."

"Of course, of course. And call me Elmira."

Wow.

Never in my life had I seen the old crone be so civil. *Call me Elmira?* Had Blue been a dragon tamer in a previous life? I hurried down the perfectly edged path behind her, eager to put some distance between myself and Elmira in case the spell broke.

"How did you know about the birds?" I asked when we got back into the horrible rental car.

"Easy. She has four bird tables, six feeding stations, bird boxes galore, and at least ten different kinds of bird food. Plus there was the thing with the cats. Think about it—she tossed all the kitties out in the forest to keep them away from her feathered fiends."

"No, I meant how did *you* know about the birds. Lesser goldfinches? Nyjer seed?"

"Oh, I briefly dated an ornithologist. Most boring two months of my life."

"Then why'd you date him?"

"He had a nine-inch dick, and he knew how to use it. Always the quiet ones, right?" She groaned and laid her head on the steering wheel. "Dick's always been my fucking downfall. I've taken a vow of celibacy now."

I nearly said, "Same," but I managed to bite my tongue. "So you don't really like birds?"

"I'm indifferent."

"What about cats?"

"My mom has a cat, and I get along with him well enough, but I'm more of a dog person."

"I can't believe you got Elmira to talk."

"Everyone will talk; you just need to phrase the questions appropriately."

And it seemed that Blue knew how to do that, unorthodox or not.

"So, what's next?"

"Next, I need to find Gerilee Kroger. I remember her from the gas station—she said she was moving to Idaho. Or it might've been Iowa, which would be a pain in the ass because now I have to go visit her."

"You can't call?"

"A witness with the potential to be this important, you talk to in person. If she was fucking your dad—" Ouch. "—then she was closer to him than most people. She might be able to shed light on his actions and state of mind back then. And for whatever reason, she didn't become your stepmom, so chances are she doesn't much like him anymore."

"Do you have to be so blunt?"

"Tact costs extra. Herb Pettigrew's gonna cover for Rey Mendez, but I'll bet you a snow cone that Gerilee'll dish any dirt she has."

"A snow cone? What, are you twelve?"

"So I like snow cones—sue me."

16

———

ROMI

"And *this* is why I used to spend so much time at the office." Davis cursed under his breath and tossed the phone onto the coffee table, where it skidded across the polished wood until it hit a vase of peonies. "No matter how much you pay people, they still manage to screw things up."

"What happened?"

"The company I'm trying to sell a stake in, the buyer's finance team found an error in the revenue forecasts. The business is solid enough, and it was a genuine mistake, but the buyer's the nervous type and now he's getting cold feet."

"Do you need to go back to New York?"

"It would make life a hell of a lot easier if I could speak with him face to face."

"Then you should go."

Davis strode over to me, took my hands in his. "What about you? Do you want to come back early?"

"I think that maybe I'll stay a little longer. If Blue makes any progress on Mom's case, then I want to be here. And besides, my next shoot is in Klamath, so it seems dumb to fly to the East Coast and then back again a week later."

"True. Klamath Falls?"

"No, just Klamath. Kind of odd because the last time I spoke with Ishmael, he was talking about an eerie lakeside ambience, but I guess he changed his mind."

Which he did with frustrating regularity. Make her hair pink, no, orange, no, pink. Put her in the green pumps. Heavens above, not those green pumps, *those* green pumps. Are you colour-blind? Ooh, too high, *too high*. No. No, no, no. Let's just have all the models go barefoot. At least the intergalactic space maiden aesthetic had fallen by the wayside.

"Ishmael?" Davis's mouth twisted into a grimace. "Is he going to make you wear a golden fishing net again?"

"It wasn't a fishing net; it was gilded mesh."

"You could have caught a good-sized bass with that skirt."

Davis did have a point there. "I think the mesh trend died at the end of last season."

"Forgive me if I don't send flowers. Will you be all right here on your own? With everything that's going on?"

"I'll just hole up here at the hotel until Blue gets back. She thought she'd only be a couple of days."

I'd offered to go to Iowa with her, but she said she'd be more efficient on her own. Okay, so what she'd actually said was that if I kept "helping" the way I had at Elmira's, then my shins would end up black and blue. Which would no doubt give Ishmael a conniption. And I had to admit that yesterday, Blue had handled both herself and the fire-breathing monster better than I ever could.

"I'll get back as soon as I can, and I'm only a phone call away."

"Honestly, don't fret. Things are...okay. With Aaron, I

mean. Awkward, but bearable. And I really want to see this through."

"Let me know if Bartlett causes problems. Right now, I'm wishing I hadn't nudged him out of New York."

Huh? "What do you mean, nudged him out of New York?"

"A year or so ago. After you got off the phone with Luca and began ranting about how Aaron was considering earning his chops at one of the more prominent city firms and that New York wasn't big enough for the both of you. Well, I had words in a few ears and made it clear that any firm he landed a position with wouldn't get any future business from me."

A chill ran through my bones. "You prevented Aaron from getting a job?"

"You seem upset?"

"I... I'm not sure how I feel." Shocked. Definitely shocked. "I mean, I didn't want to run across him in a restaurant, but..."

Davis squeezed my hands. "Sweetheart, I'm sorry if I did the wrong thing."

"You only did what you thought was right."

And really, it was me who'd pushed Aaron out of New York, wasn't it? I let off steam one night, and a powerful man with more connections than a city substation had taken my words literally. That left me feeling...guilty. Oddly guilty. For years, one of my main complaints against Aaron had been that he'd set back my career. And now I'd done the same thing to him, albeit inadvertently.

Sure, he seemed happy here with Asa, and he was creating a home out of Deals on Wheels, but who knew what heights he could have reached at a big New York firm?

Aaron was smart, seriously smart. I'd held him back in the same way that he'd held me back.

Though I was happy now. Kind of. I had plenty of work, a new business venture, and Davis. But I'd lost a friend—a good friend—in the process.

A lover.

The man I'd once dreamed would be my future.

"What can I do to make things right?" Davis asked. "You want me to get Barlett another job? I can do that."

"I'm not sure. This...this has all come as a surprise." I stepped out of Davis's hold and walked to the window. The sun was shining today, glinting off the waves. "I just need to think on some things."

"Are we okay, Romi?"

The day we left rehab—together—we'd promised to look out for each other. To protect each other. To do whatever was necessary to stop minor problems from becoming major ones. We didn't consult each other on every little action we took. I'd run interference with Davis's exes a time or two, and in his eyes, he'd merely been repaying the favour.

"We're fine." I turned, met his gaze. "We are, truly. Now get to New York before your buyer gets cold feet."

"Pass the guac?" Addy asked. "I can't believe your dad was hooking up with another woman. Do you think your mom knew? Do you think that's why he killed her?"

She'd invited herself over for dinner, but nobody minded because she'd stopped to pick up Mexican on the way. Brooke said they were rarely alone in the evenings now—there was always somebody dropping by—but I knew from her smile that she liked it that way. And Aaron's cavernous apartment was set up for entertaining with a dining table that could comfortably cater a medieval banquet, albeit with slightly more glass and chrome than the knights of old were used to.

So tonight we had Addy and also Nico, who'd come bearing wine plus a carton of mango juice for me. Had someone told him about my issues, or was he just overly observant? Although his presence might save me from talking to the hotel staff tomorrow morning—I needed to extend my stay.

Missing from our little group was Aaron. He'd piled a plate with food and then disappeared into his office. Was he really working? Or had that been an excuse? I suspected the latter. Tomorrow, I'd eat at the hotel. Which would have the added bonus of allowing me to avoid Addy's questions as well.

"How am I meant to know whether Mom knew? All I remember is that they used to yell at each other constantly."

"What about?"

"Addy…" Nico got in before Luca could. "Please, a little tact."

"It's an important question. You know, *motive*."

Luca took a steadying breath before he spoke. He'd done that a lot with Addy over the years. "We were kids, Addy. Neither of us can remember what the yelling was about. We tried our best to keep out of the way."

"But if he did want your mom gone so he could replace her with a side piece, then why didn't he keep seeing Gerilee-the-slut?" Addy clapped both hands over her mouth. "Hey, maybe Gerilee found out? Maybe she found out what he'd done, and he threatened her into keeping quiet? Ohmigosh."

"Adeline." Nico said her name as a statement. "Adeline, if you stop talking for the rest of this meal, I'll gift you a weekend break at the Peninsula."

"Wow, really?"

"Yes, really."

"Will it include spa treatments?"

He sighed. "A massage and a facial."

"When you say 'talking,' do you mean entirely? Or just about murder?"

"Please say 'entirely,'" Luca muttered.

"I meant about murder, but if you stay totally quiet, I'll throw in a manicure too."

"Then my lips are sealed. Uh, oops." She mimed zipping her lips and tossing away the key. "Mmm-mmm."

Ah, the blissful sound of silence. I basked in it for a moment—we all did. When we were in high school, Addy had held a sponsored talk-a-thon to raise money for an African orphanage, and she hadn't shut up for a full sixteen hours, which, it turned out, had just been practice for adulthood.

"Nico, while we're on the subject of the hotel, is it possible to stay a bit longer?"

His expression turned pained. "I'm afraid not."

"It doesn't have to be in the same suite. Any room would do."

"We're fully booked later in the week. An online fitness guru reserved every room in the place—other than Colt and Brie's suite—to hold a wellness retreat. We had to offer a small discount, but rest assured it was a business decision and nothing to do with the thought of a hundred women in yoga wear." Addy threw a nacho at him, thankfully sans guacamole. "If it would help, I do have guest rooms in my private residence."

"Don't you dare even think about it," Luca practically growled. "*We* have a guest room. Romi, you can stay here. I don't know why you didn't just ask in the first place."

I knew exactly why I hadn't asked, but no way could I tell Luca that.

"We didn't want to be any trouble, and you barely know Davis, and…"

"Then maybe we should get to know him? You've been together for over two years."

"I guess."

"And he's back in New York anyway."

Brooke beamed at me. "I'll make up the bed. This'll be great, all of us back together. Remember when we used to have sleepovers?"

"But I'm not sure how long I'll be in town. Maybe I won't leave for weeks."

"Even better. We've missed seeing you around."

Shit. *Shit, shit, shit.*

But I couldn't turn them down. They'd be hurt, and worse, they'd be suspicious.

"Then how can I say no?"

"And you're welcome to use the spa and gym at the Peninsula any time," Nico added.

A kind offer, really sweet, but all I could think about was how I was going to explain this latest mess to Aaron.

17

AARON

"Hey."

Romi was the last person I'd expected to see in my office on Monday evening, but there she was, large as life and beautiful as ever. But she didn't look happy. Had Brooke sent her to drag me back to the dinner table?

"Hey."

"Have you got a minute?"

"Sure."

She stepped inside and closed the door behind her. So... this wasn't about dinner?

"There's a problem."

With the food? With the case? With Davis? He seemed to have vanished from the scene tonight. Or had I fucked up in a way that was not yet apparent?

"You'll have to elaborate."

Romi stopped just inside the door, shifting from foot to foot as if she might run at any second. We got clients like that occasionally. Asa called them landmines—take one wrong step and the results were liable to be unpleasant.

I stayed firmly put behind my desk.

"Getting justice for Mom is important to me."

"I never imagined that it wouldn't be."

"So I want to be around as much as possible while Blue does her thing."

"Understandable, and I promise to keep out of your way."

"That might not be so easy."

Romi looked nervous rather than pissed, which naturally made me nervous too.

"Oh?"

"I thought it would be easy to stay longer at the Peninsula, but Nico said it's fully booked later on in the week. A wellness retreat. A hundred women practising yoga."

Uh-oh. The last time the Peninsula had hosted a group of female fitness enthusiasts—a triathletes' training camp— Nico corrupted at least three of them, then tried to set me up with his leftovers. My insistence that I wasn't looking to date or even hook up fell upon deaf ears. Perhaps I should have been grateful for his efforts, but after Romi ran my heart through the garbage disposal and Clarissa shredded what was left of it, I'd embraced the single life. Work kept me busy. Asa had built his firm on a solid base, but there was still room for expansion.

"So Nico offered me his guest room..." Oh, hell no. "And I thought Luca was gonna take his head off." Which was the appropriate response. "Although it was really kind of Nico, especially considering that he barely knows me." No, Nico had an ulterior motive, and if he *was* the Bad Samaritan, then he was also dangerous and I didn't want Romi anywhere near him. "So Luca said that he and Brooke also had a guest room, and I couldn't think of a polite way to say no, so now I'm staying here."

Shit.

"How long for?"

"Blue committed to working on the case for a month. But I've got modelling jobs booked, so I won't be here the whole time."

"I can't just up and take a vacation for a month. Not right now. I've got cases too."

"That's not what I'm asking."

"Then why are you here?"

Romi took a tentative step forward. "I... Because... We both messed up. In New York, we both messed up, and I'm sorry for my part. And the more time that passes, the more I miss what we used to have. The friendship. Being able to pick up the phone and call you when I'm feeling down, meeting for lunch just because, even your dumbass jokes. I realise we can't go back to the way things were, but do you think...? Hell, I don't even know."

"Do you think we could salvage the ability to have a civil conversation?"

"Yes, that. Can we try?"

It was more than I'd ever dared to hope for.

Romi was right—we'd both made mistakes. But hers had come from a place of pain. She'd always preferred to dull the agony of her childhood with alcohol rather than talking about it, and the drugs had been a natural extension of that tendency to self-medicate. A way for her to escape her own mind. I was the one who should have known better, who should have reacted calmly instead of panicking and forcing her into a recovery centre.

In fact, that whole night had been a mistake. I'd given in to a lifetime of temptation and tried to take our relationship someplace it was never destined to go. When I was a kid, my father once said to me, "Only a fool chases the sun when he's got the earth." My parents had both been content with what they had—a small but comfortable home in Baldwin's Shore, jobs as an accountant and a secretary, a two-week camping trip each year, and a sensible Honda minivan.

Romi was the sun. Bright, beautiful, and dangerous. I'd flown too close, and I'd been burned.

Then I'd tried picking the sensible, dependable option in Clarissa and gotten burned again.

And Mom and Dad's safe, comfortable lives had been snuffed out in an instant when a semi ran a red light and hit the minivan.

There had to be a lesson in there somewhere... But hell if I could work out what it was, and I hadn't even had a drink tonight, mainly because I'd removed all the wine from my apartment out of solidarity with Romi. Hmm... Was I meant to invest in an armoured vehicle and stay single for the rest of my life?

Gee, wasn't that a cheery thought on a Monday evening...

"Sure we can try being cordial, Buttercup."

"So, do you, uh, do you want to come out for dessert? Addy brought churros."

"Give me a minute to finish up here."

"Wait, you're actually working?"

"Kind of. I've been looking for people who worked in the Cavan Arms at the time of your mom's disappearance."

"Really? Have you had any luck?"

"Asa remembered the name of one of the barmaids, and I think I've just found her on social media."

"Asa never struck me as the type of guy who'd drink in the Cave."

"He doesn't, but a number of his clients do, so it pays to keep abreast of who's who."

"Did you tell Blue about this?"

"You mean did I voluntarily call a woman who wants to remove my testicles and mount them on a plaque? No, I didn't."

"She's good at her job."

"If she improved her people skills, she'd be better."

"Her ex was a lawyer. I think he screwed her over in the split."

"Heav'n has no rage, like love to hatred turn'd, nor hell a fury, like a woman scorn'd," I quoted. "But even if Blue has what is to her mind a good reason for behaving the way she does, I still value certain parts of my anatomy, and I do *not* dress like a frat boy."

Romi tilted her head to one side and grimaced.

"*You* think I dress like a frat boy?"

"It's the pastel shirt. Try wearing a darker colour next time. And also a pair of jeans. Tell me you don't own boat shoes now?"

"Nico invites us out on his boat sometimes. It's a perfectly legitimate reason to wear them."

She buried her head in her hands.

"They're comfortable."

"Maybe if you just wore them in the house..." Romi came closer, stopped three feet from my chair. She was wearing perfume today. A scent with vanilla undertones I recognised from one of her ad campaigns last year because, like a sap, I'd taken a sniff when I dropped by the perfume counter to pick out a gift for Clarissa. "Does the barmaid you found still live around here?"

"She moved to Eugene."

"You want me to pass the information to Blue?"

"Blue's busy. I figured I could talk to Nolene myself."

"You're not a detective."

"No, but I've taken plenty of depositions, and don't forget I interned at both the NYPD and the Office of the Attorney General when I was in New York. I know how to ask questions. Plus I worked as a bartender, and our female customers always told me I was a good listener."

Too good a listener. I'd lost count of the number of times I'd been stuck behind the bar at the end of a shift, trying not to yawn as women confided in me about affairs, divorces, egotistical bosses, traitorous friends, the darkness of grief, various transgressions... The list went on. At least they'd tended to leave generous tips.

"You *are* a good listener. If you go to talk with Nolene, can I come?"

If a potential witness saw Serena's daughter, that could garner some sympathy for the cause. But Romi might also turn out to be a loose cannon—she had a tendency to speak before she thought on occasion. From a purely logical perspective, the pros and cons balanced out. But from a personal point of view, spending time with Romi would be a good thing. Possibly painful too—in the way that wanting what you couldn't have always hurt—but it might get us talking properly again.

"Sure you can come, Buttercup. If she'll agree to see us, that is."

"If I was a woman, I'd agree to see you."

"You *are* a woman."

I had first-hand knowledge of that fact.

"Oh, yeah. A woman and a dork, right?"

I had to smile. "A woman and a dork."

18

———

AARON

"Sorry, but I just can't be certain whether Rey Mendez was in the Cave that day. It was twenty years ago, and my memory's not what it was. A Thursday, you say?"

I put Nolene Parnell in her mid-sixties, a sturdy, moon-faced woman with deep dimples and a ready smile. She'd been working in the yard when we arrived, her cheeks pink from the exertion. A natural hostess, she'd offered us sweet tea and led us to chairs and a table set out under a pergola in the backyard. Too cold to sit outside, really, but she was doing us a favour by talking, so I gave Romi my sweater and made the best of it.

"That's right, a Thursday."

"Rey used to come in for a drink most afternoons." And the rest. Nonna said he used to prop up the bar every evening too. "A hard-working man like that has to unwind after a long day out on the land. Jeb Robertson used to start his crew on the dot of six thirty, come rain, come shine. But Thursdays... Around that time, Rey often used to be missing on Thursdays." Nolene cast a sideways glance at Romi. "He had personal matters to attend to."

Romi stiffened, but she stood her ground. "If you mean he was screwing Gerilee Kroger, I already know about that. And Jaycee Billings."

"Oh. Oh dear." Nolene cleared her throat, uncomfortable. "Sometimes after a woman has children, she loses her...well, her *desire*. And men, they have needs. Thursday was Gerilee's day off, if I remember right. I'm real sorry about your momma. I always figured she had enough of small-town life and ran away to the city."

"Why do you say that?"

"Serena, she always seemed like she was meant for more, you know? Rey was a catch when he was younger, a real hard worker, but Serena... With her looks, she could have been a model."

"He wasn't a catch—" Romi started, and I grabbed her hand under the table and squeezed. Then realised what I'd done and let go in a hurry, but at least she stopped talking.

"What did Rey say after she left?"

"Well, naturally he was upset, *real* upset. And a little annoyed too. Serena took the car, you see, and Rey's truck had given up the ghost not so long before, so he was stuck without a vehicle. Bob Herbert always gave him a ride to work, and Gerilee would pick him up for their...you know, but losing his independence, it was hard. And money was tight with two kids and only one wage coming in. Then there was the childcare... I don't suppose it was easy being a single parent."

Stay quiet, Romi.

"Mrs. Parnell, did Rey ever voice what he thought had happened to Serena?"

"He said she must've run off with another man, and if he ever got his hands on him... Well, I'm sure you can imagine."

"Which man?"

"Now that you mention it, I don't think he ever did say. But he was sour about it for months. I suppose that was a tiny bit two-faced of him on account of he was still seeing Gerilee, but at least he stuck around to provide for his family."

Only if by "provide for his family" she meant that he'd drunk himself into oblivion while Nonna made sure Romi and Luca didn't starve was that statement accurate. But like so many abusers, Rey Mendez was practised at hiding the monster within. Plenty of acquaintances found him personable, charming even, while his nearest and dearest suffered.

I asked more questions, going over the same ground from different angles in an attempt to shake something loose, but no new information emerged. To summarise, Rey had seemed more annoyed by losing the car than by losing Serena, and irritated at the prospect of having to curb his drinking time to look after a house and kids. And Nolene hadn't known the cabin in the forest existed either.

In short, she'd be a better witness for the defence than for the prosecution.

The trip had been a complete bust.

At least, it had when it came to the case. In regard to the Romi situation... Well, we'd made it to Eugene without her sniping or giving me the cold shoulder, so I was taking that as a win. And she hadn't stayed silent either. No, she'd told me about her modelling job in Klamath next week—she'd booked Selwyn to drive her there at four a.m., apparently— and then she'd asked me about my work. Why had I moved back to Baldwin's Shore? I'd been honest and told her it hadn't been my first choice, but things were working out okay. I had a steady job and good friends, and my half-finished apartment was a hell of a lot nicer than any place I'd have been able to afford in the Big Apple.

Post-rehab-Romi seemed calmer. Mellower. And also more careful. Gone were the random ramblings about life and the impulsive streak that had gotten us both into trouble over the years. Including the last time we'd driven this route together. Seventeen-year-old Romi had wanted to go to the country fair over in Veneta, and of course I'd offered to take her. I'd been driving an ancient convertible back then, a Ford that leaked when it rained, but at least the lack of a roof meant there was plenty of room for Romi's stuffed bunny in the back seat. Peter. *Petey.* An eight-foot-high furry pink abomination wearing yellow overalls and a mutinous expression. I'd begged Romi to leave him behind, but my pleas had fallen on deaf ears.

"But I never win anything. Ditching him would be bad luck."

"How do you figure that?"

"Like, it would make me seem ungrateful."

"No, it would make you seem sensible."

"Can you help me carry him to the car?"

If it had been Brooke asking, Petey would never have made it out of the fairground, but it was Romi.

"I'll take the feet."

If Petey had been the only critter we'd encountered that day, I'd have considered the trip a success, but five minutes after we'd paused briefly to take pictures of a rainbow—and when I say "we," I mean Romi—she screeched, "Stop, stop, stop!"

I hit the brakes, then asked the sixty-four-thousand-dollar question. "Okay, what did we stop for?"

"Back up."

"Why?"

But Romi was already out of the car and running back along the pavement, heading for... Was that... Was that a dead raccoon?

Yes. Yes, indeed it *was* a dead raccoon.

Fuck my damn life.

"Aw, look!"

"At what? The guts all over the road?"

"Don't be so gross. It's got a baby." *Oh, shit.* I knew what was coming even before Romi turned those doe eyes on me. "Aaron, could I please borrow your shirt?"

"Buttercup, we're not taking a baby raccoon home with us."

"Fine, I'll use my own." She stripped down to her bra at the side of the road and scooped the tiny ball of fur into her arms, then hit me with a smile. Assault with a deadly weapon. "Isn't he just the cutest?"

"No."

"Liar."

"What the hell are we meant to do with a raccoon?"

"I guess maybe take it to the veterinarian?"

Arguing would have been pointless. Even at the age of nineteen, I'd known that all too well. I also knew that I was ridiculously, stupidly, and hopelessly in love with Romi, so if she wanted to take a half-dead baby raccoon to see Dr. Stockton, we'd be taking a half-dead baby raccoon to see Dr. Stockton. Plus her bra was slightly see-through, and every time I looked at the raccoon cradled against her chest, I got to enjoy the view.

"The veterinarian... Sure, why the hell not?"

Why not? Because the cop who pulled us over five miles later, no doubt intrigued by the giant bunny in the back seat and the half-naked brunette in the front, had other ideas. Two minutes and one lecture about public-decency laws later, Romi had charmed him into lending her his windbreaker and he was escorting us to a wildlife rehabilitator in Coos Bay.

No, life had never been boring with Romi, and I kind of missed her crazy ways.

Had Maple Mountain tamed the wild child within her? Or was that Davis's doing? They'd been together for more than two years now, and I couldn't imagine him playing taxi driver to a raccoon. But she was clean and sober, so much as I wanted to hate him, I couldn't. Romi's well-being was more important than my feelings.

"That didn't go well, did it?" Romi asked when we were on our way back to Baldwin's Shore.

"It could have been better."

"*A good father.*" Romi spat the words. "Nolene thought Dad was a good father. Why are so many people blind to the way he acts?"

"People only see what they want to see, and even when they find out the truth, they don't like admitting to their own short-sightedness."

"People suck."

Did she have to say that? Because now all I could think of was that night. My cock in her mouth.

"They do," I murmured, then shut that image firmly away. "Any news from Blue?"

"She's arrived in Iowa, but she said it might take a couple of days to find Gerilee and convince her to talk."

"I'd tell her anything she wanted to know just to make her go away."

"Hey, whatever works. Although if Gerilee's got anything

in common with Elmira, she and Blue will probably end up besties."

"Great. Maybe Blue can move to Iowa and hang out. Do you mind if we pick up lunch on the way home? I've got an afternoon meeting when I get back to the office."

"You have any place in mind?"

"The Steak and Shake? I may have omitted to mention that there's been one tiny change to the menu—Vi added an almond-milk version of her chocolate milkshake after Josie Bennett developed a dairy allergy."

Romi twisted in her seat, eyes wide. "You're telling me that Vi does a vegan version of her famous chocolate milkshake?"

"Yup. I tried one, and it was surprisingly drinkable."

"You've made my day. My week. My year. I'm gonna order two. No, three, plus fries and onion rings. And then I'm gonna drag my ass out of bed an hour early tomorrow and run because I'll still need to fit into the sample size next Tuesday."

I ran most mornings, but it was too soon to offer to go with her. Baby steps were better than no steps at all, and I didn't want to push my luck.

"My treat."

"Perhaps this day isn't turning out so bad after all? Just keep your fingers and toes crossed that Blue finds something useful."

"Toes as well? You'd better not complain if I walk funny."

That's what I said, but if I'd known what Blue was going to find, I'd have sawn my fingers and my toes off at the roots and stuffed the bloody stumps into my ears. Because Blue Carver was about to tip Baldwin's Shore on its sleepy small-town head.

19

ROMI

"*D*id you fill this with rocks?" Colt asked as he hefted my fifth suitcase onto a luggage cart.

"I just bought a few bits and pieces in the boutique." Including a rather lovely driftwood sculpture titled "Healing Soul" that would look fabulous in Davis's Florida beach house. Made by none other than Deck, whose talents were wasted in Baldwin's Shore. His pieces would sell for a fortune in a New York gallery. "It's important to support the local economy."

"How did you ever manage to go backpacking? Did you rent a Sherpa?"

Packing to go to Europe had been the hardest challenge of my life. I'd folded, rolled, and crammed everything into one giant rucksack, then nearly collapsed when I tried to pick it up. But no way was I leaving that fourth pair of shoes behind. Or my hair straighteners. Or the six packages of anti-blister Band-Aids, and believe me, I'd needed every single one of those.

"No, I just got really strong."

And also pulled a back muscle. Then I met a charming

Danish guy who'd helped me to carry things. Milas had been handsome and kind and sweet, and boy, he'd had stamina, but still...he wasn't Aaron. In those days, I'd harboured a secret longing to move to New York after I'd travelled for a year or two, to convince Aaron to give "us" a go away from Luca's disapproval. Then I'd been scouted in a mall in Paris, and two weeks after that, I'd walked the runway in my first show, terrified but exhilarated beyond measure.

And for as long as people were willing to pay me a stupid amount just for wearing clothes, I had to take the money. It was too good to turn down. I'd used a chunk to pay off Nonna's medical bills, put way too much of it up my nose, and then banked the rest. I had nice things now, but I didn't live extravagantly, and Davis insisted on paying for everything while we were together. He was old-fashioned that way.

I heard running footsteps behind me, and two seconds later, Kiki barrelled into me full-force. "You're leaving?"

"I am."

"Why?"

"Because some other people already arranged to stay here. But I'm not going far."

"Romi's going to stay with Brooke and Luca," Colt told her.

"Can we visit?"

I crouched down to her level. "Of course you can."

"And then you can visit us. We're getting a new house." Kiki thrust a piece of paper toward me. "Look!"

Wow, she'd been busy. Both sides of the paper were covered in drawings—ponies, a fairground wheel, a swimming pool, and three people I assumed were Colt, Brie, and Kiki.

"Who's this?" I asked, pointing at a fourth figure.

"That's me as well. I'm ice skating."

"Kiki's nothing if not ambitious," Colt said. "Brie asked her what she'd like at the house, and these are her ideas."

"*Some* of my ideas. I've got more."

Colt raised his eyes skyward. "Heaven help us all."

"You want to be an architect when you grow up?"

"What's a architect?"

"A person who designs houses."

"When I grow up, I'm gonna be a princess."

I raised an eyebrow at Colt.

"It's under discussion," he muttered, his cheeks turning a delicate shade of rose. "We're just trying to find 'normal' at the moment."

For him and Brie, "normal" meant buying the town's derelict paper mill and using the land to build their dream home. Putting down roots in Oregon. Not for the first time, I wondered what it would be like to have a place of my own. I could afford to buy a property ten times over, but despite travelling the world, I hadn't found anywhere I loved enough to stay permanently. My mail got sent to Davis's New York penthouse, but my heart? My heart was still wandering.

And after yesterday, also slightly confused.

I'd spent half of my life loving Aaron, and then that love had turned to hate in a heartbeat. Or had it? Over milkshakes and fries at the diner, I'd felt a hint of what we used to have. The easy camaraderie, the connection. And if I wasn't careful, those feelings could tip the new life I'd built for myself upside down.

"Heard anything from Blue yet?" Colt asked, snapping me back to the reason I was in town in the first place.

"She watched Gerilee from a distance yesterday, and

she's going to try approaching her today if there's a good opportunity." Gerilee was married now, a mom with two young children. Blue didn't want to plough in while Gerilee was with her family and risk getting shoved straight out the door. Softly, softly was the best approach with this one, she said, and I had no choice but to trust her. "But I spoke to the barmaid from the Cave with Aaron, and that was a bust. She thinks Dad's a good guy. Can you believe it?"

"Men like him are good at pulling the wool over people's eyes."

"How dumb must she be? I mean, she remembered he was more upset about the car than about Mom. Didn't that raise any red flags?"

"Some men don't deserve a family."

And others would move heaven and earth for theirs. "Brie and Kiki are lucky to have you."

"Yeah, well..." Aw, it was cute when he got embarrassed. "Anyhow, I asked around and found another name for you and Blue."

"I thought you weren't meant to be 'asking around.'"

"Call me an anonymous source."

"Whatever works. What's the name? I mean, who?"

"Arlette Strong. She worked as a barmaid at Beer Me Up around the time your mom was there. If your parents had a serious fight, your mom might've mentioned something to a colleague."

Another barmaid. Great. "Does she still live in the area?"

"Heard she's in Coquille."

"Maybe if Blue takes her time in Iowa, I could speak to Arlette with Aaron?"

"You've got Aaron doing legwork now?"

"Don't sound so surprised. He's not a deputy. He doesn't have to follow your dumb rules."

"Guess things just seemed a little strained between the two of you last time you were here, that's all."

Shit.

"If I was off, it's because I was burying my mom, okay? And Aaron's been busy with work."

Colt merely shrugged. "So, you and Davis French, huh? Gotta admit, that wasn't the type of guy I imagined you ending up with."

Colt was too damn perceptive. Time to shut this down.

"That's rich coming from a man whose future father-in-law wears a crown."

Now he laughed. "You got me there. And before I forget, Brie told me to ask you to dinner tomorrow night."

"Here?"

"Aaron's place. We don't have a proper kitchen in the hotel suite, and she's decided she's playing chef." Colt pulled a face. "So if you can come up with a good excuse, I'd advise you to use it."

"Brie's that bad of a cook?"

"Let's put it this way... Her head bodyguard sent his men on a firefighting course, and her father insisted the architect include the mother of all sprinkler systems in the new house."

"Thanks for the warning."

But I knew I'd be there. It was only now that I was back among friends—some old, some new—that I realised how lonely I'd truly been for the last few years. I'd had Davis, my rock, but after rehab, I'd taken a step back from the other people I used to hang out with. If I'd returned to the party scene, I wouldn't have been able to resist the lure of my old vices, and...why had that mattered? Because deep down, I'd always known Aaron was right. If I'd kept treating alcohol as a soft drink and drugs as candy, I'd have danced myself into an early grave.

I just hadn't wanted to *admit* he was right, not out loud.

I hated being wrong.

Hated messing up.

Life with Davis was so easy. So smooth. We complemented each other like yin and yang, but there'd never been that heat I felt with Aaron. Never would be.

And now that those embers were being stoked again, I realised what I'd been missing.

* * *

"What the hell?"

I froze halfway into the abomination of a dress I was trying to pull on, no doubt giving Aaron an eyeful of my ass. Nothing he hadn't seen before, but *fuck*, this was awkward.

Awkward squared.

Everyone had been out when I arrived at Deals on Wheels, but Luca had given me a key and the alarm code with strict instructions to arm the perimeter again once I was inside. When the light turned green, I'd headed up the ramp. Sunlight streamed through the French doors that led to the roof terrace, a beautiful space dotted with palm trees and colourful plants surrounded by a metal-and-glass railing and with a glimpse of the sea in the distance. I'd figured nobody would mind if I borrowed it for a couple of hours.

"Could you just pull the bottom down? Or up? I think I'm stuck."

He tugged on the hem, my head popped through the neck-hole, and hurrah, I was able to move my arms again.

"Shit, I ruined my make-up."

"I'd tell you that you look beautiful anyway if I didn't think it'd earn me a slap. But Buttercup, that's the ugliest dress I've ever seen. Tell me it's for your blog?"

"You've been reading my blog?"

Aaron took two exaggerated steps back before he uttered a careful, "Yes."

Two and a half years ago, still miserable from rehab and bored because I didn't have much work to do, I'd been browsing social media when I came across a post from a young British fashion devotee. Hazel had bought a dress from one of those social media ads—you know the ones, designer knock-offs for a bargain price—and needless to say, it looked nothing like the picture. She'd added the caption, *Only a supermodel would look good in this*, which was of course a lie.

After some back and forth, she'd mailed me the hideous outfit all the way from London, and the blog *Not Even a Supermodel...* had been born. We posted photos of original designer dresses, laughable shots of me wearing the shady versions, and links to "inspired by" pieces from legitimate retailers so people looking for affordable fashion didn't get ripped off. We'd gradually expanded to include articles about the fashion industry and life in general, and now we had sponsorship deals with various designers and retailers. Hazel used her share of the ad income to pay for her university tuition, and I enjoyed having a creative outlet. Plus if I could stop a small percentage of people from losing their money on poorly made clothes, I considered that a victory.

Hence the dress. A skintight neon-yellow abomination, too long in the body and too short in the sleeves. The front was more creased than ruched, the asymmetric hem appeared to be accidental rather than intentional, and it smelled odd. Kind of plasticky. Yeuch.

Was it weird that Aaron had been reading the blog? Although it wasn't as if I'd kept it a secret—quite the opposite, in fact—and maybe, just maybe, I'd taken a nose through his bio on the law firm's website. There was a photo too. Aaron looked good in a suit. But no way would I ever admit that I'd bookmarked the page.

"Yes, it's for the blog. Hazel mailed another package of dresses, and Davis's assistant forwarded them to me here." Readers sent us the outfits now, and we had an endless supply. Today, I'd model a dozen, tweak the pictures in Photoshop, and then send the results to Hazel to upload. I motioned Aaron to the side. "You're in front of the camera."

He took two more steps back and pointed at his chest. "You might want to blur out certain areas before those photos go near the internet."

Aw, hell. This damn dress was see-through as well. At least I was wearing panties.

"Wipe that smile off your face."

"Trying."

I nearly threw the camera remote at him, but knowing my luck, it would probably have broken. And besides, half of the world had seen my boobs. I couldn't afford to be shy in my line of work.

"Try harder. What are you doing here, anyway?"

"I took Vega to the office with me this morning, but the client I'm meeting with this afternoon is scared of dogs, so I had to bring him back home. Figured I should warn you he's in there."

"Thanks." When Aaron turned to leave, I stopped him. "Uh, I might have a problem."

"Oh?"

"Now that I'm in this dress, I'm not sure I can get out of it. Davis usually helps me, but he's not here, and..."

"Want me to find you a pair of scissors?"

Secretly, I wanted him to peel me out of the vile outfit, but if I asked, he'd probably think I'd lost my mind. And perhaps I had? Cue another trip to Maple Mountain...

"Scissors would be great. What are you doing tomorrow?"

"Why?" he asked, glancing left and right like a cornered animal. "How many dresses do you have to try on?"

"This is nothing to do with dresses—Colt just found the name of the barmaid who worked with Mom at Beer Me Up, and I thought we could go talk to her if Blue isn't back. If Mom told her that Dad threatened her, that would be evidence, right?"

"Unfortunately not—it would be hearsay. But if she saw bruises or your mom cried while she was telling the story, that would count as an eyewitness account and would therefore be evidence."

"Do you have to be such a lawyer?"

"Sorry. Where does the barmaid live?"

"Coquille."

"I have court tomorrow and probably Friday too, but we could go one evening?"

"Friday evening? Brie's cooking dinner at your place tomorrow."

A look of horror came over his face. "I'm definitely working late tomorrow."

"Her cooking's that bad? I thought Colt was exaggerating."

"Yup, it's that bad."

"Need a secretary?" I offered a sultry smile, and I knew it

was sultry because I'd practised it a thousand times in the mirror. "I could take dictation, sir."

But Aaron didn't bite.

"What happened to spending quality time with your brother? You know how to work a fire extinguisher, right?"

"If I'm going, then so are you, buster."

"We'll see. Friday evening for the interview?"

"Friday evening works."

Or so I thought. Until Blue tipped that carefully made plan on its head.

20

⸻

ROMI

Say what you wanted about Blue, but she sure did have an impeccable sense of timing. My phone rang two minutes after Brie had served the main course, just as I was wondering how not to eat the rest of it.

"Excuse me a moment."

Her face fell, and a touch of guilt niggled at me.

"I'll put yours back in the oven to keep warm."

"Might be a little blackened for that, princess," Colt said.

"You think? I didn't want to undercook it this time."

"Ah, the medium-rare chicken," Aaron murmured beside me. "An interesting concept."

I conjured up a smile. "I'll be back in no time."

Brie's two bodyguards looked at each other and smirked as I headed for Brooke and Luca's apartment—the farther I got from Brie's vegan meatballs, the better, plus I'd nearly chipped a tooth on a Hasselback potato. How ironic that she had muscle to follow her everywhere, but the biggest danger came from her own cooking. And I noted they'd declined to eat with us.

"Hey," I said as I hurried up the ramp to the second floor. "Is there news?"

"There is, but I doubt you want to hear it."

My heart plummeted. "Gerilee couldn't remember?"

"Oh, she remembers all right. Herb's alibi for your dad is bullshit—which we already knew—but Gerilee's is the real deal."

Was this a sick joke? "She gave him an alibi?"

"She picked him up from work that day. He was with her for the whole afternoon and most of the evening too."

"What if she got the day wrong? It was twenty years ago. Or maybe she's just covering for him the way Herb did?"

I'd never understand how my father convinced people to do his dirty work, but I couldn't deny that he managed it somehow.

"She didn't, and she's not. First, you need to understand that Gerilee hates your father. When I told her why I was there, her first words were, 'What shit did he pull now?'"

"It didn't end well?"

"No, and I can't see her lying for him. She remembers the day in question because the next morning, Rey called her to rant that your mom had disappeared and what the hell was he meant to do with you and your brother? He didn't know what time you went to school, or how to make a packed lunch, or when you went to bed. He wanted Gerilee to come over and do laundry. Apparently, that was the beginning of the end."

"Because of laundry?"

"Slippery slope, she called it. She was twenty years old, looking for a bit of fun with an older man because boys her age—and I quote—fumbled around down there like they were rollin' a cigarette, then thrust away for less time than it took to smoke the thing and expected a girl to be grateful.

She believed Rey to be an improvement in that department."

A little bit of vomit came into my mouth. "Please, spare me the details."

"Didn't plan on getting graphic. Anyhow, their relationship was purely physical until your mom disappeared. Then Rey started pushing for more, and by more, I mean he wanted Gerilee to cook and clean and babysit."

"I don't remember her doing any of that."

"That's because she didn't. And when she told Rey she wasn't interested in bringing up somebody else's kids, he slapped her and told her she was nothing but a whore anyway."

Ouch. But I struggled to feel sympathy for her. She'd brought trouble on herself by messing around with a married man.

"And yet she's still providing him with an alibi?"

"She said it wouldn't be right to let an innocent man go to jail, even if he's an asshole. Besides, her brothers saw to it that he didn't raise a hand to her again. Do you recall your father being slightly bruised around that time?"

"No, I don't." Although he hadn't been home much. "What if Gerilee's lying for some reason? Where does this leave us? With the case, I mean? What do we do next?"

"There isn't a case against your father, not now."

"But there *has* to be a case. Who else would've killed Mom? There must've been a mistake with the times, or the date, or..."

"Whether he did it or not, no jury would convict. Gerilee's testimony would be enough to introduce reasonable doubt."

"You don't know that for sure. You're not an attorney."

"No, I'm not, but I was—ugh—married to one. And this isn't my first rodeo. I get that you're emotionally involved, but if you take a step back—"

"How can I do that? How? My mom's the one lying in a cold grave. And before that, I had to live with that...that *beast* for eighteen years." I felt my blood heating, heard my voice rise to a near screech, but I couldn't stop. "So don't you dare tell me to take a step back. Somebody has to stand for my mother, and right now, it seems like I'm the only person willing to do that."

"If you try to turn this investigation into a crusade against the wrong person, that's not standing for your mom; it's letting your own emotions lead you down a dead-end road."

"You don't know my dad. You don't realise what he's capable of."

"Maybe none of my four stepfathers were as shitty as him, but believe me, I've come across my fair share of motherfuckers. Look, I'll be back tomorrow, and I'll turn in my report. You can decide whether you want to carry on with this, but if you do, you've gotta accept that we'll be looking for someone other than Rey Mendez."

"But—"

"My cab's here." Blue's voice softened infinitesimally. "Think things through, and I'll see you in the morning, okay?"

Then she was gone, and I was adrift.

Free of my bubble.

Untethered from the carefully constructed reality I'd been living in for the past three years.

And while I was down, while I was shaken, an old friend came to visit, and by "old friend," I meant that lifelong acquaintance who's nice to your face and then stabs you in the back.

A ghoul.

A devil in disguise.

And when he whispered sweet nothings in my ear, I walked to Luca's kitchen.

21

———

AARON

"Romi? You okay?"

She'd been gone for an hour. Luca figured she was just steering clear of Brie's cooking—and who could have blamed her—but I knew better. Romi was a diva, but she also liked to please people. Her whole childhood, she'd sought her father's approval without once getting it, and old habits died hard. If she was all right, she'd have come back for dessert.

"No." The giggle that followed made my gut twist. "Not one little bit."

I found her sprawled on Brooke's grey leather couch, her head hanging over one end, and the bottle of red next to her had barely a teaspoon left in the bottom. *Fuck.* Fuck, fuck, fuck, she'd found Brooke's cooking stash. I'd told my sister to get rid of it, to pour it all down the damn sink, but she'd said it would be fine. That Romi had recovered and sauces didn't taste the same without a splash of wine, and the alcohol burned off anyway.

Sauces. Who the fuck cared about sauces?

"Romi, what did you do?"

"I only...drank...a tiny bit." She held up a hand, forefinger and thumb pinched together. "Why does my head hurt so much?"

Romi groaned as I hauled her up to sitting, and as soon as I let her go, she slumped sideways. This was bad. Really bad. Romi had six stages of drunkenness, and I knew them well. Too well. Stage one, and she mellowed out. The anxiety she constantly carried with her eased, which might have been considered a good thing, but she never knew when to stop. When she got to stage two, she was chatty and fun and the life and soul of the party. If it weren't for the liver damage, that wouldn't have been such a disaster either. But she inevitably reached stage three, misery, followed by tears and then—oddly —giggles. Once she started giggling, the puking soon followed.

"If you haven't touched alcohol since you went to rehab, then you've lost your tolerance." Plus, by any regular person's standards, she'd drunk more than a "tiny bit," but since I valued my manhood, I wasn't about to point that out. What the hell had Blue said to her on that phone call? "You only drank the one bottle?"

Back in the old days, two hadn't been unusual for Romi on a bad night.

"I..." Another giggle. Shit. "I think so?"

Brooke had a million cushions piled around the place, so I grabbed half a dozen and used them to prop Romi upright. If past experience was a reliable indicator, I had less than five minutes to either find a bucket or get her to a bathroom. Given that the buckets were outside in the storage shed with the decorating equipment, the bathroom seemed like the better bet at this stage.

"You need to stand, okay?"

"Oh, no. No, I can't. The room...all spinny."

"Come on, I've got you." Slowly, slowly, I pulled her to her feet. Despite her height, she didn't weigh a whole hell of a lot, and I steadied her with an arm around the waist while she swayed and stumbled toward her bedroom and the sanctuary of its en suite. "Take it easy, no hurry."

"Don't let go."

I'd dreamed of hearing those words from her lips, but not under these circumstances. "I've got you. Just a few more steps and we're there."

"Aaron? I feel weird. Kinda...sick?"

Fuck it—I picked her up and carried her the rest of the way, and I just had time to pull her hair back before she peaked at stage six and unloaded the contents of her stomach into the toilet. And while she retched, I considered the best way to murder Blue Carver. Whatever she'd done, it had upset Romi enough to end a hard-won stretch of sobriety, and I'd wager the news had also been broken with Blue's usual lack of tact.

"You're okay, Buttercup. Better out than in."

When the heaving stopped, I passed Romi a wad of tissue and knelt beside her while she wiped her mouth. My beautiful disaster.

No, not mine.

The only woman I'd ever truly loved wasn't mine anymore, and she never would be again. How could I compete with Davis French and his millions?

Tears tracked down her cheeks as she dropped back to stage four. Her olive skin had paled several shades, and that thick dark hair hung limp around her shoulders.

"Romi, Romi, Romi," I whispered. "What happened?"

"Dad... Dad...he's getting away with it."

"With what? Murder?"

"With everything. Ev-ery-thing. Scot-free. No trial, no jail, not even...not even a shmack on the wrist."

Terrific, now we had slurring. "Blue said that?"

"He has an abil...abil...abili."

"An alibi? We already knew that."

"Another one. A *better* one. His little slut... She was with him. Hates his slimy guts, but she was still with him."

"Blue's certain?"

"That's what she says. Reasonal...reasonable doubt. Damn lawyers."

"Yeah, we're all assholes."

That got half a smile out of her.

"What about a civil case? Could you do that?"

"Sadly not."

"Why? *Why*? I can pay. I have money."

"But your father doesn't, and that's the remedy in a civil prosecution. True, the burden of proof is lower—preponderance of the evidence versus beyond-reasonable doubt—but I can't send your father to prison. The best you could hope for would be damages for losses incurred by your mom's death, which your father couldn't afford to pay anyway."

"I...what?"

"We'll talk in the morning, Buttercup. First, you need to sleep this off."

"Dinner, I should be eating dinner." Romi groaned and put her head in her hands. "Luca's never gonna let me hear the end of thish. And Davis, he'll be so dipa...dispa...mad at me. I cracked. I broke. I drank."

"I'll deal with Luca, tell him you're not feeling well. Which is technically true."

I'd feel guilty keeping him in the dark, but Romi was fragile right now, and she didn't need her brother's disapproval weighing heavy on her shoulders. When she was stronger, she could tell him herself. Or not. I had no right to make the decision for her.

"What about Davis?"

"That's your problem to deal with, I'm afraid. Promise me you won't drink any more wine tonight?"

"My mouth...it tastes *horrible*."

"I'll get you a glass of water. Do you promise?"

Romi looked up at me with those big brown eyes and bit her bottom lip. My dick twitched. I was a sick, sick man.

"I promise."

22

ROMI

Soft knocking on the door woke me, but the *rap-rap-rap* echoed inside my skull and made my head throb. Why did it hurt so bad?

Blue's call... Dad's alibi... The wine... Puking everywhere in front of Aaron... Slowly, my fuck-ups from last night came back to me in all their horrifying glory, and I wished I could flush myself down the toilet. Was that Aaron at the door now? Or Luca? I hoped for Brooke, but my run of bad luck continued.

"Who is it?"

"Aaron." Rats. "Can I come in?"

I couldn't very well say no, could I? He'd held my hair back as I vomited. That had earned him an apology, at least.

"Okay."

The door opened, and I smelled coffee. Liquid gold. And was that a tray Aaron was carrying? I hadn't realised just how hungry I was until that moment, but now my stomach grumbled.

"I made you a grilled cheese. Thought you might want breakfast."

"You mean the un-cheese you used to make? The vegan version?"

"Yes. You remember that?"

How could I ever forget? Aaron's offer was…sweet. Delicious too, and more than I deserved. One of his little secrets was that he cooked almost as well as Brooke did. They'd had the same teacher, after all—Nonna. I pushed myself up to sitting, then shuffled over so he could perch on the edge of the bed.

"Thank you."

"How are you feeling?" he asked.

"Urgh. Is that a package of Tylenol?"

"Yup."

"My hero." Because this was Aaron, the coffee beans were freshly ground as well, and I inhaled deeply before I blew on the steam. "Where's Luca? I'm surprised he hasn't come to check up on me."

"He was called out early. Myron Berwick's garage got broken into, kids probably, but Myron sounded upset and nobody wants him to have another heart attack. Brooke's taken the dog for a walk. She didn't want to wake you before she left."

"What did they say last night? Did they ask questions?"

"One or two, but I deflected. Brie was worried she'd poisoned you, but I assured her that wasn't the case."

"I should apologise."

"That would only lead to more questions. Plus she mentioned taking cooking lessons, which can only be a good thing. I've brushed my teeth three times, and I still can't get the taste of last night's crème brûlée out of my mouth." Aaron waited for me to take a sip of coffee. "Romi, we have to talk about what happened."

"Are you gonna send me back to rehab?"

"Do you think you need to go back to rehab?"

I didn't want to go to Maple Mountain, but yesterday, I'd scared myself. When I'd taken that bottle out of Brooke's cupboard, I'd wanted to put it back, to walk away, but my brain had switched onto autopilot, and the next thing I knew, the bottle was nearly empty and I was lying on the couch.

"I don't know," I whispered. "Aaron, I couldn't stop. Everything...it was too much."

"Let other people take some of the load."

"I tried that with Blue."

"And she gave you news you weren't ready to hear." Aaron nodded to himself. "The stress has been building for the past month, and you made a mistake."

"A *mistake*?" I'd ruined three years of sobriety, the longest period I'd survived without a drink since I was, oh, ten years old and sneaking beer out of Dad's stash. "I've gone back to square one."

"No, you haven't. You've taken a step down the ladder, but you'll get to the top again. You knew you shouldn't drink the wine, right?"

I nodded.

"Once upon a time, you offered me coke like it was candy."

Yes, and I'd never forget the look of shock on Aaron's face. Shock mixed with horror and disappointment. *Sickened and sad and all things bad.* The end of the beginning, the beginning of the end.

"Please, don't remind me."

"My point is that back then, you didn't realise it was a problem. Now you do. Your sandwich is getting cold, Buttercup."

So it was. I took a bite, then another, and I might have

moaned as un-cheese oozed out. I wished I was better at making it myself, but my cooking abilities were closer to Brie's than to Brooke's.

"If the lawyer thing doesn't work out, you could become a chef."

"Fortunately for the restaurant trade, lawyering's going pretty well. And you're trying to change the subject."

Busted. "Because I don't want to think about the other stuff."

"When's Blue coming back?"

"This morning." What time was it? Eight o'clock? Late o'clock, Nonna used to say—she'd always been an early riser, but for me, the day didn't start properly until noon. "Is it too late to go to the airport?"

"You want to meet Blue there?"

"No, I want to fly to Australia."

Aaron smiled, and I felt a flutter in my belly. A flutter that told me I was in trouble. It had been far easier to handle my feelings when he was being an asshole, and now I was tangled up with another man. And I wouldn't—couldn't—hurt Davis. Davis... What was I meant to tell him about last night? We'd sworn to be honest with each other, and he'd always confessed his setbacks. But sending a few emails at midnight paled into insignificance compared to downing a whole bottle of wine.

"Want me to come with you when you talk to Blue?" Aaron asked.

"You'd do that?"

"I wrapped up in court yesterday, so I've already cleared my schedule."

Tears prickled, but I blinked them back. My emotions were all over the place lately, but this morning, the overwhelming feeling was one of gratitude. I'd screwed up, but despite that, despite a rocky patch filled with more boulders than pebbles, Aaron was still by my side.

"I need her to look harder. To find a way to prove the timings are wrong. If Dad has an alibi for Thursday afternoon, then he must've killed Mom some other time."

"Have you considered the possibility that maybe he didn't do it?"

What?

"Are you kidding? Who else would have wanted to hurt Mom? Dad has a violent streak, you know he does, and they fought all the time." The yelling. I'd never, ever forget the yelling. He'd yelled from the moment he walked in the door, although the times he got quiet were scarier. Silence meant the fists were coming. Or the belt. "Actually, fighting makes it sound like she hit back, and she didn't, I'm sure she didn't. And he already lied about one alibi, don't forget that."

"Your mom was pretty. She turned heads. Playing devil's advocate, a stranger passing through could have grabbed her."

Oh, thank goodness, Aaron was back to being an asshole now.

"How many people 'pass through' Baldwin's Shore? It's at the end of the freaking world."

"That was only an example."

"A bad one. And Dad didn't even report Mom missing."

"Maybe he figured she'd left, the same way everyone else did. Don't forget the note."

"Or maybe he knew exactly where she was."

"I just think you should look at the alternatives, that's all. Don't forget what Nolene said—that Rey was annoyed about your mom vanishing. Not dejected, not worried—angry. If he'd killed her, I'd have expected him to feign some kind of sorrow, but he didn't. And then there's the car. Logic says that he'd have found a way of keeping it."

"Not if it was full of bloodstains. What about forensic evidence, huh?"

"Firstly, criminals didn't have the same knowledge of forensics twenty years ago, and secondly, you're giving your father credit for a level of intelligence he doesn't possess."

"But—"

"Just hear Blue out, okay? I asked around after you hired her, and people say she's not the easiest person to get along with..." Aaron rolled his eyes. "...especially if you happen to have passed the bar exam, but she did have a reputation for getting results."

"Do you think we should carry on investigating? Be honest."

"If I had the money to spare, I would. Maybe your father won't get what he deserves, but your mom might."

Justice. Mom deserved justice. And if money couldn't buy justice, then what was the point in having it?

"You're always so damn sensible."

He murmured something that sounded suspiciously like, "Opposites attract."

"What was that?"

"Nothing, Buttercup. Drink your coffee."

23

AARON

Romi passed me her phone.

Blue: Fog at airport. Flight cxld. New 1 lands 3 hrs l8r.

She'd followed it up with three swearing emojis, so I figured she wasn't happy about the situation, but I couldn't say I was disappointed. The less time I had to spend with Blue Carver, the better. Plus the delay meant I'd have Romi to myself for longer, and the selfish, sadistic part of me didn't mind that idea.

"She's getting a cab from the airport?"

"She drove her rental car there, but I'm not totally sure it'll make the trip back."

Shame. I took a seat on the couch, and since Brooke was out, I put my feet up on the coffee table.

"How's your head?"

Romi had finished the grilled un-cheese, swallowed two Tylenol, and taken a shower while I answered my emails. The rest of the morning was ours.

"The pills helped."

"What do you want to do while we wait for Blue?"

Priority number one was keeping Romi calm after last night's upset. When we were teenagers, she'd been happy to go to the beach or the diner, and in New York, we'd probably have watched a movie or, if the sun was shining, taken a walk in Central Park. But we'd grown apart. I didn't know her anymore, not the way I used to. What did she do with Davis in her free time? Actually, scratch that question. I didn't want to think about it.

Romi shrugged.

"Watch TV? Go to the coffee house? Head to the beach for an hour?"

"Could we visit Arlette?"

"Maybe we should leave that to Blue?"

"But Blue isn't here."

"She's on her way."

Romi put her hands on her hips. "*You* were the one who talked about justice for Mom. You think I'm not capable of keeping my head, don't you? That's why you're trying to wriggle out of this."

Whatever I said, it would be wrong. Telling the truth seemed like the lesser of two evils, otherwise Romi would keep pushing, pushing, pushing, and we'd end up fighting again. These days, spending time with her was like ice skating across a frozen lake on a sunny day—pleasurable but dangerous. Possibly even deadly, because if she broke my heart again, I wasn't sure I'd recover.

"I have my doubts."

Right decision. The bluster went out of her, and the roller coaster of emotions continued as she sagged onto the couch beside me.

"Sorry. I'm sorry I acted so crazy last night. I don't know what's wrong with me. My thoughts are all jumbled, and every time I try to straighten them out, tears get the better of me and I end up in a mess. Usually, I speak to Davis about this stuff, but he's not here, and there's some big business deal, so I don't want to bug him all the time, and..." She swiped at her eyes with a hand. "Here I go again."

I passed her a handkerchief. "You can talk to me. If you want, I mean. I appreciate that I'm a poor substitute."

She stared at the square of cloth. "Since when have you carried a handkerchief?"

"Since this morning. After last night, I thought it might be prudent."

"Oh."

"It's clean. Addy's mom gave me a box last Christmas."

"I thought she always gave you socks?"

"Guess she decided to change things up. So...Arlette? Will you let me do the talking?"

"I won't say a word."

That wasn't entirely true. Romi talked plenty to begin with. Turned out Arlette remembered her—although Romi didn't remember Arlette because she'd been six years old when they last met—and after offering her condolences, Arlette wanted to hear all about Romi's life as a jet-setting model and, perhaps more importantly, as Davis French's girlfriend.

"You two are one of those power couples, aren't you? I saw him on that *Making of a Millionaire* show."

"He has a good head for business."

"And he's a real hottie. If I was ten years younger..."

Make that thirty. Arlette was on the far side of seventy, close to thirty years older than Serena would have been had she lived, although she dressed like a woman half her age. Her skirt was shorter than Romi's, lime-green satin that matched her hair, and she'd stuck an oversized daisy behind one ear. Perched on a leopard-print couch, Arlette was a monument to dubious taste.

But Romi took Arlette's interest in good humour and told tales of some of the more outrageous outfits she'd had to wear. Cotton-candy dress, anyone? I'd seen the pictures—another of Ishmael's creations, unsurprisingly—and spent far too long fantasising about what it would have been like to eat it off her.

Only after fifteen minutes and a glass of iced tea was I able to get a word in edgewise.

"Arlette, we were hoping to ask a few questions about Serena Mendez."

"Oh, Serena, poor Serena." Arlette grasped both of Romi's hands in hers. "The story's been all over the news, and she was such a sweet girl, too. Always smiling, even with... Well, I'm sure I don't need to tell you how things were at home. Your father..."

Arlette shook her head in disgust, and I breathed a sigh of relief that she hadn't joined Nolene Parnell as a card-carrying member of Rey Mendez's fan club.

"You knew what he did to Mom?" Romi asked. Vow of silence, my ass. But she was keeping her head, so I didn't interrupt.

"She tried to hide the bruises, but I knew. No woman walks into that many doors." Arlette lowered her voice. "My sister's first husband was the same way. A cruel man. Week after week, I told Paula to leave, offered her my spare room, but you know what she said every time? *He's promised he'll change, Arlette.* But men like that never do."

"You said her first husband—she left eventually?" I asked.

"Only after he pushed her down the stairs in front of the

children. Broke her arm in three places. The bone was sticking right through the skin. But her second husband's a real good guy. Worships Paula, so he does. Treats her like a queen."

"What did you think had happened when Serena disappeared?"

Arlette scrunched her lips to one side. "I guess I wanted to believe that she went of her own accord, but I always wondered why she left the children behind." Arlette focused on Romi again. "She loved you and your brother very much. Carried your pictures in her purse, never stopped talking about the two of you."

Tears pooled in the corners of Romi's eyes, and...fuck it. I took hold of her hand. When she didn't pull away, I hoped she'd take whatever strength she needed because this had to be hell on her.

"You weren't worried enough about where she'd gone to raise your concerns with the authorities?"

I'd read the report filed with the sheriff's office three times, even made notes on it, and Arlette's name hadn't been mentioned. Unless the file was incomplete, which was another possibility. Twenty years, things went missing...

"I thought if she *had* gone to start a new life, she wouldn't want anyone looking for her, not the police and certainly not that husband of hers."

"Did she say or do anything that made you think a new life was a possibility?"

Or had it just been wishful thinking on Arlette's part? A case of not wanting to get involved?

"Well, yes."

Hmm. "Could you elaborate?"

"She told me she wished she'd never come to Baldwin's Shore. That marrying Rey had been the biggest mistake of her life, but she couldn't regret it entirely because he'd given her two wonderful children."

Hardly surprising, but that still didn't show intention. "A lot of people have regrets."

Arlette laughed. "Can't get to my age without wishing you'd done a few things differently. Anyhow, Skip used to let Serena borrow that clunky old laptop of his on our breaks. You know, to send emails? Never did get along with computers myself. My Dennis handles all that electronic business, and a good thing too, otherwise the bills wouldn't be paid and we'd be getting those demand letters left, right, and centre. But Serena, she was good at the internet. One time, I walked into Skip's office and she was looking at pictures on a realtor's website."

Romi gripped my hand tighter. "Why? Why was she looking at real estate? She was planning to move?"

"I don't know whether she was or she wasn't, but when I commented, she said it was her dream to live in New York City."

Curious. "As in an aspiration, or something she was working toward?"

"That's a question I've asked myself a thousand times. But at the time, I thought maybe she was serious. And to tell you the truth, I was relieved, because those bruises were getting harder for her to hide."

"Wouldn't have been easy for her, starting off alone in a new place."

When I'd first moved to New York, the size of the city was overwhelming. My first roommate stole half my stuff, my second apartment had mould, and I was pretty sure I'd fractured my hand by punching a mugger. I'd nearly left after the first semester, but I'd stuck it out, and the city gradually grew on me. Then Romi began spending more time there, and leaving wasn't an option anymore.

"Now, here's the thing. I don't think she was planning to go alone."

"You already said that—she wanted to take her kids."

"No..." Arlette lowered her voice to a conspiratorial whisper. "I think she had somebody else."

Ice slid up my spine like a glacier. Slow, but heavy. "And when you say somebody...?"

"A man. Another man. Not something I agreed with, but honestly, who could blame her?"

"My mom was having an affair?" Romi's voice came out hollow.

That Rey had been cheating was bad enough, but Serena as well? Two wrongs didn't make a right.

"I don't know that for sure, dear. But she kept her phone real close in those last few months, and she kept glancing at it. You know, checking for messages. And sometimes, her face would soften and she'd get this happy little smile... She looked the way I felt when I first met my Dennis. And then one of the customers would call for more drinks, and that smile would just slip right off her face."

"Do you have any idea, any idea at all of who was messaging her?"

"I always figured he must be a rich gentleman, since Skip said she had wages owing and she didn't collect those before she left. We always got paid on Fridays. But now it turns out she didn't run off after all, so who knows? She ended up in that horrible place." Arlette shuddered. "My grandson and me, we were talking about it only the other night. The cabin, I mean. Oh, he wasn't meant to go there, but kids are kids, aren't they? Always doing what they're not supposed to."

"Your grandson went to the cabin where Serena was found?"

"Once or twice, so he said. It wasn't derelict back then, just a warm, dry place where..." Arlette glanced between Romi and me, then at our joined hands. Raised an eyebrow. "Well, I'm sure you already know what young boys and girls get up to."

"Did he notice anything unusual?"

"Only the smell. Like something had died, so he said. They thought it was a wild animal, and all the time it was Serena."

Fuck, if they'd only called the cops back then, there would have been a chance of solving the mystery. Now, the forensic evidence had degraded to nothing and people's memories weren't much better.

"Did you ever see Serena with a man?"

"We didn't spend time together outside of work. Maybe we'd pass in the grocery store from time to time, but apart from that..."

"How about *at* work? Did anyone call in to talk with her? Did she pay extra attention to any of the clientele?"

"Not that I can recall. But my Dennis says I'd forget what to buy at the grocery store if I didn't write a list. The New York thing, it stuck in my head because that's where I always thought she'd gone, but visitors and conversations... I just don't remember."

"Who else worked at the bar with you?"

"Back in those days? Well, there was Skip, but he's..." Arlette pulled a face.

"In prison, I know."

"Prison! I couldn't believe it when I heard. He was always such a kind man. A little odd, but never violent. Guess it just goes to show that no matter how well you think you know a person, they can always surprise you."

"You have no idea how true that is. Did anybody work at Beer Me Up besides you, Skip, and Serena? What about the lunchtime shift?"

"Oh, that was Mindy. Or Sindy? Maybe Sandy. I'm not real sure. She was always leaving as I arrived, and she came from out of town."

"Any idea where she is now? Do you have contact details?"

"Haven't seen her for years. And then there was Larch. At least, I think that was his name. I recall it was something to do with trees. He was an odd boy. I think Skip met him on one of those internet forums, and the next thing we knew, he was living in a trailer out back and hunting for UFOs whenever he wasn't serving drinks. Between you and me, I think he was too wacko even for Skip. Now, Larch, he moved to Montana. To one of those communes. Said the government was tracking us and monitoring every word we said, so he was going off-grid." Arlette snorted. "I pity the poor schmuck who has to listen to Dennis and me all evening. *Have you seen the remote, what's for dinner, where's the cat?*"

So that was a no, then.

"If you do recall anything else that might be useful, could you let me know?"

"Oh, sure, sure." When I handed over a business card, she smiled. "A lawyer? I always said you were a smart one."

"I didn't realise you remembered me."

"You and your little sister, cute as buttons. A real tragedy what happened to your parents." She was still shaking her head when she showed us to the door. "A real tragedy."

24

ROMI

My *mom* had been having an affair? No. No, Arlette must have gotten it wrong. Mom wouldn't have done that. Would she?

"That was interesting," Aaron said as he opened the car door for me.

"Interesting? *Interesting*? You think my shitshow of a family is *interesting*?"

"I didn't mean it in a bad way."

"In what world is my mom cheating on my dad as well as my dad cheating on my mom good?"

"It opens up a new avenue of investigation."

"Does it? If Dad found out, he'd have killed her for sure, but you already said he didn't do it."

"If she was seeing another man, he's either a potential suspect or a potential witness." Aaron's voice softened. "I know it hurts, Buttercup. All of this hurts, and I guess that sometimes I come across as callous because I'm looking at things from a step further back."

Callous? No, not callous. Aaron wasn't being deliberately cruel. Blunt, yes, but not cruel. And my mind was churning.

My whole life, I'd cast my dad as the bad guy and my mom as the good guy. And while Dad was still a sadistic son of a bitch, it seemed that Mom might not have been the angel I'd always thought. The idea sat wrong in my gut, like a plate of fries eaten half an hour before a photo shoot.

"I'm sorry I snapped. It's just that my mind's a mess right now. *I'm* a mess."

"I'll give you as much help as you want to get through this. As much help as you'll accept. But I know things are still...shaky between us, and I don't want to overstep."

He'd held my hand. When we were speaking to Arlette, he'd held my hand, and I hadn't let go. Hadn't *wanted* to let go. But Aaron was right—we were still tiptoeing around each other, and our relationship was strained compared to the old days. But I saw a chink of daylight now. Perhaps in time, we'd find our way back to the way things used to be? Was it possible? I hoped so.

An image of *that* night flashed into my head, Aaron naked underneath me as I took whatever I wanted from him. Which version of the old days did I want to go back to?

And what the hell was I meant to do about Davis?

Fortunately for a procrastinator like me, my phone rang and saved me from having to answer the question.

"We're okay." I squeezed Aaron's hand, then picked up.

"Where are you?" Blue asked. "I'm at your brother's place, and you're not."

"I went to visit somebody."

"When are you coming back? We need to talk."

"How long until we're home?" I whispered to Aaron.

"A half hour, give or take."

"You're with your brother? Or the lawyer?" Blue's tone twisted at the end, making "lawyer" sound like a dirty word. When I hired her, I'd thought her hatred of the legal profession would be an advantage, but now I realised it could be a problem instead.

"I'm with Aaron. He's been helping me."

"Here's a tip—ask yourself one question: what's in it for him? And when you get back, I've got something to show you."

I ignored the first part.

"Can't you just tell me?"

"Nope."

Arguments left me drained, and arguments over the phone were the worst.

"Okay, well, we'll be there in a half hour."

Aaron gave a heavy sigh. "Want me to drop you off? I can go to the office."

"Would you stay?"

"Will I need to borrow Luca's body armour?"

"I'll throw myself in front of you if she goes for her gun."

Finally, he cracked a smile. "How can I say no to that offer?"

<hr>

When we arrived back at Deals on Wheels, Blue was out of the Honda, looking up at the front facade.

"Are the bathroom fittings made of gold?" she asked when we got within earshot.

"Huh?"

She pointed at a camera just below the roofline. "I've seen banks with less security."

"The Bad Samaritan's broken in twice," Aaron told her. "I'm keen to avoid it happening a third time."

"What'd he steal?"

"Nothing that I know of."

"Then what was the point?"

"He left notes."

"Notes?"

"The last one told us how to get to the cabin in the forest."

"That's..." Blue searched for the right word, settled on "weird." Also weird was that Blue was being civil to Aaron. Had curiosity overridden her hostility? "How'd he get in?"

"The first time? We don't know. The second time, he climbed onto the roof."

She stared at the wall, fifty feet of vertical brick. "How?"

"You're asking the wrong person." Aaron moved past her to unlock the front door and disarm the security system. There were sensors everywhere. "Come in. Do either of you ladies want a drink?"

My first thought was "vodka," my second thought was "don't you dare," and what came out of my mouth was, "I wouldn't say no to juice."

"Blue?"

"Coffee."

"Cream? Sugar? A pint of my blood?"

"Strong and black."

"Ah, just like your soul."

Aaron ducked toward the kitchen before Blue managed to throw anything at him. She had to settle for glaring as he walked away. If looks could kill...

"What did you find?" I asked her.

"The car was bugging me. A body's easy to hide—you can bury it, burn it, chop it into little pieces—" Great, now I felt sick. "—but a ton of metal, not so much. So either somebody drove it away, to another county or another state, or they didn't."

"Wow, that really narrows things down."

This time, it was me on the receiving end of Blue's glare. "I was on the plane—middle seat, economy, keeping the expenses in check—and a jackass from New Jersey had the aisle seat. His hand kept landing on my leg, so my elbow landed in his nuts, and he screamed bloody murder. Long story short, he was a frequent flyer on that route, and the cabin crew moved me to business class with free champagne."

"What does this have to do with my parents' car?"

"I had peace and time to think, and also free Wi-Fi, so I started doing some research." She reached into her giant purse and pulled out a laptop. "Did you know that on Google Earth, you can go back in time? View historical imagery?"

"I don't much use Google Earth."

Blue just shrugged. *Never mind.* "Well, I do, and I found this."

She showed me a fuzzy green screen, rows of lumpy broccoli, and pointed at the centre.

"Are those trees?"

"Yes, and the cabin. See?"

Not really, but I didn't want to admit that. "Okay."

"And look at this here."

"The red dot?"

"What colour was your mom's car?"

It dawned what she was trying to tell me. "That's it? The car? It's still there?"

"I think ten years ago it might have been. Either that or there was an anomalous pixel in the photo. Step forward in time, and it disappears, but that could be because the area got more overgrown. The driveway's gradually disappearing too."

"Holy shit."

"What's holy shit?" Aaron came back with a tray holding my juice, plus coffee for him and Blue.

"Blue found Mom's car."

"Really?"

She took her coffee. Peered at it suspiciously. "Fifty-fifty. I still need to check."

"Now? Can we go now?" How long would it take to reach the cabin? Forty minutes? An hour? "At least then we'd know."

"Go where?" Aaron asked.

"To the cabin. Blue thinks the car's near the cabin."

"You two are *not* going to the cabin alone."

Who was he to tell me what to do? "In case you haven't noticed, I'm an adult."

Technically. Sometimes, I still felt like a clumsy teenager and way, way out of my depth. When I was small, the grown-ups around me had seemed so smart. So capable. But I realised now that it had all been an illusion. Mostly, adults were just better at bluffing. There were exceptions—Davis, for example—but for the most part, we were swans. Serene on the surface while paddling furiously underneath.

"I have a gun," Blue added. "Plus a black belt in aikido."

"And the Bad Samaritan has a sniper rifle and hangs out in that area. Nobody goes near that section of the forest without proper planning and precautions."

"Who died and made you boss?"

"Who died? So far, Romi's mother and a kidnapper dressed as Ronald Reagan."

Blue closed her eyes and let out a long breath. "Sorry, I shouldn't have said that."

Somebody had to play mediator. "Aaron's worried, that's all. We can go on the weekend once we've had time to make a plan. Is tomorrow too soon?"

A little of the tension in Aaron's jaw loosened. "I'll talk to Colt and Luca. And we also need to consider what this might mean—if the car was left in the forest, why?"

Blue's contriteness didn't last long. "Isn't it obvious? Serena met someone at the cabin, and they had their own transport. Which again rules out Romi's father because (a) he didn't have access to another vehicle, and (b) he was probably drunk. And after the perp killed Serena, they drove the car farther into the forest to hide it. Maybe they knew the area real well and figured it wouldn't be found? Or maybe her death was an accident, and they panicked afterward? Or they could have come from out of town and planned on being far away by the time anyone discovered the car or the body."

"That doesn't narrow things down much."

"We've barely started putting the puzzle together. As we find out more, the pieces'll slot into place."

So Blue said, but at the moment, what we had was a bunch of jigsaws jumbled into one big pile, and every single one had key parts missing.

The discovery of Mom's car—if it *was* the car—raised more questions than it answered.

And left me more confused than ever.

25

AARON

Eleven o'clock on Saturday morning, and seven of us were en route to Blue's red dot. We'd all pored over the satellite pictures yesterday evening, and while none of us could say definitively that the dot was a car, we couldn't be sure it wasn't either.

And Colt and Luca agreed we had to check.

We'd tried to leave Romi and Blue behind, and Blue said no problem, she'd just drive there herself, which promised to create more problems than it solved. So Romi and Blue were being chauffeured by Luca, and I was shotgun in Colt's truck. Brooke was at work, thank fuck. She'd begged us to wait until tomorrow so she could come too, which was why Luca and I had decided we absolutely had to go today.

Brie had also wanted to join us, but Colt said no, her security team said no, and somebody threatened to call her mother, so she was sulking at the Peninsula with Kiki and we'd brought Kasper, one of her bodyguards, as a concession. Couldn't say I was upset about that—before he joined the Valetian Royal Guard, he'd been in the Danish special forces, and he knew more than any of us except Luca about war. And with the Bad Samaritan lurking in the shadows, it felt as if we were stepping into a combat zone.

Deck had also come along for the ride. Colt thought the extra muscle might be advantageous, and Deck had shown up with a machete. A fucking machete. Said it would come in useful if we had to cut through any undergrowth, and I only hoped he knew what he was doing. Today would be enough of a challenge without a visit to the emergency room.

At least this morning, we'd be able to drive right to the cabin instead of taking the Bad Samaritan's trail through the forest. That cut the risk down to a tolerable level. A quick recon of the area beyond the clearing to check whether there was indeed a car lurking in the undergrowth, a prayer beside the cabin where Romi wanted to lay a bunch of flowers, and we'd be home in time for a late lunch.

That was the plan, anyway.

A plan I soon realised was up shit creek, quite literally, when Deck and Luca—who it turned out had his own machete—hacked their way through a clump of buckthorn and found...a large pond. Or possibly a small lake. Either way, it was a heck of a lot of water, and it was right where the coordinates said Blue's red dot should be.

"Aw, hell," Luca groaned.

"What? What is it?"

Romi stumbled forward from behind and would have landed on her face if I hadn't grabbed her arm. She might have been elegance personified on the runway, but sure-footed she was not. We used to hike in the hills around Baldwin's Shore when we were teenagers—me and Romi, Luca, Brooke, occasionally Addy and Colt—and if someone was going to trip over, it was invariably her. She'd once confessed that her biggest fear was face-planting on the runway in a pair of the ridiculous shoes she got paid to wear. So far, she'd survived intact, but if you knew her well, you could see her shoulders tense whenever she approached steps.

"Why is there a lake here?"

"At a guess? Too much water and nowhere for it to go."

"Oh, ha-ha. Very funny. Why isn't the lake on the satellite pictures?"

"Are we in the right place?" Blue asked.

"More or less." Luca checked the satnav unit in his hand. "The satellite images were low-res, so we could be a little way out, but we're in the vicinity."

"Try skirting around the lake?" Deck suggested. "If we check a hundred yards on either side, that should cover all bases."

"After you." Luca stood for a moment, studying him. "What unit were you with?"

"One I don't much like to talk about."

Deck had been military? He'd never mentioned that, not once, and we'd spent a reasonable amount of time together when he was working on my apartment. Come to think of it, he hadn't said much about his past, period. We'd spoken of his childhood in Georgia, his parents' divorce when he was a teenager, the motorbike he'd rebuilt with the help of his grandpa, his sculpting, weekend camping trips he took to Olympic National Park when the weather was good, football, the brick grill he wanted to build, but now that I considered it, there *was* a big chunk of time missing in the middle.

And when I watched him more closely, I realised Luca was right. He moved with the same smoothness as Kasper and Luca himself. Precise, fluid movements. Comfortable despite the difficult terrain.

Who exactly *was* Decker Langdon?

"There's a stream here," Kasper called. "Shallow enough to wade across."

"Elmira mentioned a stream," Romi said, tripping along behind me. At least if she fell forward, she could grab my backpack. "She said her great-uncle Ralph used to fetch water from it." She shuddered. "Imagine not having a faucet."

"Did she mention a pond?"

"I don't think so."

"No," Blue said. "She didn't. And why would there be a pond halfway up a damn mountain?"

The answer? An enterprising beaver. Its dam was a sight to behold, a masterpiece of rodent construction that spanned the whole way across the ravine. And if I wasn't mistaken, that was a muskrat lodge at the far side. When I was a teenager, I'd taken a forestry job to earn money for college, and I'd learned a bit about Oregon's wildlife that summer.

"Is this a good news/bad news situation?" Kasper asked. "As in, the red blob we're searching for is probably here, but underwater?"

Romi let out a squeak of frustration. "So what do we do? Can we dismantle the dam?"

I had more bad news. "It's illegal to remove a muskrat lodge."

Blue muttered something that sounded like, "Fuckin' lawyers."

"What muskrat lodge?"

I pointed. "See those reeds and sticks on the far side?"

"What if we just...I don't know...took down the other side of the dam?"

"Beaver's not gonna be happy about that," Deck pointed out.

"Doesn't investigating a homicide take precedence? We can put the logs back afterward."

Colt played devil's advocate. Brave man. "We don't know for certain that the car's even in there."

"Well, we have to find out. It can't be that deep, surely?"

Deck hunted around until he found a suitably long branch, hung onto an overhanging tree, and probed the water near the bank. The bottom was damn near six feet down, probably seven or eight feet closer to the middle, a sludgy brown soup that could have been hiding a car, a serpent, or Skip's missing hoard of gold.

"Maybe we should call Detective Payne," Colt suggested. "Let him deal with this."

Luca sucked in a breath. "If I had any confidence he'd do his job, I'd agree to that, but we all know he'll just jot a footnote in the file and go back to his coffee."

"You did swimming in the Rangers. I remember. You told me some guy got kicked off the course because he nearly drowned on the first day of training. And you..." Romi pointed at Kasper. "Brie said you were in special forces. Didn't you have to swim too? And in deeper water than this?"

"We did," Kasper grudgingly admitted.

"Well, there we go. Problem solved."

Deck snorted a laugh, then quickly straightened his face, no doubt in case Romi turned her sights on him next.

Luca pinched the bridge of his nose. "It's not an outrageous idea. I'm sure Nico has wetsuits we could borrow."

"He has scuba tanks too," Kasper said. "They use them for the tourists."

"Great, so can we go back and get them?" Romi again.

I almost pitied Luca, having to argue with her. Rey said she was pig-headed, and Nonna had gone with "strong-willed," but either way, when that stubborn streak made an appearance, you'd be better off arguing with a rodeo bull.

"By the time we've driven to the Peninsula, talked to Nico, assembled the equipment, and gotten back here, we'll have lost the light. But tomorrow should be doable."

Logistically feasible, yes, but there was one small problem. "What about Brooke?"

"You can just explain to her that she needs to stay with Brie."

"Why do *I* have to explain?"

"Because you're her brother."

"And she's gonna be your wife, which gives you certain responsibilities."

Deck chuckled. "I like the way you all think Brie'll sit in her hotel suite for two days running." He patted Colt on the shoulder. "Good luck, buddy."

"Kasper's responsible for her security."

But Kasper saw things differently. "As Aaron said, there are expectations for a fiancé."

"We're not engaged."

"Everyone knows it's only a matter of time."

"Shoulda brought popcorn," Blue said. "This is more entertaining than I thought it'd be."

"It's not— Holy fuck." The curse tumbled out of my mouth as Romi sprinted past in her underwear, tripped over a tree root, and belly-flopped into the water with her arms flailing.

What the hell was she doing? My heart leapt into my throat, but I'd only taken two steps when Luca shot past me, swiftly followed by Kasper and Deck. The three of them dove into the pond with considerably more grace than Romi had managed, one after the other.

"Get the blankets from the back of my truck." Colt threw his keys at me. "In the storage box."

My heart told me to go after Romi, but logic said there were three people who were all far better suited to the job than I was. And when they got her out of the water, the bigger risk was hypothermia. Luca carried space blankets in the first aid kit in his truck, so I'd grab that too. The cool-headed bastard had shed his jacket on his way to the pond, and the keys were in a pocket.

"I'm fine, get off!" Romi shrieked. "Let me look for the damn car!"

Yeah, better them than me.

When I got back with blankets, medical supplies, and as much spare clothing as I could find, Romi was huddled against Blue on the bank while Luca, Deck, and Kasper duck-dived in the pond. It didn't take long for them to centre on one area on the opposite side.

"There's something down there," Luca shouted, treading water. "Could be a car."

Right now, I was more worried about Romi. Blue had wrapped a coat around her shoulders, but she was still shivering.

"Here, use this instead."

I unwrapped one of the foil blankets, trying—and failing—not to look at Romi's perfect tits as she unpeeled the jacket.

"Th-th-thanks."

"Put this fleece over the top. You should go sit in the truck with the heater running."

"No way."

"If you get sick, you won't be able to help with the case at all. And don't you have a photo shoot next week?"

"Yes, *Dad*."

Blue nudged her. "Relax. She's tougher than she looks. A fucking lunatic, but tough."

Dealing with Romi or Blue was difficult. Butting heads with both of them? Impossible.

"Use your shirt to dry your legs and put your pants back on. Socks and boots too." I turned back to the pond. "Luca, you gonna be long out there?"

"Fuckin' hope not."

Kasper dove under as Deck surfaced. How long had he been down there? A minute at least. Whatever he'd done in his past life, it was clear he was at home in the water. Was that why he'd settled in Baldwin's Shore?

"Look what I found." Deck waved something thin and slimy in the air. "The licence plate."

Blue stood up. "Is it legible?"

"Yup."

He wiped some of the gunk away and called out the digits. I'd read the missing persons report twenty times over, learned the damn number by heart, so I didn't need Blue to tell me what I already knew: we'd found Serena's missing vehicle.

26

ROMI

"You okay in there?" Aaron asked. "I've left clothes outside the door."

"I'm fine. And I don't need to go to the hospital."

He'd asked a hundred times on the drive back. I'd traded places with Kasper and ridden in Colt's truck because I wanted to avoid a lecture from Luca. I still got a lecture from Aaron, but it was a smaller one, and he'd also lent me his jacket which meant I couldn't complain too much.

Now I was hiding in his en suite while Deck used the family bathroom upstairs. I'd definitely gotten the better end of the deal because Aaron's shower was big enough to turn a cartwheel in, and I could also delay the inevitable scolding from my brother for a little longer.

"You're not still shivering?"

My eyes rolled automatically. "Nope."

"You want something to eat?"

"Not in the shower."

"When you get out?"

"Grilled cheese?"

I heard the smile in his voice. "Don't stay in there too long, or it'll get cold."

Over scalding coffee and sandwiches, we held a conference around Aaron's dining table. We'd found the car, but now what were we supposed to do with it?

"Let's just take the dam down," Blue said. "The water'll drain away in, what, a day?"

Colt shook his head. "And it'll wash out the surroundings. We can't keep this hidden from the state police. Payne's a jackass, but he's a jackass in charge of the case, and it wouldn't be right to cut him out of it. Plus if there *is* any evidence in the vehicle, we'll need a forensics team to go over it."

"That'll take forever."

"Twenty years have passed already. Another month won't make much difference."

Luca nodded his agreement. "If we want any chance at a criminal prosecution, we have to maintain the chain of evidence. Which means getting the cops involved and then waiting. Guess they'll need to consult the Baldwins too, seeing as it's their land."

"Payne spoke to EJ when they cordoned off the cabin, and apparently, he didn't even recall it was his. Had to go back to the office and check the records. Said his father must've dealt with the lease."

"If he doesn't much care about that piece of land, let's hope he doesn't object to it being flooded."

I didn't like the idea of involving Detective Payne again, but deep down, I understood that Luca and Colt were right. Aaron would side with my brother too, I knew it. And

Kasper, because he struck me as the kind of guy who played by the rules. Which left Blue and possibly Deck as the holdouts, so Blue was about to be overruled.

When she was, she just shrugged.

"You're the boss. But I'm still only sticking around for three more weeks."

Then we had to hope Payne pulled his thumb out of his ass and got on with the job. Thankfully, I had a shoot to distract me this week—two glorious days in Klamath working for Ishmael, who was demanding at the best of times. At least that would pay for Blue's fees with enough left over for milkshakes.

What I thought at four a.m. on Tuesday morning was, *Fuck, you've got to be kidding me.*

What I said was, "My gosh! I'm so sorry to hear that. You just let me know if there's anything I can do to help."

Selwyn, who'd promised to drive me to Klamath in time for hair and make-up at nine o'clock sharp, had tumbled down the last half-dozen stairs at home, landed awkwardly, and was on his way to the hospital with a suspected broken ankle. His grandson had been terribly apologetic but, quite understandably, had bigger concerns than Ishmael's impending nervous breakdown.

Which left me with a huge problem. Where the hell was I going to find a car and driver in the early hours of the morning? My laptop. I needed my laptop. But where had I left it? Not in my suitcase—I hadn't planned on taking it to Klamath because I could get email on my phone and Ishmael would be working us from dawn till dusk if the past was any indication. I'd been using it last night... After dinner... In Aaron's apartment...

Shit.

It was downstairs.

Which gave me three options—I could squint at my phone screen for a solution, or wake Luca, or go and get my laptop. Aaron didn't lock the door to his apartment. Why would he? His sister and his best friend were the only other occupants of the building, and all the security was on the outer perimeter.

I tiptoed through Luca's living room, then hurried down the ramp. Surely there'd be a twenty-four-hour car service in Coos Bay? There were nightclubs in the downtown area. Bars that stayed open late. People who needed to get to the airport for an early flight or Portland for an early meeting. If I offered to pay double, then maybe—

"Shitting fudging fuck!" I clutched my bare foot as I hopped around in near-darkness, spewing every curse I could think of and a bunch I made up. Were my toes broken? They sure felt like it.

The light blinked on.

"What the hell's going on?"

Aaron stood there in a pair of boxers, a gun in one hand and his hair delightfully dishevelled. *No, not delightfully anything. Call it messy.* Hmm, he'd spent time in the gym, hadn't he?

"Why the hell is there a box in the middle of the floor?"

"So I don't forget to take it to the office in the morning."

"That's a stupid place to leave it."

"In case a burglar trips over it?"

"I'm not a burglar."

"Which brings us back to my first question."

"I need to find alternative transport to Klamath, and I thought it would be quicker if I used my laptop."

"What happened to Selwyn?"

"According to Deon, he fell down the stairs. Do you have the number of a cab firm in Coos Bay?"

"You hate cabs."

"I also hate the idea of giving Ishmael an aneurism, but that's what's gonna happen if I don't get my ass to this shoot. Do you have a number?"

"Want me to drive you to Klamath?"

I froze. After all of our history, after the way I'd blanked him for three years, he'd do that?

"Are you serious?"

"I'm always serious. Apparently, I need to loosen up and take the stick out of my butt every now and again."

He remembered. He remembered the words I'd said to him right before I undid his belt and sucked his cock. Words I'd never forget and had later grown to regret.

"Don't you have to go to the office?"

"I'll have to drop the files off for Asa on the way. As long as there's an internet connection available, I can work remotely for a couple of days."

"I'm sure there'll be internet. Ishmael's people took care of the hotel booking, and he freaks out if the Wi-Fi's less than stellar."

"What's the name of the place? I can book myself a room."

"Ishmael promised me a two-bedroom suite. Originally, I thought Davis might come with me, but then his schedule changed."

Aaron looked at me curiously. "You don't share a room with Davis?"

Oh, no, no, no, I couldn't be having this discussion, not now.

"That's the way we prefer things. He's an early riser."

All of which was true, so why did it feel as if I was lying?

Deep down, I knew the answer.

I just didn't *want* to know the answer.

But Aaron merely shrugged. "Okay."

"Okay?"

"Give me ten minutes to take a shower and throw some essentials into a bag."

"I should leave a note for Luca. Let him know you've come with me."

"Or you could call him?"

"No, I think I'll leave a note."

Luca was still annoyed at me for jumping into the pond on Saturday, and even though his teenage pact with Aaron had gone the way of the dodo, I still didn't want him to get the wrong idea about the two of us. Or maybe it was the right idea? I just didn't know. What I did know was that I needed to speak with Davis, face to face.

And take a long, hard look at my future.

27

AARON

The man I recognised as Ishmael lay on a Pepto-Bismol-pink velvet chaise longue, or a chaise lounge as Nonna had insisted on calling it even after our neighbour at the time, a Quebecois named Emile who'd spent most of his free time playing the violin—badly—had explained multiple times that "chaise longue" was the correct French for "long chair." Maybe Nonna did it to annoy him? I couldn't have blamed her if that was the case. Even now, the sound of string instruments set my teeth on edge.

Anyhow, Ishmael was lying on his chaise, sighing dramatically as an assistant frantically fanned him with a clipboard. He wore a skintight tangerine catsuit with platform boots and a feathered collar, also orange, but a darker shade. Probably he'd call that burnt butterscotch or honeyed ember or spiced carrot or some other bullshit. His hair was green, the colour of grass, square at the sides and flat on top as if somebody had mown it. A white butterfly perched over one ear. Or was it a flower? I didn't want to get close enough to find out.

"This is a disaster. A *disaster*."

Romi had warned me the man was a drama queen, but this was taking things to a whole other level.

She approached gingerly, practically tiptoeing.

"I'm not late. It's still two minutes to nine, and I checked my watch against that website with the atomic clock."

"Romina, my *darling*." He reached up for her hands and clasped them in his, then pulled her closer and air-kissed her twice on each cheek. "My fallen angel. You're perfect. It's everything else that's a *catastrophe*."

"It is?" As Romi spoke, the fan-girl shook her head, panicked, but Romi didn't heed the warning. "What happened?"

"We're *homeless*."

The guy was on a fancy chair in the middle of a field. There wasn't a building in sight. What did he mean, homeless?

Romi was puzzled too. "I don't understand?"

"We have nowhere to lay our heads. Nowhere to bathe. Not even a coffee machine."

"Then why did you arrange an outdoor photo shoot?"

"I mean tonight. *Tonight*."

"But we have hotel rooms. Your assistant sent me the confirmation."

"Amaryllis got confused between Klamath and Klamath Falls," Fan-Girl whispered. "The only place around here with vacancies has three stars and half the amount of rooms we need."

Romi looked at Ishmael, then back to Fan-Girl. "I see how that could be a problem."

"We're trying to fix it, I swear. But this area is, like, desolate, and we're not scheduled to finish shooting until ten tonight."

And the schedule saw them starting again at sunrise.

"Romina must have sleep," Ishmael mumbled. "We can't have bags under her eyes. She *needs* to look fresh."

Fan-Girl gave a nervous giggle. "Amaryllis is calling hotels right now. Oh, there's Anders. I need to...uh..." She passed the clipboard to me. "Just keep fanning."

Was she joking? She was joking, right?

Romi gave me a "well, what are you waiting for?" look, and I gave a few half-hearted flaps. The four-hour drive and the prospect of working from a hotel bar for two days, I didn't mind, but I hadn't signed up for this.

"Who's Anders?" I asked.

"A colleague," Romi said, grimacing.

"A *star*."

I ignored Ishmael.

"What's the problem?" I mouthed.

"Later," Romi whispered. "Ishmael, should I head to make-up?"

"Yes, yes. We'll head to the first location at ten, and you need to look tippety-top." He gave his fingers a chef's kiss. "*Perfetto*."

Romi backed away and motioned me to put the clipboard down. Ishmael would either have to fan himself or pass out—I didn't much care which.

"Anders?" I asked as Romi headed toward a marquee set up on the far side of the pasture. Outside, a handwritten sign said "Staging Area."

"Anders isn't my favourite person to work with."

"Why?"

"Because he thinks he's smarter than everyone else. He has a PhD in...something, but he couldn't make any money with it, so—in his words—he's been forced to sell his body."

"Sounds like a great guy. He's arrogant?"

"More bitter. But very, very pretty."

"And Amaryllis?"

"Ishmael's other assistant."

"Someone called their kid that? Didn't the DHS get involved?"

"Her name's Amy, but she changed it to sound more exotic. And don't say anything about names in front of the girl who gave you the clipboard."

"Dare I ask why?"

"Because her parents couldn't decide between Mackenzie or Kennedy or Kayleigh, so they called her Mackennedeigh—with an E-I-G-H at the end. We all call her Kenny, but she's still real sensitive about it."

"Noted. Want me to search for a hotel?"

"Amaryllis and Kenny'll be calling every single hotel, guest house, and rental agent in the area, trust me." Romi pointed toward a satellite dish. "There's your Wi-Fi. Wish me luck."

"You'll knock 'em dead, Buttercup."

I'd never get sick of watching Romi work. In New York, I used to go to her shows when I could, but I hadn't seen her do a shoot in a forest before. Ishmael might have been a demanding oddball, but I had to concede he could design good clothes when the mood took him. Romi looked ethereal in delicate dresses that floated on the breeze. Today, she was posing in a forest of redwoods, a nymph among giants. I took a break from reviewing documents to observe for an hour.

She was a natural in front of the camera. Fluid, expressive, stunning. So was Anders, unfortunately. Even as a straight guy, I could see why he'd made it as a model. But I still wanted to knock his damn head off, especially when he whined about bugs or allergies or pinching shoes every five minutes. No wonder Romi couldn't stand the guy.

"Do I look sultry enough?" she asked at lunchtime. "Ishmael seems happy with the pictures, but I just really want to knee Anders in the nuts. He keeps bitching about mosquitos, but there are no freaking mosquitos."

"You look perfect, as always."

"No need to suck up. I'll still give you one of my..." She picked up a blob of what might have been wilted spinach from her plate. "Whatever this is. In fact, have all of them."

The spread Kenny had arranged for lunch was also in Klamath Falls, and no doubt delicious. Ishmael had waved his arms, huffed, and told her to donate the food to the homeless. The hotel rooms too. When she raised the question of whether the Linkville Plaza would be happy to host people from a shelter, he'd simply fixed his gaze on her.

"They can have good Twitter or bad Twitter. Ask them which they'd prefer."

She'd bobbed her head, stumbling as she backed away. "I'll get right onto that, Ishmael."

Sometimes, the crazy guy wasn't so awful.

"I'm good with my cheese sandwich, thanks," I told Romi.

Although I used "cheese" in the loosest sense of the word. The saran wrap it came in probably had more flavour.

"Uh-oh. Here come Amaryllis and Kenny. They seem nervous."

Which made me nervous too.

"Good news, everyone!" Kenny chirped, although she looked close to tears. "We've arranged hotel rooms really close by. They're a little drab, but we're gonna brighten them up this afternoon with a few little extras. Unfortunately, existing bookings mean some people will have to share, so we hope you'll all be understanding."

Amaryllis spoke up. "And the local steakhouse is gonna cook up a special dinner for us after we've finished shooting for the day. To speed things up, we're asking everyone to make their menu choices in advance, so we're gonna leave a pile of slips right over here next to the board with the room allocations."

She gave us a thumbs up and a pleading look, and then the two of them practically sprinted out of sight.

"Don't worry, I told them we weren't, you know, together," Romi said.

Even so, I didn't think I was going to like this.

And I was right.

Anders. I got Anders. Who gave me a filthy glare and started complaining right away.

"Why does Romi get her own room? We're meant to be on an equal footing, therefore I shouldn't have to share either."

One of the make-up artists gave a long-suffering sigh. "Because after you take Ishmael out of the equation, there's an even number of men and an odd number of women."

"Find another woman, and I'll share," Romi said, and then her face fell as she perused the menu.

Shit.

I sidled up to her. "How bad is it?"

"I can have a baked potato with no filling and an ear of corn."

Davis would probably have arranged for dinner to be flown in from LA, but my budget didn't run to that.

"Want me to go hunt food while you finish up here? If I

can't find a decent restaurant, we could have a carpet picnic in your room."

"Like the old days?"

The old days. When she'd fly in late to JFK and hire a fucking limo to get to whichever shitty apartment I was renting a room in at the time. She'd always been the night owl to my lark, and we'd sit up until the early hours putting the world to rights, always with a bottle of wine back then. Even though she knew a seemingly infinite number of people with swanky apartments in NYC, she often chose to crash on the air mattress I kept specifically for that purpose.

I'd wanted her in my bed.

But I'd been too afraid of rejection—and also of Luca's reaction—to tell her how I felt. I was a geek, she was a goddess. What did I have to offer her? Nothing but myself, and until the night she'd made a move on me, I wasn't sure that would be enough. So I'd cast myself in the role of friend and confidant, tried but failed to keep her on the straight and narrow where her party habits were concerned.

The old days.

They were bittersweet.

"Sure, Buttercup. Just like the old days."

28

———————

ROMI

Me: I can't sleep.

Two a.m., and I should have been dead to the world after spending hours in the forest. At nine p.m., Ishmael had decided he wanted dimly lit pictures of me running between the trees in an evening gown and a pair of stilettos, which was basically my worst nightmare. I'd been so terrified of tripping that I'd been stiff and awkward, and we'd had to do a million takes before Ishmael was happy. At least we were on the beach tomorrow. Sand was better than leaf litter.

Aaron had come through with dinner, though. I'd been expecting PB&J and possibly a portion of fries, but his picnic was a vegan's dream. Nachos with cashew sauce, tofu taco bites, enchiladas, even dairy-free churros for dessert.

"Where did you get all this?" I'd asked.

"From a food truck in Crescent City. Google to the rescue."

"It's amazing."

My room, sadly, was not. Amaryllis and Kenny had done their best by adding a vase of fresh flowers and brand-name shampoo, but it still stank of stale sweat, and no way was I putting my bare feet on that carpet. Plus the headboard had been banging against the wall in the room next door on and off for the past four hours.

Aaron: Join the club.

Me: Does Anders snore?

Aaron: Worse. He's chanting.

Me: Chanting? Why?

Aaron: Who knows? If I open my mouth to ask, he shushes me.

Was chanting better or worse than enthusiastic grunting? A tough question, and not one I cared to know the answer to. I should have brought earplugs. What if I put cotton balls in my ears? Anything was worth a try.

It wasn't just the sexcapades of the folks next door keeping me awake, though. Luca had called earlier. They'd come to an arrangement with Detective Payne, and the state police were going to drain the pond tomorrow. EJ had granted permission to do whatever was needed. Payne hadn't been happy that we'd gone renegade, apparently, but his irritation had been tempered by the fact that we'd done his job for him *and* he'd get to take all the credit. I wanted to be there, but instead, I had to model swimwear on a day forecast to be unseasonably cool.

The cotton balls didn't work. The walls were thin enough for me to hear the woman squeal, "Danny!" and although I wanted to vomit, I was also reminded just how long my own dry spell had been.

Me: Still awake?

Aaron: Strongly considering going to sleep in the car.

The couple next door fell silent as I considered my next move, but my mind didn't. Aaron had a long drive back tomorrow, and he needed to sleep. And I had a couch. Three years ago, I wouldn't have hesitated to offer it, but after all our ups and downs... Would it be weird?

Probably, but I decided I didn't care.

Me: Want to borrow my couch?

Aaron: Better than being bailed out for murder.

He padded through my door five minutes later, duffel bag in hand.

"If you laugh at my pyjamas, I'm sending you straight back to Anders."

His lips twitched, but he kept his tone serious. "Hello Kitty is no laughing matter."

"It's Pusheen."

"I didn't want to look too closely in case you thought I was a pervert. What the hell is a Pusheen?"

"A fatter, cuter cat. I found you pillows and a blanket. The blanket smells a bit fusty, but..."

"It's fine." Aaron brushed hair away from my eyes. "Get some sleep, Buttercup. You've got another long day tomorrow."

That was the moment I realised I still loved Aaron Bartlett.

I probably always would.

The question was, what was I going to do about it?

***

"Get it off!"

I flew out of bed, across the room, and straight into the wobbly table.

"Ow!"

My thigh throbbed where it had connected with chipped veneer, and in the moonlight, I saw Amaryllis's carefully placed vase teeter for a second, then upend onto

Aaron. He knifed up, dripping water and freesias and gypsophila and curses.

"What the fuck?"

"There's something in bed with me," I hissed. "Shit, shit! I'm sorry about the water."

"What do you mean, something's in bed with you?"

"I felt it crawling up my leg."

"What time is it?" he groaned.

"Uh, I don't..." I lifted his wrist, checked his watch. "Three thirty."

"Where's the light switch?"

A cockroach. It was a cockroach. Aaron grabbed a shoe and flattened it, only for three more to crawl out from under the bed to inspect their fallen comrade. This was a nightmare. A real-life roach motel. I pinched myself to check I was still awake, and unfortunately, I was.

Splat. Splat.

Splat, splat, splat, splat.

"Where are they all coming from?" he muttered.

"Become a model, they said. It'll be glamorous, they said. Travel the world in style, they said."

"There's a hole in the damn wall. Don't suppose you've got any duct tape in your giant suitcase?"

"If I did, I would've used it on Anders earlier."

"Then find me a towel."

By the time Aaron had blocked up the hole and disposed of two dozen roach corpses, it was four a.m. and I could barely keep my eyes open. Which, given the circumstances, I had to view as a good thing.

"My hero," I said weakly.

"I'd better go see if Anders has finished chanting."

"What's wrong with the..." I pressed a hand on the couch, and it squished. "Oh."

"Call me if any more roaches show up, and I'll come to get rid of them."

"Okay, but—" Hell. "Just sleep in the bed, Aaron. It's plenty big enough for two."

He went rigid. Didn't move for a full five seconds. Then he walked stiffly to the window and stared out at the stars.

"Not a good idea, Buttercup."

"Why? I swear I won't molest you in my sleep."

He wouldn't look at me. Why wouldn't he look at me?

"Why? Because I can't make the same promise."

I stood behind him, laid a hand on his shoulder and felt him tense under my touch.

"I don't mind."

He spun to face me. "Well, I do. You're with Davis, and I'm not the kind of guy to steal another man's woman, no matter how much I might want her."

I wanted to tell him the truth. *Needed* to tell him the truth, but it wasn't my truth to tell.

"It's complicated."

"Understatement of the damn century, Romi."

"I'll sleep in the car."

"The hell you will."

"You need the sleep more than I do. I can rest on the ride back to Baldwin's Shore."

"Fine. *Fine.*" Aaron stormed across the room and began throwing pillows into a line down the middle of the bed. "Pick a side."

"I don't care."

Without another word, Aaron climbed into the side next to the window, turned away from me, and pulled the quilt up to his chin. Why was he so annoyed? Yes, this was awkward, but I thought we'd both grown up in the last three years. Whatever. It was stupid o'clock already, and I had to get up at six.

We'd have to deal with this in the morning.

I closed my eyes, and three seconds later, the headboard started banging against the wall again. "Artie," the woman screamed. "Harder, Artie."

I'd died and gone to hell.

From hell to heaven.

I woke in Aaron's arms. My head rested on his shoulder, and my legs were tangled with his. In sleep, he looked peaceful, somehow younger than his twenty-eight years without the weight of responsibilities and expectations weighing down on him. Me? I felt like a thief for stealing this little bit of time with him that I wasn't supposed to have. But I still couldn't make myself move away.

I knew I'd done wrong the moment his eyes flickered open. In an instant, serenity turned into a storm of irritation, and he swore under his breath.

"Romi, stop biting your lip unless you want me to do it for you."

Do it. The words balanced on the tip of my tongue, but Aaron was already out of bed and striding toward the bathroom, muttering.

"Don't be angry with me. Please, don't be angry."

"I'm not angry with you; I'm angry with myself."

"You shouldn't be. Can't we just go back to the way things used to be?"

"I hoped we could, but it's hard." And so was he. I'd missed that little factoid before, but when he turned, it was all too obvious. "I love you. I'll always love you. Even when you hated my rotten fucking guts, I never stopped loving you. And it hurts like hell that I can't have you."

He loved me? Aaron loved me? That was... That was *everything*. I longed to tell him I felt the same, to show him all the ways I felt it, but this wasn't the right time. Not yet.

Because *Davis*.

I loved him too, just in a different way.

"I'll fix things. I promise I'll fix them."

"Buttercup, whatever you do, someone's gonna end up getting hurt. I just don't want it to be you."

Aaron slammed the bathroom door, and five seconds later, I heard the shower running. One step forward, two giant leaps back. But I wouldn't give up. I hadn't clawed my way to the top of a competitive industry by being a damn pushover. Aaron was mine, and I was his.

He just didn't know it yet.

29

ROMI

According to Luca, the extrication of Mom's car had been something of an anticlimax. The crime scene technicians had carefully removed part of the beavers' dam, a tsunami of water and sludge had flowed away down the hill, and the slimy red Ford had finally been revealed. An arborist cut away enough of the trees and undergrowth for the cops to winch the vehicle onto a truck, and it'd been taken away for further examination. This morning, we had a call with Detective Payne to hear the provisional results.

"I made the cake with no eggs," Brooke said. "Tell me if you like it, and I'll make it again."

"I will," I promised, even though I wasn't hungry in the slightest.

Aaron didn't want to be there, I could tell. But Luca had checked he was free before he confirmed the time with Payne, so Aaron had been all out of excuses. Things weren't right between us. He was avoiding me again. Not in the same way as before—he was still friendly and polite in front of everyone—more that he was avoiding being *alone* with me.

And yet he loved me.

The journey back from Klamath had been uncomfortable all around, a vacuum of stilted small talk and long, painful silences. In the end, I'd feigned sleep and made it easier for both of us. And now here we were. Dancing around each other like two goofy teenagers in high school. The only saving grace was that we'd finished the shoot an hour early after Anders got stung by a jellyfish, which shouldn't have been funny, but I swear I saw Ishmael chuckling when he thought nobody was watching him.

Which brought us to today.

Aaron had borrowed a conference phone from work and set it up on the table in the dining room. Even though it was nine o'clock on a Thursday, everyone had shown up for the party. Darla was covering for Brooke at the Craft Cabin, Aaron had juggled his meetings, and Luca and Colt had taken the morning off, although they were on call in case of an emergency. I'd say nothing ever happened in Baldwin's Shore, and growing up that had been true, but in the last year, the town had seen more drama than through the whole of my childhood. Or maybe the darkness had just been better hidden back then?

Payne called right on time, so at least the man had one redeeming quality.

"Luca Mendez?"

"That's right, sir."

My brother acted deferential, but I didn't miss the way his lip curled on the "sir."

"And do you have that sister of yours with you?"

"Hi, Detective Payne."

"Aaron's here too—Aaron Bartlett—and Blue Carver."

We'd agreed ahead of time to keep quiet about the others. Payne had termed this a family call, and nobody wanted him to hold back on the details if he thought he had a larger audience.

"I didn't realise you'd have company."

"Aaron is our family attorney, and my sister retained Blue to assist in any way possible. We all know how difficult budget cuts have made both of our jobs."

"Okay, I'll allow it." As if he had a choice. "As you know, our technicians spent some time going over your momma's car yesterday, and I did promise to keep you informed of progress. Sorry to say there hasn't been much, not in regard to the vehicle, anyway."

Well, that was a let-down.

"Not much or none?" Aaron asked.

"As I'm sure you understand, we didn't hold out a whole lotta hope for the forensics. In the years the car's been underwater, most everything useful has been washed away, and any organic matter would have degraded in any case. We did have one interesting find, though."

Hurry up, hurry up. Now isn't the time for a dramatic pause.

"And?" Blue asked.

Thank you.

"There was a gold coin in the glove compartment. A one-ounce American Eagle. Do either of you kids recall your momma owning such a thing?"

My knowledge of gold was limited to the jewellery form. But I'd inherited my love of all things sparkly from Mom, and if she'd shown me a trinket as shiny as real gold, then surely I'd remember? Dad called me a magpie—not in a cute, quirky way, but more because he saw me as a pest.

"She never showed me a gold coin," I said.

Luca added his agreement. "Our parents barely got by. If they'd had money to spare, they'd have spent it on food, not gold."

"Or alcohol," I added under my breath, then louder, "How much does a gold coin cost, anyway?"

"Almost two thousand bucks, according to my research."

"And back then?" Aaron asked Payne.

"Uh, well, I'm still checking out that side of things."

Blue shook her head in disbelief, and Luca reached for Aaron's legal pad to write us a note.

Price of gold increased 7x over past 20 yrs.

Guess there were some benefits to his brief stint as head of security for an Eritrean gold mine. My clunky math said that when Mom disappeared, the coin would still have cost several hundred dollars, which my parents didn't have. So how did it get into their car?

There was one obvious answer. Who'd lived in Baldwin's Shore and had a whole bunch of gold?

"Skip," Aaron and Luca said at the same time.

"One step ahead of you, boys." Payne was clearly pleased with himself for managing the most basic of deductions. "Went over to the prison to talk to him yesterday, but he didn't have much to say. Doesn't know nothin' about nothin', and that was his final word on the subject."

"Which doesn't mean he's innocent," Aaron pointed out.

"Rest assured, we'll continue looking into that angle, but it's not the only lead we have." Payne's tone turned downright smug. "Do you have any recollection of a man named Derek Wright?"

Everyone shook their heads no, and Luca answered for all of us. "No, we don't."

"According to county records, he lived on the same street as you for a brief period that coincided with the time of Ms. Mendez's disappearance. Today, he's serving life in the

Arizona State Prison system for the murder of three women he met through personal ads."

Aaron recovered first, speaking before I managed to breathe again.

"How did they die?"

"Through strangulation."

"Evidence suggests Serena Mendez suffered blunt force trauma to the head."

"We never did find her hyoid bone, so the ME can't rule out strangulation post or prior."

"I doubt Serena used personal ads either. She was married, albeit unhappily."

"Serial killers have been known to refine their methods. I'll be travelling to Phoenix tomorrow to speak with Wright, see if I can get some answers for you folks. He's never getting out, so he has nothing to lose by talking."

Nothing to gain, either.

"Wild fucking goose chase," Blue muttered, and I was inclined to agree with her. Mom had left a note. She'd planned to move away. And even if she'd done the unthinkable and gotten involved with a serial killer, how would he have known about the cabin? I'd had no idea it was there, and neither had Luca, or Aaron, or Colt, and we'd lived in Baldwin's Shore for most of our lives.

"Ever heard of Occam's razor, Ms. Carver? Often the simplest solution is the correct one."

"Ever heard of a killer's signature? Derek Wright—aka the Scottsdale Strangler—killed every one of his victims after their first date. In their own beds. He posed them, wanted them to be found. Serena Mendez was hidden in a crawl space in an empty cabin in the middle of nowhere. You say Occam's razor, I say your sister moved to Phoenix and you want to drop by for a visit on the department's dime."

Payne's silence told me Blue was absolutely correct. He probably had steam coming out of his ears by now.

"You say you didn't find much in the car, *Detective*." She managed to make the rank sound like an insult. "What didn't you find?"

"I don't follow."

"No suitcase? No duffel bag? No keepsake box filled with mementos?"

"Nothing like that," he admitted.

"Serena Mendez left a note saying she was leaving town, yet she didn't take so much as a change of clothes with her?"

"Perhaps she planned to pick them up later?"

"Good luck in Arizona, Mr. Payne." Blue reached out and disconnected. "What a waste of fucking space."

"Maybe we weren't finished talking?" Aaron said.

"Feel free to call him back on your own time. I'm sick of wasting mine."

I was on Blue's side, but I also didn't want to antagonise Aaron any more than I already had.

"How did you know all that stuff?" I asked. "About Derek Wright and Payne's sister?"

"Number one, I'm a true-crime podcast junkie, and number two, I do my homework. What happened to the note? It was mentioned in the deputy's report, but I didn't see it on the file."

"Because it wasn't there," Colt told her. "Either it wasn't kept, or it got misplaced."

Lost to the sands of time.

"Shame. Would've been interesting to get a look at the handwriting. Or was it typed?"

I might have forgotten the exact wording, but I could still

picture the note, a snapshot in my mind. "It was handwritten."

"You don't believe Mom wrote it?" Luca asked.

"No, I don't believe she did. Think about it—she lived with an abusive husband. If she was planning to leave, she wouldn't have informed him of her intentions before she'd packed. That would've been asking for trouble."

"Are you suggesting the killer left the note?"

"I'd say that's a reasonable deduction."

A chill ran through me. "But the note was inside our house."

"It was."

The chill turned to a full-on freeze. "Then the killer was *inside our house*."

"Yes."

"Could you at least try to sound horrified?"

"What do you want me to do? Fling my arms around and gasp?"

"I don't know!"

"Look, I understand why it's upsetting. But if that's the way it went down, then it's not necessarily a bad thing."

"And how exactly do you come to that conclusion?" I asked.

"Because it tells us a lot about the perp. You were alone in the house, right?"

I nodded.

"So if the person we're hunting for was unstable, or bloodthirsty, or bore a grudge against your whole family, then we wouldn't be having this conversation because you'd be dead too. No, they're smart. They targeted your mom specifically and then tried to cover up the crime. And it was somebody close to her. Close enough to imitate her handwriting and fool your father, close enough to know your home had no security and they weren't likely to get caught. You said before that there was a spare key hidden somewhere?"

"Under a rock in the yard," Luca supplied. "Mom figured me and Romi would lose a key if we carried it around with us, and it wasn't as if we had any shit worth stealing."

"So maybe the killer knew about the key, or maybe they got lucky."

"Or picked the lock."

Blue shrugged. "Or picked the lock. Whatever, we've narrowed down the list of suspects considerably. We're also looking for someone who's smart enough to plan in advance and ballsy enough to carry out that plan. Tell me, who would your mom have trusted enough to agree to meet them in a remote location? Family, friends, this mysterious lover Arlette seems to think she had? A colleague?" Blue paused, thinking. "Skip?"

"You think Skip did this?" Luca asked.

"What if she found out where he'd hidden all that gold he stole? Maybe she tried to blackmail him? He'd have had four million good reasons for shutting her up. I'm putting him at the top of my list."

I tried to reconcile Blue's suspicions with the Skip I'd known. Or thought I'd known. He'd always been a strange guy, big on conspiracy theories and not so hot on following the rules. I'd run into him from time to time with Mom, and back in those days, he'd had a big old crow named Barbara that used to ride around on his shoulder like a pirate's parrot. By the time I was old enough to drink in Beer Me Up —think sixteen, not twenty-one because as I said, Skip didn't pay much attention to the rules—Barbara's soul had passed on, but her mortal remains still perched on a rainbow behind the bar between an ugly little leprechaun and a twisted lump of metal Skip swore came from a flying saucer.

"He just didn't seem the type," I said, thinking out loud.

"He didn't seem the type to rob an armoured truck either, and yet he did."

I had to concede that Blue was right.

But despite his oddities, and yes, the whole robbery thing, Skip had always seemed kind, the type of guy who walked women to their cars late at night and stepped in if a girl's date was acting like a jerk. From time to time, he'd slipped me a free package of chips "for old times' sake" and asked if I'd heard from Mom. Did he genuinely care? Or had he just been covering his tracks?

And more importantly, how would we find out?

30

ROMI

When Blue said she was putting Skip at the top of her list, I thought she'd spend a few days researching on her laptop and then go out and talk to people who'd known him. Perhaps contact the cops who'd investigated the robbery and get their views on Skip's character. Who, incidentally, wasn't called Skip at all. His given name was Seth Hoffman, and his eventual arrest might have flown under the radar if not for the fact that he came from a wealthy New York family who'd disowned him when his outlandish views diverged from their conservative ones.

Anyhow, Blue had skimmed over steps two and three in favour of a more direct approach, which was why we were currently in the rust bucket of a Honda, on our way to the Idaho State Correctional Center. I had my doubts we'd make it that far, but when I'd voiced my concerns, Blue had just patted the hood and told me not to be so negative.

She'd also told me to keep quiet about our visit in case Luca or Aaron tried to stop us from going.

"Why do you think he chose the name Skip?" I asked.

"Either a sense of humour or an incredible lack of self-awareness."

"I didn't realise you could just visit people in prison like this. Isn't there some sort of procedure you're meant to go through?"

"Yup. But I know a guy who knows a guy who works there, and he fast-tracked our visitor applications. When you get my expense claim, that's what the basketball tickets are for."

"You bribed a corrections officer?"

"He's more of an administrator, and 'bribed' is such a dirty word, don't you think? I prefer 'incentivised.'"

"What if you get caught?"

"You reckon he's gonna tell? He won't."

"Do you think Skip will see us? What if he refuses? We'll have driven ten hours for nothing."

Actually, it'd be more like eight hours because Blue didn't make any allowances for my nerves.

"He probably won't remember me, but he'll see you."

"How do you know that?"

"Because he'd have bumped us off his visitors' list yesterday if he didn't want to talk."

"What if he does that this morning?"

"My basketball buddy's keeping an eye on it. And I bet Skip's also curious. I only met him a handful of times, but I remember him the way you do—a fruitcake with a dislike of the authorities, which means he won't have discussed much with Payne. And even if he's a closet psychopath, he'll want to know what's going on with Serena. You're the bait."

What did she mean, bait? Was this why she'd insisted I come yet been kind of hazy on the details?

I swallowed hard. "You're kidding, right?"

"Relax—he can't do anything to you in a prison. There

are guards. But you're Serena's daughter, and he'll want to find out who you've become. Trust me—you're our ticket inside."

"You think he'll say anything useful?"

"Who knows? We'll tread softly, softly, ask for his help. Don't go in heavy about the gold or suggest that he might've been involved with your mom's disappearance because that'll shut him down. He's never revealed what he did with the loot, even when the cops offered him a deal. So if he wants to keep his lips sealed, he will, but... Keep your fingers crossed."

If the thought of prison hadn't been enough to keep me away from drugs in the past, my experience at the Idaho State Correctional Center was enough to keep me clean for life. How much had I spent on rehab? Thousands, when all I'd needed to do was drop by for visiting hours.

Blue had warned me about the dress code in advance. No short skirts, no revealing tops, no denim just in case— heaven forbid—someone mistook me for an inmate. But even though I wore slacks, ballet pumps, and a turtleneck, that didn't stop a man with bad breath from searching me before we went inside.

"Do you have any electronic devices, cash, or tobacco about your person?" He sounded bored, as if he was reading a grocery list.

"No, none of those."

"Do you understand that if you act disruptive or fail to obey staff instructions, your visit will be terminated?"

"Yes."

"Hold out your hand."

He stamped it, but there was nothing there.

"Shows up under black light," he explained. "Next."

The table was bolted to the floor, and so were the chairs. Blue appeared worryingly at ease as she chatted with a corrections officer, and people kept looking at me. Men, mostly. I'd grown used to people's stares over the years, but today, it felt as if ants were swarming under my skin. Was I about to have a conversation with my mom's killer?

Skip had aged since I saw him last, more than the eight years that my time away dictated. The greying beard didn't help, but it was more than that—the lines around his eyes had deepened, and he had an air of weariness about him, a gauntness that his baggy shirt couldn't hide.

"Ladies," he said, sliding into the seat opposite. "Romi, it's good to see you again. Circumstances aren't as I'd like, but they are what they are." He focused on Blue. "You a friend of Romi's? Your face is familiar, but I can't quite place it."

"Yeah, we're friends. I came into Beer Me Up once or twice, back in the day." She held out a hand, and Skip shook it. "Blue Carver."

"Got that much from the visitor sheet. I'd say I was surprised to see you, but after that detective showed up... Did he ask you to come?"

Blue's lips quirked into a smile. "Nah, he doesn't know we're here. He's busy chasing his tail in Arizona."

"Don't surprise me. The man couldn't find his own asshole if he passed gas. Romi, I'm sorry to hear about your momma."

"Thank you. It was a shock, but all I want now is closure."

"That I can understand."

"To state the obvious, Detective Payne ain't doing much

of a job," Blue said. "And you know what they say—if you want something done, do it yourself. So, we're asking around. Mind answering a few questions?"

"Not for the cops, but for you…" He reached across the table and squeezed my hand, not in a pervy way but more of a fatherly gesture. I still had to suppress a shudder. Was physical contact even allowed? The officers didn't seem too concerned. "And besides, I don't got much else to do in here." He glanced toward a camera on the far wall. "Serena was the best waitress I ever had, but she wasn't just an employee, she was a friend too. A friend with a good soul. I'll do what I can. Got eyes and ears on us though, so keep it clean, girls."

Blue nodded. "Understood."

"The detective said they'd ruled out Rey Mendez?"

"Unfortunately," I ground out through gritted teeth.

"Guess that's the biggest surprise in all of this. When she first disappeared, I figured something bad had happened, but nobody would listen to me back then."

Blue took over again. "You went to the police?"

"The next morning. Tried calling the house a dozen times before I reported her missing, even drove over there, but Rey told me to get lost—not quite so politely as that— and that was when I got ahold of Deputy Kidd. Turned out EJ Baldwin had already been in touch because Serena hadn't shown up for that job either. But even with the two of us reporting in, the sheriff's department didn't take the issue seriously, just said she was a grown woman and there was no indication of foul play."

"She left her kids behind."

"Think I didn't tell them that? I even called the sheriff himself, but he said the children were with their father, so she hadn't abandoned them. I kept an eye out, made sure the two of you were going to school as you should."

Should've played truant. Honestly, I'd rather have taken my chances with the DHS.

"You said 'when she first disappeared' you thought something bad had happened. What changed?"

He did? I hadn't even picked up on that.

"You're a sharp one, aren't you?"

"Most people tell me I'm blunt."

Skip guffawed at that. "Blunt or not, you're right. I only started to think differently when I got the note."

I stiffened. "What note?"

"Through the mail. A pretty little postcard. Said she was sorry for leaving without notice, and she hoped I could forgive her, but she'd had a chance for a better life, now or never. That once she got settled, she'd come back for you and your brother. I believed... I guess I *wanted* to believe that she would."

"How long after she disappeared did the postcard arrive?"

"Two weeks to the day, I remember that. I should have realised, realised it wasn't from her, but at the time... It looked like her handwriting. She signed it 'Rena'—I used to call her Rena for short—and added a heart at the end, the way she always did when she left notes for a friend."

"Did she write many notes?" Blue asked.

"All the damn time. Liked to cheer people up with those inspirational quotes and doodles. Smiling through the sadness, I always thought."

I remembered the notes. She used to put them on my pillow, in my book bag, in my lunch. Luca had inherited the trait, although when we moved apart, the smiley Post-its had turned into emailed memes.

"Did you give the postcard to the police?"

"What good would that have done? Figured she was better off with the other guy, anyway. I pinned the card on my refrigerator, always hoping she'd keep her word, but after a year or so, I tucked it away. I was disappointed in her. But now I'm disappointed in myself because I should've known she wouldn't have behaved that way, especially after — It doesn't matter."

"*Everything* matters."

"She didn't pick up her last paycheck." Which tied in with Arlette's recollection. "Rena lived hand to mouth, and if she'd waited one more day, she'd have had money in her pocket for a fresh start. I recall thinking that whoever she'd run off with, he must've been a rich fella."

The same thing Arlette had said.

"Arlette thought she might've been having an affair."

I was glad Blue was doing the talking because the words would have stuck in my throat. At least this way, I could just sit back and process. Skip's story, it all sounded plausible, but what about the gold coin? Why did Mom have it?

"Yes, she was having an affair."

When I glanced sideways, Blue had a gleam in her eyes totally at odds with the ice in my veins. "You know that for certain?"

Skip nodded. "She said it was complicated." He reached for my hand again. *Stay still, stay still.* "I'm sorry, my love. I understand this can't be easy. And I know some people will judge her for the affair, but she needed a little happiness in her life, and I'd say she got it."

My last hope that Arlette had been wrong evaporated into the stuffy air of the visiting area, and I was left with more questions than answers.

"Who was she having the affair with?" I whispered.

"Now that, that she didn't tell me."

"But you must have had an idea," Blue prompted.

Skip tilted his head from side to side. "Maybe I did. Rena was good with the customers, real chatty and always had a smile. Friendly, but professional. Got the job done. But I did notice there was a fella she spent more time with than the others."

"Who was he?"

"Ted. First name was Ted, but I don't know his last name. Something to do with the paper mill. Not one of the regular workers, a consultant or a manager in town for some project or another. Rented a place from the Baldwins, one of those beach houses at the end of Shore Road. You know the ones?"

I nodded.

"Stayed there for months. A rich fella, as I said. And he left about the same time as Rena did. Never did see him again after that week."

Blue tapped her two forefingers together, the others interlinked like a church with a tiny steeple. I'd noticed she did that when she was thinking.

"When you say she 'spent more time,' do you mean outside of work?"

"Never saw them together outside the bar."

"When would Mom have had time to get involved with another man?" I asked. "She saw us off to school in the mornings, cooked dinner in the evenings. And the rest of the time she worked, or cleaned, or cooked, or shopped..."

"But working for the Baldwins, she didn't clean every rental property every day," Skip said. "Only once a week plus changeovers unless the vacationers paid for extra service. And from what she told me, the Baldwins left her to get on with things unless there was a complaint, which knowing Rena's work ethic, I can't imagine would've happened often."

Blue nodded. "And if Serena wanted a tryst, what better place than an empty home with a choice of beds?"

My stomach heaved. "I feel sick."

"Try to swallow it down," Skip advised. "The guards don't much like it when people vomit."

I choked out a laugh. Same old Skip. He'd used exactly the same tone in Beer Me Up when a patron overindulged and he suggested she head to the bathroom before she ruined her shoes. Funny—even though Skip had been outed as Seth Hoffman, he hadn't reverted to his old accent. There wasn't a hint of New York in him.

Blue kicked me under the table—a warning to keep my stomach under control, presumably—and a corrections officer swung his head in our direction. I flashed him a smile, and he grinned back, then caught his boss's eye and turned stony-faced again.

"You said that when Serena didn't come back, you tucked the card you received away. Any chance it might still exist?"

"I doubt it. After I got arrested, the judge decided I was a flight risk, so I never went back to the bar, and then they confiscated the place. Said I'd bought it with the proceeds of a crime."

Blue merely raised an eyebrow.

Skip chuckled. "Couldn't much argue with that."

"The bar's called Applejack's now," I told him. "I haven't been there, but Brooke said a girl from New Jersey runs it."

"Guess I should wish her luck. Anyhow, I don't know what happened to my stuff, but if you happen across Barbara, do me a favour and take care of her."

"Sure."

He grew weirdly earnest, took both of my hands in his this time. "Promise me you will. She'll bring you good luck."

"Okay, okay, I promise."

The crow had been cute when she was alive, strutting across Skip's desk with that jaunty walk of hers, but dead? I'd never understood why people felt the need to preserve their pets that way. I mean, would you stuff Grandma and mount her in a glass cabinet? Still, if I found Barbara, I could put her in the shed at Deals on Wheels as a favour to Skip. It wasn't as if Luca was short of space.

Blue wanted to roll her eyes, I knew she did, but she just gave a one-shouldered shrug. "Speaking of the proceeds of a crime, you know we've gotta ask about the gold coin found in Serena's car. Tongues are a-wagging, and it's all too easy to cycle through the various scenarios and land on blackmail."

"Is it illegal to give an employee—who's also a friend—a little birthday bonus?"

"You *gave* the coin to Serena?"

"Told her to keep it hidden away from that son of a bitch she was married to, or he'd waste it on himself. Not in a bank, though. Banks are nothing but fronts for corporate theft and government corruption."

At least Dad hadn't pulled the wool over Skip's eyes. Those were perhaps the strongest words I'd ever heard from him. And I wanted to believe him about the gift, I did, but he'd lied about so much in the past.

He picked up on my hesitation. "You look troubled, my love, but I speak the truth. Ask Arlette about the coin—I did the same for her. Good women, both of them. And I'm glad you and your brother took after Serena and not your father."

"So am I."

"Tell me, what's happening in Baldwin's Shore now? I don't get so many visitors. Did that new resort ever get built?"

We stayed for another half hour, talking about the past and present, and every so often, Blue would steer the conversation back to Mom, but we didn't glean any other useful nuggets of information. At least Skip had talked. And when Blue asked him why—out of curiosity—he'd stolen millions in gold and then chosen to run a bar in Oregon instead of, say, Antigua, he'd just laughed.

"Didn't do it for the money. I got no need for all them fripperies."

"Then what'd you do it for? Not the glory. The challenge?"

"No, for Caro." An unspeakable sadness came into his eyes, and he lowered his voice so it was barely audible. "My boss's wife."

"*She* needed the money?"

Blue had shown me the reports on the theft, and I'd even skimmed the court transcript yesterday. Nobody named Caro had been mentioned.

"Can't spend cash in heaven. He bullied her so bad that she took the only way out she could. When I heard the news, then and there I swore I'd make him pay. Didn't turn out to be so hard in the end. Like so many capitalists, he was all about the bottom line, so he'd cut back on the costs. I asked around. Talked to the girls in the office. The truck I was driving, the GPS tracker was faulty because he was quibblin' over the quote to fix it, and he'd skimped on the insurance. Plus he'd taken to doubling up on loads, carrying more than he should in order to save money on gas. I knew if that gold disappeared, so would his business. So I made it disappear. No regrets." He looked around the visiting area, at his fellow inmates and their families, some angry, some resigned, some talking quietly with tears in their eyes. "This place ain't so bad. Keep myself to myself. I'll be out in five." He cracked a smile. "Then maybe I'll give Antigua a try."

The more time I spent with Blue, the more incredulous I grew that she'd been working as a hot dog. And when she got to Europe, she planned to take shifts as a bartender in a ski resort. What a waste.

What a damn waste.

Blue had a gift. She could read people like books and ferret out the details that everyone else missed. Pick through a mountain of junk and find the one gem hidden in the middle. She was born to be an investigator.

And after today, I was determined to help her see that.

31

———

AARON

"Tell me again why you're here?" Taya Swann asked. "Brooke was kinda vague on the phone."

Romi and Blue had arrived back from Idaho in the early hours. From *Idaho*. When Luca found out where they'd gone, he'd nearly taken off after them, but they'd gotten too much of a head start and we both knew Blue wouldn't listen to him anyway. He didn't want Romi going near a prison. Neither did I, if I was honest, but she wasn't going to come to any harm. And with the amount of shit that had happened in Baldwin's Shore recently, she was probably safer in a state penitentiary.

Luca had chewed the girls out when they got back, Romi nodded in the right places and Blue didn't, and then they told us they had two new leads from Skip, plus they'd bumped him down the suspect list. Serena hadn't been the only person he'd offloaded stolen property onto. Arlette had also received a coin, although Blue said she'd been really cagey about admitting it over the phone. Skip had given her that coin fair and square, she said. How was she meant to know if it was stolen?

As a lawyer, I had to see her point. American Eagles didn't have serial numbers. Nobody could prove the coin Arlette had been gifted was part of the spoils from Skip's robbery.

"You said you kept some of Skip's stuff when you took over?"

Taya nodded. "I was on a budget. Still am, and it was cheaper to stack it in the cellar than rent a dumpster. I sold the flying saucer on eBay, but nobody wanted a rubber alien or a pickled potato shaped like Gene Kelly's head."

"Mind if we take a look?"

"Be my guest. Take anything you want."

"We're after something specific—a postcard. Do you recall seeing one?"

"A postcard? Who from?"

"From a murderer."

"Like Ted Bundy or John Wayne Gacy? That might be worth a few bucks."

"From the person who killed my mom," Romi said from behind, a hitch in her voice.

I'd acted like a jerk last week when I let emotions get the better of me, but now I'd removed my head from my ass, and I needed to make amends. Which was why I'd volunteered to hunt through a pile of Skip's junk for the metaphorical needle in the haystack. The fact that Blue was here too was the frosting on the cake—if we found the needle, she'd probably stick it right through my dick.

"Well, shit. I'm sorry, really sorry." Taya backed away. "And I don't think there's much in the way of paper left. The roof leaked, and some of it had gone mouldy, so I burned most of it soon after I came here. Uh, the door's right over here behind the bar."

The doorway was so low that Romi and I had to duck to

get through it, and the cellar didn't give us much more headroom. Although in terms of floor space, it was bigger than I'd expected, extending the whole length of the building. The end nearest to us was tidy and functional, with casks set in three sections—one row connected to the taps, another group with red stickers that presumably meant they were empty, and a larger cluster just waiting to be consumed. Next to the casks sat a felt-topped card table surrounded by dusty wooden chairs. Wouldn't have surprised me if it was as old as the bar itself. Asa once told me that in his youth, underground poker games took place every Wednesday and Sunday, and some of the players had been real sharks.

Beyond the card table was a cobwebbed mess.

"Good thing we don't have Addy with us," Romi whispered.

Addy and spiders weren't a good combination. She'd have run screaming, and she wouldn't have stopped until she reached Canada.

"*Hoarders* meets *The X-Files*," Blue muttered. "Shoulda gone to the paper mill first."

That was this evening's job. And probably every evening's job for the next month.

When Romi relayed the possibility that her mom's lover had worked for the paper mill, I'd expected that Blue would need to spend her remaining time on the job tracking down ex-employees of the now-defunct company in the hope that one of them recalled a manager named Ted. She'd already struck out with Baldwin Estates. Marianna Baldwin had been full of apologies that she didn't remember the guy— she'd been new to the job back then, assistant to the previous office manager—and said they only kept rental records going back seven years as their accountant recommended. And the old manager had retired years ago, to New Mexico, she thought, or maybe it was Nevada.

Marianna did at least remember Serena, but said she'd been a quiet woman, kept herself to herself, just came into the office at the start of each shift to pick up supplies and again at the end to check the next day's task list, report any problems, and drop off dirty linen. Cleaning products were ordered in bulk to save money, and linen was laundered by a company based in Coos Bay who delivered to the office. Serena had always been reliable, Marianna said, which was why she'd called EJ when Serena didn't show up at work on that fateful day.

Asa had given me the names of a couple of other people who'd worked at the paper mill, but neither of them knew Ted, and both said that management hadn't made a habit of mixing with workers on the factory floor.

But then Colt and Brie showed up for dinner with bodyguards in tow, and Kasper recalled that when he'd assessed the old mill building for potential purchase, he'd seen an archive room full of filing cabinets. When he'd opened one or two drawers out of curiosity, he found papers inside.

And it was possible that some of those papers were personnel records.

Of course, they should have been destroyed or moved to a secure location, but who would volunteer to do that if they weren't getting paid? I still remembered the announcement that the mill was closing. I'd only been thirteen at the time, but I'd understood the shock, and I'd never forget the funeral-like atmosphere. The news had come out of the blue, the poor shape of the company's finances covered up by management in the hope of attracting much-needed investment, and employees had been given less than a week to clear their desks and lockers. Many had quit on the spot amid rumours that their final paychecks would bounce.

And a once-thriving town had been thrown onto its deathbed.

Many residents had moved away in search of work, and with fewer customers, other businesses had closed down too. The Mexican restaurant, Frankie's Feet & Fashions, the hardware store. Only a decade later, as the digital economy grew and remote work became a possibility, did Baldwin's Shore finally start to recover. Most of our clients at the law firm still came from Coos Bay, but over the past couple of years, Asa had noticed a shift, especially after the new resort opened. Folks were gradually coming back. Brie's presence didn't hurt either—she'd unintentionally put the town on the map, and so many reporters followed her around that Mary at the coffee house had added an Inkslinger's Special to the menu.

"I doubt the paper mill's ready yet," I said to Blue, and she scowled. "Kasper said the electrician wouldn't be finished until late afternoon."

The archive room was in the middle of the building, a dusty tomb with no windows. Since electricity to the place had been cut off long ago, Brie's team was arranging for a generator and temporary lighting so we could see what we were doing.

In the cellar of Applejack's, we had half a dozen bare bulbs, but there were still shadows in every corner. Probably bugs too.

"Think this place has cockroaches?" Romi asked.

Great minds think alike. "If it did, they'd find their way upstairs and Taya would fix the problem." I hoped. "Come on—the sooner we get started, the sooner it'll be over."

Four hours later, we'd been through every box in the

place without finding the postcard. But Romi had ferreted out Barbara the crow, and now she wanted to bring the moth-eaten bird home with us. And it wasn't just the crow. Its feet had been wired to a wooden rainbow, the end of the rainbow was stuck in a cauldron of plastic coins, and there was a damn leprechaun perched on the edge of the pot. "Tacky" didn't even begin to cover it. But now Romi stood in the parking lot, clutching the thing to her chest with surprising ferocity.

"Are you kidding?" I asked. "Tell me you're kidding."

"I promised Skip, and I don't break promises."

No, she never did. Back when I was applying to law schools, I hadn't thought I stood a chance of getting into NYU, but Romi had promised she'd bring the champagne when I got accepted. The day after I received the letter, she'd shown up outside my apartment at two a.m. with a bottle of Cristal and a "Congratulations" card, already drunk on whatever they'd served her on the plane. I still had the card. Inside, she'd written, *I told you so, brainiac.*

"Okay, fine. We'll find a nice closet for her."

Blue was clutching a small plastic hula doll, one of those cheap things people put on their car dashes. If I recalled correctly, Skip used to keep it on a shelf behind the bar alongside a model of the Wallowa Lake Monster and an alleged meteorite.

"You're keeping that?"

"So?"

"You don't strike me as the hula-girl type."

"Yeah, well, I always wanted to go to Hawaii. Saved up for years so I could. Then the stinking low life I married cancelled our trip to Oahu because he got invited on a corporate golf retreat and he wanted to make partner."

"Why didn't you just go by yourself?" Romi asked.

"Because he promised he'd pay for a new trip as soon as his next case was over, but there was always another case after that, and another, and another, and then we got divorced. Funny how he still had time to fuck his paralegal, though."

"Whoa, I'd have set his balls on fire for that."

"I set his Lexus on fire instead, and he had me arrested. Lied about a bunch of shit to make me look crazy. So this..." She jabbed the doll's head into my chest. "*This* is a reminder that someday I'll get to Hawaii, and when I do, I'm gonna throw the signed Seahawks jersey I swore I didn't have into Kilauea."

If I were in her position, I'd probably have done the same. "I'm beginning to understand why you hate lawyers."

"Glad we're on the same page."

Her phone rang, and I was saved from further snark when she stepped away to take the call. Romi was putting a brave face on things, but I knew she was disappointed that we hadn't found the postcard.

"You okay?" I asked.

"I'm okay. It was a long shot, right?"

"We already have an idea of what it said from Skip."

"I hoped there might be a fingerprint. Or DNA on the stamp."

It was possible there might have been—prints had been found on paper forty years after deposition, and DNA could stay intact for twenty years too. But knowing that wouldn't make Romi feel better.

"Chances are the prints would've been smudged. And the culprit could have chosen a self-adhesive stamp or used water to wet it."

"I know, but—" Romi rushed past me. "Hey, are you all right?"

I turned and saw Blue's ashen face. Her white knuckles where she gripped the phone.

She shook her head, her usual bravado replaced by uncertainty and, if I wasn't mistaken, a hint of fear.

"My... My mom's house is on fire."

32

AARON

Blue and her mom lived in a small ranch-style home on the outskirts of Coos Bay, but by the time we got there, there wasn't a whole lot left of it. The roof had caved in, and soot-blackened water ran out of the open front door. Even though the fire had been extinguished, acrid smoke still tainted the air, clawing its way into my lungs. Made me damn glad I'd paid the extra to install a sprinkler system at Deals on Wheels.

"Mom!"

Blue leapt out of the car and ran to the far side of the lot where half a dozen women were poking around the overgrown bushes. One woman stepped back, her face red and tear-streaked. The two embraced. Usually, Blue talked about her mother with irritation rather than fondness, but when it came down to it, family was family.

"Thanks for driving us," Romi said.

"What are friends for?"

Blue might have acted tough, but she'd been shaking after the phone call. The last thing we needed was a car accident to deal with.

"Still…" Romi slipped her hand into mine and squeezed. "Thanks. What do you think they're looking for?"

"I'd imagine some kind of pet."

"A pet?" Her hands flew to her cheeks, and she looked to the house. "She said her mom had a cat. Do you think…?"

"Let's go help, okay?"

When we got closer, we could hear them calling for Woody, and one of the ladies was waving a fillet of salmon so I had to assume we were indeed dealing with a feline. I couldn't imagine he'd have stuck around in the yard while the fire crew did their worst, but Romi joined the search while I spotted a deputy I knew by the fire truck and went over to get the low-down.

"First on the scene, Jeff?"

"Second. Young Vincent got here first."

"Any idea what happened?"

"Whole place was in flames when I pulled into the driveway. You know the occupants?"

"Mother and daughter. The daughter's a…" I hesitated to call Blue a friend, but telling the deputy she was a pain in my ass wouldn't get me very far. "She's a friend of Luca Mendez's sister. Deputy Mendez? Over in Baldwin's Shore."

"Yeah, I've met him." Now Deputy Jefferson nodded toward Romi. "That's Romina Mendez?"

"Yes."

He gave a low whistle. "The pictures don't do her justice."

No. No, they didn't. And I didn't like the way he was looking at her either. "Getting back to the fire…"

"Big ol' blaze. Know anyone with a grudge against either of them?"

"Why? Do you suspect arson?"

"Can't say for certain, but the place sure went up fast.

Sniffer dog's gonna be here soon, and then we'll find out. So, any issues you're aware of? I know full well you keep your ear to the ground, Bartlett."

"I've never met the mother, but let's just say that Blue Carver's personality can be a little abrasive. And I know there's an ex-husband kicking around."

"Divorce amicable?"

"Far from it. And—" Shit. "And there was fire involved. She torched his car. I believe she lived in New York at the time. The NYPD should have a file."

"So she's a firebug? Reckon she might've been involved in this one? Insurance job?"

"Absolutely not. She's been with Romi and me all morning. No, I was wondering about retaliation."

"Retaliation..." Jeff nodded to himself. "Guess if this turns out to be deliberate, we'll have to start somewhere."

"We will."

And Blue surely would too. I couldn't see her sitting back and leaving the hard work to the cops. But what would that mean for the investigation into Serena's death?

Three hours later, the arson dog had confirmed what we suspected: that the fire had been intentional. Plus the cat was still missing, and Blue...well, she seemed lost too. Subdued. It was quite disconcerting.

An hour ago, she'd rallied enough to visit one of the neighbours, a grey-haired lady named Janie who lived two houses down on the other side of the road. Janie came to the door in a wheelchair, a pile of knitting in her lap. When she saw Blue, her eyes widened and she held out both hands.

"You're all right! Oh, thank the good Lord you're still breathing."

"I'm okay."

"When I saw those flames, I'm telling you my heart threatened to give out."

"The police said you called 911?"

"Not two minutes after I saw the smoke. First, I thought that fella on the far side of you was havin' a cookout—wouldn't be the first time he's burned his food—but then the smoke got thicker, and I thought to myself, Janie, why would Rolie be cookin' on a Tuesday afternoon when his wife's at work? He might grill the steak, but he ain't no good at makin' the fixins to go with it."

Blue smiled faintly. "We can always count on you to know what's going on."

"What happened? Did that cat of your momma's knock into something he shouldn't?"

"The fire investigator's still looking into that. We can't find Woody."

Janie laid a hand on Blue's arm. "I'm sure he got out, sweetie. Your momma always left that window open for him at the back."

"I know."

And Blue also suspected that was how the arsonist had gained entry to the property. She'd said as much to the investigator earlier. Of note: her ex had visited the house a number of times and was aware of her mother's habits.

Damon Mercier. When she spat the name, I realised I'd heard of him. He'd been part of the defence team for a suspected mafia boss, and photos of the celebrations after the man got acquitted had made the front pages. Some said he'd gotten to the jury. Others questioned whether the judge was crooked. Me? I thought the attorneys hadn't done a bad job, and juries were often unpredictable.

But I still thought Damon Mercier came across as a self-centred jackass.

What the hell had Blue seen in the man?

"Maybe Woody's just hiding?" Janie suggested.

"I hope so. Janie, what else did you see? Before the smoke? Were you at the window all afternoon?"

"Always am, sweetie." Janie's smile faltered for a heartbeat. "Don't got nothin' else to do. Saw your momma leave for work this morning, then Wendell Jacobs came by, deliverin' flyers for his window-washin' venture. Gotta admire a young man with a good work ethic."

"What time was that?"

"Well, let me see… I'd had my lunch, so around one o'clock? Not so long before you came back. Did you forget something, sweetie?"

"What do you mean? I came back after the fire."

"Really? I coulda sworn it was your car turned into the driveway earlier. That black one you've been driving these last couple weeks?"

"That's back in Baldwin's Shore."

"Oh, well then, I don't know who it was."

I did. And judging by the anger that flashed in Blue's eyes, so did she.

The arsonist.

"The car was a Honda?" she asked. "A Civic?"

"I don't know one model from another, but it was small and black, that's for sure. Or maybe dark blue. My eyesight's not what it used to be."

"Did you see the driver?"

Janie scrunched her mouth, thinking. "Can't say that I did. The sun was on the windshield, real bright."

"What about when the car left? Did you see it leave?"

"'Bout fifteen minutes before I saw the smoke, but only the back end as it disappeared up the road. I dropped a stitch, you see, and I didn't want to ruin this sweater."

Blue went over the whole sequence of events twice more, but Janie came up with nothing new. The car was small and dark coloured—that was all she could recall. It was more than we'd had before, but it still wasn't much. And when we got back to the smoking remains of the house, Blue shut down again.

Romi wrapped an arm around her shoulders. "What now? I mean, what can we do to help?"

"I need to find out where Damon is."

"You think he did this?"

"Who else?"

"Want me to make a list?" I asked.

But she didn't snap back. No, something was seriously wrong.

"I know I'm not the easiest person to get along with, but how many people would risk jail? And besides, Damon said he'd pay me back for the Lexus."

"You don't think flying here from New York to set your mom's house on fire is a bit...extreme?"

"You didn't see how angry he was after I cut one arm and one pant leg off every single one of his designer suits."

I could see a man being upset by that in the heat of the moment, but months later?

"How long since you broke up?"

"Two years, but we only signed the papers three months ago. I thought it was finally over."

That sigh... Now she sounded defeated. This wasn't the Blue I knew and tolerated.

"I'm on friendly terms with a couple of cops at the NYPD —want me to see if they can ask around?"

"How do *you* know New York cops?"

"Because when I was a student, I interned at the NYPD, and unlike some people, I understand the value of building relationships."

"I *do* build relationships. Just not with assholes."

"She does," Romi confirmed. "Maybe for one tiny minute we could forget that Aaron signs off his emails with 'Esquire'?"

"I don't actually do that."

"Shhh. Blue?"

She mustered up an overly saccharine smile. "Sure. I'll play the game. Please, kind sir, could you call your buddies in the NYPD and have them toss that scheming pig in a jail cell?"

"Can't guarantee the jail cell, but I'll call them. The house belonged to your mom—could she have been feuding with anyone?"

"Mom? No way. She's too nice. A pushover. That's why we're incompatible as roommates—she smothers me with kindness, and it's suffocating. Plus she lets people take advantage of her, and it drives me crazy."

"What about your dad?"

"He hotfooted it to Maine when I was nine. Married a high-school teacher in Windham and forgot all about us. Did I mention he was a lawyer too? I should've treated that as a learning experience, but more fool me. And before you ask, Mom's boyfriend is a lazy jerk who expects her to wait on him hand and foot, but even if they'd had a fight, committing arson would take brain cells he just doesn't have."

"He lives with her?"

"Nah, he has an apartment across town. He was waiting for me to move out so he could move in."

"You didn't win him over with your charming personality? I'm shocked."

"Screw you." Ah, there was a hint of the old Blue, but the insult still lacked conviction. "I told him that if he moved his stuff in while I was there, I'd toss it out on the lawn and change the locks whether Mom liked it or not. She'll probably stay with him now." Blue's laugh was hollow. "The irony."

"What about you?" Romi asked. "Do you have somewhere to go?"

"Guess I'll find a motel." She closed her eyes. Steadied her breathing. "Gotta buy clothes as well. And I might need to delay my trip to Europe so I can help Mom. Fuck. *Fuck.*"

I couldn't believe I was about to do this, but in that moment, I saw her vulnerability. The soft core she tried to keep hidden.

"If you need a bed, I have a spare room. Assuming you can manage to avoid choking on your pride, you're welcome to stay there for a month or two."

"Why? Why would you say that? Because you feel sorry for me?"

"Sure, we can have ourselves a regular pity party. I'll supply the snacks and Romi can bring the non-alcoholic wine."

Blue didn't want to accept. Judging by her sour expression, the prospect of taking charity—and from an NYU law graduate, no less—pained her. But she was on a budget, and she wasn't stupid.

"I'll stay until I can get something else sorted out. Uh, thanks."

"You're welcome."

33

ROMI

I hadn't expected Aaron to lend Blue his spare room, but nor had the offer shocked me. That was the type of man he was. He did the right thing, even when it cost him.

Which made my decisions about the future easier to make.

Life was going to change.

And soon.

But not today.

We'd received one small piece of good news this morning—Blue's mom's cat had shown up on Janie's porch, miaowing to get in. The bad news? Her mom had indeed gone to stay with her good-for-nothing boyfriend, and his apartment complex didn't allow pets. So Blue had headed to Coos Bay to pick Woody up, and we were all hoping he'd get along with Brooke's dog because Vega spent as much time in Aaron's apartment as in Brooke and Luca's. Colt said he had plenty of spare cat food, and after Brie had taken Kiki and Sophie Snyder to school and finished some errands—amazingly, she carpooled the school run like a regular mom, just with the addition of bodyguards—she'd promised to come over with the food plus a few clothes because she and Blue were roughly the same size, widthways. Blue was a little shorter, but she could make do.

At five minutes past eleven, the slamming of car doors outside told me she'd arrived, and when I opened the front door, I realised that Brie's idea of "a few clothes" and mine were mighty similar. A girl after my own heart.

"Could you grab one of those bags?" she asked. "Kasper likes to keep his hands free."

A second bodyguard was wheeling a pair of fancy leather suitcases, another had an enormous bag of Kitty Krunchies, and a fourth carried what looked like a small furry mansion. I raised an eyebrow.

"It's a cat cabana," Brie explained. "Nico donated it to the cause. He offered a hotel room as well, but I told him Aaron had already come through with accommodation."

"The room might come in useful if Blue and Aaron end up at each other's throats."

"Ah, the lawyer thing."

Brie deposited a suitcase in Aaron's living room, and I parked the one I'd wheeled in next to it.

"Yeah, the lawyer thing. Nice luggage."

"Is it? I think it was a gift. One of those freebies people always send in the hope that I'll use it and give them extra publicity. Blue can keep it."

If she sold the set on eBay, the cash would probably go a good way to rebuilding her mom's house. "I'll let her know."

"I hope this stuff fits. If it doesn't, I can always get more."

"I sent out an SOS to some friends in the fashion industry, and people are already promising to send clothes for Blue and her mom. Homeware too. Plus one guy offered the use of a condo in Florida, but I doubt Blue will go."

"Who can blame her for wanting to stay with her mother?"

"It's not that. She says her mom smothers her, but we had to talk her out of flying to New York to confront her ex."

Late last night, after she'd had time to stew, she'd been about to drive to the airport. Only Aaron's assurances that his contacts were looking into the issue had stopped her from getting on a plane.

"She's far braver than— Hey, I think she's back. Shhh, shhh, act normal."

I nearly burst out laughing. For Brie to tell anyone to act normal when she was surrounded by bodyguards and a boutique's worth of designer gear was stunningly ironic, but even so, she was far less pretentious than I'd expected. And so, so sweet.

Blue walked in with a cat carrier, and I got my first look at Woody—a big black-and-white ball of fluff with burs sticking out of his fur. When they got closer, I caught a whiff of yesterday's smoke still clinging to him.

"I'll put him in my room for now," she said. "Let him settle down."

"He looks scared."

"Took me an hour to coax him into the carrier."

"How's your mom?"

"Heartsick about some of the stuff that burned up— photos, trinkets, things that can't be replaced—but okay. I snuck Woody in to visit with her and then spoke to the insurance company, started the ball rolling."

"Everything was covered?"

"The salesperson talked her into every possible add-on. She's insured up the wazoo."

"Brie brought you a few clothes."

Blue's gaze landed on the suitcases. "What did you do? Rob a department store?"

"Could you picture the headlines if I did that? Because I can see them now." Brie spread her hands. *"Princess Piggy Commits Another Crime Against Fashion.* No, this is just stuff I don't need anymore. If you don't want it all, perhaps we could donate what's left to the ladies in Brooke's support group?"

After struggling to find help herself, Brooke had started a group for survivors of sexual assault and domestic violence. More people came than she'd ever imagined, and now they met twice a month at the Craft Cabin to talk over coffee, cakes, and crafts. Perhaps I could help to provide clothes as well if they were needed?

I was about to make the suggestion when Blue's phone rang.

"I've got to take this," she muttered. "Might be the insurance company."

But it wasn't.

I heard a man's voice say, "Don't hang up," then she paled a shade and disappeared out the front door.

Who was he?

And why was she worried?

Something to do with the fire?

"Any idea who that was?" Brie asked.

"Not a clue."

I suspected that yesterday's events had shaken Blue up more than she cared to admit, but I didn't know how to help.

***

"Think we should let the cat out?" I asked Brie.

Woody had been miaowing in his carrier non-stop.

Everything was set up—the cabana, food and water bowls, and a litter tray Darla had dropped off. Brie and I had drunk two cups of coffee each, plus shared the last of a raspberry vegan mousse Brooke had left in the refrigerator. But there was no sign of Blue.

"What if he runs off?"

"He can't get outside."

"No, but if he decided to hide in this place, we might never find him. Do you think I should send Frederik and Bjørn out to look for her?"

"She can't have gotten far. Her car's still here." But Blue's phone was going straight to voicemail, and she'd left almost two hours ago. Plus somebody had burned her home down yesterday. True, she hadn't been inside, but what if it was a warning of things to come? "Actually, maybe it wouldn't hurt for them to find out where she is."

But there was no need. Before Brie's bodyguards had finished their strategy conference, Blue walked through the door, and this time, she had a bounce in her step.

"Are you...okay?" I asked.

She'd taken a trip to mood-swing city for the last forty-eight hours. Which was understandable—I just hadn't expected to see her smiling.

"Not really. We need to get to the paper mill."

"That's it? We need to get to the paper mill?"

"Yeah."

"Wait. Wait a second. You ran out of the house with a face like thunder, disappeared for two hours, and now we have to go to the paper mill? We were ready to send out a search party."

"I just went for a walk. I think better when I walk."

"Who was on the phone?"

Since she wasn't going to volunteer the information, I

decided to be blunt. I'd learned that from Davis. He'd told me that instead of hoping people picked up on what I didn't say, sometimes it was better to ask a direct question, even if I was afraid I wouldn't like the answer. At least then I could deal with a concrete response instead of wondering about what-might-have-beens.

"Damon."

"Your ex?"

Blue nodded. "I don't know who Aaron sent to roust him this morning, but he was spooked and he was angry."

"Sorry." I felt I should apologise on Aaron's behalf. He took enough flak from Blue.

"Talking to that asshole's never pleasant, but this morning, it added clarity. He denied everything—I'd expected nothing else—but some of what he said made sense." Blue huffed. "Fuck, I hate admitting that, but Damon isn't stupid. I hate admitting that too."

"So what did he say?"

"I pointed out that he'd promised to pay me back for ruining his car, and he said he'd already gotten his revenge in court. And I guess he did. Took me to the cleaners, ruined my reputation, played every trick in the damn book. As far as he was concerned, it was over. We were finished. I was nothing. And his new girlfriend's pregnant, so why would he risk committing a felony?"

"I guess that does make sense."

"Yeah. So I said that if it wasn't him, then who? And he said that I'd most probably been poking my nose where it didn't belong again, and pissing people off comes so effortlessly to me that I should just make a list of everyone I've spoken to in the last month and start from there."

"What a charmer."

"Tell me about it. But what have I been doing for the last month? Apart from dressing up as a fucking hot dog?"

Uh-oh. I was beginning to see where this was going. "Investigating my mom's death."

Blue snapped her fingers. "Exactly! Although it doesn't feel as if we've gotten very far, we've hit a nerve somewhere, and we've hit it hard enough to send someone scrambling into damage-control mode."

"You think the same person who killed my mom set your mom's house on fire?"

"It makes more sense than anything else I've come up with so far. My mom doesn't have enemies. And my last case as a PI was over three years ago, before I moved to New York. It's possible somebody with a grudge has gotten out of jail recently, and I'm not gonna ignore that, but it doesn't feel right. Most of the criminal work I did was for defence lawyers. I got people off rather than sending them to prison. A couple of times, exonerating one party led to a different suspect, and some of those suspects got convicted, but I asked Damon to check into them, and he did. Grudgingly, but he did it. They were mostly cases he was involved in. And every criminal who got convicted because of my investigative work is still locked up."

"So what happens now? I'll totally understand if you want to quit the case. I don't want anyone else to get hurt either, and I'm so sorry about your mom's house. I have money, and—"

"I'm not a fucking quitter."

"But—"

"Whoever the perp is, they just made a big mistake. A clusterfuck of big mistakes." Blue counted off points on her fingers. "One, they underestimated the opposition. Two, they told us they're still local and close enough to be nervous. Three, they're connected enough to know where I live. Not an outsider. Four, we know we're on the right track with the investigation. Five, we know they drive a small dark car. Six, they won't have an alibi for yesterday afternoon. Seven, they chose a time when the house was empty, so their intent was to distract rather than kill. They're not bloodthirsty, but they *are* scared. Eight, they might be scared, but they're also confident enough to act in broad daylight. Nine, they've got enough to lose that they're willing to take risks. Ten, we can rule out Skip for sure. Eleven, shit, I've run out of fingers, but you get the picture."

Yes, I did get the picture, and the artist was channelling Francisco Goya.

Kasper stepped forward and addressed Brie. "Your Highness, perhaps you should consider returning to Valetia temporarily?"

"No way. And for crying out loud, stop calling me 'Your Highness.' I thought we'd got past that?"

"What if they come after you again?" I whispered. "After *us*."

Blue's smile was a little scary. "This time, we'll be ready."

34

AARON

The good news? Nobody who worked in the admin department at the paper mill appeared to have thrown anything away, ever. The bad news? That left us with stack upon stack of archive boxes and cabinets filled with everything from invoices to budgets to lunch menus to résumés, and there was no discernible filing system.

Oh, and did I mention the dust?

We'd taken to wearing disposable masks to keep the worst of it out of our lungs, but it still got into our hair, our clothes, our pores. We'd been at this for three days now. And when I said "we," I meant everyone Romi and Blue had managed to co-opt into helping. Me, Luca, Brie, Colt, Brooke, Deck, Nico, Addy, even Darla, Paulo, and Asa when they weren't working, although Blue had balked at having Asa there at first. She didn't want anyone on the team who'd (a) lived in Baldwin's Shore at the time of Serena's death and (b) been old enough at that time to commit the crime. Only when I'd pointed out that on the afternoon when our friend in the small black car had been setting fire to her mother's house, Asa had been in court with witnesses including a judge, a jury, and several curious reporters had she relented. Plus there was the fact that Asa drove a yellow Corvette. He said that every man was entitled to a midlife crisis, and he'd just waited until the kids left home to have his.

I'd been working under the premise that having more people on board could only be a good thing, but that was until Davis fucking French had shown up to lend a hand in a suit and shoes that probably cost more than I earned in a month.

"Tell me again why we're doing this," Addy complained.

"Because it's a lead, and we've got precious few of those."

Blue and the cops were both hunting for the black car, but apart from a kid who'd been shooting hoops along the road and thought that maybe he'd seen the vehicle at around that time and that possibly the driver had been wearing a red ball cap, we'd struck out. Homeowners in that area didn't go in for security cameras. Why would they when they had Janie?

"What about this?" Brie asked. "It's an invoice from E. Findley for consultancy services. Could the E stand for Edward? Ted?"

"Put that in the 'unlikely' pile," Colt told her. "The E. Findley invoices carry on after Serena died, and we think our man left the area."

Since by Blue's reasoning, our killer was still around, we didn't believe Ted was the man we were looking for in that respect, but if he'd been close to Serena in those days, then he might be able to shed some light on what was going on in her head. On what might have possessed her to meet a murderer at a cabin in the middle of nowhere.

As we shortlisted candidates, Blue began researching them. So far, she'd tracked down three men—two Edwards and a Theodore—but all denied knowing Serena. One supplier, two employees, and it turned out neither of those employees had begun working at the mill until after Serena's death.

It was slow going. Today, we'd added five more names to the "possible" pile, and the others were making noises about dinner. I'd rather have stayed in the archive room all night than chat over pizza with Davis and Romi, but in light of the psycho creeping around, we'd made an agreement—none of us would spend time alone until this was over.

However long that took.

If Davis's arm around Romi's shoulders during dinner had left me queasy, the sight of them tiptoeing off to her room after dessert turned my stomach. She didn't make a big song and dance about it. Just slipped away.

Fortunately, there were enough people present that I could do the same. I headed for my office, for the bottle of Scotch hidden in my desk drawer and the secret staircase that led up to the roof terrace. The subterfuge had been Brooke's idea. When we were kids, she'd daydreamed about marrying into royalty and living in a castle, and although she'd swapped out Prince Charming for Luca, she'd still put "secret room" at the top of her wish list when we were designing the apartments. Now there was an opening at the back of the closet in Brooke's craft room, and behind it lay a cosy nook with a beanbag chair and a bookshelf. A door on the far side led to the staircase that ran from the first floor to the roof, not a feature we often used because we had the ramp, but it sure came in useful when a man wanted to dodge dinner guests.

My secret room was more practical. Thanks to advice

from Brie's security team, we'd hardened it into a panic room, installed a separate phone line, and moved the security-monitoring equipment in there. With the Bad Samaritan on the loose, it seemed like a prudent move.

I poured myself a drink, swung the bookcase to the side, and headed up the stairs. Other than the great room, the roof terrace was my favourite space in the building. It spanned a third of the second floor, and in the days of the dealership, Jackson Pettit used to park cars up there for show, and they sure had been a talking point. Now, I'd had the waterproofing repaired, replaced the wooden railing with glass and metal, and Brooke was busy creating a jungle at the far end. Palm trees, frilly flowers, a hammock, lounge chairs, strings of twinkly lights, a little metal dining table... Luca had bought a grill last week. I wanted to add a hot tub eventually, but it was way down the bottom on the list of priorities. Right now, security came at the top.

From the far corner, the sea was just visible through the trees near the water's edge, and on a quiet night, I could hear the waves too. I stretched out in Brooke's hammock, trying to think of the future and not the past. My love life was a disaster. First I'd lost Romi, and then Clarissa had cheated on me earlier in the year. And no matter how many times I said I was taking a break, Addy kept trying to set me up with everyone from her reflexologist's sister to Taya Swann.

Once Romi went back to New York, things would be easier. I could focus on the business again. Get my head back in the game.

"You're a hard man to find."

Fuck. I nearly fell out of the hammock, and Scotch spilled all over my shirt. Davis stared down at me, irritatingly suave and somehow not dusty in his expensive suit, as I struggled to a sitting position.

"Perhaps I wanted some time to myself?"

Davis ignored me and pulled up a seat. "I hear you're in love with Romi."

Double fuck. Tread carefully, Bartlett. Davis French had the power to ruin me if I said the wrong thing.

I forced a laugh. "Who told you that?"

"She did."

Triple fuck. Romi, what are you playing at?

"Maybe you misunderstood?"

"No, I most definitely didn't. You love her, you'll always love her, and even when you thought she hated your rotten fucking guts, you never stopped loving her. Sound familiar?"

Was Romi trying to wreck my life?

And was Davis...smiling?

"Okay, fine. So I feel the way I feel, and it was inconsiderate of me to tell her. But rest assured I won't act on my feelings, and she'll be going back to New York soon in any case."

"I'm sure she'll be disappointed to hear that. On both counts."

"I don't understand."

"Romi thinks she's staying in Baldwin's Shore."

Were we even having the same conversation? If our roles were reversed, I'd probably have knocked Davis's block off by now.

"You seem remarkably calm about this."

"I've only ever wanted Romi to be happy." Davis leaned back in Brooke's dainty metal chair and steepled his hands. "I suppose I should start at the beginning. Romi assured me I could trust you, and I need your word that anything we discuss this evening goes no further than this rooftop."

What could I do but agree? Yes, jumping over the railing was an option, but not a particularly appealing one.

"You have my word."

"Good. This wasn't a conversation I envisaged having tonight, but as I'm sure you know better than I do, Romi can be impatient. Where do you think we met? Romi and me?"

I was lost. "Uh... At a party?"

Romi had said as much during magazine interviews. I'd read far too many of them during the stalkerish phase I most certainly wasn't proud of.

"That was a set-up. We actually met several months before at the Maple Mountain Recovery Center." Holy shit. "We're both addicts, you see. Romi likes to snort and sip her poison, whereas I prefer to finagle and fuck mine."

Well, gee, this wasn't a conversation I'd expected to be having tonight either.

"Why are you telling me this?"

"So that you'll understand. Romi isn't my girlfriend. She's a good friend, but she's not my girlfriend." Davis sighed. "Neither of us enjoyed rehab, but we both knew that what came afterward would be a hundred times harder. So we devised a mutually beneficial arrangement. A two-person support group, if you like. We'd each do whatever it took to keep the other on the straight and narrow, as well as providing other benefits." Davis held up a hand. "Not that kind of benefits. Although we share a bed on occasion for appearances' sake, I've never had sex with Romi, and nor do I ever intend to."

How much of that Scotch had I drunk? He actually sounded as if he was serious.

"You're already well-versed in Romi's issues," Davis continued. "For my part, I agreed to help her to get her career back on track and ensure she avoided people and events that might lead her back into temptation. I also fend off interested men, including a singer she dated for five minutes three years ago who's convinced their break-up was a mistake."

"Rocki?"

"I see you've had the pleasure. The moron still keeps showing up at inopportune moments. And in return for setting him straight, Romi helps me to maintain sensible work hours and acts as my beard."

"Your beard?"

What did facial hair have to do with any of this?

"I'm gay, Aaron."

What? My expression must have given away my shock because Davis managed a tight smile.

"Good. You're surprised, which was exactly our intention. The world I operate in, the people I deal with, they're very conservative. Homosexuality is frowned upon, and I believe that if my preferences became widely known, my ability to make the deals that I do would suffer. Romi would tell you I have two loves in life—making money and fooling around with young men, the former in preference to the latter. And thanks to her, I can fly under the radar when it comes to my out-of-hours indulgences. As long as I have one of the world's most beautiful women on my arm, it never occurs to anyone that I might prefer cock to pussy."

This...this was *not* the man I thought I sort of knew.

"Weren't you married?"

"My wife spent most of our marriage fucking her yoga instructor. She thought I didn't know; I couldn't have cared less as long as she was discreet, which she was. But the time came when she wanted to start a family, so we agreed to part ways. I wish her all the best."

"That still doesn't answer my question: why are you telling me this?"

"The fake-relationship element of my and Romi's arrangement was never supposed to be permanent. In fact, it's lasted longer than I ever hoped it would, but I always knew that eventually, she'd want more than I could offer. In fact, I wondered whether she'd swallow her pride and find her way back to you."

"What do you mean, swallow her pride? She was furious at me for years."

"For pushing her into rehab? Yes, you could have been kinder about it, but we all know that if you'd merely made the suggestion, she'd never have gone. An ultimatum was what she needed. Not that she'll admit that. Early during our time at Maple Mountain, I once made a comment to that effect, and..." Davis grimaced. "I'm sure you can imagine how that went."

Was it weird that I was starting to like this guy?

"Why did you go to Maple Mountain? Suggestion or ultimatum?"

"Neither. Heart attack."

"What?"

"At my desk. Just a mild one, but it scared the hell out of me. Back then, my diet was shocking, my stress levels were off the charts, and I took no exercise outside of the bedroom. I had a stent inserted and started going to the gym, but reducing the stress was a challenge. Admitting I needed help was difficult, but the alternative was worse. Or, as Romi put it, the choice between burial and cremation." Davis smiled. "Our girl has a way with words."

"Our girl?"

"Romi and I are going to put out a press release.

Amicable break-up, plan to remain friends, blah, blah, blah. And we *will* remain friends."

"What are you saying?"

"I'm saying that she can tell you the rest herself. I'll let her know you're up here."

35

ROMI

"*H*ey." Aaron was standing on the far side of the terrace, looking toward the ocean. Davis had done his part, but now it was up to me. And I was so freaking nervous. My palms were sweating, and the weight of a thousand bad decisions tugged at my heels as I walked toward the man I loved.

When he turned, the soft glow of fairy lights left his face half-hidden in shadow, and I couldn't read him.

Did we stand a chance?

"Why didn't you tell me?" he whispered.

"It wasn't my story to tell. I made a promise to Davis, and I don't break promises."

"He's an interesting guy."

I had to smile at that. "Isn't he?"

"Maple Mountain, huh?"

"Yup. Workaholic meets alcoholic." Funny how hard I'd once found it to say that word. "We met in the library. He went there to read; I went there to cry." Aaron's horrified expression made me wince. "Don't worry, it turned out okay."

"I wish I could've been there for you."

"I... I wasn't in a good place back then. But I'd like to believe that everything happens for a reason, and Davis was the friend I needed at that time in my life."

"That's really all you are? Friends?"

"That's all we've ever been. I know how it looks—he's older, ridiculously rich, male—but I'm sick of conforming to expectations. And it's been such a relief to spend time with someone who didn't have an ulterior motive. We mapped out our expectations beforehand, signed the contract in blood..." Oh, Aaron's face... "Relax, I'm kidding. Something just clicked for us. Parts of our lives meshed neatly together, and we figured, why not act as each other's shields?"

"I saw a picture of you on vacation together, and you looked so damn happy, and I thought..."

"The one with the gold bikini?"

He nodded.

Figured. That photo had made every gossip page in the universe, which had been our intention. Davis had needed to head off a hysterical ex-fuck-buddy who was threatening to breach his NDA and go public, and I'd wanted to send a message to Rocki and Aaron as well as getting my name out there again. So we'd taken a trip to Saint Lucia, made sure everyone knew we were there, and fooled around on the beach. And I mean *fooled* around.

"We knew the paparazzi were watching. Right before they took that shot of him kissing me, I whispered, 'Just imagine I've got a dick' into his ear, which is why he couldn't stop laughing."

The captions had ranged from *Carefree and in Love— New York's Newest Power Couple?* in the classier publications to *Romina Frenchies French* in the trashy British tabloids. We'd both gotten exactly what we desired out of the show.

If you can't beat 'em, use 'em.

"Why are you telling me all this? Why now?"

"You said you loved me. And I... I screwed up. I screwed everything up, and it was easier to keep blaming you than to blame myself. And it took until now for me to see that. To understand that you weren't the monster I'd turned you into in order to avoid facing my own demons." This was hard, so hard. My head was a jumbled mess, and dammit, I couldn't stop the tears. "Aaron Bartlett, I've never loved anyone the way I love you. So I guess what I'm saying is that I'm clean now, and maybe one day if—"

He was on me before I finished the sentence, my face cupped in his hands, his mouth pressed to mine. I gasped, and that was all the invitation he needed. Our tongues duelled, his fingers tangled in my hair, and those stupid tears kept on coming.

"Say it again," he demanded.

"Say what?"

"You know what."

"I love you?"

He wrapped me up in his arms, buried his face in my hair. "I love you so fucking much."

My heart thudded in my chest, and I could feel Aaron's doing the same against his ribcage. I had him. I had him back. The future would be hard, I didn't doubt that, but as long as we were together, the challenges would be worth it.

Our next kiss was slower, languid, smooth heat that turned to fire in my veins. I hooked a leg around his hip, ground against his hardening cock because I'd gone for three long years without him, without any man, and I craved an orgasm that wasn't self-induced. I wanted to touch him, taste him, ride him.

Aaron's hand slid up my thigh, and he squeezed my ass hard.

"*Mine.*"

"Yours."

I slipped a hand between us and palmed his length through his pants. *This* was mine, and I intended to make the most of it. Except when I began to undo Aaron's belt, he put a hand out to stop me.

"Wait, what if somebody comes?"

Oh, honey. "Somebody's definitely gonna come."

He traced my smile with a fingertip. "I'm serious."

"Good. So am I."

"Your brother is downstairs. I don't know if you've heard what happened with him and Brooke..."

When Aaron caught them in a, uh, compromising position? Luca had told me the bare bones of it, and I'd filled in the blanks.

"He said you've got a good jab for a southpaw."

"I'd rather he didn't return the favour."

I dropped my voice to a whisper. "Then you'd better fuck me quietly."

"Are you trying to kill me here?"

"If you stroke out, I promise to call 911."

He muttered a curse, but this time when I reached for his buckle, he didn't try to stop me. I stroked him, the smooth, hard steel of him, and tightened my grip when he shuddered.

"Are you still on the pill?" he asked.

"Yes."

I dropped to my knees and took his cock in my mouth, my breathing ragged as I tried to slow my racing heart. I missed this. I'd missed the filthy taste of him, but he didn't allow me more than an appetiser before he fisted his hand in my hair and pulled my mouth up to his again.

"No more. I'm coming inside you."

"Technically, my throat is inside me."

"Romi..."

"Does this mean you're not gonna come in my ass either?"

Aaron snorted and covered his face with one hand.

"What? I was only asking."

He spoke against my lips. "I think I'm going to like the new, dirtier version of you."

A door slammed, and we both snapped our heads around, but nobody appeared on the terrace. Still, it was a reminder that we weren't entirely alone.

Which made it all the more delicious when Aaron's hand snaked under my dress, when his fingers pushed aside the barely-there panties I was wearing.

"Silk?"

"Of course they're silk. You didn't think I'd show up for this in polyester, did you?"

I'd nearly worn a garter belt too, but I'd been afraid that might jinx things. As it was, I could smell my own arousal on the sea breeze, and I wanted—no, I *needed*—Aaron to screw me senseless.

"You're soaked, Buttercup. So damn slick."

"Then maybe you should start calling me Buttercunt? Just during sex, obviously. Not in front of my brother."

Aaron's eyes widened. Then his lips twitched. A second later, we both dissolved into laughter and I began to realise the benefits of bringing a clear head to the bedroom—uh, to the terrace—rather than being zonked out on drink and drugs. This was *fun*.

And also hella hot.

"I love you."

"I love you too, *Buttercunt*. But you're gonna have to stop talking now."

"Okay." I mimed zipping my lips. Then I unzipped them again. "Permission to use my mouth for other stuff, sir?"

"Just bend over the fucking table," he growled.

I did as I was told, ass in the air, waiting. Anticipating. I hadn't expected to feel his palm, to hear the *crack* of flesh on flesh, but damn, I liked it. A moan slipped out. No, not a moan—an *invitation*.

"Okay?" Aaron asked, his lips brushing my ear.

"You'd better pull my hair."

He nudged my legs apart farther, farther, then tore off my panties. Two hundred bucks' worth of designer silk and lace fluttered away. A worthy sacrifice. Then he slid a finger inside me and stroked. Was that weird mewling coming from me? Shit, it was, but at least I wasn't screaming.

"More," I gasped.

"Good things come to those who wait."

"Patience isn't one of my strengths."

"So we'll have to practise."

But he did take the finger away, and I felt the weight of his cock resting between my ass cheeks, thick and hot, as he leaned forward to pepper kisses across my shoulders. Was he deliberately stalling?

"How do you get this dress undone?"

"There's a zipper at the side. Why do you smell of whisky?"

"Made the mistake of trying to drink in a hammock."

A second later, he pushed the straps off my shoulders, unhooked my bra, and cupped my breasts in his hands, distracted for a moment as he caressed my skin. My nipples were as hard as his cock, more sensitive than I ever realised was possible.

"Men and their toys," I murmured as I shuddered under his touch.

"I'm like a kid on Christmas morning."

"Dear Santa, please fuck me hard."

"Don't you ever stop?"

"No, but I thought men liked that?"

Finally, finally, he pushed inside me. Stretched me and filled me. This was why I'd abstained for three years—because deep down in a place I'd refused to think about, I'd known no man would ever measure up to Aaron but...well, Aaron.

"Hard and fast, Buttercup. We can do soft later."

"Less talking and more screwing, Aaron."

He didn't say another word. Deft fingers came to my clit, and it turned out men *could* multitask after all. I was so wound up, it didn't take much. A few hard thrusts and I clenched around him, using my own hand to muffle my cries because both of his were busy. I thought I was done, spent, as I clung to the table for support, but Aaron didn't quit, and only when I shattered for a second time did he empty himself into me with a soft groan.

Oh my. Oh *my*.

He'd destroyed me. Ruined me. My legs were shaking, and if it wasn't for the table's support and his arm around my waist, I'd have collapsed into a boneless heap.

"I love you," he murmured.

Do not fuck this up, Romi. Not again. Not ever.

"I love you too."

How I got through the rest of the evening, I had no idea. We cleaned up as best we could, and then Aaron snuck back downstairs using a hidden staircase I hadn't even known existed. I followed a little later with a detour via my bedroom to tidy my hair, spritz myself with perfume, and put on fresh underwear.

We'd agreed to wait for the right moment to break the news of our relationship to Luca. Aaron was nervous about his reaction, and Davis also needed time to get his ducks in a row. We'd have to let my brother and Brooke in on his secret, probably Colt and Brie too, because he'd still be in my life.

But that didn't stop me from tiptoeing into Aaron's room that night. He'd promised me soft, and he kept his word. Twice. Now in the early hours, I lay at his side, my head on his chest and his arms around me, possessive even in sleep. This was how our first night together should have ended, but I'd been too stupid, too scared, too insecure to realise that at the time. I'd been terrified that if we fell asleep, when he woke up, he'd regret everything.

That he wouldn't love me anymore.

But now I understood. If Aaron could love me today, after what I'd put him through, he'd love me forever.

My whole life, I'd tried to fit in. I'd started drinking because the cool kids did it, and then I couldn't stop. The same with drugs. I'd hated the person I'd become, but two men had shown me it was okay to like the girl still lurking underneath. Me and regular Romi, we got along okay now. All those puzzle pieces that had bamboozled me for so long were gradually slotting into place.

And one day, one day soon, I'd become the woman I was always meant to be.

36

AARON

When Jackson Pettit had offered me the chance to buy the derelict shell that had been Deals on Wheels, this was the life I'd dreamed of. A spacious home built just the way I wanted it, good friends close by, a comfortable job I enjoyed, and Romi sitting on my breakfast bar in a dusky-pink silk robe, swinging her bare feet as she ate grilled un-cheese for breakfast.

She loved me.

She fucking loved me.

It was official: I was the luckiest man on earth.

"Food okay?"

A nod.

"Want anything else?"

Another nod.

"Care to elaborate?"

She beckoned me toward her with one crooked finger.

"Mmm-hmm."

What do you know? It turned out that Clarissa cheating was the second-best thing ever to happen to me. Because now the stars had aligned and the gods had smiled down and I had my girl.

Romi wrapped her legs around me, and I stood on tiptoes to kiss her. A waterfall of dark hair tumbled around us, and I tucked some of it behind her ear, remembering the way it had felt in my hands last night. At first, I worried I'd been too rough with her, but she assured me she liked it that way.

Her lips were so soft, and those breathy little moans, they—

"Oh, for fuck's sake."

We sprang apart, and I cursed myself as I added "ability to walk really fucking quietly" to Blue's list of superpowers. What I really needed in this place was more doors.

"Aren't you meant to be banging the rich dude?" Blue asked Romi.

"So that's, uh, it's a really long story."

"Let me guess... He's gay, and you're his cover."

Romi turned ghostly pale. "Uh... I..."

"What makes you think that?" I asked.

"Davis is forty-two, he has no children, and he's been married once to a woman who popped out a kid ten months after the divorce. So either he has problems in that department, or he wasn't much interested in her. Based on other information, I'm gonna plump for option B. He's got a reputation for being hard and ruthless, yet out of the limelight, he's smooth but not pervy. Safe. I've met a lot of assholes in my line of work, but he isn't one of them, even if he acts otherwise on occasion. And you..." She nodded at Romi. "You obviously felt the same because you glommed onto French two and a half years ago right after treatment for 'exhaustion' when you were probably feeling fragile, and you're still with him today."

"You've been digging up dirt on us?"

"You call it digging, I call it research. I like to know who I'm working for. Moving on, you've obviously got some weird history with Mr. NYU Law here, and you weren't afraid to hook up with him under the same roof as French. You need to scream quieter."

Romi's cheeks went from white to red. "None of that tells you Davis is gay."

"No, I picked up on that when I caught him checking out Paulo's ass. Ergo: sham relationship."

"Oh, hell." Romi's words came out as a croak. "Please, you can't tell anyone. His reputation—"

"Cool your jets—I don't talk shit about clients. Or friends. Is that actual grilled cheese? Or weird fake cheese?"

Strangely, I was inclined to believe her about keeping quiet. Blue was the human equivalent of a power drill to the head, but she wasn't a bullshitter.

"Do you want a grilled cheese?" I asked her. "A real grilled cheese?"

She nodded.

"And coffee?"

"Definitely coffee. I came out here to tell you I found the guy."

Romi gave her a blank look. "What guy?"

"Esquire really did screw your brains out, huh? Ted. I found Ted. Also known as E.B. Rockman, Engineering Consultant. But he and his wife were just running out the door to church, so we've gotta call back at twelve thirty, Florida time. Does Luca know about you two?"

I gritted my teeth. "Not yet."

"Then you might wanna get that shiny shit off your lips before he comes downstairs. Just a tip."

Romi grabbed a sheet of paper towel, and two seconds

after I'd wiped away pink-tinted gloss with—shit—a hint of sparkle, the front door opened. People were gonna have to learn to knock around here.

"Luca! Guess what? Blue found Ted," Romi said, jumping down from the counter.

"Thank fuck for that. I'm still sneezing dust from that damn archive room." He gave Romi a hug. "So, who is he? *Where* is he?"

Blue took over, checking her watch. "Florida, but I've arranged to call him after lunch. Which gives me time to drive to Coos Bay and visit with Mom first."

"Not on your own," Luca warned.

"I'll go with you," Romi offered. "But only if Aaron drives."

"Why? What's wrong with my driving?"

"You treat every trip like it's the Indy 500."

"The Brickyard's an oval. You're thinking of the Monaco Grand Prix."

"Whatever, I'm not riding with someone who thinks a stop sign and a yield sign are the same thing."

"The road was clear. There was nothing coming."

"There are *rules*."

Spending a couple more hours with Romi wasn't exactly a hardship, but for Luca's benefit, I made it sound like one.

"I'll drive, okay?"

Romi beamed at me. "Can we stop for milkshakes?"

"Sure, Buttercup, we can stop for milkshakes."

"Yes, I remember Serena. Not sure I ever knew her surname, but I remember her. A beautiful young lady with the personality to match. You're saying she's missing?"

I put Ted Rockman in his mid-fifties, a trim man with salt-and-pepper hair and a weathered face. He waved his hands as he spoke, and the tan line along one wrist told me he was a golfer. Probably put in his years and then retired down to the Sunshine State. Blue had suggested a conference call, and he'd countered with a videoconference, said he liked to see who he was speaking with. So Romi, Blue, and I were seated around my desk, with Luca and Colt off to one side since they weren't technically meant to be there. Davis had joined us too. Only fair since he was paying half of Blue's fee, but after last night, I wasn't sure how to act around him.

Anyhow, we'd done the introductions, and Blue had moved on to the issue at hand.

"Serena's not missing anymore," Blue said. We'd agreed she'd do most of the talking. "Her body was found last month."

"I'm sorry to hear that." Ted sounded as if he meant it. "But I don't understand—what does that have to do with me?"

"You left town around the same time she vanished."

Blue let that sit. Gave Ted time to digest the news. Caustic as she might be on a normal day, I had to acknowledge that she had a good interview technique.

"And you think... You think *I* had something to do with it?"

"I'm afraid it's an angle we have to consider."

"You're not the police, though? I don't have to answer your questions?"

"We're just providing extra manpower." Blue gave a lopsided shrug. "Cutbacks, always cutbacks. And no, you're under no obligation to answer any of our questions, but we'll be passing all the information we find to Detective

Payne, and I'm sure he'll get in touch soon." She threw in a chuckle. "Aldrich is an experienced investigator, but also a suspicious old coot, and I know the first thing he'll say is, 'Blue, why wouldn't Mr. Rockman answer the questions? It's only the guilty who have something to hide.' If you could help to avoid that, it'd make both of our lives easier."

"I guess I do see how that could look bad."

"Can you work with us to get your name ruled out?"

"I'll do what I can, but we're talking twenty years ago. All I can tell you is that my contract with Workman Paper came to an end, and I left Baldwin's Shore as planned. Heard the whole group went bankrupt in the end—which wasn't a surprise to me after what I saw there—so I doubt there's anyone left to confirm that."

"What issues were there at the mill?"

"You think that's linked to Serena's death?"

"No, I'm just curious. When the mill closed, it killed the whole town."

"Oh, well, I was brought in to review the manufacturing processes and systems, and I was able to implement some efficiencies, but there was only so much that could be done without capital investment. And management hated to spend money on anything but themselves. The organisation was rotten at the top, if you want my opinion."

Good move. Let him talk about an unrelated subject, get him comfortable.

"They took what they could, and screw everybody else?"

"In a nutshell. With all the cheap imports available, making a profit was becoming more difficult, but there are always people willing to pay more for a premium product. They could have updated the lines and restructured, but they bled the company dry instead. What happened to the old mill building? Someone turn it into a hotel or something?"

"Not quite—the new hotel got built a little way along the coast. The mill's still standing, but it was sold recently."

"To a developer?"

"No, to a private buyer. A family."

Ted gave a low whistle. "That's a lot of property for a family. My wife and I are quite happy here in a condo."

"How long have you been married?"

"Celebrated our fifteenth wedding anniversary last month."

"So you met after your Baldwin's Shore days?"

"That's right. I took a job in New Hampshire, and we lived there for a few years, but Sue has Raynaud's syndrome —you know what that is?"

"A circulatory disease?"

"Yes, yes. Turns her fingers white when she gets too cold, so we decided to move somewhere warmer."

"I can see why you didn't come back to Oregon. Last winter was no joke. Snow, snow, everywhere, rain when it wasn't snowing."

"Guess I must've gotten lucky when I was there."

"Tell me, before you left, when was the last time you saw Serena Mendez?"

Blue's previous questions had also served a second purpose—they'd established a baseline, shown us how Ted talked when he was being honest, when he wasn't under pressure. Any changes in his speech patterns, mannerisms, or demeanour could indicate a lie. On screen, Ted's gaze flicked up to the left as he remembered the past, but he didn't look away for more than a second or two.

"When did I last see Serena? That must have been...the day before I left town. I paid for a twice-weekly clean, and she came by to spruce the place up and bring fresh towels. Should've cancelled really, but I knew she had kids, and I figured she could use the money. And seeing her was always a bright spot in my day. The work at the mill, it wasn't easy. Too much infighting, always nitpicking over costs and timescales. Anyhow, I was packing my belongings, and since there wasn't much in the way of cleaning to do, we shared coffee instead."

"Can you remember what you talked about?"

"That day? Not in any great detail, no. As I said, it was twenty years ago. I gave her a good tip, though."

"How did she act? Did she strike you as worried about anything? Nervous?"

"Nervous? No, not that I can recall."

"You said you couldn't remember what you talked about in any great detail—does that mean you have a vague recollection?"

"I expect I wished her good luck for the future, offered to show her around town if she ever made it to Colorado—that was where I was based at the time. She'd asked me all about Boulder, how much it cost to live there, what the people were like, whether it was easy to find work. I got the impression she was considering a move away from Baldwin's Shore."

New York, Boulder... She'd wanted to leave, but she hadn't made any concrete plans?

"And when you got this impression, did it sound as if she wanted to leave alone or with her family?"

Ted looked genuinely perplexed. "Well now, that's not a question I've ever given any thought to. I'd assume with her family? Although she didn't mention her husband much, and I heard from other people that he wasn't the nicest man to be around. But her kids..." He focused on Romi. "You...

She spoke about you all the time. No, I can't imagine she'd have gone alone."

Blue went in for the kill. "I'll be upfront with you, Mr. Rockman. Some of Serena's friends have suggested she was having an affair, and you were put forward as a possible candidate."

His eyes widened, and I had to say the video call was an excellent idea. I got to see Ted Rockman's shock in full colour all the way from Florida.

"No, oh, no. I wasn't involved with Serena that way. Definitely not. She was a married woman."

"Unhappily married."

"Even so... No, that wasn't me. But maybe..." In the silence, I could practically hear the wheels turning. "Maybe you should talk to Mr. Baldwin."

"Which Mr. Baldwin?" I asked. "Senior or junior? East Baldwin passed away two and a half years ago."

"East was the father?"

"Yes."

And Easton the Third would have been barely out of diapers at that point.

"If you see the family, please pass along my condolences. But I didn't mean him; I meant his son. EJ, was it? He used to spend time with Serena too."

"They both worked for Baldwin Estates at that point."

"Not in the office." A pause. "I don't wish to speak ill of Serena, but there were several occasions when I saw the two of them coming out of the house next door to mine. Another rental, I understand, but it was empty most of the time, so I thought it was slightly odd that they should be in there, but I just assumed there was some sort of maintenance issue they were trying to solve, and... You should speak to Mr. Baldwin."

That son of a bitch.

I thought back to the original sheriff's report, to the brief notes I'd read a hundred times. When EJ reported Serena missing, he'd said he didn't see her the previous afternoon because he'd been out and about, checking up on the various properties they owned. Alone. *No alibi.*

Luca's thoughts had clearly gone along the same lines because Colt was trying to stop him from reaching the door. Trying and failing. Davis grabbed an arm, and Romi jumped up to help.

Blue managed to keep her composure, and dare I say it, she sounded almost chipper.

"Thanks very much for your help, Mr. Rockman. We sure will talk to Mr. Baldwin. You mind if I call back with any follow-up questions?"

"I suppose that would be okay."

"Hope you enjoy your golf game."

"How do you know I'm going to play golf?"

"Just a lucky guess."

The screen faded to black, and Luca was already cursing.

"That *motherfucker*. I'll kill him."

Romi dug her nails into his arm. "No! Because then you'll go to jail, and if you think I'm visiting you in *that* place every week…"

At least she'd learned something from her trip to see Skip. "Think of Brooke as well, buddy."

"Maybe we should hand this over to Aldrich Payne now?" Colt suggested, but Blue vetoed that idea.

"Are you kidding? No way. We're just getting to the interesting part, and Payne would screw it up."

Luca turned on her. "The *interesting* part?"

"Well, how would you describe it? Look, I'll go talk to EJ,

see what he has to say. Ten bucks says he caves under pressure."

"He's dangerous. If he killed my mom, he's dangerous."

Luca was right. "Apply pressure in the wrong way, and EJ might lash out. You're not going alone."

"No, I'm not." Blue's grin was downright terrifying. "*You're* coming with me."

37

AARON

*W*hy me?

Sure, Blue had explained her reasoning —that I wasn't part of Serena's family, I wasn't a deputy banned from working on the investigation, and I had a cool head—but still, *why me*?

"Come in."

EJ Baldwin agreed to see us at his office on Monday morning, probably because Blue had sat down in the reception area and made it clear she wasn't leaving until we'd spoken with him. Baldwin Estates occupied a converted barn on the edge of the Baldwin property. The building was decked out in light wood and a colour scheme of navy and plum, with fresh flowers in a vase on the reception desk and paintings of the town hanging on the walls—corporate but not tasteless. A large conference room took up one side of the space, with smaller offices for EJ, Marianna, Parker, and Easton the Turd at the rear. Parker's door was closed and Easton's was open, the younger son conspicuous by his absence. He'd always been a work-shy fool, even when we were at school. Marianna watched with mild curiosity as we filed into EJ's corner office.

"Should I bring coffee?" the receptionist asked.

"That won't be necessary. Thank you, Natalie," EJ said as he closed the door behind us. "I don't normally take meetings without an appointment."

Blue didn't say a word.

"What's this about?"

Still she stayed silent. EJ picked up a pen, began fidgeting with it. *Click, click. Click.*

"Look, if you're not even going to speak, then you can leave. I don't have time to waste."

"You know what this is about."

"Do I? How is that possible? You haven't told me, and nor would you tell Natalie."

"You didn't think you could keep your secret forever, did you?"

Click, click, click, click, click.

"What secret? I don't have any secrets."

But EJ had paled a shade.

"I can't decide whether it was ballsy or stupid of you to report Serena missing. On the one hand, you drew attention to yourself, but on the other, who would suspect the caring boss?"

"You're judging me for showing concern over an employee?"

"No, I'm judging you for killing your mistress."

Ah, fuck.

EJ leapt to his feet, quite ashen now. "How dare you come in here and make such baseless accusations?"

"Why'd you do it? Did she threaten to tell your wife? You were still married to Justine at that time, weren't you? Did she want money to stay quiet?"

"You have no idea what you're talking about."

On balance, I had to disagree with that statement. EJ was full of bluster, but his knuckles had turned white where he gripped the edges of the desk, and unless I was mistaken, I'd seen a slight tremor run through him as well.

"Don't I? The woman you were having an affair with just happens to show up dead in a cabin you own, and we're expected to believe you had nothing to do with it?"

"I didn't! Everyone knows Rey Mendez killed her. The man's a brute."

Of note: EJ still hadn't denied the affair.

"Ah, you made a mistake there. Yeah, Rey was an asshole, so much of an asshole that he was screwing around too. Guess where he was at the time Serena was murdered?"

"I... I..."

"That's right—with his side piece. No love lost between them now, but she did confirm his alibi. So who does that leave, EJ?"

Click, click, click, click, click.

"What's wrong? Cat got your tongue?"

"I didn't kill her."

"You know what? You can tell that to the police."

Blue moved to get up, but EJ blocked the door. I stood too. I rarely used my size to intimidate, but I had two inches and thirty pounds on him, and I'd be damned if I was going to let him threaten Blue.

But she waved me away.

"First you wanted us to leave, and now you want us to stay?"

"You don't understand."

"What don't I understand? Everything you've said so far has been bullshit."

"I didn't kill Serena. I *loved* her." Oh boy. "I loved her."

EJ slunk back to his desk and sank into his chair. Blue sat too.

"Talk," she instructed. "From the beginning. Don't leave anything out."

"Where do I start?" he muttered, then sucked in a breath. "Okay. *Okay.* I'd been seeing Serena for a year when she disappeared. Maybe a little longer. Dad had put me in charge of repairs and maintenance, and cleaning fell under that remit too. So we were often out at the same properties together, and I guess... I guess we were both lonely. Yes, I was still married to Justine, but that wasn't going well." He sighed. "I mean, have you met Justine? What was I thinking?"

The guy was a prick, but I had to empathise with him on that score. Justine Ashbrook-then-Baldwin-now-Vincent had the personality of a hand grenade. Whenever she'd shown up at school to collect the kids, everyone else used to wait inside the building until she'd gone, including the principal.

"So you'd been doing the nasty with Serena for a year?"

EJ winced. "You make it sound so sordid, and that's not how it was. At first, we just used to talk. But then one thing led to another, and yes, our relationship turned physical. I'm not proud of the way we snuck around, but that was the way it had to be."

"Why?"

"If Rey even thought she was involved with another man, he'd have killed her. At first, I thought that's what happened, but then I got the note."

Another note?

"What note?" Blue asked.

"She left it in my desk drawer." EJ tossed the pen onto his blotter and tore both hands through his hair. "I found it after I'd reported her missing. We were planning to leave town together, not right away, but soon. I'd already told Justine that I wanted a divorce. But Pop had insisted on a prenup to protect the family money, and there was an adultery clause that went both ways. Most of the property was still in Pop's name, but I owned the home we were living in at the time—the villa near the Peninsula—and if Justine had found out about Serena, she'd have ended up with the house. And I needed that money to start a new life for the two of us, somewhere far away from here."

"Just the two of you?" Anger bubbled through my veins on Romi's behalf. "What about her kids?"

"The kids too. That was part of the deal, and I was looking forward to getting to know them. I'd have gone anywhere for her."

So why not say the four of them? The kids had been incidental, hadn't they?

"The note?" Blue prompted.

"She said that Rey..." EJ closed his eyes, and his Adam's apple bobbed as he swallowed. "That Rey had forced himself on her, and she couldn't stay another night with him. She had an old friend in Idaho, and she was going to stay there until the divorce came through. Then we'd pick up the kids and run."

"And you didn't think, as the months passed and she didn't show up, that maybe there was a problem?"

"Of course I did! I was quietly freaking out every damn day. But then I received the second note."

How many damn notes had the psycho sent?

"And what did the second note say?" Blue sounded sceptical, and I honestly couldn't blame her. If Romi had vanished without leaving a forwarding address, I'd have moved heaven and earth to check she was okay.

"That she'd fallen for somebody else in Idaho, and she realised that what we'd had, it hadn't been love, just a temporary infatuation. She wished me all the best." EJ spat the words. "Said she hoped I'd meet a nice girl and move on. And I was angry, okay? I was angry that I'd turned my life upside down and she'd skipped out on me. As the weeks passed, I convinced myself that she was right—it hadn't been love. I'd been intoxicated by her touch, blinded by her beauty, and what I'd felt, it hadn't been real. And I pushed her out of my mind. What else could I have done?"

Was EJ that naive? Or was he merely an excellent actor? If what he said was true, he'd kept his silence for twenty years, and nobody had suspected a thing.

"You could have asked more questions," I told him.

"I wish with all my heart that I had. When I heard her body had been found, the bottom dropped out of my world."

"And yet you continued to keep your secret."

"Rey Mendez still lives in this town, Aaron."

"How do you explain the fact that Serena's body was found in a cabin your family owns?"

"I don't. I mean, I can't. I didn't even remember the damn place until the police started asking questions. Pop used to rent it to some old couple for a pittance, because who else would want to live out there? Maybe he tried to find another tenant when they moved on—who knows?—but by the time I inherited the portfolio, the cabin was nothing more than a footnote on a spreadsheet."

"You own that whole hill?"

"Yes. A company was interested in buying logging rights a year or two ago, but their offer bordered on insulting, and when I discussed it with Marianna and Parker, we decided to leave the area to the wildlife rather than invite bad feeling from the folks in town. There'd already been enough uproar about the new resort. But now I wonder if we could have discovered Serena sooner and laid her to rest."

Blue changed tack. "Where were you last Tuesday afternoon?"

"What? What does that have to do with anything?"

"Humour me."

"I don't... I can't... Tuesday..."

"Do you have a calendar?"

"Uh, yes, yes." EJ turned to his laptop, clicked the mouse a few times. "Last Tuesday... Oh." His face took on a green tinge. "Now I understand. Somebody saw me there, didn't they? At the cabin?"

That wasn't the answer I'd been expecting.

"You mean the cabin where Serena's body was found?" Blue asked.

"Yes, dammit! Yes."

"And why, pray tell, did you go to the cabin?"

"I know it sounds ridiculous, but I just wanted to feel close to her again. I was on my way to a networking event in Coos Bay when I found myself thinking 'what's the point?', so I turned the car around and drove to the forest. I took her flowers. Wildflowers—they were her favourite because she said they survived against the odds."

"And you were alone the whole time?"

"Yes, but why does that matter? The police took all the tape down. After they removed her car, a detective called to tell me they'd released the scene."

"Why does it matter? Because this is the only case I'm working on right now, and somebody burned down my home on Tuesday afternoon. I don't think that was a coincidence."

"And you think *I* did it? Have you lost your mind?"

"How do you think it looks? Somebody lured Serena out to a cabin in the middle of nowhere, *your* cabin, and it must have been somebody she knew and trusted. They killed her and dragged her body into the crawl space to rot for twenty years. And right after I started asking questions, someone targeted me too. You don't have an alibi for Tuesday, and you didn't have one for the day Serena disappeared either. Tell me, EJ, what am I supposed to think?"

"I was *meant* to meet her that afternoon, at one of the houses on Shore Road. She didn't show up."

"Oh, this just gets better and better."

"I think... I think I should get a lawyer."

Speaking as a lawyer, that was probably a smart idea. Disappointing, but smart. "That's your choice."

As we filed out to the parking lot, Blue tipped her head toward two vehicles in the "Director" slots next to the front door. A dark blue Honda compact with a "MARI B" vanity plate, and a metallic black Toyota hybrid.

"Small dark cars," Blue murmured.

Yes, they were. Another "coincidence."

38

ROMI

"So what happened?" I asked. "Did he do it?"

Blue headed straight for the kitchen and Aaron's coffee machine. "Wait until Colt and Luca get here. I'm not answering the same questions twice."

I turned my attention to Aaron and gave what I hoped was a winning smile.

It sort of worked.

"We don't know," he told me. "That's the short version."

Brooke ran in. "Well? What happened?"

"He won't dish the dirt until Colt and Luca get here."

"Not even to me? Your favourite sister?"

"You're my only sister. And they'll be here in five minutes —we called them as soon as we left Baldwin Estates."

When Blue decided she was taking Aaron with her to question EJ, I'd been a little peeved about being sidelined, but in light of my new "don't fuck this up" mantra, I'd gone along with the plan. And I'd also been glad to spend some time alone with Davis. With everything changing for us, I wanted to show him that he was still an important part of my life, that I wouldn't be ditching him now Aaron had come along. And Davis had agreed that we should tell my little bubble here in Baldwin's Shore about his sexuality. Secretly, I thought it would be good for him to have a place where he could be himself. The whole of my adult life, I'd been dreading coming back to the town I'd run from, but now that I'd slotted back into a...kind of better version of my old life, I regretted staying away for so long. I'd forgotten what it was like to be surrounded by friends. People I could trust to have my back. Old friends like Brooke, Colt, and Addy, and new friends too.

Brie and Blue.

My brother.

And Aaron.

I felt whole, perhaps for the first time ever, and I wanted to share that with Davis.

"They're here," Brooke called from the window.

I still couldn't get used to seeing my brother in his uniform. From teenage rebel to sheriff's deputy—it was quite the leap. But at least now that he was here, we'd get some answers.

Aaron leaned against the counter that separated his kitchen from the great room, coffee in hand. The mug had obviously been a gift from Brooke because it had "World's Okayest Brother" written on it in royal-blue script.

"Where's the best place to start?" he asked.

Blue held up her phone. "Let's just play the whole conversation back, and then we can take questions at the end."

"You recorded EJ? You do realise that in Oregon, recording a private conversation without the consent of all parties is a crime?"

"Only a misdemeanour. Why do you think I didn't tell you?"

Aaron sucked in a tortured breath, but he didn't complain when Blue pressed "play." To my ears, EJ sounded nervous, defensive, and as the conversation continued, I understood why. And suddenly I was glad I'd been bumped from the interview team. Relieved I hadn't had to face him. The man claimed he'd wanted a life with my mom, wanted to be a father to Luca and me, and when things hadn't gone his way, he'd spent the next twelve years ignoring us while Dad made us suffer. If I'd been in that room, I'd have rammed a paperweight into his whining mouth.

When Blue talked about Mom's body rotting in a crawl space, Luca left Brooke and gave me a hug.

"I wish you didn't have to hear this."

Blue had only been doing her job, I understood that. Trying to provoke a reaction from EJ. But it still hurt.

"If it gets justice for Mom, it's worth it. Do you think it was EJ?"

"Honestly, I don't know. At best, he's a coward, and at worst, a killer, but I don't know which."

"So what do we do now?"

"With EJ lawyering up, I think we're at the stage where we need to speak with Aldrich Payne." Luca must have caught my look of disgust—I just couldn't help myself—because he tried to placate me. "Look, I don't like it any more than you do, but we can't arrest anybody, and we can't get search warrants. Basically, we have no power here."

"Much as it pains me..." Aaron grimaced. "Shit, sorry. Much as it annoys me, I agree with Luca that it's time to get the police involved again. Present what we've found and see where it takes us. EJ had the means and opportunity to commit both crimes, and potentially a motive too, but if he *is* guilty, he deserves an Oscar for the performance in his office."

"You don't think he did it?"

"I'm trying to put myself in a prosecutor's shoes. There's no forensic evidence, and the circumstantial evidence is tenuous. If I were the DA, I wouldn't take this to court right now. We need more."

"So we'll have to get more."

Blue hopped up onto the counter, the zipper on her leather jacket clinking against the grey granite.

"Can I just throw a wrench into the works?"

Aaron groaned. "Is 'no' an acceptable answer?"

"I actually have another candidate in mind. Did you notice the intercom light in EJ's office was glowing green?"

"What intercom light?"

"On the wall. An old-fashioned thing. I bet East Baldwin had it installed back in the day. Anyhow, somebody was listening to our conversation today."

"Who?"

I saw the moment it hit him. The shock mixed with the horror.

"Marianna," he whispered.

Blue smiled, but there was no mirth in it. "Means, motive, and opportunity. She worked for Baldwin Estates alongside East and EJ, so there's a good chance she knew about the cabin. And the note was *in EJ's desk drawer.* Motive? She married into money. And I bet Serena would have trusted her. 'Hey, would you mind cleaning up this old cabin? Kinda out of the way, but East thinks it's got rental potential. All those city types looking for a back-to-nature experience. I'll meet you there, give you a hand.' Yeah, Serena would've gone."

My knees went weak. Aaron took two steps toward me, then thought the better of it and let Luca and Davis hold me up. Marianna? No. No, how could she? She'd always seemed so quiet, so unassuming, the amiable stepmom who joined the PTA and did her best in the face of open hostility from Justine. Once or twice, she'd given me a ride home when it was raining.

"Are you sure? I mean, how would she have known EJ was seeing Serena?"

"They worked together. Even if people think they're being discreet, the truth can be all too obvious to those around them." Blue flicked her gaze toward Aaron. Thanks for the reminder. "And no, I'm not sure, not by a long shot, but I think we should consider the possibility."

"But Marianna's, what, five feet four? Mom was six inches taller than her. Stronger."

"Marianna could have come up behind her. One good swing with a bat or a rock or a saucepan, and she'd be out like a light."

"Could she have dragged her into the crawl space?"

"Let's find out, why don't we? Lie down."

"Huh?"

"Lie down. I'm two inches taller than Marianna, and you're two inches taller than your mom. Let's see how far I can drag you."

"Is this a good idea?" Aaron asked.

"What, you want to volunteer as tribute?"

"Yes."

Luca gave him a curious glance. Uh-oh.

"Aaron, I can do my own dirty work. Where should I lie?"

Blue grinned. Oh, she was enjoying this. "Right here is as good a place as any."

Five minutes later, I had bruises on my hips, my ass, and my shoulders, and we'd established that it would indeed have been possible for Marianna to move Mom into the crawl space, especially if she was hopped up on adrenaline. Aaron looked as if he wanted to drop-kick Blue off the roof, and I felt quite, quite sick.

Marianna.

Had Mom considered her a friend? Chatted with her? Confided in her? I'd come to Baldwin's Shore hoping my dad would go to jail, but he was still walking free, and instead, the culprit seemed more and more likely to be the last person I'd have ever suspected.

"Guess I'd better write that report," Blue said.

"That's it? That's the end? You write the report and we're done?"

Blue had committed to a month, and she still had a week left on the job. There were so many loose ends. Detective Payne couldn't tie a square knot if he had an instruction video, and I'd bet my favourite Louboutins that EJ Baldwin's lawyer would walk all over him.

"Oh, no, we're not done. My mom's still crying over lost family photos and heirloom jewellery that can't be replaced. We are *not* done. Look, I'll put off my trip to Europe for a couple of weeks, okay? Spend some time helping Mom and work the case the rest of the time."

A lump came into my throat. For all her brashness, Blue was a good person, and we needed her.

"I'll pay you extra."

"I don't even care about the money anymore. I just want this beast to get what they deserve."

39

AARON

"I'm doing everything I can." Detective Payne picked at a stain on his tie. Egg yolk or mustard —I didn't want to get closer to find out which. "But all we've got right now is theory and conjecture. Adultery isn't a crime."

We'd given him a week. A week to follow up on our report and connect the dots. I'd used the time to catch up on work, and Blue had visited her mom each day, plus spent hours arguing with the insurance company. How did I know that? Because in keeping with our "safety in numbers" policy, I'd packed up my laptop and driven her to Coos Bay each morning. Her mom was sweet but...suffocating. She hovered constantly, flitting in the background, asking if I wanted coffee or cookies or a casserole to take home because a man shouldn't go hungry. She never stopped talking. The boyfriend seemed the type who liked a little lady at home in the kitchen, so in that respect, they were a good match, but I saw now why Blue wanted to move to Europe.

And Blue, she still complained about lawyers on a

regular basis, but unless I was mistaken, there didn't seem to be the same animosity behind the bitching. I had to view that as progress.

Romi had flown to New York with Davis for a modelling job. On the one hand, I was envious because he got to be with her and I didn't, but on the other hand, I understood now how their relationship worked, and I could see the guy cared for her. She'd explained their living arrangements—she had her own bedroom suite in his Upper East Side penthouse, and that was where she kept her belongings. It was the closest thing she had to a home. For now. Was it too soon to clear out half my closet?

Don't run before you can walk, Bartlett. We still had to break the news to Luca, and preferably before Thanksgiving dinner in two days' time. Davis and Romi were coming back, and Brooke had invited half the town over, but since she was also cooking, I couldn't get upset about that.

"Did you interview EJ Baldwin?" Blue asked.

"Yeeeeeees." Payne stretched out the word as if he were speaking to a small child. "But he didn't say much, as is his right."

"What about Marianna?"

"Yes, I spoke with her too. She said that she had no idea there was anything going on between EJ and Serena all those years ago, and would she really have married the man if she thought he was capable of murder? I have to see her point there."

"She 'said.' What if she lied? What if *she* killed Serena?"

"Don't you think you're clutching at straws here? She came across as genuine, and she didn't request a lawyer. And as your report indicates that you believe the murder of Mrs. Mendez and the arson attack on your mother's home are inextricably linked, we can rule Mrs. Baldwin out."

Payne sat back in his chair, pleased with himself. "She has an alibi for Tuesday afternoon."

"Which is?"

"Apart from a brief trip home in the morning, she was in her office working."

"Alone?"

"No, she was with..." He consulted his notes. "Joel Morris, financial controller, Tracie Langley, marketing assistant, and Natalie Olsen, receptionist."

"And you confirmed that?"

"Ms. Carver, I've been a detective for longer than you've been alive. You think I'd make a rookie mistake? Ms. Olsen made Mrs. Baldwin a cup of coffee at ten thirty, saw her leave at approximately eleven thirty and return just before noon, and took her lunch at twelve thirty, as was her habit. Mrs. Baldwin then worked until four thirty, at which time she attended an appointment at the hair salon."

I thought back to the floor layout at Baldwin Estates. "Was Marianna's office door open or closed during the day?"

Payne opened his mouth. Snapped it shut again because he clearly hadn't asked *that* question, then hedged, "There were three other people present. One of them would have noticed if she'd tried to sneak out." He held up a hand to shush me before I could enquire about the possibility of bathroom breaks. "And Ms. Olsen's desk overlooks the parking lot. She confirmed that apart from the half-hour trip before lunch that we're already aware of, Mrs. Baldwin's car didn't move until late afternoon. I understand that Deputy Mendez and his family want to get to the bottom of this, but I've spoken to the prosecutor, and at this time, he doesn't see a way forward. All we've got is circumstantial evidence."

Then the prosecutor was as lazy as Detective Payne.

Sixty years ago, DNA analysis had been in its infancy, forensic techniques were limited, and AFIS didn't exist, but cases still got solved. Security cameras weren't a thing, not every crime had an eyewitness, and confessions were rare, but murderers still went to jail. In the right hands, circumstantial evidence was gold.

"Can we speak with the prosecutor?" I asked, struggling to remain diplomatic. In an ideal world, he should have been speaking with us already, but he'd shown no inclination to start a dialogue. Probably because he knew we'd ask difficult questions.

"I can put in the request, but I doubt anything will happen until after Thanksgiving. And remember, double jeopardy means we only get one shot."

Then take the damn shot. Do something rather than nothing.

"I'll tell Luca Mendez to expect a call."

Romi pressed a soft kiss to my shoulder. "I wish we could stay here all day. No work, no responsibilities, just us and a king-sized bed."

"Me too, but people might ask questions."

And by "people," I meant Luca. Romi and Davis had arrived in Baldwin's Shore yesterday evening, and half an hour after she'd pretended to go to bed, she'd snuck downstairs and into my arms. I hated going behind Luca's back, but not enough to give up a night with my girl.

We'd tell him tonight. During dinner. We'd planned it over the phone, even got Davis's input since he was meant to be a master at negotiation, and although I'd rehearsed the speech a hundred times in my head, I still reckoned there was a fifty-fifty chance I'd have to duck afterward.

"Maybe tomorrow we could have a lie-in?" Romi said.

"Sure, if I'm still breathing."

"Can we have pancakes for breakfast today? I mean, you might be eating through a straw tomorrow, so you should make the most of being able to chew while you can."

"Is that supposed to make me feel better?"

"No, but as long as Luca doesn't punch you in the nuts, I promise to take your mind off the pain."

"Thanks, I think." I gave her one last kiss—that would have to last me the rest of the day. "Wait here while I check the coast's clear."

By the time Brooke and Luca showed up, Romi and I were an appropriate distance apart and the pancakes were cooking. They'd gone out early to run errands before Luca started his shift, although nobody was gonna complain if he clocked in a few minutes late in the name of community service. Theoretically, he worked eight hours a day, five days a week, but in practice, overtime was the norm and he was on call twenty-four seven. At the moment, as he neared the end of his field training, he was riding with Colt, but soon he'd be patrolling on his own and they'd work separate shifts.

Brooke ran over and threw her arms around me. Sisterly affection? No, she just wanted pancakes.

"Tell me you made enough for everyone?"

See?

"Romi and Blue are first in line, but you can have the next batch."

"You're the best."

"Did you drop off Mr. Bertrand's medication?"

"Yup. Plus I delivered cookies to Mrs. Petronelli, Mrs. Anderson, and Selwyn. His leg's on the mend, thank goodness. Mrs. Anderson wanted to know if the rumours about the Baldwins were true, and I neither confirmed nor denied."

"What did she hear?"

"That maybe EJ killed Serena, and there was some kind of cover-up. Did you tell people that?"

"Not me. Blue?"

Blue shook her head. "It must've come from the cops. That department makes a sieve look watertight."

"Well, if Mrs. Anderson knows, then everyone knows," Brooke said. "Romi, are you coming to Coos Bay with us? I need to go to the big grocery store, and Blue wants to check on her mom."

"Are you driving?"

"Sure, I can drive." Brooke glanced out the window. "Looks like rain—better take a coat."

If only I'd realised that watching the girls eat pancakes —with fruit for Romi, maple syrup for Brooke, and syrup, fruit, *and* cream for Blue—was just the calm before the storm. Romi sent me a text as the car left the driveway.

R: Miss you already. Your cock tastes better than pancakes <3

"What are you smiling about?" Luca asked, heading for the door. Colt was waiting for him outside, ready to go deal with the first issue of the day. On a normal week, the town was quiet. Mostly, the two of them dealt with drug issues— usually opioids—and domestic violence. The latter was something Luca took all too seriously in light of his father's assholic tendencies.

He was a good cop, although sometimes I wished he wasn't so perceptive.

"What am I smiling about? Nothing."

But if I'd known what was to come, I'd have run after Romi and kissed her like I meant it, pacts and punches be damned.

40

ROMI

"This is a heck of a lot of food."

I read down the list Brooke had given me. It ran to three pages. Since Paulo was invited to dinner tomorrow, he'd agreed to swap shifts with Brooke so she could take the day off to cook, but if she planned to use all of these ingredients, she'd need an entire week.

"If we take a page each, we can pick up our items and then meet at the register. Divide and conquer, right?"

All very well in principle, but if we paid together, then how would I hide the chocolate sauce and whipped cream I planned to buy for Aaron? I'd picked up a pair of cufflinks and a belt in New York, but those gifts weren't *fun*. And if he was still alive later, then we were definitely having a whole night's worth of entertainment.

Blue groaned from the back seat. "Do we really need all this stuff? Won't the other people bring dishes? My mom's planning to make a pumpkin cheesecake."

"Maybe they will, but I said for people just to bring themselves, so we can't rely on donations."

But no way would guests show up empty-handed. Addy's

mom baked for fun. "Whatever you do, don't buy champagne. Davis is having three dozen bottles of Cristal delivered. And it's meant to be a surprise, so act shocked, okay?"

"Cristal?" Brooke looked at me, wide-eyed. "Are you serious?"

"Yes. Watch the road!"

"Sorry, sorry. But *Cristal*. Wow." Then she turned curious. "Will you be all right with everyone else drinking?"

I couldn't lie and say it would be easy, but I was in a better place now.

"I'll deal, and I wouldn't want you guys to miss out."

As Brooke drew up to a stop sign, she reached out to squeeze my hand. "You know if you ever want to talk..."

The first shot came out of nowhere.

Didn't register right away.

Just a *bang* that could have been a firecracker or a car backfiring.

Then a window shattered, and Brooke was screaming, and I was screaming, and Blue was yelling, "Drive, drive!"

Somehow, Brooke managed to get her foot onto the gas, and we shot through the intersection, but too far, too fast, and there was a truck coming. She screamed again as metal crunched, and then we were spinning, spinning into the trees. An explosion made my ears ring, and then...nothing.

Only silence.

All around me, I could see white, and I wondered if I might be dead, but then somebody wrenched my door open, and I realised the white was the airbags, and there was a gun.

"Get off! Get away from me!"

"Are you hurt?"

Panic coursed through me, hot and fierce, and I kicked

out, clawed at his face, but Deck just grabbed both of my hands in one of his and held them still.

"Gotta get out of the car, Romi. There's someone in the trees with a gun."

I focused on the pistol in his hands. "You! You've got the gun!"

"But I wasn't the one shooting. Brooke?"

The only sound was Blue groaning in the back, and my heart stuttered. "Brooke? Brooke!"

"Romi, you need to hide behind a tree and keep your head down. Get something solid between you and the shooter while I help Brooke and Blue. Can you do that?"

"I-I-I think so."

"The shooter's on Brooke's side of the car. I'll cover you while you run. You have your phone?"

"Yes."

"Call your brother. Ready?"

I could barely breathe, but I nodded.

"Go."

Run? I struggled to even stagger. Broken glass crunched under my feet, and I jumped as Deck fired a shot across the road. Nearly fell. Another shot. But then I dove behind a sturdy tree and crouched, waiting for the next bullet to fly.

Call Luca. Deck said to call Luca.

I fumbled the phone out of my pocket, praying it wasn't broken and also thanking Ishmael, who'd made the dress with pockets in the first place. Part of his regular line, not the outlandish outfits he showed on the runway to get column inches, so comfortable and— Who cared? *Brooke might be dead.*

"L-L-Luca?"

He picked up on my fear in a heartbeat. "What's wrong?"

"There w-w-was an accident. Someone shot at us, and we c-c-crashed."

"Where? Where are you?"

"Pine Cliff Road. The intersection with Little Creek Lane. Deck's here, he's helping, but... Brooke..."

"I'll be there."

How long would he take? Was the shooter still in the forest, watching, waiting? Or had he run when he realised Deck had a gun too? Should I go back to help? I heard a *thump*, risked a look around the tree, and saw Blue kicking her way out of the back door. Hell, oh hell! Her arm was crimson. Her shoulder... Blood was dripping from her hand...

I tore the bottom off my dress and pressed it against the wound. Blue gasped but held the wadded wool in place.

"Brooke?" I asked.

"Deck said she was breathing."

A siren sounded in the distance, and I sagged back against the damp bark. *Luca was coming.* Wind whipped at my hair, and I wanted to scream at the damn sky as the first fat drops of rain fell. Was the bleeding slowing? At least Blue was conscious and cursing—I was more worried about Brooke at this moment.

I heard a car engine, looked up to see a yellow SUV with a pair of kayaks strapped to the roof. A man, well, more of a boy, stepped out. He couldn't have been more than twenty.

"What happened? You crashed?"

"Get down," Deck shouted. "There's a shooter in the woods."

The guy dropped like a stone. "Holy shit, man."

One, two, three more cars stopped—which wasn't surprising since it was a main road—and when no more shots came, I began to suck in ragged breaths. Would the psycho really try again with an audience?

"Do you think he's still there?" I asked Blue.

"Not if he's got more than one brain cell. Or she."

"She?"

"Marianna. Duh."

"You really think…?"

"I think a woman can shoot a gun as well as a man."

Colt and Luca's patrol car kicked up gravel as it slowed. Luca was out and running before it came to a complete stop, and Colt quickly followed, both of them heading for the car.

"What happened?" Luca asked. "Where's Romi? Brooke?"

Deck stayed eerily calm. "Guy in the woods was taking potshots at Brooke's car. She floored it out of Little Creek Lane and hit my truck. Got knocked out briefly."

"Romi?"

"Romi's okay. Blue's bleeding."

"The shooter?"

"Ran when I fired a couple of warning shots. Don't think he expected anyone to fight back."

The shooter was gone? Thank goodness. I staggered to the car, my knees threatening to give way. "Is Brooke all right? Is she awake?"

A shaky voice came from the car. "I'm all right."

And then Aaron was striding toward me, worry etched into his forehead.

"I'm—"

I started to say I was okay, but he didn't stop, just cupped my cheeks in his hands and crushed his mouth to mine. His kiss was better than any medicine, but didn't he realise we had an audience?

"I've never been so scared as I was when Luca called five minutes ago," he whispered. "Where's Brooke?"

"In the car."

"What the fuck?" Luca asked.

Aaron wrapped an arm around my shoulders and turned to face him. "I'm in love with your sister. If you need to punch me, get it over with because I need to see Brooke."

Luca took in a bracing breath, and I knew he was struggling for control. "Later. We'll talk about this later. Can you handle things with Colt? Because I need to go after the shooter."

He what? "Are you crazy? He's got a freaking gun!"

"So do I."

Deck straightened. "I'll come with you."

"You sure you want to do that? How did you end up on the scene, anyway?"

"I was on my way to Baldwin Estates when Brooke's vehicle ricocheted off my bumper."

"Baldwin Estates?"

"That uptight receptionist called me. Said the fire door was jammed and needed fixing *right now*." Deck shrugged. "I'm a carpenter, not a handyman, but cash is cash."

"EJ couldn't fix it?"

"He promised to do it yesterday, apparently, but he didn't, and now he's not there." Well, wasn't that interesting? "And in answer to your other question, yeah, I'm sure I want to come with you. I like the idea of a psycho running around with a gun about as much as you do."

"Then let's go."

Blue appeared beside me, still dripping blood. "Did somebody call an ambulance?"

"Ambulance is on its way," Colt said. Aaron had already climbed into the passenger side of the car, and I heard him talking softly to Brooke, reassuring her. "Everything's under control."

Was it? *Was it?*

What about the next incident, and the next one? Would this ever stop?

41

ROMI

"Worst Thanksgiving Eve ever," Brooke croaked from her hospital bed.

I couldn't argue with that. Even the Thanksgiving Eve I'd spent at Maple Mountain had been better than this, and I'd been angry at everything and everyone back then. Now? Now I was just furious at whoever had put us all here at the medical centre.

Brooke had a mild concussion and a whole bunch of cuts and bruises. One jagged tear on her thigh had needed stitches, and her car was on its way to the great junkyard in the sky, but she'd recover.

Blue had come off the worst. She was out of surgery now, at least. Her humerus had been pinned back together, and the doctor said she was lucky the shot hadn't done more damage. The final insult had come when they removed what was left of the bullet and found it so deformed that linking the remains back to the gun that fired it would be difficult, if not impossible.

But we were alive. We were all alive, and that was the most important thing.

Although when Luca arrived and found Aaron's arms around me, there might be a different outcome...

My phone pinged. Speak of the devil.

Luca: Be there in five.

"What's wrong?" Davis asked as my palms began sweating. He'd met us at the hospital and insisted we have private rooms, specialist consults, additional scans, whatever was necessary.

"Luca's on his way. Maybe Aaron could go down the fire escape?"

Brooke nodded at the jug of water on her rolling table. "Throw this over them. That's what worked last time."

We'd already let her in on the secrets—about Aaron and me, and about Davis—and she'd gushed congratulations, then offered to introduce Davis to Paulo. She'd been joking, of course, but Paulo was actually closer to Davis's type than she might have imagined. He liked younger men, the fun ones, the more flamboyant the better. Opposites attract, right? But if he took one of his boy toys to the ultraconservative luncheons he attended, his peers would have a meltdown. The same peers who patted him on the back when I showed up on his arm in a short skirt and skyscraper heels and a rainbow of make-up. Double standards much? I'd worn shorts to a corporate picnic once. Three grubby old men had fondled my ass.

"I'm not running," Aaron said. "If Luca's pissed, then he's pissed."

Blue grinned from her seat next to Brooke's bed. The seat she absolutely shouldn't have been sitting in. The doctors had tried to make her stay in bed, but she said rest disagreed with her, so they'd grudgingly compromised on a wheelchair.

"Good for you. You should be happy. *Everyone* should be happy."

"Even you? I thought you took pride in your grouchiness?"

"Even me. I feel *great* today. No grouching here, no siree."

"What pills did they give you?"

"Uh, all of them, I think." She used the arm that wasn't in a sling to point toward Davis. "Why don't you just tell everyone about your love of dick? Then you could avoid all this skulking around."

Bless Davis, he didn't kill her. "Because it would affect my ability to do business."

"Don't you already have, like, a billion dollars? How much more business do you need to do?"

"No, I don't have a billion dollars, not yet. But someday I will. When I told my ninth-grade teacher that, she laughed at me. Told me that kids from families like mine didn't walk on Wall Street, or words to that effect. So when I get that final zero, I'm dedicating it to Mrs. Kajinski. And after that, then maybe I'll come out."

"Well, I hope you get the extra zero soon, but in the meantime, we'll just all be..." She put a finger to her lips and glanced around furtively. "Shhh."

I kind of liked Blue on drugs. Too bad it wouldn't last.

Davis simply smiled. "I appreciate that."

Footsteps sounded in the hallway outside, heavy boots, and Aaron's arms tightened. It was showtime.

Luca walked into the room, followed by Colt, and neither of them looked thrilled. Perhaps we should offer them some of whatever Blue was taking? The first thing Luca did was kiss Brooke on the cheek, carefully so he didn't press on her bruises.

"How are you feeling, sweetheart?"

"Like I got hit by a truck. How did the whole forensics thing go? Did you catch him?"

Luca shook his head. "He got away. Me and Deck tracked him to a stand of trees, but the visible trail disappeared after that. He could've gotten into a vehicle."

"He?" Blue asked. "You say it was a 'he'—how do you know it wasn't a 'she'?"

"Deck caught a glimpse of the shooter as he ran off. Only for a second, and from the back, and he says it's more his subconscious speaking than any particular attribute he can put his finger on, but he thought it was a man."

"That sounds concrete."

"He's got good instincts."

"Was it EJ?"

Luca shook his head. "We checked the whereabouts of EJ and Marianna this morning—first thing we did—and they were both at a business breakfast in Portland. Some 'maximise your profits in real estate' conference. Started yesterday, they attended a dinner and stayed overnight, and there're about a hundred witnesses."

"So who does that leave?"

Brooke shuddered. "The Bad Samaritan? He shot at you guys before."

"We discussed that on the way over, and it doesn't feel right. The Bad Samaritan wouldn't have missed, and the crime scene investigator who came over from Coquille thinks Blue was hit by a ricochet rather than a direct shot. There's a sign for the picnic area thirty yards before the intersection with a chip of paint scraped out of it, and the doctor recovered similar paint from Blue's wound. Still needs to be analysed, but that's the theory the CSI's working with at the moment. Romi heard two shots, and the second also went wide."

"So maybe he *meant* to miss for some reason." Brooke knifed up, then winced. "What if EJ and Marianna hired him to scare us?"

Blue snorted. "And how would they have hired him? From Craigslist?"

"I don't know. It's just an idea. Do you have a better one?"

"Not right now," she admitted.

Colt shifted uncomfortably. "It's also possible... Shit." He closed his eyes for a second. "It's also possible that the Bad Samaritan was the man who rescued you."

"Deck?" Brooke was incredulous. "You can't be serious? Why would you say that?"

"When we went out to the cabin to search for Serena's vehicle, Luca identified Deck as former military. An operator. And Kasper doesn't like questionable folks being around Brie, so he did some digging."

"Into *Deck*? Where is Brie, anyway? Did she stay at the hotel?"

"After the shooting, she got summoned back home. Nobody wants her in danger, and I have to agree with the move. Too many unknowns right now."

"And Kiki? She's with the Snyders?"

"She went with Brie."

Colt's voice was thick, and I knew how hard it must have been for him to send his daughter away, especially on Thanksgiving. But where would the next attack come from? Baldwin's Shore used to be such a safe town, and now it felt like a sleeping volcano waiting to blow.

"What did Kasper find?" Luca asked.

"That Decker Langdon died twenty years ago. Just one month after Serena."

"Then who...?"

"We don't know yet."

"Is that another reason Brie flew back home?"

"It factored into the decision, yes. If Deck was driving the truck today, then he couldn't have been in the trees with a gun, but he's lying about his past."

"So who *was* in the trees?" Blue asked. "Dammit, I was so sure it was Marianna. If she's ruled out, who's left?"

"Dad?" I suggested, although that was more wishful thinking than anything else.

Blue shook her head. "That alibi was solid."

"Then who? It feels as if we're starting again at the beginning, except this time the villain's levelled up while we're still floundering around in a sea of dead ends."

Luca sat on the edge of the bed and clasped Brooke's hand. "We need to take a step back and regroup. Brooke and Blue need to heal."

"Do you know how long it takes for bones to knit?" Blue asked. "We can't sit out for that long."

"It's been a tough day for everyone. Let's get some sleep and talk about this tomorrow. We've got a tracking dog arriving at first light, and then we need to comb through the forest."

A tracking dog? "Won't the scent be gone by the morning?"

"No, it'll linger for twenty-four hours at least."

"Even though it's been raining?"

"The shower didn't last long enough to wash away the trail."

"Won't the dog just follow you since you also walked through the forest?"

"Apparently, it's trained not to. The shooter must've been

lying in wait, and if we can find his nest, the dog'll track from that."

"What about Thanksgiving?"

"I spoke to Addy, and she's been calling everyone we invited over. We'll eat together, just the seven of us, and rearrange the big dinner for a later date."

I grabbed onto that thread of hope. "Seven of us? Does that mean you're not gonna load Aaron into a casket?"

He nodded at Davis. "Surprised you haven't done that already."

Davis smiled. "I'm happy for them."

"Why do I get the impression that I'm missing a big piece of this puzzle?"

"Because you are; I prefer men."

Seeing Luca completely and utterly speechless was a once-in-a-lifetime event, so I took a moment to treasure it. The glorious sound of his silence.

"Davis is and always has been a close friend, but we've never been romantically involved."

"But you said—"

"Actually, I never did. We just showed up to places together, I pawed him in public, and everyone assumed. Including you."

"You've been living together."

"His apartment is six thousand square feet. It's plenty big enough for two, and he's the best roommate *ever*." I wriggled out of Aaron's grasp and smooched Davis on the cheek, just to wind up my brother. "He makes a mean cup of coffee, he showers daily, and he always remembers to put down the toilet seat."

"Seems I've got big shoes to fill," Aaron muttered.

"Can you try to be happy for us too?" I asked Luca. "Please?"

He met my gaze, his face solemn. Then slowly, slowly, his eyes crinkled and he broke into a grin.

"I don't need to try. I *am* happy for you. Couldn't think of a better man to take care of my little sister. If Aaron fucks up, then clearly I'll have to pound him into dust, but yeah, I'm happy for both of you."

42

ROMI

"Best Thanksgiving ever." Brooke popped a snickerdoodle into her mouth, and she wasn't lying. "Tell it again, tell it again."

When a night of observation hadn't revealed anything concerning, the doctors had released Brooke at lunchtime. Aaron had picked her up along with Blue, and then he'd cobbled together a Thanksgiving dinner with ingredients we had in the kitchen while Brooke offered advice from the couch. And while he was cooking, people kept dropping by with food and sympathy.

Ginger pumpkin cheesecake and a greetings card from Blue's mom.

Fruit-and-nut trifle and flowers from Mrs. Crowe.

Apple cranberry pie and a crocheted blanket from Darla.

Cookies and handmade candles from Paulo.

The snickerdoodles and a set of coasters from the Snyders.

Crystal wine glasses and a good Merlot I couldn't drink from Nico.

Nico had shown up yesterday too, and he'd offered us his spare rooms and the services of his security team in case we felt uncomfortable at Deals on Wheels. But if we let the shooter scare us away, then the enemy would have won. This place was our home. At least, it was Brooke's home, and Blue's temporary home, and I hoped one day it might be my official home too. Anyhow, it felt like home, and that was the important thing.

So we'd stayed.

And Brie sent a set of fancy furniture for the terrace plus a hot tub and a mobile freaking crane to install it, because of course she did, which was awesome but also awful because I'd secretly ordered a hot tub as well, so now we'd have two hot tubs if I couldn't swap it for something else.

Perhaps a sauna?

Or a cabana?

Now Luca and Colt were back, we had food, food everywhere, and the day was going considerably better than yesterday.

"Only took us ten minutes to find the spot where the shooter hid," Luca said. "Broken twigs, trampled grass, a tuft of dark blue fabric on a branch where he caught his shirt. Couple of shell casings he forgot to pick up or more likely panicked and left behind when Deck started shooting back. And then the dog picked up his scent, and we followed the trail all the way to the Baldwins' front door."

He'd already told the story once, but I'd never tire of hearing it.

"Times like this, I wish I'd become a deputy instead of a lawyer," Aaron said.

Hmm... Aaron in a uniform? I wouldn't mind that. Although he looked pretty damn sexy in a suit too. I leaned into him, and he kissed my hair, and this was just...perfect.

"So we knocked," Luca continued. "And the maid answered. Told us what we already knew—that EJ and Marianna had been gone all of the night before last, but also that Mr. Parker had left for the office at eight yesterday, and the girls drove off five minutes after to go plan some shindig."

Sara, Kayleigh, and Lillian had started their event-management business right after Sara left school. Translation: Kayleigh and Lillian swanned around at the parties, basking in compliments, while Sara did all the work. Think I'm kidding? I'd been to one of their functions in Portland a few years ago, a ball organised for some forgettable D-list celeb eager to capitalise on their five minutes of fame, and Sara had spent hours running around like a blue-assed fly checking on food and waitstaff and performers while the twins sipped champagne and chatted for the entire night. You only had to look at them to know who carried the company—Sara wore boring black pants and sensible shoes while the gruesome twosome teetered around on stilettos, constantly tugging down their hems.

Colt picked up the story. "But Mr. Easton was in yesterday, so Ms. Lopez said, apart from a couple of hours in the morning when he 'went for a walk.'"

Luca tried to keep a straight face. "Turns out that six months of being called 'Oi, you' hadn't exactly endeared Easton the Turd to the poor woman, so she didn't mind telling us that when he got back, he was sweaty and kinda nervous."

"And when we asked her real nice, she took us up to his room and found the shirt he wore for his 'walk' yesterday in the laundry hamper. A dark blue shirt. With a tear out of it."

"So we got to arrest him over Thanksgiving dinner, and

no matter how long I spend with the sheriff's department, I'm sure this'll always be the highlight of my career."

"When I'm seventy, I'm gonna look back on this day with fond memories and a happy tear in my eye."

Brooke held up her glass. "We should make a toast. To the best Thanksgiving gift any of us could ever hope for. Easton Baldwin the Third locked up in jail."

"Hope you put the cuffs on nice and tight," Aaron added.

Luca smirked. "Wasn't about to miss that opportunity."

Of course, Easton hadn't gone quietly. No, he'd screamed and yelled blue murder, cursing Colt and Luca and their vendetta against his family, Blue and her meddling, and my general existence. And in the middle of all the yelling, he'd blurted out that he'd only meant to scare us, and it was Brooke's fault that we got hurt because she was a terrible driver, and she wasn't even meant to be in the car anyway because Aaron should have been behind the wheel.

Aaron.

He'd been targeting Aaron and Blue.

They'd driven that route each day for a week, and at roughly the same time, although we didn't yet know how Easton had become aware of their schedule because at that point, Marianna told him to shut his stupid mouth and ordered EJ to call a lawyer.

The best part? Luca and Colt had caught Easton's confession on their body cams, so there almost wasn't a need to match the shell casings they'd found to the gun Easton had used. But just in case, they'd confiscated every firearm in the house and taken them all to the lab. The search and the paperwork had taken time, which made them late for dinner, but who cared about dry turkey? Or, in my case, shrivelled stuffed mushrooms? That's right—nobody. Tonight, we were celebrating. One piece of scum was out of the way, and the fact that it happened to be Easton the Third made the victory so much sweeter.

"Did he say anything about the fire?" Blue asked.

Way to put a downer on the evening.

"No, but from what I've seen today, I doubt he's smart enough to be our arsonist. He'd have driven over in his Porsche with the top down, and we'd probably have him on video buying a can of gas from the nearest gas station too."

"So we're back to EJ? Either covering himself or protecting Marianna?"

"Or Parker?" Brooke suggested. "He's not as dumb as Easton, and since this seems to be a family affair…"

Luca took a sip of his drink. He'd indulged in one small glass of wine and then switched to water because he wanted to stay alert, just in case. It wasn't lost on me that he had a gun strapped to his hip. So did Colt, and somebody had lent Blue a pistol because hers had burned up at her mom's house.

I felt safer than I had at this time yesterday, but danger still lurked in the background.

"We'll check into Parker's alibi," Luca said. "But we'll do that tomorrow. For now, let's just forget about the Baldwins and enjoy dinner. They've taken enough from us already."

They had, and while I still wanted justice for Mom, I'd grown to realise that we couldn't let her passing overshadow the rest of our lives. She'd have wanted us to be happy. I had so much to be thankful for—Aaron, Davis, Luca, my friends, my health, a steady job.

Too much to lose.

Justice had a price, but how much was I willing to pay?

43

AARON

*T*here was a piece missing from the puzzle.

A clue we hadn't found yet.

And it was bugging the hell out of me that I couldn't see what it was. Blue too—she'd gone into a funk these last few days, although I suspected that was partly because she'd finished her course of happy pills. I'd grown used to having her around the place now. It was like having a pet gremlin. Just don't get her wet or feed her after midnight.

She couldn't go in the hot tub until her cast came off anyway, which was another source of misery for her. The rest of us had tried it out, although that led to a very awkward conversation with Luca about precisely what we could and couldn't do in there because neither of us wanted to sit in each other's jizz. Pointing out that Romi swallowed would probably have resulted in another visit to the hospital, so I'd agreed to a "no fucking in the hot tub" rule. At least he hadn't said anything about the lounge chairs.

Ah, speaking of the gremlin...

She walked across to the breakfast bar and took a seat

opposite Romi and Davis, her face like a thundercloud whose puppy had died.

"What got your goat? Or is it just my general presence, as usual?"

"Everything."

"You can't narrow it down a tiny bit?"

"Why do you care?"

"Because your scowl is hurting my eyeballs."

"Okay, fine. My arm's throbbing, I barely slept, and I lost my job."

Romi looked puzzled. "Huh? But we didn't fire you."

"I'm talking about the job in Europe. They won't hold it open until my arm heals, and it's not as if I can stay here forever. I didn't even manage to solve your case."

"You got further than the police."

"Further isn't finished."

"It was colder than Alaska before you started. You're a great PI, and I really think you should consider working in that field again."

"In case you hadn't noticed, I don't exactly have a glowing reputation."

No, but she was good. Better than most of the investigators Asa or I used. "If you can find it within yourself to work for a lawyer, I can throw a few jobs your way."

Blue pondered that for a moment. "Maybe."

"How do you feel about corporate work?" Davis asked. "Legit stuff." He gave a wolfish smile. "For the most part, anyway."

"Business research? I've done that kind of thing in the past, but my lack of diplomacy lets me down."

"You'd be reporting to me, and I like to hear it straight."

"Working for you?"

"Freelancing. But between Aaron's jobs and my projects, you'd be busy for the next year or so. Probably longer."

"Depends on when you make that billion, huh?"

Davis gave the faintest smile. "Something like that."

"Would I have to go to New York?"

"There might be some travel involved, but I'd anticipate that much of the work could be done remotely. And as Romi is fond of pointing out, my penthouse is six thousand square feet, so I should be able to find you a bed."

"I still want to keep working on Serena's case."

"Good. That'll make Romi happy. Tell me, if you went on instinct alone, who do you think is the culprit?"

Not Parker—he had an alibi for the fire. So did Easton the Third, unfortunately. They'd both been in Coquille buying a new pool table for their games room. Parker would have to get used to playing alone, though, because Easton was going to do jail time. Not as much as I'd have liked, but the DA was going for attempted murder. Oh, Easton claimed he'd been aiming wide, but one of his shots had still hit Blue, and what did he think was going to happen when he started firing indiscriminately?

But back to the main event...

There was no hesitation on Blue's part. "My head says EJ, but my heart says Marianna."

"Why?" Davis asked.

"You said instinct."

"But there must be a reason."

"There's something off about her. She hides it, but not well enough. And if EJ was serious about Serena, then Marianna's the one who ultimately benefitted from her death. But now I have to tiptoe around in case I set off her or one of her sociopathic stepkids because I really don't want my mom or any of you people to get hurt again."

"How's the house rebuild going?"

"They tore down what's left. They're saying six months for the new place, but maybe if I cry on the phone, they'll get it done faster. At least Mom's content fussing over the layabout." She turned back to me. "I'll look for a place of my own, okay? If I've got an income, I can afford rent. But I'm not giving the Baldwins a cent, so I guess that puts me at a disadvantage around here."

"No hurry. But when you're ready, try speaking to Addy's mom and dad. They've got a garage apartment Brooke recently moved out of."

"It's still empty?"

"They only rent it to people they know because they don't want strangers messing around on their property, but I'll get Addy to put in a word. Now, do you want breakfast before I head to work? Or are you just going to sit there feeling sorry for yourself all day?"

"Maybe I could eat a pancake."

"Romi?"

She beamed at me with that million-dollar smile, and I'd never get sick of the sight.

"I wouldn't mind a pancake either."

I made hers with oat milk, then added blueberries and sliced bananas. Davis had already nibbled on fruit with his decaf. Said he was trying to keep his ticker healthy. This afternoon, he'd fly back to New York, and I'd actually miss him. When he wasn't hashing out deals over the phone with ruthless efficiency, he had a strangely calming presence. I saw what Romi saw in him.

Never thought I'd say *that*.

But a week on from Thanksgiving, it was time to start getting used to the new normal. A future not just with Romi in it, but with *us*. A future I once thought I'd ruined. I'd asked her if she might want to move in with me someday, and she said, "If by 'someday' you mean tomorrow, then yes." Good thing I'd built a big closet because seven-eighths of it now belonged to her.

Brie and Kiki were on their way back, and we'd dropped the "safety in numbers" policy in favour of "watch your back." We couldn't live in fear forever.

If we did, the monster would win.

The new normal lasted less than a day.

A few hours, in fact.

The call came in the afternoon as I was finishing up a meeting about Mr. Simonson's will. Via Lois, who'd been Asa's admin for as long as anyone could remember, and who now acted for me as well.

"I'm sorry to disturb you, but your sister's on the phone, Aaron. She says it's urgent."

My spine stiffened. Brooke wasn't a drama queen, and she wouldn't have asked Lois to interrupt if it weren't essential.

"Would you excuse me? Lois can see you out, and I'll get those changes made by next Tuesday."

Mr. Simonson used the prospect of an inheritance to "keep the grandkids in line" and changed his will monthly depending on which of them was in favour, which made him somewhat of an asshole and also one of my best customers. I shook hands and left Lois to placate him. She was a seasoned pro at that, and Brooke was more important.

"You okay?"

She spoke in a hushed voice. "Can you come over to the Craft Cabin?"

"What is it? Is everything all right?"

My first thought had been "hostage situation," but although there was a quake in her voice, there was also a hint of excitement. Excitement, but she was trying not to show it, like when teenage Luca had invited her to a party and she was pretending to stay chill.

"Yes, yes. But there's somebody here that you *need* to speak to. *Right away.*"

"Who?"

"Please, can you just come?"

"You're safe?"

"Totally safe, but you need to come."

Now I was curious as hell. Who was at the Craft Cabin, and why was Brooke so insistent that I needed to drop everything and hotfoot it over there?

"Give me ten minutes."

44

AARON

"Sara?"

What was Sara Baldwin doing in the break room among half-finished knitting projects, the remains of a pineapple upside-down cake, and Darla's cat? She looked skittish, shifting from foot to foot as if she might bolt out the back door at any moment.

"I'm not supposed to be here."

"Then why *are* you here?"

"I told Parker I needed to pick up more watercolour paints. Uncle EJ said I should buy them mail order from now on, but as long as he doesn't find out..."

"We won't tell him you're here," Brooke assured her. "Will we, Aaron?"

"Our lips are sealed. Why are you here?" I asked again.

"I wanted to warn you. About Easton."

Sara was definitely the more worried out of the two women. Was she always this jumpy? I hadn't spent much time with her in the past, but Brooke used to chat with her at school, and she'd mentioned that Sara had started coming to her painting classes earlier in the year.

"What's Easton done?"

Apart from trying to kill three people.

"Nothing else, not yet anyway. I know he's not meant to come near you now, but Marianna's riling him up again, the same way she did last time, and he's got such a foul, foul temper..."

"Are you saying Marianna's encouraging him to breach his restraining order?"

"Maybe? I don't know! I'm just saying that she knows what buttons to push to make him mad, and right now, she's pushing every single one of them."

"You said she did this before?"

Sara nodded. "When you began asking questions, and that private investigator too. Marianna started going on and on about how you were trying to ruin our family, how you and Luca had always been jealous of what we had and now that you're some big shot with a fancy law degree, you're trying to throw your weight around. Easton, he's never liked you because you're smarter than he is, or Luca because of all the fights they used to get into..." The fights that Easton had lost every time. "And after Brooke and Luca got him banned from the bar at the Peninsula, that hatred only grew. So Marianna fans the flames. She manipulates him, and Uncle EJ doesn't even see it."

"Can you give us an example? Something she's done?"

Preferably something useable in court.

"So before he shot at you, she just happened to mention over dinner that you and the investigator—Blue?—you drove to Coos Bay every morning. 'Mr. Big-time Attorney's probably cheating on that whore he calls a girlfriend,'" Sara mimicked. "'Screwing around with his hired gun so she'll spread lies about us.'"

Rage burned inside me, but I tamped it down. Forced myself to remain calm.

"How did she know we were going to Coos Bay? Was she watching us?"

"I-I think Natalie told her. The office assistant at Baldwin Estates? She lives in Coos Bay, and she said she saw you. Natalie's a spiteful shrew as well. She and Easton are—" Sara clapped a hand over her mouth as if she suddenly realised she'd said too much. "Sorry, that's not really relevant. I guess... I guess I just wanted to say that y'all should watch your backs."

Behind Sara, Brooke gave me a "See?" half-shrug. Sara had told her this, but she'd wanted me to hear it for myself. And perhaps see what else I could get.

Slowly, carefully, I took a seat in the chair by the cat's bed, trying not to spook Sara any further.

"Why do you think Marianna's so upset about this?"

"I already told you!" Sara's voice rose. "She says you're trying to destroy the family."

"But if she didn't do anything, if your uncle didn't do anything, there's nothing to be afraid of."

"She said the cops frame innocent people all the time."

"We're not the cops. We're just a group of friends trying to get to the bottom of why somebody dear to us died."

Brooke took Sara's hands in hers. "We both understand what that's like. To lose our parents without getting to say goodbye."

Sara's parents had died in a car crash, the same as mine and Brooke's had. Day to day, it got easier to live with the pain, but it was always there in the background, a dull ache that never quite went away. For Sara, maybe it was worse. My parents had been hit by a drunk driver running a red light. Rumour said—well,

Kasper's research suggested—that Sara's mother had been shot before the car rolled down the embankment. Sara had been the sole survivor of what most likely wasn't an accident.

How much did she remember?

Enough that a tear slid down her cheek.

"EJ admitted he had an affair with Serena," I told her as gently as I could. "We'd be remiss if we didn't follow up on that."

"He wouldn't have killed her. He doesn't have it in him. When Lillian's cat dropped a half-dead mouse in the living room, he couldn't even put it out of its misery. He took it to the veterinarian instead."

"What if it was an accident? A fight that went too far?"

Sara shook her head. "No, no, no. EJ just doesn't do confrontation. He leaves that to Marianna."

I thought back to Blue's theory, her instincts, and decided *fuck it.*

"Is *she* capable? Marianna?"

Sara would make a terrible poker player. I watched as the emotions crossed her face—fear, disgust, discomfort. What didn't I see? Surprise.

Instead, we got the smallest of nods. "Y'all don't know her the way I do."

Oh, I wouldn't be so sure about that.

"Tell me why you say that. Why you think she's capable."

Now Sara sat down too. Well, perched on the edge of the couch, but it was better than making a run for it.

"She's...complicated."

"Complicated how?"

"I've spent years trying to fathom how her mind works." A sigh. "At heart, she's a horrible, selfish person, but she hides it. She hides it so well. Her parents used to have money, but they lost it, and I think when she met EJ, she saw him as a way back to her old life."

"A meal ticket?"

"Not just a meal ticket—the whole package. The chance to have what her parents had—love, wealth, a good name in the community."

"She loves him?"

"Oh, yes. When it comes to EJ, she has a jealous streak a mile deep and two miles wide. And she's not a trophy wife, absolutely not. Who do you think runs Baldwin Estates? Because it isn't EJ. He just tinkers around with the properties. Marianna and Parker do all the hard stuff. Maybe that's why EJ turns a blind eye to her worst qualities?" Sara blew out a breath. "Or maybe I've been reading too many psychology books? Growing up in that family was *hard*, and after Grandpa died..."

"I'm so sorry," Brooke said. "I wish I'd known how you were feeling. I could have... I don't know... We could have hung out or something. But you're here now. Can I get you a drink? A coffee?"

Brooke meant well, but for crying out loud, this wasn't the time or the place.

"No, no, I shouldn't stay. I shouldn't be here."

Sara began to rise, and I groaned inwardly. For the first time in my life, I wished Blue were with me instead. She wouldn't take her eyes off the prize, and like Marianna, she knew which buttons to push. Which thread to tug on to unravel the whole damn sweatshop.

What would Blue do?

Sara's lack of surprise, that was the key. There was a big jump from petty jealousy and gold-digging to murder and a cover-up. And yet Sara had made that leap. Why? She'd been thinking about the puzzle as much as we had, hadn't she? And she had the missing piece.

"Who else did Marianna hurt, Sara?"

She paused, her ass a foot off the seat.

"I-I-I'm not sure. I mean, I don't know for certain that she did."

"But you suspect?"

Her voice dropped to a whisper. "She carries a knife in her purse."

A chill ran through me. "And she's used it?"

"Not on a person, not that I know of." Sara slumped back onto the couch. "That was an awful evening. The worst. We were working a party over in Coquille, a birthday celebration for a friend of Uncle's, so he and Marianna attended. The alcohol budget was...generous, and some of the guests overindulged. *Most* of them overindulged. A blonde woman was flirting with EJ, and Marianna didn't like that, not one bit, but I kind of... forgot about her when this pig of a man old enough to be my father cornered me by the coat closet and stuck his hand up my dress." She gave a hollow laugh. "That'll teach me not to wear pants. I thought I was gonna puke, so I stepped outside to get some air, and that was when I saw her. Marianna. Coming back to the ballroom, tucking the knife into her bag. But she didn't see me."

"What had she done?"

"I think she slashed the flirt's tyres. I only found out when we went to clean up the next morning and the blonde woman was having hysterics in the parking lot."

"Did you report your suspicions to anybody?"

"You mean the police? It wasn't as if I saw her do it. I told Grandpa, and he said Marianna wouldn't have left any proof, so what was the point in dragging the family name through the mud for nothing?"

"He knew what she was like?"

Sara nodded. "When Darla first started working as his nurse, I overheard him telling her to keep her distance from EJ and watch her step around Marianna."

"Were there ever any incidents between Marianna and Darla?"

"No, I don't think so. I mean, not that I'm aware of. Darla just heeded Grandpa's warning and stayed out of her way, which is what I do as well."

"Is Darla working today?" I asked Brooke.

"Nuh-uh. She has Thursdays off."

We could follow up later if necessary. I took a long, slow breath. Blue had been right. So far, she'd been right about everything except possibly…

"The fire?" I asked Sara. "Did you hear about the fire?"

The change was unmistakable. She paled one full shade and began trembling. And asshole that I was, I hoped that her distress meant good news for our case.

"You know something?"

"I think… I think she tried to frame me. She set me up, and I didn't even realise until Parker told me about the rumours flying around town."

Well, this was new. "How did she set you up?"

"The fire was three weeks ago on a Tuesday, right?"

"Yes."

"Well, I was sick that day. Horribly sick, and it came out of nowhere. First thing, I felt fine, but then I threw up my breakfast. Lillian looked up the symptoms on the internet and told me I had either gastroenteritis or an intestinal blockage, and she said I should go to the emergency room, but then Marianna told her not to be ridiculous and it was only a virus. And I honestly felt so bad that I just wanted to go to bed."

"And did you?"

Sara nodded. "Marianna came to check on me at lunchtime and brought me a mug of herbal tea to help me stay hydrated, and after I'd slept through the afternoon, I felt human again."

"How does that lead to Marianna framing you?"

"I got sick so suddenly, and then I got sleepy—too sleepy—so quickly. Juana had the day off, so the only person who saw me at home was Marianna, and I bet you ten bucks that if the cops asked her where I was that afternoon, she'd hedge and say that, well, I *could* have snuck out. That maybe I faked the whole thing, when all the time *she* drugged me."

"You believe she slipped something into your drink?"

"Kayleigh takes sleeping pills. She wouldn't have noticed if a couple went missing."

"Why would Marianna go to those lengths?"

"So she could borrow my car. I know people think we're rich, and it's true Grandpa left me money in his will, but I won't get access to that until I turn thirty, which means I still have to budget. I'm real careful with my spending. When I parked my car on the Monday, I'd just filled it with gas, but when I got into it on Wednesday, the tank was only three-quarters full."

"What car do you drive?"

"A Toyota Corolla."

"Colour?"

Brooke answered for her. "Black. I saw Sara drive in."

"It's actually dark green—they call the shade 'myrtle'— but everyone thinks it's black. Am I crazy? I've been over this a hundred times in my head, and I don't want to believe it, but Marianna... She's all smiles in public, and she paints herself as a kind-hearted saint, but that's not who she is."

"What about her alibi? Natalie said she spent the whole day in the office apart from the trip to visit you."

"As if Natalie would notice. She spends most of her time sexting Easton."

"There were also two other people present."

"So Marianna probably climbed out the window. She did that once before when the door to her office jammed. It's an old building, and there's a damp problem, and...never mind."

Sara's account explained how the crime *could* have happened, but the difficulty lay in convincing a group of strangers that it had indeed gone down that way. Was it enough? I believed Sara, but would a jury? If I were defending Marianna, I'd turn Sara's words against her, use the so-called evidence to sow reasonable doubt. *Sure, judge, my client could theoretically have done it, but the prosecution's only evidence is the say-so of another suspect.*

"Would you testify to this? Make a statement?"

Another tear tracked down Sara's cheek. "I'd lose everything. My family, my home, my job. If I did speak in court, do you think Marianna would go to prison?"

I longed to say yes. I desperately wanted to reassure her that justice would be done and Marianna would pay for her transgressions, but I'd seen juries acquit in cases more solid than ours.

"I'll need to go over the evidence. Speak with Blue. You have my word that unless we believe there's a good chance of conviction, we'll keep your name out of this."

Brooke passed Sara a tissue. "I'm so sorry you're caught in the middle. If you ever want to talk, I'm always here."

"I suppose it's been good to get things off my chest. At

home, I feel like a square peg in a round hole. A Baldwin, but not a Baldwin, if you know what I mean?"

"Maybe when things cool off, we could have lunch together? In Coos Bay or Coquille, somewhere away from your family."

"I-I think I'd like that." Sara sniffled again and wiped her eyes. "Sometimes... Sometimes it's awkward when people are kind. I never know what to say."

"How about a hug instead?"

At times like this, I was so proud of my little sister. She had what Marianna lacked—empathy and compassion. I could trust her to handle that side of things while I tackled the bigger problem: what the hell were we meant to do about Marianna Baldwin?

45

AARON

The tableful of snacks Brooke had put out lay untouched, and the wine sat uncorked. Nobody had much of an appetite this evening. We'd been over the evidence again and again—what we had, what we didn't have—but every time, we came to the same conclusion.

Blue huffed as she sat back. "We don't have enough. Even with Sara, we just don't have enough."

"So what now?" Romi asked.

What indeed? Luca, Colt, and Brooke had joined us for this extended family conference, and Luca took it upon himself to summarise our limited choices.

"Option one, we can turn the new information over to Aldrich Payne, keeping Sara as an anonymous source, and hope the prosecutor's brave enough to act. But that's dependent on factors outside of our control, and we'd still be at the mercy of a jury. Option two—probably the safest— we can back off and let this case go to the grave."

"That's not a freaking option."

"Figured you'd say that. Which leaves option three: we keep digging, very, very carefully. At least now we've got a single suspect to focus on, and we know where the threat's coming from. Brooke, do you think Sara would feed us more information?"

"I don't know. Maybe? If I can catch her alone, I could ask her."

"Do that."

"So we're going with option three?"

"We should be democratic about this. Hold a vote."

"Well, I vote option three."

"Me too," Romi said, which didn't surprise me in the slightest. "Blue?"

After a moment's hesitation, she nodded. "I can't let this go."

Colt didn't look too happy. "I don't want to put Brie and Kiki in any danger. Easton the Third's out on bail, and from what Sara said, he's still liable to do something stupid. Stupider."

"What about delaying things for a while?" Luca suggested. "When does Easton come up for trial?"

Of course, Easton couldn't just do the honourable thing and plead guilty. "He's out on a security release, so it could be weeks until the arraignment. Months until the trial."

A heavy silence descended. None of the options were palatable, but neither was the prospect of somebody else getting injured or worse. Which was perhaps why I voiced the idea I'd been mulling over since the meeting with Sara. An idea that would see me disbarred if it ever came out that I'd proposed it.

"There is a possible fourth option." Five heads swung in my direction. "Over the past several months, we seem to have cultivated a backup justice system here in Baldwin's Shore. One that skips the trial and goes straight to the punishment."

Luca got there first. "You're talking about the Bad Samaritan?"

"He seems to be here to stay, so I'm suggesting that in the absence of a good alternative, we might consider utilising his services. Justice by proxy."

"Use him to do our dirty work?" Romi asked. "Like how Davis and I couldn't get rid of the paparazzi, so we got them to tell the story we wanted instead?"

"Yes, kind of."

"Except there's a good chance Marianna might wind up in the morgue," Colt pointed out.

"Well, excuse me if I can't spare any sympathy. Maybe we should ask my mom what she thinks? Oh, that's right, we can't because she's dead."

Harsh, but true.

In the end, it came down to the evidence. "We're closer to this than any jury would be. We know the players personally—hell, so does the Bad Samaritan in all likelihood—and we've seen a side of them that won't show in court. If Marianna makes it as far as the dock, you can be sure she'll play the bewildered yet doting wife, so sorry for Serena's death and confused as to why anyone would think she was involved. And we should credit the Bad Samaritan for his self-restraint—he didn't kill Brooke's stalker."

"He might as well have," Colt muttered.

"Nor did he lay a finger on Elmira Fairbanks. So far, he's selected penalties that fit the crimes."

Luca chimed in with a reminder. "He also saved our lives, buddy."

"We don't even know who the Bad Samaritan is. How would we make our request? Pin a flyer on the noticeboard in the grocery store?"

"Based on current information, we have two reasonable

candidates—Nico and Deck. We spend time with both of them. All we'd need to do is slide details of the investigation into conversation, then sit back and wait a few weeks, which Luca suggested doing anyway. Put words in ears, and hope nature takes its course. If one of them acts, then he acts, and if not, then what have we lost?"

"I don't like it." Colt let out a heavy sigh. "But I like the idea of Brie and Kiki getting caught in the Baldwins' crossfire even less."

So we had Colt on board, and I'd always thought he'd be the hardest to convince. Slowly, everyone else nodded. We had our plan. Now we just had to execute it.

And hope our local vigilante took the bait.

46

ROMI

When Aaron came up with his plan to delegate justice, nobody said how hard the waiting would be. Luca had shared our suspicions with Nico during an early-morning gym session, and Aaron had gone over the evidence with Deck as they built a pergola over the hot tub.

Deck... Brie's people were still digging into his background, as was Blue, but so far, they'd found zip regarding his true identity. His prints weren't in the system. The real Decker Langdon had been eleven years old when he lost his life, knocked off his bicycle near Fort Collins by a hit-and-run driver who'd never been caught, so Blue thought that maybe there was a connection to Colorado, but none of her enquiries had borne fruit. What were we going to do about him? Well, right now, we were following the old adage: keep your friends close and your enemies closer. Or potential enemies, anyway. Did Deck wish us harm? Luca and Aaron knew him best, and they were inclined to believe not.

And hadn't he been the one who shot back at Easton the Third after the accident?

I'd forever be grateful for that.

Anyhow, both Deck and Nico had expressed suitable horror at the prospect of Marianna walking free, but neither had offered to push her down a flight of stairs. Not that I'd really expected them to, but still, the anticipation was unbearable.

Two weeks later, I'd spent several days working in LA, gone to three parties on my own, only one of which was fun, and supervised the installation of the sauna. We'd put it on the roof near the hot tub, our own little open-air spa. My next project was a movie theatre in one of Aaron's empty rooms—comfy couches, a big screen, a soda machine, and a popcorn maker. And Barbara, probably. We still weren't quite sure what to do with the stuffed crow, but I'd promised Skip that I'd take care of her, and I would. And perhaps he was right about her bringing me luck? I had Aaron now. My perfect man. The movie room would be my Christmas present to him. And speaking of Christmas, we'd invited everyone who should have come to Thanksgiving over for one huge celebration.

Brooke was cooking.

And I was in charge of decorations.

Which was why I was currently on my way to Main Street—I needed to visit the Craft Cabin for sparkles as well as pick up ingredients for dinner and fill my prescription for birth control, something that had gone from "why bother?" to absolutely essential in the last few months. Although Aaron still refused to christen the hot tub, and I had no idea why.

I was browsing toothbrushes when I bumped into her.

Quite literally.

The bitch from hell.

As Marianna stepped back, her amiable expression

twisted into a sneer, but not before she'd checked we were alone.

"Surprised you didn't go running back to New York with your tail between your legs."

"Baldwin's Shore is my home."

She gave a dismissive shrug. "Now that you've called off the hounds, maybe you'll live to enjoy it?"

Fury burned through me. How dare she be so...so nonchalant?

"I know what you did."

She leaned in close, her smile pure malice. "But you'll never prove it."

And then she sauntered away, leaving me shaking with anguish and rage and regret that I hadn't recorded her spite for posterity. People should know who she was.

Although I'd never have admitted it, when we'd made the decision to send the Bad Samaritan after Marianna, I'd had a few lingering doubts. Had we interpreted the evidence correctly? Were we being too harsh? What if we'd gotten it wrong?

But now? Now, I knew she deserved everything she got and more.

"I need red and green ribbon," I told Brooke, then burst into tears.

At least I'd managed to avoid breaking down in front of Marianna.

"Hey, hey, what's wrong? Paulo, can you cover?"

"Sure thing, sweet cheeks."

Brooke shepherded me to the break room and shifted a box of yarn so I could sit on the couch. What was wrong with me? I'd stayed strong through the funeral, through the fire, through the car crash, and yet a five-second conversation in the drugstore had broken me.

"What happened?"

"Marianna happened." Voice hushed, I told Brooke what she'd said and how she'd said it, the way her face had morphed from benign to malevolent in the blink of an eye. "She might not have confessed in words, but I felt the meaning in my core."

"Wow. That's ballsy."

"She caught me by surprise." I held out a hand. "Look, I'm still trembling."

"I know it's hard, but think of this as a good thing—none of us needs to second-guess our decision anymore. The Bad Samaritan can do his worst, and if Marianna shows up in a body bag, we don't have to feel any guilt."

So we were on the same wavelength. "At least there's that."

"Don't let her ruin Christmas. We'll pick out ribbon, bake way too many cookies, drink wine and mango juice, and enjoy our new home." She twisted her mouth to one side. "Although Luca's being really weird about the hot tub."

"My gosh, Aaron too."

"You mean...you know?"

"Yes!"

"Why?"

"I have no idea. He was okay with the sauna, but I nearly passed out from heatstroke. Pro tip: take a bottle of ice water in with you."

"I definitely will." Brooke held out a hand. "Shall we go ribbon shopping?"

"Did somebody say ribbon?" Paulo burst through the door, ten different shades of ribbon draped over his shoulders and pom-poms hanging from his ears. "Ta-da! I'm an expert on ribbon."

"He's on something," Brooke muttered, but I had to smile.

She was right—I needed to put Marianna out of my mind and make the most of my first Christmas in my old-new home.

47

ROMI

'Twas the night before Christmas, and all through the house...was chaos.

Okay, it was only lunchtime, but Addy and Paulo had walked in ten minutes ago, so I couldn't see the situation improving any time soon. But that was okay.

This time last year, it had just been Davis and me, sharing a bowl of popcorn and watching *The Grinch*. Now at twenty-six years old, I was about to celebrate my first proper Christmas since Mom died. And despite everything that had happened in the past several months, it would be a *good* Christmas, not because of the food or the decorations or the gifts, but because of the people.

Darla followed behind Paulo, and Deck had already arrived. Davis had flown in yesterday and Blue was still with us, although she'd be moving into the Crowes' garage apartment in the new year. We were helping her to redecorate on account of her arm still being strapped up.

After some negotiation, Colt and Brie had stayed in Baldwin's Shore for Christmas, although they'd had to promise to spend New Year's Eve with Brie's family. Which meant Kiki was currently decorating the dog with tinsel and coloured ribbon. Luckily, Vega was taking her affections in good humour, and Woody had wisely run and hidden.

A powerful engine sounded outside, and Aaron mouthed, "Nico."

I had to confess to being a little disappointed. Both of our candidates for the Bad Samaritan were here for the festivities, but Marianna Baldwin was still alive and kicking. Kicking small puppies, probably. It seemed like the sort of thing she'd do. I'd seen her outside the grocery store an hour ago and given her a wide berth.

"Romi, my darling..." Addy had let Nico in, and he made a beeline straight for me, carrying a potted plant. "There's wine in the car for everyone, but I've noticed you don't indulge, so I brought you this."

"A...tree?"

"A mango tree. The lady at the garden centre assured me it would grow well in a container."

Aw, that was actually kind of sweet. "Thank you."

"And congratulations on your new contract."

The ink was barely dry, but I didn't ask how he'd found out. Nico just seemed to know stuff. Anyhow, I'd signed a three-million-dollar deal to become the global spokesmodel for a new make-up line, which would pay for the new coffee machine Aaron wanted with plenty left over to invest. Plus Ryse had hit half a million in total revenue last week, so there were two reasons to celebrate tonight.

"Again, thank you."

Paulo trotted up. "Everyone's here now?"

"Yes, I think so."

Blue's mom and her boyfriend, Addy's parents, the

Snyder family, plus Asa and his wife would be joining us for lunch tomorrow, but tonight, it was just the fourteen of us, plus Kasper and his team of bodyguards hovering around the periphery. They weren't allowed to touch alcohol, but Brooke was putting together plates of food for them.

"Excellent!" Paulo clapped his hands together. "That means we can start the party games."

Nico's eyes widened a fraction. "Are you *sure* we're not still waiting for anyone?"

"Uh, maybe?"

Who else could I invite on short notice?

"Quit stalling." Paulo took both of our hands and tugged us toward the great room. "Hey, you guys all need party hats!"

Luca took a step back. "Nobody said anything about hats."

Darla just rolled her eyes and muttered to Brooke, "Told you this would happen, hun."

A phone rang, and people frantically checked their purses and pockets, each hoping to be the lucky recipient of a telemarketing call on Christmas Eve. I'd buy a whole set of double glazing if it meant I didn't have to play Charades or Never Have I Ever: Festive Edition.

"It's me!" Luca held up his phone like a prize, then checked the screen. "Ah, shit."

Brooke stood on tiptoe to look. "Detective Payne? What does he want?"

My brother didn't look quite so jubilant anymore. "Better find out."

When he left the room, the party atmosphere went with him.

"Anyone want to help carry the wine from my car?" Nico asked. "It seems likely we'll need it."

No, I wanted to know why Payne was calling. I couldn't imagine him taking the time to wish us a happy Christmas. My nerves were fraying by the time Luca came back ten minutes later, and I couldn't read the expression on his face. If I had to guess, I'd say...incredulity?

"What? What happened?"

"You're not going to believe this, but Marianna Baldwin just walked into the police station in Roseburg and confessed. To everything. Mom's death, the arson attack, even goading Easton into shooting at you."

What?

But...but that made no sense. None whatsoever.

"Why would she do that?"

"I don't know. According to Payne, she said it was time to come clean about what she'd done. He spent three hours with her, and at the end, she signed a statement and said she'd plead guilty to everything." Luca shook his head, still disbelieving, as if this was all a prank and someone would jump out to tell him he'd been Punk'd. "She admitted that she lured Mom out to the cabin with the intention of making her back off EJ, and when Mom wouldn't, they got into a fight, and she grabbed a brass candlestick and... Yeah, we already know the rest."

"Why was it any of her business what Mom and EJ did?"

"Because in her warped mind, she thought he deserved better."

"I wish I'd scratched her eyes out when I had the chance."

"Well, I'm glad you didn't. It's better this way. When Payne asked her about Easton, she said, and I quote, 'Of course he was going to get caught, but if you saw the chance to get that idiot out of your hair for a few months, wouldn't you have taken it? Killed two birds with one stone? Or it would have if he'd been a better shot.'"

Aaron slipped an arm around my waist. "That's cold."

"Would we really have expected anything else from Marianna?"

Still, I shuddered. "I guess not. But I definitely didn't expect her to confess. She said we'd never prove it, and perhaps we wouldn't have, so why?"

"Isn't it obvious?" As usual, Blue had the answer. "Because something—or someone—scared her more than the thought of going to prison."

"But what— Oh."

The Bad Samaritan. *The punishment fits the crime.* He hadn't killed Marianna, and maybe he hadn't even touched her. He'd forced her to confess her sins and submit to good old-fashioned justice. Luca and I had closure. Mom, wherever she was, could be at peace.

Tension I hadn't even realised I was carrying seeped out of me.

A stranger had come through.

A stranger... Were they in this room? I fought the temptation to look around, to study the faces. If the Bad Samaritan wanted to remain anonymous, then we had to respect that. But later, when it was just the six of us—me, Luca, Aaron, Brooke, Blue, and Colt—we'd drink a toast to the person who'd gifted us the best Christmas present ever.

Retribution.

"*Now* can we play party games?" Paulo asked. "Do you want to start with Name That Christmas Tune or Eggnog Pong?"

Oh, thank goodness. "Eggnog Pong."

As a vegan alcoholic, I had two perfectly valid reasons to sit that one out.

"Super-duper! I made you a special eggnog with cashew and coconut milk and alcohol-free bourbon." Oh *hell.* "Darla can share it seeing as she's teetotal as well."

Colt groaned. "This is gonna get messy in so many ways."

And was Kasper sniggering?

"What if I have an allergy to nutmeg?" Davis asked.

Nice try. "You don't have an allergy to nutmeg."

"Traitor."

This time, it was Colt's phone that rang, and I didn't miss the glee in his tone when he glanced at the screen and said, "Dispatch."

The Coos County Sheriff's Department wasn't huge, and they were always short of manpower. Colt spent half his life on call, but earlier, he'd proudly told us that he'd never been rousted on Christmas Eve. In Baldwin's Shore, the bars were closed, kids were tucked up waiting for Santa, and the only public gatherings were church services.

Jinxed it.

Or not, depending on how you looked at it, and Paulo was looking at it aghast.

"No," he squeaked.

Colt answered and listened for a moment. "Sure, I'll attend. On my way."

Luca grinned. "As a Coos County deputy-in-training, I feel obliged to offer my assistance. Purely for the learning experience, you understand."

"Too damn—" Colt glanced around and realised Kiki was in earshot. "Too darn right you're coming. Assault reported at the Baldwin Estate."

The atmosphere in the room turned serious in an instant.

"Assault on who?"

"Don't have that information yet."

"Who reported it?"

"A hysterical female."

A hysterical female? My money was on Kayleigh or Lillian, then. Oh boy, it was all happening tonight.

48

AARON

Whoever came up with the phrase "the lesser of two evils" had never had to decide between wrangling the Baldwin twins and playing Paulo's party games. But in the end, chivalry won out.

"I'm not a deputy, trainee or otherwise, but do you need a hand with the hysterical female?"

Romi's eyes narrowed, but rather than bitching, she conjured up a smile. "I could help too? I've had plenty of practice at placating people."

"Aw, Buttercup, I wouldn't want to deprive you of Paulo's vegnog."

"I can drink it when I get back."

Her unspoken words? *Or pour it down the sink.* I brushed my lips over hers, ignoring the scowl.

"Enjoy naming that tune."

"Sometimes I hate you."

But she didn't, not anymore, and we both knew it. I gave her hand a squeeze and grabbed my car keys from the counter. If Luca and Colt had to transport a prisoner, then

I'd need my own vehicle to get home. Good thing I hadn't started on the wine yet.

Who the hell was being assaulted? I kept my fingers crossed for Easton, but if our schooldays were anything to go by, he was more likely to be dishing out the punches than taking them. Unless he'd come across another Luca. I lived in hope.

Colt turned on his light bar and pulled ahead, leaving me to follow within the speed limit. But I wasn't too far behind, and when I turned into the Baldwins' driveway—at least someone had thought to leave the gates open—and saw the scene illuminated by Colt's headlights, the only words I could utter were, "What the fuck?"

EJ staggered around, followed by Rey Mendez, who'd clearly been drinking. But that hadn't stopped him from pounding EJ's face into something resembling raw meatloaf. Kayleigh and Lillian were shrieking like demented ring girls and swatting at Rey ineffectively as he moved in for another swing. EJ blocked, but not well enough. Ouch.

"Steal my wife, motherfucker?" Rey landed a jab to EJ's ribs. "I'll teach you to steal my motherfuckin' wife."

"She...she couldn't stand you."

"Still wore my fuckin' ring."

Parker sat on a low wall to the side, hands in his pockets and legs crossed at the ankles, watching. Sara stood behind him with her arms wrapped around herself, her frame rigid. Well... Looked as if Romi might get another Christmas wish after all. The only question was, would Luca arrest his father or would he leave it to Colt to do the honours?

While the two of them worked out who to grab, I headed for Sara. Kayleigh and Lillian could wait.

"You okay?"

"Not really."

At least she was honest.

"Has anyone tried to break them up?"

Parker made a soft sound that could have been a laugh. "Times like this, it's difficult to know who to root for."

"Not your father?"

A shrug.

Sara bit her lip. "EJ's gonna be upset you didn't help."

"What's he going to do? Fire me? He can't. Somebody needs to run the company in Marianna's—" Cough. "Absence."

"No love lost?" I asked.

"Between my father and me? No. His whole life, people have bailed him out. First Grandpa, then Marianna. He's never had to face the consequences of his own actions, or the lack of them." Parker nodded toward the bleeding men. "Until now."

Sara winced as another blow landed. "Aren't Colt and Luca gonna stop them?"

"I expect so." Eventually.

"Kayleigh! Watch out!"

Kayleigh swung around to see what Sara was yelling about, and EJ's elbow connected with Lillian instead. She hit the deck and began wailing.

"Actions have consequences," Parker murmured.

Cold.

He was a year older than me, and throughout our schooldays, he'd always seemed distant. Aloof. I'd assumed he avoided mixing because he thought he was better than us, but he didn't seem to like his family much either. What made Parker tick?

That was a question for another day because I'd

promised to assist with Kayleigh and Lillian, and if they kept up with the screeching, we'd all suffer permanent hearing damage. Colt and Luca were getting ready to move in as well, Luca on his father and Colt on EJ. Good decision. Luca's special-forces training should let him drop Rey without too much trouble.

And it did. A minute later, it was all over. Rey and EJ lay on their fronts, cuffed and moaning, and the twins were huddled together crying. I'd offered them tissues and whatever sympathy I could dredge up, and Sara had found ice for Lillian's rapidly swelling cheek. She'd have a black eye in the morning. Or, as Parker put it, "No Instagram Christmas selfies for her."

Like I said, cold.

Colt had called for an ambulance to take EJ to the hospital, and I'd texted Romi to let her know the good news. Although it was in bad taste, I might also have snapped a picture or two and sent those too. Her reply?

R: Is there video? :)

"What happened?" Colt asked. "What set this off?"

Kayleigh and Lillian both started talking at once.

"That monster! He just came out of the dark and started hitting Daddy."

"Right in the face. *Pow, pow, pow.*"

"He was lying in wait."

"He broke his nose!"

"And he stinks of whisky."

"He pushed us too."

Colt nodded. "Parker?"

"That about sums it up. Dad went to Roseburg to see Marianna, and when he arrived back, I heard the car door slam, and then the shouting started."

"How did your father react to news of the confession?"

"He's still at the 'disbelief' stage."

"EJ was on the ground when we got outside," Sara said. "But then he kicked Rey's legs, and Rey fell over, and they started wrestling around."

"Someone should tell Rey to lay off the drink. It does nothing for his coordination."

Even so, he'd managed to do a reasonable job on EJ, and as Parker had said, whose side were we meant to be on?

"Speaking of drunks, where's Easton tonight?"

"Probably out breaking his bail conditions." Parker's nonchalant shrug said he didn't care. "I should go take dinner out of the oven."

He strolled off, and Sara stared after him. This was possibly the most dysfunctional family I'd ever had the misfortune to meet. Only Sara seemed vaguely normal.

"Is he always like that?" I asked her. "So detached?"

She gave the briefest of nods. "I guess... I guess we all cope in different ways."

"How do you cope?"

Shit, now her eyes were watery.

"I just take one day at a time."

"Look, we're having drinks at our place tonight. You'd be welcome to join us."

It would mean keeping Marianna-and-EJ-related talk to a minimum, but I'd feel like an absolute shit sending Sara back into that house with two harpies and a robot for company. Brooke would welcome her, and I couldn't see Brie or Romi being upset. Blue might be irked, but what was new?

Sara made an effort to focus as the ambulance trundled along the driveway toward us. EJ sounded as if he was sobbing, but quite frankly, it was nothing more than he deserved. His inaction—whether through wilful stupidity or cowardice—had let a killer walk free for twenty years, plus he'd benefited financially from the deal. Marianna had been a better businessperson than East or EJ. Having that ruthless streak undoubtedly helped.

"I shouldn't come, not tonight."

"Too soon?"

"Too soon. But thanks."

Once the medics had given Rey a cursory check over, Colt and Luca stuffed him unceremoniously into the back of their cruiser. Apart from one weak protest of, "You'd do this to your own dad?" Rey hadn't had much to say for himself.

"You'll be okay here?" I nodded toward the twins. "With them?"

Sara nodded. "Maybe I'll take a lesson from Marianna and slip them a couple of sleeping pills."

"That's the spirit."

"I hope you have a good Christmas," she said softly.

I would. I most definitely would. With Marianna and now Rey locked up for the holidays, it couldn't get much better.

And the gifts just kept on coming. Quite literally.

Romi threw back her head as she rode me, her hands on my thighs. She'd woken me up with a kiss on the cheek and a striptease, and I hadn't even finished unwrapping her before my cock weighed in on the discussion. So she was still wearing the fur-trimmed lingerie she'd bought for the occasion, and I'd never seen a more beautiful sight in my life.

"Are you close?" I asked, because I sure was.

"Oh, yeah."

She closed her eyes, slammed down, and clenched around me, her lips parted on a moan. A second later, I followed her over the edge, then pulled her tight against my chest.

"Love you, Buttercunt."

"Love you too, Slick Dick." A little giggle. "My gosh, I can't believe we made it this far."

"To adulthood?"

"To bed. Together. We survived our many, many fuck-ups, and we made it."

"Now all we have to do is survive Christmas dinner with Blue and Paulo."

"With any luck, Paulo will still be unconscious on the couch."

When Colt and Luca had finally arrived back from Roseburg, midnight was fast approaching, but that hadn't dampened the party atmosphere. In fact, their tales of Rey being locked in a cell only fuelled the celebrations. If the Bad Samaritan *was* among us, then I hoped he'd had a damn good time. We'd considered moving Paulo to a bed last night, but at three a.m., it seemed easiest to just leave him where he was. I'd slept on that couch myself in the past —by accident rather than by design—and it was perfectly comfortable.

Colt and Brie had taken a snoozing Kiki back to the Peninsula in the early hours, and Nico had hitched a ride with them, but everyone else had stayed. We had the space. When Jackson Pettit originally asked me if I'd be interested in taking the building off his hands, my first reaction had been "no way." But that night, I'd dreamed. I'd dreamed of family and friends and a big old building filled with their love and laughter. And of course Romi had been there, front and centre.

"I'd stay here all day, but I'm hungry," she mumbled.

Now here I was, living the dream.

"What time is it?" I took my hand off her ass long enough to check my watch. Groaned when I saw it was almost noon. "I should go help Brooke with the food, and the rest of the guests will be arriving soon."

"Do me a favour?"

"Does it involve hunting for your robe? Because I have no idea where I threw it."

"Could you toss some Tylenol at Davis on your way past? He doesn't do well with hangovers."

"Sure."

And I knew exactly where the robe was. I just liked Romi better naked.

Paulo, not so much.

But unfortunately, that was exactly what I got when I cracked open the door to Davis's room. The horrifying sight of Paulo's naked ass as he sprawled face down across the covers, Davis sleeping peacefully beside him.

Fuck.

The headache would have to wait. I backed away slowly, slowly, right into Romi. She'd found the robe now, more was the pity.

"What? Why do you look as if Woody shit on your Christmas sweater?"

"Shh. Paulo's in there?"

"Paulo? Then where's D—" Her eyes widened in understanding. "Oh!" Then she groaned. "Oh, no. There's no NDA. What if he didn't set ground rules? What if—"

"What if he's just feeling more comfortable with who he is?"

"I... Uh... You think?"

"I think we should go get coffee."

"But... But..." She took one last look at the closed door and gave her head a little shake. "He's happy. Okay. *Okay.* Aaron?"

"Yes?"

"This is the *best* Christmas ever."

EPILOGUE - ROMI

"Slick, did you leave this card on the counter? And the gift?"

"What card?"

"The 'Happy New Year' one."

It wasn't your usual holiday card. On the front was a drawing of three women, one in rags and two in ball gowns. Cinderella? The pumpkin at their feet confirmed that theory. Inside was another drawing, this time of three stick people behind bars—two men and one woman—and a single line printed in block capitals.

THAT WAS FUN ;) LET'S DO IT AGAIN SOMETIME.

"Ah, fuck. Get away from there. Stay down."

"Huh? Why?"

Aaron pushed me behind the counter, and not in a "let's get naughty on the kitchen floor" kind of way. No, this was more of a mild freak-out.

"What's wrong? What are you doing?"

He snatched the card from my hands and studied it. Read it again.

"This is from the Bad Samaritan."

"A holiday card?"

"That's his writing."

"Are you sure?"

"He's left us notes before."

Weird, but how else was an anonymous vigilante meant to communicate? "Aw, that's sweet. And look, he's offering to help out again."

It wasn't as if he'd even killed anyone this time. Marianna had gotten exactly what she'd deserved.

"Romi, it was on the counter. *In our home.*"

It took a second for the meaning of his words to hit. The implication. Then my veins turned to ice.

"How? How could he have gotten in? We have locks on the windows. Bolts on the doors. Cameras. An alarm."

"That doesn't seem to matter much." Aaron turned the card over. "He hasn't left a P.S. criticising the set-up this time, so I guess the changes we made after his last visit were up to scratch." Then he took a closer look at the Cinderella picture. "Do you reckon these look like the Baldwin women?"

Now that he'd said it, I saw the resemblance. "A little, but what does it mean? And why are we sitting on the floor?"

"Because the drapes are open, and we know the Bad Samaritan owns a rifle."

"Oh, please. If he wanted us dead, he'd have slit our throats while we slept."

"That's a comforting thought."

"It's the truth." I stood and reached for the long slim package wrapped in gaudy red-and-gold paper. "What do you think this is?"

"I think it's a gift for the bomb squad."

"Don't be ridiculous."

Before Aaron could stop me, I sidestepped and tore the package open. The wooden box inside had no markings, no indication of what it contained, but I flipped the lid, and just as I thought, nothing exploded.

"Aw, pretty!"

"What is it?" Aaron stood on tiptoe to peer over my shoulder. "It's a stick. A fancy silver stick. What the hell?"

"It's a wand." A jewel-encrusted wand with a silver filigree end. "A fairy godmother wand."

"And it was definitely with the card? Why would he send that?"

"Maybe because he wants us to be the fairy godmother?"

Aaron spread his hands in an "I don't get it" gesture.

"Follow the clues. Cinderella? Fairy godmother? The Bad Samaritan helped us, and now he's asking us to return the favour. Sara's got to be hurting right now—her family was torn apart."

"He wants us to give her a dress and a pumpkin coach?"

"No, dumbass, he just wants us to be the friends she needs."

Although granted, getting the dress would be easier. Ishmael probably had one in his sample closet.

"That's somewhat unexpected."

"That Sara needs friends?"

"No, that the Bad Samaritan has an altruistic side. Between the knife work and the guns and him constantly breaking into my fucking home, it never occurred to me that he might have a heart."

"Why else would he do what he does?"

"I suppose... I suppose I thought he did it for kicks."

"And also for justice. Maybe we should give him a new name? He's not bad, he's not good, he's...fairish?"

"The Fairish Samaritan?"

"Okay, so it doesn't have the same ring to it. But as long as we don't do anything to cross him, we're safe. He's a silent partner, not an enemy. Could you imagine Deck turning on us? Or Nico? Nico brought me a freaking mango tree."

And Nico was charming too—definitely a ladies' man, although he kept a certain distance. Emotional distance, not physical distance. Deck seemed to be the strong, silent type.

"I guess not."

"Well, while you work yourself up about possible snipers, I'm going to work on next winter's Ryse collection."

When we started out, I'd designed all the beadwork pieces myself as a way to keep my mind off my other vices, then produced patterns for the teams of craftswomen to make. Gradually, we'd started taking design submissions from other artists and the makers themselves, but I still liked to include a few of my own creations each season. That was my January project. Four quiet weeks of beading and bedtime fun.

And working out how to turn myself into a fairy freaking godmother.

"We've run out of the amethyst Delicas in size ten, but we've got lilac?" Brooke handed me a small package. "Would those be okay?"

For a mock-up? Yes, they'd work perfectly. "I'll take them, and do you have silver bugles?"

"Three or six millimetres?"

"Six."

A quarter inch, but since the Delicas were made in Japan, they used metric measurements along with the whole rest of the world.

"Right over here. What time should I pick you up this evening? Seven?"

"Seven's perfect."

Sara had turned down Brooke's invite to our New Year party—and honestly, that had been a good call on her part because over three weeks had passed and I still had a headache from that night—but she'd agreed to meet us for dinner at La Cantina in Coos Bay this evening. Phase One of Operation Fairy Godmother. Aaron and I had told the others about the Bad Samaritan's latest note, and of course Brooke and Addy had offered to help. Brie too, but she was in Scandinavia for another month.

Brooke leaned in closer. "So, what's the story with Davis and Paulo?"

Inwardly, I groaned. "What's he said?"

There'd been a repeat of their drunken Christmas Eve dalliance a week later, and there was still no NDA in place, a first for Davis. He said Paulo had promised to keep his mouth shut, and he didn't want to insult him by asking him to sign a piece of paper to that effect—another first.

"Nothing." Brooke glanced sideways at Paulo. He was on the other side of the store, helping a guy who could have been his twin by the yarn display. "He's said nothing; that's the whole point. And usually we hear every last painful detail. Paulo doesn't understand the concept of TMI."

"Then why do you think there's something going on between him and Davis?"

"Because Luca saw Davis give him this *look*. Is it true?"

"You can't tell anyone."

"My lips are sealed, I swear." She grinned. "Aw, that's so awesome."

"It's just casual, so Davis says."

"But still…"

A blonde came in, strikingly beautiful but too short for the runway. Too bulked up. And too…tough. She had a hard aura about her that reminded me of Blue, but when she tried to get Paulo's twin to leave, he was having none of it. Another blonde in the gift section seemed to be struggling to keep a straight face, and so was I.

"My money's on Paulo's new friend," Brooke whispered. "Have you seen how much stuff he's buying? We're gonna have to order more stock."

"You say that like it's a bad thing."

"I like to go home sometimes."

"You've been busy?"

"Online sales have gone through the roof recently. Paulo's a marketing genius."

The bell above the door jangled, but I only caught a glimpse of a dark-haired woman before she turned around and walked right out again. Weird. Couldn't she read the massive sign above the window? The tough-looking blonde exited right after, and I was glad I hadn't taken Brooke's bet.

"Well, that was anticlimactic. I thought she'd have tried a bit harder. Hey, do you want a coffee while it's quiet? I'm due to take a break."

"I'll never say no to coffee."

Pickle, Darla's cat, leapt into my lap when I took a seat on the couch. I'd never had a cat before, but I'd miss Woody when he left with Blue. Maybe Aaron and I could get a kitten? We'd already decided kids were a decision for the future, but a tiny furball would be so cute. Or a puppy? A buddy for Vega? There was a rescue centre over in Coos Bay, and—

"Did you hear that?" Brooke asked. "Sounded like a scream."

"Probably kids by the coffee house."

Mart and Mary had installed a swing set on the empty plot of land next door, and on a Saturday, all the children were out of school.

"But it's freezing outside."

"There are these things called jackets..."

"Ha-ha, very funny. You want eggnog syrup? It's low-cal and vegan."

"Are you kidding me?"

"Paulo bought it off the internet. It doesn't taste as awful as I thought it would. And we have leftover Christmas cookies, but I think those have..." She checked the ingredients. "Sorry, they have butter."

"Go on, I'll try the syrup. Make the Christmas magic last."

Or not.

Hammering on the back door made me jump out of my skin, and I wasn't the only one. Brooke dropped the cup she was holding and coffee splashed everywhere. I dove for the roll of paper towel, then glanced toward the back door and saw the terrified face of a woman through the glass panel.

"What the...?"

Brooke already had the door open. "Shauna? What happened?"

It took me a moment to recognise Shauna Weaver, another of our old classmates. She'd changed her hair since I saw her last—cut it shorter and dyed it blonde, and today, she'd accessorised with...were those brambles?

Shauna practically fell through the door, and the dog

she was holding tugged the leash out of her hand and leapt straight for Pickle. Chaos reigned as Pickle shot through the door into the store with the mutt following, and I heard squeals from Paulo and his new bestie as well as the sound of crashing shelves. Brooke had her head in her hands, but she recovered enough to ask, "What's wrong?"

Shauna was sobbing now. "I th-th-think Scooby got attacked by a c-c-cougar. In the forest."

"You saw it?"

"H-h-he's covered in blood."

So was the floor, now that she mentioned it. Freaking hell.

Brooke grabbed her phone. "I'll call Luca."

Hadn't she heard what Shauna said? "Uh, there's a *cougar*."

"Yes, and Luca has a gun. He can fire a warning shot or something, and people need to know the forest isn't safe. Can you...uh..."

She passed Shauna over to me, and I helped her onto the couch. One of the animals screeched, and I couldn't tell if it was the dog or Pickle or a damn mountain lion.

What had happened to the quiet town I used to know?

A FEW WORDS FROM THE BAD SAMARITAN…

Curious how the Bad Samaritan approached the Marianna
problem?
I've included a few of their thoughts in a bonus chapter,
FREE to members of my reader group.

You can join here:
www.elise-noble.com/coug4r

WHAT'S NEXT?

My next book will be the fifteenth instalment of the Blackwood Security series, *Pretties in Pink*.

Five years ago, Mila Carmody disappeared from her bed, and that was just the beginning. Two little girls, swallowed by darkness, never to be seen again. For Micah Ganaway, it might be the end. Arrested for child abduction, he's already been tried in the court of public opinion and found guilty. The lead detective assures him the trial is only a formality.

Private investigator Hallie Chastain isn't so certain. On paper, Ganaway makes a reasonable suspect, but in person... Things don't quite add up. Detective Ford Prestia doesn't share his partner's convictions either, but he's the new cop in town. Can't afford to rock the boat. Then he meets Hallie, and when she rocks not only his boat but his whole damn world, he finds his career isn't the only thing in jeopardy...

For more details:
www.elise-noble.com/pink

And the next book from Baldwin's Shore will be something a little different—a crossover with Blackwood Security that follows on both *Buried Secrets* and *Chimera*. If you want to find out who the Bad Samaritan is, all will be revealed in *Secret Weapon*.

As Director of Special Projects for a global security firm, Emmy Black is well acquainted with trouble, but she didn't expect to run into a proverbial nightmare in small-town Oregon. The place is just hills and trees, right? But a quest to help an injured woman soon leaves Emmy fighting for not only her own survival but the lives of many others too.

When Nine came to Baldwin's Shore, the former member of a Russian hit squad had two goals: to hide and to heal. But someone else has the same idea, and the consequences threaten to upend Nine's carefully crafted existence. With the appearance of old friends and enemies as well as a madman intent on provoking a war and—most disturbingly—an unfamiliar feeling that might be love, Nine is left with one burning question: can an assassin ever truly retire?

For more details:
www.elise-noble.com/secret-weapon

But if you'd rather preserve the mystery, then you'll want to wait for Sara's story in the fourth book in the Baldwin's Shore series, *A Secret to Die for*.

Oh, and if you'd like to see more of Ismael, you can find him in *Red Alert*, part of the Blackwood Security series.

For more details:
www.elise-noble.com/red

If you haven't read any of the Blackwood Security books yet, why not start for FREE with *Pitch Black*?

After the owner of a security company is murdered, his sharp-edged wife goes on the run. Forced to abandon everything she holds dear—her home, her friends, her job in special ops—assassin Diamond builds a new life for herself in England. As Ashlyn Hale, she meets Luke, a handsome local who makes her realise just how lonely she is.

Yet, even in the sleepy village of Lower Foxford, the dark side of life dogs Diamond's trail when the unthinkable strikes. Forced out of hiding, she races against time to save those she cares about.

For more details:
www.elise-noble.com/pitch-black

If you enjoyed *Buried Secrets*, please consider leaving a review.

For an author, every review is incredibly important. Not only do they make us feel warm and fuzzy inside, readers consider them when making their decision whether or not to buy a book. Even a line saying you enjoyed the book or what your favourite part was helps a lot.

WANT TO STALK ME?

For updates on my new releases, giveaways, and other random stuff, you can sign up for my newsletter on my website:
www.elise-noble.com

If you're on Facebook, you might also like to join Team Blackwood for exclusive giveaways, sneak previews, and book-related chat. Be the first to find out about new stories, and you might even see your name or one of your suggestions make it into print!

And if you'd like to read my books for FREE, you can also find details of how to join my advance review team.

Would you like to join Team Blackwood?

www.elise-noble.com/team-blackwood

facebook.com/EliseNobleAuthor
twitter.com/EliseANoble
instagram.com/elise_noble

END-OF-BOOK STUFF

It's early December as I write this, the start of proper winter here in England. There are fallen leaves everywhere, we've just had our first (half-arsed) flurry of slow, and there's Christmas stuff everywhere. I'm not really big on Christmas myself—just give me a few days off and some M&S party food and I'm happy.

Audit season is nearly done for the year (I'm a chartered accountant for my part-time day job), and I won't lie, it's been tough. Too much work and too few people to do it. But I'm looking forward to catching up with the Bad Samaritan in December—I should have finished that book by now, but it's ended up longer than I planned. The story of my bloody life, with writing anyway.

I've got a bit of Christmas shopping left to do, although I lucked out with stocking fillers a few weeks ago when I came across the ladies from Action for Ingwavuma, which is a charity working to support women and children in the KwaZulu-Natal province in South Africa. They sell gorgeous hand-embroidered bookmarks and super-cute beaded animals, so if you're looking for little gifts, why not give their online store a visit? To meet them felt kind of fitting as I was working on Buried Secrets at the time, and Romi's ambition for Ryse—to empower local women—is similar to their mission. Plus I sponsored a a rainwater collection system for a South African family, which is something I've wanted to do since I did the research for Judged and realised how difficult it is for people to get access to fresh water in some parts of the world.

So, what are my publishing plans for 2022? Well, I've got a schedule kinda sort of mostly almost mapped out...

Feb 22 - Pretties in Pink (Blackwood Security #15)

Apr 22 - Chimera (Blackwood Security #15.5)

Jun 22 - Secret Weapon (Baldwin's Shore #3.6 and also Blackwood Security #15.6)

Aug 22 - Hydrogen (Blackwood Elements #10)

Oct 22 - Hard Lines (Blackstone House #1)

Dec 22 - Hard Tide (Blackstone House #2)

This might change, though. It all depends on whether I have a nervous breakdown during accounting busy season. I'm only half joking about that, lol. At least I've written three of the books and half written two more, which gives me hope.

What's Blackstone House? Well, it's another romantic suspense series, one I began writing in 2018 before I got distracted (hey, squirrel) by all things Electi. Although there are new characters, you'll also see some old ones—Pale and his Choir girls, and I'm sure Emmy will make an appearance too.

Time for me to get back to work—these books won't write themselves, although I'm sure Elon Musk would argue with that assumption.

Happy New Year!

Elise

Action for Ingwavuma website: actionforingwavuma.co.uk

ALSO BY ELISE NOBLE

Blackwood Security

For the Love of Animals (Nate & Carmen - Prequel)

Black is My Heart (Diamond & Snow - Prequel)

Pitch Black

Into the Black

Forever Black

Gold Rush

Gray is My Heart

Neon (novella)

Out of the Blue

Ultraviolet

Glitter (novella)

Red Alert

White Hot

Sphere (novella)

The Scarlet Affair

Spirit (novella)

Quicksilver

The Girl with the Emerald Ring

Red After Dark

When the Shadows Fall

Pretties in Pink (2022)

Chimera (2022)

Secret Weapon (Crossover with Baldwin's Shore) (2022)

Blackwood Elements

Oxygen

Lithium

Carbon

Rhodium

Platinum

Lead

Copper

Bronze

Nickel

Hydrogen (2022)

Blackwood UK

Joker in the Pack

Cherry on Top

Roses are Dead

Shallow Graves

Indigo Rain

Pass the Parcel (TBA)

Blackwood Casefiles

Stolen Hearts

Burning Love (TBA)

Baldwin's Shore

Dirty Little Secrets

Secrets, Lies, and Family Ties

Buried Secrets

Secret Weapon (Crossover with Blackwood Security) (2022)

Blackstone House

Hard Lines (2022)

Hard Tide (TBA)

The Electi

Cursed

Spooked

Possessed

Demented

Judged

The Planes

A Vampire in Vegas

A Devil in the Dark (TBA)

The Trouble Series

Trouble in Paradise

Nothing but Trouble

24 Hours of Trouble

Standalone

Life

Coco du Ciel

A Very Happy Christmas (novella)

Twisted (short stories)

Books with clean versions available (no swearing and no on-

the-page sex)

Pitch Black

Into the Black

Forever Black

Gold Rush

Gray is My Heart

Audiobooks

Black is My Heart (Diamond & Snow - Prequel)

Pitch Black

Into the Black

Forever Black

Gold Rush

Gray is My Heart

Neon (novella)

9 781912 888481